WAGGONER'S WAY

Also by Harry Bowling

The Farrans of Fellmonger Street
Pedlar's Row
Backstreet Child
The Girl from Cotton Lane
Gaslight in Page Street
Paragon Place
Ironmonger's Daughter
Tuppence to Tooley Street
Conner Street's War

WAGGONER'S WAY

Harry Bowling

HEADLINE

First published in 1995
by HEADLINE BOOK PUBLISHING

10 9 8 7 6 5 4 3 2 1

British Library Cataloguing in Publication Data

Bowling, Harry
    Waggoner's Way
    I.   Title
    823.914 [F]

ISBN 0-7472-1294-5

Typeset by Keyboard Services, Luton, Beds

Printed and bound in Great Britain by
Mackays of Chatham PLC, Chatham, Kent

HEADLINE BOOK PUBLISHING
A division of Hodder Headline PLC
338 Euston Road
London NW1 3BH

To old and valued friends, Frank and Vi, Terry and Joan, Peter and Sue, Bernie and Barbara, and Jimmy and Joan. Not forgetting the 'Jolly Boys'.

Prologue
1944

Outside the hall it was cool, with a gentle breeze tainted by brick-dust and charcoaled timbers, but inside the atmosphere was becoming oppressive. Cigarette smoke hung in the air and the scent of cheap perfume vied unfavourably with strong smells of saveloys and pease pudding, vinegared chips and spilled beer.

An ageing musician tapped his foot rapidly and throttled his squeeze-box, leering down from the rostrum at the confused dancers who were gyrating feverishly as the tempo of the music grew faster. Bodies collided and a roar of laughter rang out as the diminutive Charlie Catchpole was sent spinning by a large, red-faced woman in a tight flowered dress.

At the end of the hall a group of men stood at the bar holding pints of ale and watching with amusement the revellers' pathetic attempts to perform the 'Gay Gordons' to the tune of 'Cock o' the North'.

'They'd be better off stickin' ter the "Lambeth Walk" or "Knees up Muvver Brown" if yer ask me,' Tom Kelly remarked with a grin.

Joe Brennen nodded as he reached into his waistcoat pocket and took out his silver timepiece. 'They'll be roundin' it up soon,' he replied as he noted the time. 'I'm off outside fer a bit o' fresh air.'

Tom put down his empty glass and briefly glanced over to where his son was standing, then he slipped his thumb through his braces. 'I fink I'll join yer, it's too bloody warm in 'ere fer me,' he said.

The two railwaymen left the hall and stepped out into the June night, their eyes immediately drawn to the mangled waggon-shed away to the right.

'It made a right bleedin' mess of that, didn't it?' Joe Brennen said as they strolled along the line of laden waggons which had been coupled up that morning ready for the journey to Brighton.

1

Tom Kelly stopped briefly to tap his pipe against the heel of his shoe. 'It was lucky it didn't land the ovver side o' the wall,' he remarked to his friend. 'It would 'ave bin carnage.'

The two men reached the end of the line of trucks and stood looking at the remains of the shed, the charred timbers and twisted girders poking up from the brick rubble and the large piece of mangled metal from the flying bomb lying some yards away on a disused section of track. They could see the damaged rooftops of the little houses beyond the yard wall and both knew only too well how fortunate their tight-knit little community had been when the flying bomb dived down just two days ago.

Joe leaned against a low embankment and watched his old friend Tom Kelly fill his briar pipe with care. Brennen was a large, portly man in his late fifties, with thinning grey hair, a wide, open face, and humorous blue eyes. In contrast Tom Kelly was slightly built, with a large mop of unruly dark hair, brown eyes, and a friendly face that was very often creased in a smile. Tonight, however, Tom was in a serious mood, and it had not slipped his friend's notice.

'When's yer lad due back?' Joe asked quietly.

'Termorrer night,' Tom replied as he sucked on his pipe. 'They'll be the first in, when it does start. I give it a few days. It can't be long now, surely ter Gawd, what wiv all the stuff passin' frew this place.'

'Yeah, it must be like bedlam on the coast,' Joe remarked. 'They say yer can't move down there fer tanks an' guns an' supplies, not ter mention the troops.'

'The Airborne's always the first in,' Tom said, almost to himself.

Joe's eyes followed the rising cloud of tobacco smoke as it drifted off slowly into the warm night air. 'Your lad's gonna be all right, Tom,' he said encouragingly. ''E can look after 'imself. Remember that time 'e fell in the river?'

'Do I,' Tom replied with a grin. ''E came in soaked ter the skin, an' did I larrup 'im? The little sod couldn't sit down prop'ly fer a week. I used ter warn 'im time an' time again about playin' on those barges, but I might just as well 'ave bin talkin' ter meself fer all the good it did.'

'Well, yer gotta be proud of 'im now, ole mate,' Joe said.

Tom nodded and stepped over the silvery rails of the track to lean on the low wall. 'Our Mary's worried sick,' he said with a deep sigh. 'She dotes on that boy.'

Joe looked up at the red-flecked western sky and reached for his pocket-watch. 'Come on, Tom, let's get back before the last dance,' he said smiling. 'I promised our Ada I'd take 'er round.'

Kay Brennen sat with her three older sisters, oblivious to what Elsie was saying, though she occasionally nodded acquiescently. Her mind was on someone else and her eyes constantly flitted to the far end of the bar where a young soldier was in conversation with a couple of older women. She felt her stomach tightening and a strange tingling running up and down her spine as she watched him furtively. He was tall and broad-shouldered and his uniform fitted him perfectly. As he turned slightly Kay saw the red square patch on the arm of his open battledress, and above it the embroidered wings. He had his red beret tucked under his shoulder flap and his service tie was loosened over an open-necked khaki shirt.

Kay looked away quickly as the young man turned in her direction, but she prayed that he would notice her. He had been over earlier and joked with Elsie, Barbara and Dawn, and he had smiled and winked cockily at her as he stood by the table. If only she had responded he might have asked her to dance. Barbara and Dawn had both danced with him but they were spoken for; though it wouldn't have been apparent to anyone, the way they flirted openly with him.

'Kay? Is there anyone in there?' Elsie said loudly.

'I'm sorry, I was miles away. What was yer sayin'?' Kay replied quickly.

'I said look at Mum an' Dad on the floor,' Elsie told her. 'Dad's steppin' all over 'er feet.'

Kay dragged her eyes away from the tall young soldier and saw her parents dancing the last waltz together on the crowded floor. They looked so happy as they held each other tightly. Everyone seemed happy that evening, even Elsie, whose marriage was a total mess. Everyone was smiling and joking together, and Kay felt sure that she was the only person in the hall who was miserable; miserable enough to die, and it was all his fault. He should have realised that she had feelings and she wasn't a child any more. Well, see if she cared. Pat Kelly could flirt all he liked with those women. He meant nothing to her.

The night sky was now a patchwork of twinkling stars, and the freshening breeze was a much-needed change from the airless hall.

Kay bit her lip and fretted at letting hardness creep into her heart; she blinked back sorry tears as she stood alone on the steps outside the social hall. Very soon Pat would be facing terrible dangers and maybe she would never see him again.

The music had ceased and people were singing loudly,

> 'There'll be bluebirds over
> The white cliffs of Dover,
> Tomorrow, just you wait and see.'

All day news broadcasts punctuated the wireless programme, and people constantly stopped each other in the street to exchange fragments of news. Mrs Thomas and Mrs Greenedge had been at each other's throat ever since Billy Thomas had kicked his ball through the Greenedge's parlour window, but now the two warring women stopped to talk together about the invasion that had taken place that very morning. Being good Catholics, Annie Thomas and Bet Greenedge went to a special midnight mass at St Luke's, arm in arm, old animosities forgotten. The Kellys went to church too that evening to pray for their only son, Patrick.

Earlier that same evening, 6 June 1944, Kay Brennen had hurried home from her job as junior assistant at the borough council library in time to catch the early evening news broadcast. Her heart ached and a vice quickly tightened on her insides as she sat with her mother in the cool parlour.

'They said the Sixth Airborne Division went in last night,' Ada Brennen told her daughter. 'They said there was only light casualties, but they always say that, don't they?'

The vice tightened further still, and Kay fought back the sickness that threatened to overwhelm her. It was madness, she knew, but she had no control over her feelings. It was love: unrequited, but filling her every waking moment.

Joe Brennen walked in from the scullery, rolling down his shirt-sleeves. 'It seems ter be goin' very well so far,' he said authoritatively.

Ada nodded. 'Please Gawd it'll all be over soon,' she sighed.

Joe suddenly noticed the sadness in his daughter's pale face and he put his arm around her shoulders. 'At least it'll be all over long before our Colin's old enough fer call-up,' he remarked.

Ada stood up and reached for the empty teapot. 'Let's 'ope so.

4

It's bin worryin' the life out o' me, the war draggin' on so,' she said. 'Colin'll be fourteen this November. 'Ow time flies. Kay's sixteen next month.'

Chapter One
1950

Bermondsey's docks and wharves provided work for large numbers of the borough's inhabitants, as did the many tanneries and food factories, but there was another crucial element of industrial Bermondsey: its railway network. The huge freight yards off the Old Kent Road were a source of employment for many more of the local people.

Rail-tracks from London Bridge Station spread out like so many metal fingers above the backstreets, along the numerous Victorian viaducts, reaching through to the suburbs and then down as far as the south coast. At first there had only been a single line, the London to Brighton Railway that ran parallel with the riverside borough's southern boundary. It had been opened in the middle of the previous century to cater for the more affluent city dwellers who could afford to leave the grimy industrial surroundings at weekends for the bracing Brighton air and the health spas. By the turn of the century a network of track had been laid and the freight yards built over an area of grassland to cater to the prospering food and leather factories. The railway system was developed until it was able to transport all the goods destined for the south of the country, and to export goods overseas, via the Southampton Docks; its importance to the well-being of Bermondsey and its inhabitants was vital.

As with the tannery businessmen, the Southern Railway Company were obliged to provide houses and tenement blocks for their ever-increasing workforce, and by the turn of the century large blocks of flats had been established. Brighton, Eastbourne and Worthing Buildings had become landmarks in the borough. Near to the large railway goods depot new backstreets sprang up, lined with the traditional two-up, two-down houses for the railwaymen and their families.

Waggoner's Way was a small railway street situated behind the Old Kent Road. Neat little houses ran its length on both sides, and the turning ended at Hastings Street to the north and Dover Lane at the southern, Old Kent Road end. Behind Hastings Street were the huge freight yards, their tentacles stretching out almost to the Rotherhithe boundary.

At each end of Waggoner's Way there were two corner shops. Joseph Mezzo's grocery shop and Jack Springer's newsagent's straddled the corners of Hastings Street, while at the Dover Lane end there was Sammy Dinsford's bootmender's and an oilshop owned by Basil Cashman, a crusty individual who was never two days alike. The Waggoner's Way folk were predominantly railway workers, although a few of the residents had inherited their tenancies and worked elsewhere.

At number 8, halfway along the little turning on the east side of the street, Joe Brennen sat reading the Sunday paper. His wife Ada was busy peeling potatoes in the scullery. She paused to rub the itch on the tip of her nose with the back of her hand and pop her head into the passage. 'Oi, Joe, are you gonna do as I asked yer an' go round ter see if Elsie's all right?' she shouted.

Joe put down the *News of the World* and sighed as he took out his silver pocket-watch. 'I was gonna wait fer a while, luv,' he called out. 'I wanted ter give that monkey of 'ers time ter get out ter the pub.'

Ada glanced briefly out of the window at the January sky and sighed in resignation as she got on with preparing the Sunday lunch. She was a slightly built woman with a trim figure, short dark hair and brown eyes. Five years younger than her husband, she handled him very competently. Ada had always allowed Joe to make family decisions and then she did the necessary adjustments and policy changes by using guile and tact. Joe understood and acquiesced, knowing that after many years of happy marriage neither of them lost out, and common sense prevailed in the Brennen household. Ada Brennen was a very shrewd woman who never forgot that she had a gender advantage, with four grown-up daughters to call on for support if need be. She considered it a favourable situation, all told, and though he would not be unduly put upon, Joe Brennen knew the score.

Barbara came out into the scullery and sat down heavily. At twenty-five, she had a dark complexion with large brown eyes and a pretty oval face. Her figure was trim and she carried herself very confidently.

'Is Jamie callin' round this mornin?' Ada asked her, realising from the expression on her daughter's face that all was not well between them.

Barbara shook her head. ''E makes me sick at times,' she said with passion. 'I'm sure it's that miserable old muvver of 'is who causes 'alf the arguments between us. All I said to 'im was...'

'Look, luv, I don't wanna 'ear. You made yer bed an' yer gotta lie on it,' Ada told her sharply.

'Yeah but...'

'Yeah but nuffing,' Ada cut in. ''Ow long you two bin courtin'? Four years? It's about time you eivver tied the knot or kissed goodbye. Crikey, Barb, you'll be an ole biddy before yer get wed, the way you're goin'.'

Barbara made a moue as she got up to slice the cabbage. Her mother was right, she had to admit. Jamie was a really nice lad who treated her with consideration and respect, too much respect at times, she felt. She should have read the situation more clearly from the start and been more assertive. It was too late now though. Jamie would not change while his ageing, ailing mother was alive. She had too much of a hold on him.

Dawn came into the scullery looking bright and breezy. She was twenty-three, pretty and with a fair complexion. Her figure was full and inclined to chubbiness and her pale blue eyes seemed to sparkle in her round face when she smiled. Dawn was a romantic who, on her own admission, had fallen in and out of love more times than she cared to remember. Her current boyfriend was a young man with high hopes of a banking career in the City, and Dawn felt that this could be 'it'.

'I've a feelin' Gordon's gonna propose soon,' she said with a childish shrug of her shoulders.

Ada nodded casually. 'That'll be nice,' she said curtly. 'I 'ope yer tell that young man o' yours ter come an' talk ter yer farvver first. Yer know yer dad's a stickler fer propriety.'

Dawn smiled sweetly and studied her fingernails. 'Course I will,' she replied. 'Gordon wouldn't want it any ovver way.'

Ada sighed as she put the last of the peeled potatoes into a large pot. She had heard her daughter go on so many times about her young men and they had all wanted to propose at one time or another. Ada had come to the conclusion that Dawn was either prone to romanticising or else she was very fickle indeed.

The front door sounded and Kay, the youngest of Ada's daughters, walked into the house. 'I couldn't get that material down the Lane,' she announced. 'The stall wasn't out this week.'

'Never mind, I'm not waitin' fer it. Next week'll do,' Ada replied.

Kay caught the smug smile on Dawn's face. ''Ow's Gordon?' she asked, probing.

'We might be gettin' engaged soon – after 'e's 'ad a word wiv Dad,' Dawn added quickly, catching the stern glance from her mother.

'Tell me more,' Kay said with a wicked grin.

'Look, if yer wanna sit around chattin' do it in the parlour, not out 'ere under me feet. In case yer've all fergot I've got a dinner ter get,' Ada scolded them.

'Dad's readin' the paper in the parlour,' Barbara replied. ''E don't like us chattin' in there when 'e's readin' the paper.'

'Don't worry about yer farvver, 'e's goin' out very soon,' Ada told them confidently. 'You ready, Joe?' she called out loudly.

'Just goin', luv,' came the reply.

'Dad's not goin' up the pub, is 'e?' Dawn asked quickly.

'I've asked 'im ter go an' see 'ow yer sister is,' Ada said with a concerned look on her face. 'That gel worries the life out o' me, what wiv one fing an' the ovver.'

'I dunno why she ever picked Ernie Gates fer an 'usband,' Barbara remarked. ''E was always flash. Really fancied 'imself.'

Ada raised her eyebrows as she reached for the packet of salt. 'People are not always what they seem,' she said, pouring a measure of salt into the palm of her hand. 'Our Elsie was impressionable an' Ernie was a man o' the world, so ter speak. It's a dangerous combination, so you lot better not ferget. I've got one no-good in-law, an' that's quite enough ter be goin' on wiv.'

Joe looked into the scullery. 'I'm just off,' he announced.

'Don't ferget ter try an' persuade 'er ter come round fer dinner,' Ada told him. 'I ain't seen anyfing of 'er or young Billy all week.'

Elsie Gates sat in front of her dressing-table mirror in Dover Lane and dabbed at her puffed eyes. 'Christ, I look awful,' she told herself aloud.

Downstairs the front door sounded and she breathed a sigh of relief. Ernie would be out all day now, thank God. It would be the Mason's Arms until they closed at two o'clock, then the inevitable afternoon drinking session with the landlord and a few of his cronies, which often went on until the pub opened again at seven. Ernie usually played cards on Sunday evenings with a few friends, and if she was lucky he wouldn't be in until very late, after she had gone to bed. What a terrible admission, Elsie thought, sighing at her image.

The pale-faced young woman had just finished dressing when her father arrived at the house. Joe Brennen gave his daughter a customary peck on the cheek at the front door and walked into the parlour. 'Where's our Billy?' he asked.

''E's playin' next door wiv Amy's kids,' Elsie replied as she self-consciously straightened an ornament on the mantelshelf.

'You all right?' Joe asked, giving her a questioning look.

'Yeah, course I am,' she replied quickly.

Joe eased himself down into a fireside chair and clasped his hands across his middle. 'Ernie's gone out then?'

Elsie nodded. 'Yer just missed 'im,' she said casually.

'Yer muvver wants you an' young Billy ter come ter dinner, luv. She's worried about yer,' Joe told her.

'Why should she be worried? We're all right,' Elsie replied defensively.

Joe looked down at his clasped hands for a few moments and then his eyes went up to his daughter's. 'Yer've not called in fer a week now, an' let's face it, gel, you only live round the corner,' he said quietly.

Elsie sat down heavily and gave her father a wan smile. 'Yeah, I know, Dad, but yer gotta understand I don't get much time durin' the day,' she told him. 'There's Billy ter take ter school, then I go straight off ter the factory. OK, I know it's only part-time, but when I come out at two there's washin' an' ironin', then I've gotta collect Billy an' get the tea ready fer when Ernie gets in. I'm tired out by the evenin'.'

'Well, what about terday? Yer can come fer dinner terday, can't yer?' Joe persisted.

'I dunno. There's so much ter do.'

'Yer muvver's gonna be upset if yer don't.'

Elsie sighed in resignation. 'All right, I'll be round as soon as I've

10

collected Billy and got 'im cleaned up. They're playin' out in Amy's yard an' they'll all be black as Newgate's knocker.'

Joe consulted his pocket-watch and stood up with a grunt. 'Fings no better between you an' Ernie, then?' he asked.

Elsie shrugged her shoulders. 'We're all right,' she replied dismissively.

Joe knew that it was no use going on and he made for the door. 'Try not ter be late. Yer know Muvver don't like to 'old the dinner up,' he told her. 'Anyway, it'll be nice fer you an' yer sisters to 'ave a chat. They all miss yer, yer know.'

''Ow's young Colin?' Elsie asked as she stood at the door. 'It's ages since I've seen 'im. 'E never seems ter be in when I call round.'

''E's gone fishin' down in Kent somewhere,' Joe replied. 'I don't s'pose 'e'll be 'ome till late.'

Elsie watched her father walk away along the turning and she sighed sadly as she went inside and closed the front door. He was beginning to look his age now, she thought. It must have been hard for him to adapt to working in the freight yard driving a shunting engine, after all the years he had spent on the main-liners. That burst ulcer had really been a blessing in disguise, though. His life had always been controlled by the clock. She had heard him say many times that seconds counted on the main-liners. Even now that he was working in a less time-intensive job, he still consulted that silver pocket-watch of his at every opportunity. God knows how he would have got on without it.

Ada leaned back in her chair after the Sunday meal was over and smiled happily at the family gathering. Only Colin was absent, and he would no doubt be enjoying himself with his friends, she thought. The girls all seemed cheerful enough, with the exception of Elsie, who was trying to put on a brave face. Joe was looking better too, although he had still not got his old appetite back after his illness.

'Stay where you are. We'll do the washin' up,' Barbara said as her mother reached out across the table.

Ada did not protest. She was looking forward to an hour in the armchair with her feet up. It would give the girls the opportunity to have a private chat, too. Dawn was good at wheedling information out of her sisters, and she would no doubt have noticed the way Elsie was. There was something badly wrong in her eldest daughter's marriage, Ada was convinced of it. Ernie Gates had the reputation locally of being a hard man and a bully, and Ada felt sure that he had hit Elsie on more than one occasion. There was the time her daughter had stayed away for two weeks; when at last she did call round there had been signs of bruising on her face. Elsie had dismissed it as a minor knock, received when young Billy swung one of his heavy toys over his head. Another time Ada had bumped into her at the market. Elsie had looked in pain and was holding her ribs. That time too she had passed it off with some feeble excuse.

Ada slipped into the armchair and smiled as five-year-old Billy left the table and came to her. He was her only grandchild and she doted on him.

'Well now, 'ow's my little man terday?' she asked, running her hand through his thick fair hair.

'I'm all right, Gran'ma.'

Ada lifted the lad on to her lap and, as soon as the girls had carried the crockery from the room, she said casually, 'Where's yer dad, Billy?'

Joe had seated himself in the armchair facing her and he shook his head quickly as Billy's eyes flickered in the direction of the scullery.

'I dunno,' he said softly.

'Do yer see yer dad much?' Ada asked him.

Billy shook his head. 'Not much.'

'Does yer dad 'elp yer play wiv yer toys?'

Again the youngster shook his head.

'Leave it alone,' Joe hissed angrily.

Ada looked at her husband defiantly, then came back to her grandson. 'Tell me, Billy, do yer like your daddy?'

'I like it better wiv just me an' Mum,' the lad replied after a pause.

Ada heard the clatter of dishes and laughter coming from the scullery and she decided to press a little further. 'Tell me, Billy. Does your daddy ever spank yer?'

Billy looked up into his grandmother's eyes questioningly and then he shook his head once more.

Joe motioned towards the door. 'Mind they don't come in,' he warned.

'Does Daddy ever 'urt Mummy?' Ada asked him in a soft voice.

Billy suddenly slid down from her lap. 'I'll go an' see if Mummy's finished,' he said.

Ada watched her grandson hurry from the room, then she turned

12

to Joe. 'That lad's bin primed ter keep 'is mouth shut. It stands out a mile,' she whispered.

Joe pinched out his cigarette-stub and threw it into the fire. 'If I found out that monkey was ill-treatin' our Elsie, or that boy, I'd swing fer 'im, I swear I would,' he growled.

Ada leaned back in her chair and shook her head sadly. 'Where did we go wrong, Joe?' she asked him.

'What d'yer mean?' Joe queried.

'Well, after all we've tried to instil into 'em as they were growin' up, an' then our Elsie goes an' picks a wrong 'un,' she said, sighing. 'Then there's Barbara an' Jamie. They've bin goin' tergevver on an' off fer four years now an' they still don't seem ter know their own minds. Dawn, too. She's 'ad more boyfriends than I care ter remember, an' every one of 'em comes a cropper after a few weeks. An' as fer our Kay, I dunno about that one, I'm sure. She's a mystery ter me.'

Joe leaned forward to pick up his tobacco pouch from the hearth. 'The way I see it, our gels are no different from anyone else o' their ages,' he replied. 'They wanna be sure they pick the right bloke before they commit 'emselves. They've seen what's 'appened to Elsie an' they don't wanna make the same mistake. There's nuffink wrong in that, surely?'

'Yeah but that's what I'm sayin',' Ada went on. 'What about Elsie? Where did we go wrong wiv 'er?'

Joe carefully rolled his cigarette and licked the paper before answering. 'I don't see that we can be 'eld ter blame,' he said finally. 'Yer gotta remember the war was on when our Elsie wed. I don't fink any of us thought much about the future. It was enough ter stay alive. It was more like, live a day at a time an' the devil take the rest, so ter speak. When yer look back, yer gotta say that Ernie was all right at the beginning. Fings seemed ter turn sour after Billy was born. P'raps she wrapped 'erself up in that lad an' Ernie felt 'is nose bein' put out o' joint, or p'raps 'e didn't want children an' blamed 'er.'

'Well, that's just the way a man would fink,' Ada said sharply. 'They want their pleasures but they don't wanna pay the price. If that flash git didn't want kids 'e should 'ave made sure himself. You know what I'm talkin' about.'

'Now look, luv, I'm not sayin' that's what the trouble's bin. I'm only sayin' it could be,' Joe replied in a mollifying tone, not wanting her to get worked up. 'Yer'll find out what's goin' on, I'm sure. I just didn't want yer blamin' yerself fer the way fings 'ave turned out, that's all.'

Ada was still frowning. 'Yeah well we'd better leave it fer now,' she said quietly. 'I'll get ter the bottom of it one way or anuvver.'

The washing-up had been done and the four sisters stood talking together in the small scullery. Elsie was careful to steer the conversation away from herself, and in doing so she inadvertently pulled the proverbial rug from under her youngest sister's feet.

'By the way. I bumped into ole Mrs Catchpole the ovver day,' she remarked. 'I 'adn't seen 'er fer ages. She was tellin' me that Pat Kelly's back in the neighbourhood. Apparently 'is marriage broke up an' 'e's livin' back 'ome till 'e sorts 'imself out.'

Barbara's wide eyes rolled from side to side in sham alarm. 'Watch out, gels. Pat the Rake's in town,' she purred.

Kay felt her face flush at the mention of the young man's name and she fought to hide her embarrassment from her sisters. It was so stupid, she told herself. It was a childish crush she had had. Patrick Kelly had never shown any interest in her, but she had become obsessed with him. It had taken her all of two years to get over the upset of him marrying the Carter girl, and just when she thought she had put it behind her, Elsie had to go and stir it all up again.

Chapter Two

Joe Brennen left his house on a cold January night for his monthly meeting with the Jolly Boys. He had shaved, put on his best blue serge suit and a collar and tie, as befitted the treasurer, and as he walked purposefully towards the railway depot, Joe was feeling relaxed.

It had been an honour to be elected as treasurer, though at first he had worried whether he would be able to perform his duties competently. That was a year ago, and now that he was established as an official within the select group, he felt a sense of pride.

The Jolly Boys had been founded after the London Blitz, when a group of Bermondsey rescue workers banded together socially to raise money for various charities. Five years after the end of the war, the group was still going strong, and although they were older now, the men still gathered together religiously once every month at the railway social club.

Joe Brennen walked into the hall and was immediately button-holed by Charlie Catchpole. ''Ere, Joe. I gotta tell yer. We've just 'ad an application fer membership from Scatty Jim,' he said, grinning widely.

Joe shook his head slowly. 'Who's put 'im up to it?' he asked, trying not to laugh.

Charlie's wizened face took on a pained look. 'I reckon it was Errol, don't you? After all, 'e works alongside the bloody idiot.'

Joe felt that Charlie was being a little hard on the man. Jim Carney could hardly be described as an idiot, more an eccentric. He was a loader at the depot who was always provoking argument by his garbled outpourings; he had an opinion on every subject of discussion under the sun, and his often controversial viewpoint set arguments flaring. He also had a knack of upsetting the loading

15

bank foremen and checkers by being deaf, when it suited him, and one rather uncharitable foreman had nicknamed him Scatty Jim.

Jim Carney had never married and he lodged with the Bradys at number 13 Waggoner's Way. He was a lonely man in his forties, tall and ungainly, and thanks to his actions and opinions and his sometimes strange behaviour, he found it difficult to make friends with people, though he was anything but stupid. Over the years he had learnt to use his peculiarities to best effect, but his playing the fool did not stop his workmates making a fool of him too. He took the jokes and pranks against him very well, nevertheless. The way he saw it, it was better to be noticed than ignored, and although it was sometimes not very nice to be laughed at, he was sure that they all meant well really.

Errol Baines was the ringleader on the loading bank when it came to pranks against Jim Carney, and the latest joke had been devised when the subject of the Jolly Boys came up.

'What are they exactly?' one loader asked during the tea break one morning.

'They're a group o' blokes who do work fer charity,' came the reply.

'Can anyone join?' another asked.

'Nah, it's a private club.'

'That ain't right,' Jim Carney chipped in. 'They should be only too glad to accept new members who'd work fer charity.'

Errol Baines nudged his colleagues. 'I make yer right, Jim, but yer see, they ain't exactly closed ter people. It's a case o' bein' particular who they accept, if yer get me meanin'.'

'No, I don't,' Jim replied, scratching his unruly dark hair.

'Well yer see, they set tests fer applicants,' Errol told him.

'What sort o' tests?' Jim asked innocently.

'Well, yer see they 'ave ter be very careful who they take on. After all, anybody could say they was collectin' fer charity, couldn't they?' Errol went on.

Jim Carney was getting impatient. 'I know that. Anybody wiv 'alf a brain would know that,' he said, shuffling about on his size thirteen boots.

'Yeah, but I just wondered if you understood,' the ringleader of the loading team said with a sly grin.

'I understand, so tell us about the tests,' Jim pressed.

'Look, if yer really serious about joinin', go in ter the club after

16

work an' see the secretary about an application form,' Errol suggested.

The big ungainly character was by now feeling very irritated. 'The tests! What about the tests? he shouted, sticking his face forward and leering.

'Oh, the tests. Well, yer gotta get four sponsors,' Errol told him, having stalled long enough to think of a suitable idea. 'They gotta say that they know yer and that you're a pillar o' society.'

'Pillar o' society?'

''S'right.'

'What's that mean?'

'Well, like doin' good turns fer people.'

Jim Carney scratched his head vigorously. 'So the four people 'ave gotta know I done somefink good?'

''S'right.'

Jim Carney spent the rest of the day pondering on what he had been told, and by the time the shift was finished he knew what he had to do.

That evening at the social club the Jolly Boys' meeting was almost over and the members were looking forward to a pint or two in the bar.

'Is there any ovver business?' the chairman concluded.

Charlie Catchpole raised his hand. 'An application fer membership from a Mr Carney.'

'Mr Carney? Anyone know 'im?' the chairman asked.

''E's a loader at the depot,' Charlie told him.

'Well, p'raps you'll be good enough to inform Mr Carney that this is a closed club an' we don't take on new members,' the chairman said, peering over his glasses at Charlie. 'Now if that's all, I declare the meeting closed.'

Joe Brennen sat with Charlie and Tom Kelly around a table in the comfortably furnished bar. 'I understand yer lad's comin' back 'ome,' Joe said, looking up from his pint.

'Yeah, fer a while, just till 'e sorts 'imself out wiv the divorce,' Tom replied. 'It's a bloody shame really, but there yer go.'

Joe nodded thoughtfully. His own daughter's bad marriage made him worry for her.

'So there's no chance of a reconciliation then?' Charlie asked.

'Nah, it's all over. They both feel the same way. I'm just glad there's no children ter consider,' Tom told him.

For a while the three men sipped their beers in silence, then Charlie turned to Joe. ''Ere, I bin finkin' about Scatty Jim,' he said. 'I ain't got the 'eart ter tell the poor bleeder 'e can't join the club. I fink I'll 'ave a word wiv Errol Baines. I'll let 'im break the news to Jim.'

Kay Brennen sat at the dressing table combing out her long blonde hair. The young woman was alone in the front bedroom which she shared with her two sisters, and in the quiet solitude she felt troubled. Until Barbara had mentioned Pat Kelly the way forward had seemed clear. David had been open and honest about his intentions and she had had to make a decision. She was sure that her feelings for him were strong enough to overcome the problems their clandestine affair would encounter, and she was prepared to accept things the way they were. David had not pressed her for an answer, but she knew she could not keep him waiting too long.

Outside the fog was thickening and Kay pulled the curtains together over the window to shut out the night. Why should the mention of Pat Kelly's name throw her plans into turmoil, she fretted? There had never been anything between them, although it must have been obvious to him how she felt about him. He must have noticed.

Kay adjusted the collar of her dressing gown and rested her chin on her cupped hands as she stared into the mirror. It was as though it was only yesterday that she had come face to face with Patrick Kelly in the street. He had just returned home after the end of the war in Europe and he was still in uniform. She remembered mumbling how nice it was to see him back home in one piece, and he had smiled at her in that lopsided way of his. It had set her heart pounding and she recalled how flustered she had got. Patrick was in his early twenties and she was not yet seventeen. She had wanted to tell him that every night she had prayed to God to keep him safe and she loved him very much, but all she could do was smile back at him and let him walk on without another word.

Patrick had picked up where he left off as far as his flirting went. The local young women knew of his reputation, but it didn't seem to make any difference. There was always some young woman on his arm, and Kay had hoped that one day he would ask her out, but he never did.

She had just turned nineteen and was feeling very grown up when

18

Patrick started going out with Eileen Carter. It wouldn't last, she remembered telling herself. The Carter girl had a reputation to match his, and Kay was determined that she would be ready and waiting when Patrick was free of her. It was not to be, and the news of his engagement to Eileen Carter came as a terrible shock. It was as though her whole world had crumbled into pieces. Even then she did not give up hope. Engagements were known to end, she told herself.

The day Patrick Kelly got married was the worst day in her life. Along with her family she had gone to the church and to the reception afterwards, and she remembered dancing with all the young men who asked her. It was a pathetic attempt to let Patrick see that she was desirable, but he obviously had eyes only for his bride. Now, just two years later, the marriage appeared to be over and he was coming back into the fold. Well, he had had his chance long ago. There was someone else on the scene now and, as far as she was concerned, Patrick Kelly had come back too late.

Elsie had enjoyed the time she had spent with her family but, as she tucked five-year-old Billy up for the night, her heart was heavy. She had not been able to fool them into believing that things were fine with her, and they had all tried in their own ways to get her to open up to them. How could she, if she were to be totally honest, she sighed? How do you tell your own family that the man in your life finds you uninspiring in bed and has lost all interest in you as a person? Where had it all gone wrong? Had she been too wrapped up in young Billy to notice her husband?

Elsie was still sitting at the foot of Billy's bed when she heard the front door open. The lad was sleeping soundly by now and she left the room quietly and went down into the parlour.

'The card game broke up early,' he said flatly.

'D'yer want some supper?' Elsie asked him.

'Nah, I'm off ter bed. I got an early start termorrer. I gotta go ter Manchester. It's a two-day trip, by the way, so don't wait up.'

After he had left the room, Elsie sagged down into the armchair. It seemed ages now since he had even called her by name. This was worse than when he used to raise his hand to her, she told herself. At least there was some passion then.

The fire was burning low and it had grown very late as Elsie sat alone in the quiet room. She glanced over to the sideboard and saw the two pictures of happier days. Ernie looked very handsome then, and she was smiling happily at his side. The other picture was of the three of them. Billy was two years old, and he looked very serious and wide-eyed in his father's arms. How soon it had all changed. Tomorrow her husband would be driving his laden lorry up north, probably feeling glad to be away. After all, it was how she felt when he went on those long-distance trips.

Ernie's voice carried down the stairs. 'You ain't gonna sit down there all night, are yer?'

Elsie sighed in resignation and turned out the light as she left the room. Not so very long ago he would have called down to her much earlier, and with a vastly different tone to his voice.

Errol Baines had decided that the little ruse should continue as there was growing interest amongst the loaders, and as soon as Jim Carney arrived for work, the prankster was ready.

'I got a call from the committee last night, Jim,' he said.

Carney's eyes widened. 'What they say?' he asked quickly.

'It's a bit involved. We'll talk about it at tea-break,' Errol replied.

'Can't yer tell me now if I've bin accepted?'

'No, I can't.'

'Yer've only gotta say yes or no.'

'Yes or no.'

Jim Carney shuffled impatiently. 'What's that s'posed ter mean?'

Baines pointed towards the line of waggons drawn up along the bank. 'We got fifty tons o' canned goods ter stick in those this mornin',' he said sharply. 'If I stand 'ere natterin' ter you fer the next ten minutes or so, we'll both end up wiv our cards, so be told.'

Jim Carney reluctantly gave in and set to work, lugging the cases of food from the sheds into the waiting waggons. His workmates were enjoying the joke and the whole affair was threatening to get out of hand.

'I reckon it's a definite no,' one said as he passed by.

'I fink Baines black-balled yer,' another muttered offhandedly.

'You're gonna be all right, Jim boy,' someone said, smiling crookedly.

'Bung 'im a quid an' yer in, no trouble,' yet another whispered.

The plot was thickening. 'I reckon it's a bloody disgrace,' a serious-faced loader said in passing.

Jim Carney was hooked. 'What is?' he asked anxiously.

'I can't say. It's a bloody disgrace, none the less.'

When tea-break arrived, Errol Baines grabbed the dupe by the arm and propelled him to one side. 'Now listen carefully ter what I've got ter say,' he told him with a stern look. 'I've just 'ad a word wiv Charlie Catchpole, that's why I couldn't tell yer before. Charlie said the Jolly Boys are only takin' one or two new members this year, so yer gotta pull yer finger out. Get four decent sponsors – not anybody, mind – an' get 'em ter give yer a good reference.'

'I bet my lan'lady would oblige,' Jim said, stroking his chin.

'Nah she's no good. It's gotta be someone outside the 'ome,' Errol explained with a deep frown.

'Gawd knows who I could get,' Jim muttered, shaking his head slowly.

'I s'pose yer could get a reference from Farvver O'Brian at St Augustine's, an' maybe the depot manager'd give yer one, as long as yer don't tell 'im I put yer up to it,' Errol said gravely.

Jim nodded animatedly. 'Fanks, Errol, I really appreciate it. I wouldn't say you told me ter see 'im, honest. 'Ere, but what about the ovver two references though?'

'I'm afraid yer'll 'ave ter sort that out yerself,' Errol told him, hiding a smile.

That evening after he had finished his tea, Jim Carney calmly announced to his landlady that he was going to church.

'When was the last time you set foot in church?' a very surprised Sara Brady asked him.

'I gotta see Farvver O'Brian,' Jim told her.

'But yer not a Catholic, are yer?'

'I might be, after ternight,' he replied.

Chapter Three

Kay left the Old Kent Road gasworks where she worked as a typist in the accounts department, and hurried along the busy thoroughfare. The day was gloomy and cold, and as she made her way towards New Cross she pulled the collar of her fawn-coloured winter coat up around her ears. Her long blonde hair was neatly gathered and tied with a black ribbon at the nape of her neck, and she had taken care with her make-up. She had wanted to look her best that lunch-time and had put on her black patent high-heels.

She saw the tall, well-built man in his black raincoat standing outside the restaurant; as she approached he came up to meet her with a smile on his handsome face. 'Yer look very nice,' he said, slipping his arm round her waist.

Kay returned his smile and let him guide her into the warm interior. ''Ow was it?' she asked as soon as they were seated.

David Mason looked down at his clasped hands for a few moments, then his eyes met hers. 'Ter be honest I was surprised by the way she took it,' he said quietly. 'It was as though she was expectin' it.'

'She most prob'ly was,' Kay replied.

The young man looked around the crowded restaurant, as though fearful of spotting someone he recognised. 'I knew she was seein' this feller and I'm sure she knew I was involved wiv someone, but we never discussed it,' he explained. 'I know it sounds very strange, but I want yer ter believe me, Kay. Since Alice 'ad that breakdown we've not slept in the same room. She initiated it in the first place by makin' all sorts of excuses why we should 'ave separate rooms, an' at first I was angry, ter say the least. It's bin more than two years now an' she's bin meetin' this bloke on a regular basis fer over a year. We've bin goin' our own ways an' no questions asked.'

A waitress came up and handed Kay the menu-folder. 'I'll be back soon,' she announced.

'Did she admit she was seein' this feller?' Kay asked as soon as the waitress had left.

'Yeah, it was all cards on the table,' David replied. 'I told Alice that I couldn't go on like this any longer, an' I thought it'd be fer the best if we made a clean break. When I told 'er I was seein' someone too she just smiled. As I said, I'm sure she knew from the start.'

'What 'appens now?' Kay asked.

'I'm movin' out at the weekend, an' Alice is gonna stay in the flat fer the time bein',' David told her. 'I've found a furnished flat just up the road, Kay. I want yer ter see it.'

Kay studied the menu. 'I fink we'd better order,' she urged him, seeing the waitress approaching.

The fish was tasty and the new potatoes and peas were cooked to perfection, but Kay had difficulty finishing her meal. She felt unusually nervous and her stomach seemed to be rebelling. Warning bells were starting to sound in her head and she could not dispel the feeling that she was willingly walking into something from which she might not be able to escape. So far it had all been innocent enough. They had been meeting now for over a month, and they had kissed and caressed whenever the opportunity presented itself, but circumstances had prevented it from developing into a full relationship. The physical desire for him was strong in her, and she knew that David felt as she did. Now that he was getting his own flat he would most probably want her to move in with him, although he had not as yet said so. Questions were beginning to chase each other in her mind. What would her parents think? And just as importantly, what had led to his marriage breaking down? Was it Alice's nervous illness alone which had precipitated it, and if so, what had led her to form a romantic attachment with another man? Could it be that David was in some way to blame for her illness? It was all so confusing and complicated, and Kay felt distressingly out of her depth.

'I'd better walk yer back, it's nearly two o'clock,' David said, cutting into her thoughts as she sipped her coffee.

They stepped out into the murky afternoon and she took his arm as they set off along the busy road. He was charming and very considerate, and he had a smile that reminded her of Patrick Kelly.

23

It was that smile which had first attracted her to him when he called to service the office machines. There had not been much to do that afternoon, and she had got into conversation with him. He had told her then quite openly that he was trapped in a bad marriage, and she had made up a story about a love affair that had soured. David had been very sympathetic and suggested that they might meet one evening to talk some more. She had agreed. Their friendship had grown very quickly and, until her sister had brought the news about Patrick Kelly returning to Bermondsey, Kay had felt it was inevitable that David Mason would be the man who would eventually take her virginity.

'Well 'ere we are,' David said as they reached the gasworks gates. 'Can I see yer on Friday evenin?'

Kay nodded. 'Usual place?'

David nodded in return and lightly held her arms, kissing her briefly on the mouth. 'Until Friday.'

'Bye, David,' she smiled.

Sammy Dinsford shovelled more coke on to the fire in his bootmender's shop and then set about cutting a pair of thick leather soles for the boots he was repairing. It was nearing six o'clock and he wanted to finish the boots before he closed for the night. Sammy was a pleasant character in his late forties, and already balding. His pale blue eyes were set in a thin face, and he had a permanent stoop from constantly sitting hunched over his bench. He had inherited the business from his father, who had realised early in life that there was a good living to be made in boot-repairing in Bermondsey. Railway shunters, loaders and maintenance crews were inclined to be heavy on footwear, as were the factory workers and rivermen, and there was never a shortage of worn-out boots stacked up for repair at the back of his shop. Arthur Dinsford had taught his son Sammy the trade and taught him well, and when he and his wife finally retired to Brighton, he knew that the business would continue to prosper.

When Sammy had lined up a leather sole to the first boot and secured it with a tack, he scooped up a handful of brads and put them in his mouth, methodically working them on to the tip of his tongue one by one as he used them to secure the sole. He worked quickly, hammering each brad home around the edge of the new leather with one blow from the wide flat file.

The tiny kettle was starting to boil, and Sammy took a break to

24

make a cup of tea before he trimmed the soles. He was sitting cross-legged at his bench, enjoying the short respite, when Danny Adams walked in.

'Watch'er, Danny boy. 'Ow yer doin?' he asked him.

The stocky young man stood rigidly at the counter and placed his clenched fists on the lino-covered surface. 'I come fer me boots,' he said gruffly.

Sammy winced as he got down from his high stool. 'I gave 'em ter yer last week,' he told him.

'I put 'em in fer repair.'

'Yeah, I know, but I gave 'em ter yer last week. Don't yer remember?'

'I dunno,' Danny replied, staring down at the coke fire.

'I tell yer what,' Sammy said with a disarming smile. 'Go an' 'ave a look indoors. If yer can't find yer boots come back an' see me an' we'll sort somefing out.'

Danny stood for a moment with a vacant look in his dark eyes, then he nodded and turned stiffly to the door. 'See yer, Sammy,' he said as he stepped out of the shop.

'See yer, Danny.'

The bootmender shook his head sadly as he set to work on the boot strapped on the last. He had known the Adams family for years now, and he recalled what a fine specimen of a man Danny had been when he joined the Airforce at the outbreak of war. The young man had flown in Lancasters and had been on twenty bombing missions as a tail-gunner when the tragedy occurred. The bomber had been badly damaged during a night raid on Bremen and was limping home to its East Anglian base when one of the two remaining engines failed. The plane came down on farming land a few miles short of the airfield, and Danny was pulled out from the blazing wreckage by a farmer. All the other members of the crew perished. Danny spent many months in hospital recovering from head injuries: finally he had been discharged from the service on medical grounds.

Sammy Dinsford had been kept informed of Danny Adam's condition by the young man's widowed mother, who often popped into the shop for a quiet chat. She confided to the friendly bootmender the concern she felt for her son, who did not seem able to hold a job down, nor form any friendships. As she explained, Danny was not a belligerent man, in fact he had always been quiet and sensitive from a child. The problem was he suffered brief losses

25

of memory, or vacant spells as Dot Adams preferred to call them. He had found work on a building site and at a local sawmill, but he tended to wander off on occasions, or sit staring absently into space, and he had subsequently been sacked for laziness.

Sammy finished nailing the sole to the second boot. He trimmed the protruding leather and filed it smooth before adding a touch of black dye and running a wax round the edges of both boots to waterproof the leather. As he was tying a name tag to the repaired pair, Danny Adams walked in the shop once more. Sammy could see immediately from the look in his eyes that the young man had recovered.

'Sorry about that, Sammy,' he said, smiling sheepishly. 'Me ole lady said I'd better pop in an' tell yer not ter worry about those boots. I got 'em on.'

'Yeah, I noticed as yer walked out the shop. I called out but yer didn't 'ear me,' Sammy lied as he returned a smile.

'I'm startin' work next week,' the young man told him.

'That's good news. Whereabouts, Danny?'

'The Old Kent picture 'ouse. I'm gonna be an usher.'

'Well yer'll be able ter see all the pictures fer nuffink,' Sammy said, grinning.

'Yeah, an' if I come over a bit dizzy I can always sit down,' Danny told him.

'Yer'll be in the warm too. It's a nice place the Old Kent picture 'ouse.'

Danny waved a cheerful goodbye as he left the shop, and Sammy sighed sadly as he gathered his tools up and threw them in a box under the bench. He could visualise the young man in a long coat with braided epaulettes and cuffs, and the peak cap that went with the uniform, and he shook his head as he thought what a shame it was. That sort of job was for an elderly man, not a strapping young bloke like Danny Adams. He would be in for a bit of a ribbing too, once the local Herberts found out he was working as an usher.

Sammy raked out the fire, locked up his shop and set off home to New Cross.

Father O'Brian sat back in his comfortable armchair in the study and felt at peace with the world. The cardinal's visit had gone off very well, and the restoration fund was beginning to grow encouragingly. Very soon he would be taking his winter holiday, and he was looking forward to seeing his hometown of Cork once more. Father O'Brian was in his sixties and had spent more than thirty-five years in the working-class areas of London. For twenty years now he had been parish priest at St Augustine's, Bermondsey, and had got to know many things about the diverse members of his flock. He knew them all by name, and took comfort in the knowledge that they all held him in grateful high esteem.

Father O'Brian was suddenly jerked upright in his chair when Sister Albertina tapped on his study door, announcing that he had a visitor by the name of James Hubert Carney who would like to discuss an urgent matter.

The priest frowned as he bade Albertina show him in. The name Carney did not ring a bell, and he was willing to bet a month's plate collections that the man was not one of his flock.

'Sorry ter trouble yer but . . .'

'Won't you sit down, my son?' Father O'Brian said, smiling benevolently as he looked up at the tall stooping figure of Scatty Jim framed in the doorway.

Sister Albertina gave the newcomer a curious look before she departed and Jim turned to her and lowered his head in an exaggerated gesture of reverence before taking a seat facing the priest.

'How can I help you?' Father O'Brian asked, seeing the strained look on Jim's face.

'Well, yer see, I'm in a bit of a fix really. Well not exactly a fix, but I gotta sort o' get meself sorted out wiv the form an' Bainesy reckons I should come an' see yer about if yer'll sort o' do the honours, so ter speak,' Jim explained.

Father O'Brian gave the visitor a blank look and stroked his brow with the tips of his fingers. 'Mr, er . . .'

'Carney's the name, Farvver, but you can call me Jim.'

'Yes, Jim, well I'm afraid you've left me a little confused. Tell me. Are you a member of our church?'

'Nah, as a matter o' fact I'm a bit of a mixture, so ter speak,' Jim replied, crossing his legs and leaning back in his chair.

'A mixture?'

''S'right. Yer see, my ole man – I mean me farvver, well, 'e was a Methodist. Now me muvver, she was an out-an'-out Wenlocker.'

'Wenlocker?' Father O'Brian repeated, frowning.

Jim Carney smiled. 'Yeah, that's what they used ter call the ole gels who was always in the Magnet. The Magnet's that Wenlock 'ouse at the Bricklayer's Arms. D'yer know it?'

The priest shook his head slowly, wondering if he had inadvertently admitted a raving lunatic into his study. 'I'm wondering if you've come to the right place, Mr Carney, er Jim,' he said. 'Maybe the Methodist minister would be more able to help?'

'Nah, you're me man. Bainesy said you're the best bloke ter see, sorry, I mean priest. 'E reckons I should see you.'

'You mention this Mr Baines. Who is Mr Baines?'

''E's me ganger at work,' Jim told him. 'I'm a loader at the railway goods yard off the Ole Kent Road, yer see. Now Bainesy reckons I should get a reference from yer.'

'A reference? But I don't know you at all,' the father gasped.

'Yeah, I thought about that, but I got this idea yer see an'—'

'Now now, just a moment,' the priest cut in. 'What exactly do you want a reference for?'

Jim's face was lit by a radiance from within. 'I wanna be a Jolly Boy,' he said solemnly.

'I'm sure you do. We'd all like to be jolly boys,' Father O'Brian replied, realising with a sinking feeling that he was indeed talking to a madman.

'Ah, but yer can't. It's a closed shop. Not everybody can be a Jolly Boy,' Jim told him quickly. 'I got it all worked out, though.'

'I'm very pleased to hear it,' the father said slowly, his eyes wide and staring.

Jim Carney uncrossed his legs and leaned forward in the chair. 'Now, if I was ter come round 'ere, say two nights this week an' 'ave a bit of a sweep up an' clean yer winders, 'ow's about that? I could give yer pews a bit of a polish as well. They look like they could do wiv it. Then yer'd know I was doin' good an' then crash bang wallop, zomper zompers, frew the card. The way's clear ter givin' me the reference. What yer say, Farv?'

Father O'Brian got up and made for the door. 'I need to talk to someone. I'll only be a minute,' he said quickly, giving his visitor a forced smile and muttering a silent prayer.

Jim sat back and sighed contentedly. That wasn't too bad, he thought.

Father O'Brian stepped out into the stone-floored corridor and beckoned Sister Albertina urgently. 'Sister, I think we've got an unbalanced person in there,' he said a little breathlessly, motioning to the study with his thumb.

'Holy Mary Mother of God!' the sister gasped.

'Now, we must stay calm,' the priest said quickly. 'I want you to stand by that phone. If you hear me call out, ring the police immediately. I just pray that the man proves to be harmless. I'm worried though. He started talking gibberish for a moment.'

When he re-entered the study, Father O'Brian tried to put on a brave face. 'I've just had a word with the cardinal, Mr Carney, I mean Jim,' he began. 'Now I've been informed that as you are not a Catholic, I can't give you a reference, but I'm sure that if you see the Methodist minister at your local mission he'll be more than happy to oblige.'

Jim Carney's face dropped for a second or two as the words sank in, then he suddenly brightened. ''Ere, I could change to a Catholic. I could sign the forms now if yer like.'

'I'm sorry, but it's not as simple as that,' the priest replied in a hesitant voice.

'Oh well, if that's yer attitude, I'm sorry I troubled yer,' Jim said sharply as he stood up and turned to the door. 'I'm bleedin' glad I ain't a Catholic.'

A very relieved Father O'Brian watched his visitor stomp off and then he hurried out to Sister Albertina. 'We can breathe easily now, my dear,' he said with a sigh. 'Oh, before you leave, there is one more thing. I'd like you and I to take a look at the pews.'

Chapter Four

As a cold January sun rose over Waggoner's Way the little turning behind the Old Kent Road was coming alive. As on every Saturday morning, a ritual was taking place: women were out whitening their front doorsteps while children played together, windows were being cleaned with newspaper and vinegar, and the rag-and-bone man appeared, pushing his barrow into the street and shouting his unintelligible cries. A steady stream of humanity passed to and fro: laden shopping-baskets and bags were carried into the houses, and when the chores were finished it was time for a chat on the freshly whitened front steps.

''Ere, luv, I'm sure our Jim's got religion,' a buxom Sara Brady announced.

'Not Jim Carney,' Dot Adams replied, tucking her hands into her apron. 'What makes yer fink that?'

'Well, the ovver night 'e got all spruced up an' when I asked 'im where 'e was off to, 'e told me 'e was goin' ter see Farvver O'Brian at St Augustine's,' Sara went on.

'That's strange.'

''E's a bloody strange one if you ask me.'

Emily Toogood from number 12 came along puffing. She set her shopping-bag down at the Bradys' front door. ''Ere, I've just come from Mezzo's,' she announced. ''E's put 'is eggs up tuppence a dozen.'

'I dunno why yer don't go down the Blue. It's cheaper than goin' ter Joe Mezzo's fer yer eggs – an' yer butter, come ter that,' Dot told her.

'Yeah, I keep sayin' I'm gonna give 'im a blank, but yer know 'ow it is. That Blue's a long drag, especially when yer short o' time. I've got so much washin' an' ironin' ter do an' it looks like it's gonna be a dryin' day terday,' Emily explained.

Joe Brennen turned the corner. As he passed the chatting trio he waved out.

''E's got 'is 'ands full,' Sara remarked knowingly.

'Wiv those gels of 'is, yer mean?' Emily queried.

'Yeah. There's three of 'em still at 'ome an' I 'eard that Elsie's 'avin' problems wiv 'er ole man,' Sara confided, nodding her head in the direction of Dover Lane.

'That Ernie Gates is a right nasty sort o' bloke,' Dot ventured. 'I wonder why she ever got 'iked up wiv the likes of 'im. Elsie's a nice pleasant gel.'

Sara looked along the street in both directions and then leaned forward. 'Guess what I 'eard? Pat Kelly's marriage is on the rocks.'

'No,' chorused the other two.

''S'right. Mrs Kelly told me that they've split up an' 'er Patrick's gonna come back 'ere till fings get sorted out,' Sara revealed.

'Pat Kelly's a real tasty feller,' Emily drooled. 'If I was a bit younger I wouldn't mind 'avin' 'is shoes under my bed.'

'I fink yer'd 'ave ter join the queue,' Dot laughed. 'D'yer remember when 'e come 'ome on leave that time just before the invasion? 'E did look smart. I could 'ave fancied 'im meself.'

''E was in the Airborne, wasn't 'e?' Emily queried.

'Yeah. Bloody mad lot they were,' Dot replied. 'Pat Kelly's mob got dropped over there before the rest went in. I bet it was a right ole do.'

''Ere, Dot, 'ow's your boy gettin' on?' Emily asked her.

Dot Adams shook her head sadly. ''E's worryin' the life out o' me, ter tell yer the trufe. 'E's only gone an' got 'imself a job up the Old Kent picture 'ouse.'

'What as?' Sara asked.

'Why, a bloody usher, would yer believe?' Dot told her. 'Wait till they find out round 'ere. 'E'll be a right laughin'-stock.'

''E'll be all right,' Emily said encouragingly. 'At least the lad's not lazy.'

'I can't get over it,' Dot groaned. 'I can just picture 'im now in that bloody long coat down to 'is ankles an' that great big cap. It makes me wanna cry every time I fink about it.'

Along the street, another conversation was taking place. Charlie Catchpole had been nagged into cleaning the windows at number 1 when the lumbering figure of Errol Baines came into the turning.

'What you doin' round 'ere?' Charlie asked him.

'I'm collectin' me boots from Dinsford's,' Errol replied.

'Scatty Jim's bin ter see the priest at St Augustine's, so I understand,' Charlie said.

Errol's ruddy face broke into a wide grin. 'Yeah an' 'e's asked ter see the depot manager as well,' he chuckled.

'Yer better watch out your little joke don't get out of 'and,' Charlie warned him. 'Yer know what that manager's like. If Carney lets on it was you who put 'im up to it, you're gonna be fer the 'igh jump.'

Errol waved away Charlie's fears. 'Ole Preston ain't too bad,' he replied. ''E knows we 'ave Jim Carney on a lump o' string at times. 'E's more concerned about the work gettin' done. At least we've got a good team on our shift, an' there ain't anuvver shift ter touch us.'

Charlie Catchpole had to agree. He had worked at the depot for many years as a shunter and Errol Baines's team certainly had a very good output record. 'Just watch yer step, that's all. It's all right taking the piss out o' Scatty Jim as long as nobody gets 'urt,' he warned.

Errol nodded. 'I'm gonna tell yer somefink, Charlie,' he said. 'The way I see it there's a lot o' lonely people in this world an' Jim Carney's one of 'em. 'E's never bin married an' as far as I know 'e ain't got a livin' soul as kin. Now where's that leave 'im? All 'e's got is Sara an' Stan Brady. They're Jim's only kin as far as 'e's concerned. Then there's us workmates. Now you know as well as I do that Jim's a very awkward bloke ter get along wiv. Yer gotta admit 'e does get on yer nerves at times. The fact 'e's always leavin' 'imself open ter ridicule makes the rest of the blokes take an interest in 'im, if only ter take the piss. Now I got a few little thoughts about that. I honestly believe Scatty Jim deliberately leaves 'imself open ter piss-takin', just so 'e can be the centre of attention. It's the same in big families, like the sort o' family I come from. One member of the family does strange or stupid fings just ter get noticed. You fink about it. I tell yer straight, Charlie. As far as me an' the lads are concerned, Jim's OK. We wouldn't see nuffink bad 'appen to 'im.'

When he walked away, the elderly shunter stood at his front door pondering what he had said, and Errol Baines went up a little in his estimation.

At the junction with Hastings Street, Joe Mezzo had his grocery shop. Joe was Maltese and in his mid-fifties; he had been in the country since he was a child, the son of a merchant seaman. Joe too had joined the merchant marine when he was nineteen and served as a deck-hand throughout the war, getting torpedoed twice. He and his wife Maria ran a very efficient grocery shop, and Joe enjoyed being a shopkeeper almost as much as he enjoyed a gamble. The only cloud in Joe Mezzo's sunny sky was food rationing. Having to fill in endless forms and certificates irritated him, though Maria did most of the clerical work. It irritated him too having to limit his customers. The answer to that, as far as Joe saw it, was to make it clear to the regular delivery drivers who called on him that he was in the market for a bit of 'bent gear', as he described it. The response surprised even him. Eggs, sides of bacon, cases of tinned hams and fruit all found their way into the back of his grocery shop.

On Saturday morning Joe was breaking open a case of tinned pears in the storeroom when PC Fuller looked in. 'Maria said you was out 'ere,' he puffed, sitting down on an upturned crate.

Joe straightened his aching back and grunted. 'I got a fresh cut put away, Al,' he told the constable. 'You an' your missus are gonna enjoy it, I tell yer.'

Albert Fuller was quite aware of what Joe Mezzo was getting up to, but he found it more profitable to turn a blind eye to the devious goings on. As he saw it, no one was getting hurt, and the local people were all eating better than they would have been on their basic rations. 'Cheers, Joe,' he said as the grocer handed him a flat packet which contained slices of freshly cut shoulder ham.

Joe watched the policeman tuck the packet away under his tunic, and he took out a corona cigar from his waistcoat pocket. 'Yer don't smoke these, do yer?' he said.

PC Fuller shook his head. 'I've give 'em up,' he replied, smiling. 'What wiv the fags an' the weight I'm puttin' on, I ain't got a prayer o' catchin' anybody in a sprint.'

Joe laughed, and after getting his cigar properly alight he sat down facing the officer. 'Tell me, Al, what's the s.p. on this new super?'

The policeman's face took on a serious look. 'Cranley's 'is name. A bit of a stickler by all accounts, but a fair-minded bloke,' he replied. 'The bad news is, there's a new DS in the station. Detective

Sergeant William Moody. Apparently 'e's moved up from Clapham. Used ter be a PC in this neighbour'ood, so there's no pullin' the wool over 'is eyes. Sergeant Moody knows the score, an' I'll give yer a bit of advice. Now this is strictly between you an' me, Joe. Moody's crooked. 'E'll be gettin' 'is back'anders soon as 'e susses out the manor, but don't you go tryin' ter prime 'im up if 'e turns up 'ere. Moody don't take bribes from small fry, no disrespect intended. 'E'd put you away soon as look at yer, but the big boys'll get away wiv murder if they reach fer their cheque-books.'

Joe Mezzo nodded. 'I understand, Al, an' fanks fer warnin' me. Pop in on Monday afternoon when it's a bit quiet, an' I'll bag yer up a few tins o' fruit fer the kids. We gotta look after them, don't we?'

'Cheers, Joe,' PC Fuller said as he stood up. 'I'll see yer then.'

Maria hurried into the storeroom as soon as the policeman had left. 'What's wrong?' she asked anxiously. 'What yer bin an' gorn an' done?'

'I just tried ter bribe Fuller wiv a side o' bacon an' I'm comin' up the Ole Bailey next week,' Joe said, grinning.

'You just be careful. A copper ain't ter be trusted,' Maria warned him, her large dark eyes growing wide with concern.

Joe patted her on her ample bottom and grinned. 'There's no need ter concern yerself, sweet pea,' he told her. 'Your Joe is as pure as the driven snow.'

'Yeah, an' I'm the virgin queen,' she growled as she left the room.

At number 8 Waggoner's Way, the Brennen girls were assembling. Dawn and her elder sister were already there when Kay walked in.

'I was just sayin' ter Babs. I fink Danny Adams is gettin' worse,' Dawn told her. 'I passed 'im this mornin' in the turnin' an' 'e didn't seem ter know me.'

Kay shook her head as she unbuttoned her coat. 'It's a real shame,' she replied. 'I remember 'ow 'e always used ter come up an' talk to us. 'E was a good-lookin' boy too. 'E always seemed ter be 'angin' round our Elsie.'

'Danny's still a nice-lookin' boy,' Barbara remarked. 'It's just that vacant look on 'is face that makes 'im seem different.'

Kay sat down and kicked off her shoes. 'Anyone got a pair o' stockin's I can borrer?' she asked. 'I've got a ladder in mine an' I'm goin' out ternight.'

34

'I got a pair you can loan, long as yer don't ladder 'em. Is it the same feller?' Dawn inquired.

Kay nodded. 'Yeah, David's takin' me up West ter the flicks.'

'When yer gonna bring this mysterious David 'ome fer us to inspect?' Barbara asked, giving Dawn a quick glance.

The youngest of the Brennen girls shrugged her slim shoulders. 'Pretty soon,' she replied casually.

''Ere, Kay, 'e's not married, is 'e?' Dawn asked smiling.

'Yeah, an' 'e's got seven kids,' was the sharp reply.

'Oops, sorry I spoke,' Dawn said, pulling a face.

Ada Brennen walked into the house carrying a laden shopping-bag. She puffed loudly as she set it down just inside the door. 'Any tea in the pot?' she asked, looking around at her brood.

'I'll go an' put the kettle on,' Barbara volunteered.

'Is Colin in?' Ada asked as she slumped down into the armchair.

''E's gone down Millwall. It's a cup game, so 'e said,' Dawn replied.

Ada looked up at the clock on the mantelshelf. 'Yer farvver's late,' she remarked as she kicked off her shoes.

''E's in,' Kay told her. ''E's out in the yard.'

'What's 'e doin' out there?'

'I dunno, but 'e's bin bangin' away fer ages.'

'Gawd, 'e ain't mendin' that rabbit 'utch, is 'e?'

'Is Dad gonna start keepin' rabbits again?' Dawn asked.

'Over my dead body,' Ada said sharply. 'I remember the last turn-out. First it was chickens, an' when it come ter wringin' their necks you lot kicked up blue murder. Then it was rabbits. None of yer would touch rabbit stew so we 'ad ter get rid of 'em.'

As Barbara was pouring out the tea, Joe walked into the parlour.

'What you bin doin' out there?' Ada asked him.

'I bin puttin' a new door on me toolshed,' he said, grinning smugly.

'What was the matter wiv the old one?' Ada queried.

'It wouldn't stay shut. Besides, it was fallin' ter pieces,' Joe told her. 'The rain was blowin' in an' all me tools were gettin' rusty.'

'That's 'cos yer never use 'em,' Ada countered.

'Well, fings are gonna change,' Joe said, taking a cup of tea from Barbara. 'A man needs an 'obby, somefing to occupy 'is mind, an' I've decided ter take up carpentry seriously.'

Ada's eyes went towards the ceiling. 'I'll believe it when I see it,' she answered.

'You just wait,' he said smiling. 'I'm gonna get a new saw an' a couple o' chisels, an' I'm gonna sharpen up that ole plane.'

'Well, when yer ready let me know an' I'll give yer the list,' Ada replied, smiling at the girls.

'What needs doin?' Joe asked her, his eyebrows raised.

'Well, there's the cupboard door that needs a bit took off it. Then there's the girls' bedroom door. It won't shut prop'ly. The floorboards in our bedroom are split on your side o' the bed, not ter mention the weavverboard that's missin' from the front door. Want me ter go on?'

Joe looked a bit deflated as he took a sip of his tea. 'Soon as I get me tools sorted out, I'll start doin' the jobs,' he told them all.

'I got a better idea,' Kay cut in. 'Why don't yer get Danny Adams ter do the jobs? It wouldn't cost much an' Danny's pretty good at carpentry.'

'That's right. 'E used ter do a lot of odd jobs fer people in the street,' Ada added. 'Danny done a smashin' job on Mrs Rowe's front door. 'E even varnished it afterwards.'

'I dunno,' Joe said, stroking his chin. 'I know the lad's pretty 'andy wiv an 'ammer an' nails, but it's the way 'e is.'

'What d'yer mean, the way 'e is?' Ada said sharply.

'You know what I mean,' Joe replied. 'The lad 'as these blackouts or whatever they call 'em. We'd never be sure 'e'd finish the job once 'e started. I don't fancy 'avin' floorboards stacked in the corner fer weeks on end.'

'Give 'im a chance, Dad,' Kay urged him. ''E wouldn't want much an' it could be the makin' of 'im. It'd be like a tonic really.'

Joe nodded thoughtfully. Ada's little inventory had made him feel a little less enthusiastic about becoming a handyman around the place. 'Yeah, all right,' he said. 'Ada, you 'ave a word wiv Dot Adams. Tell 'er yer want Danny ter pop in an' take a look at what wants doin'. 'E can give yer an estimate.'

'In the meantime, can yer take a quick look at the dressin'-table drawer in our room, Dad?' Dawn asked him. 'It keeps jammin' an' there's all my underclothes in there.'

'Better leave it ter Danny, luv. I ain't got me tools sorted out yet,' Joe told her as he leant back in his chair and closed his eyes.

Chapter Five

It had started to rain late on Saturday afternoon as Ada Brennen crossed the turning and knocked at the house directly opposite hers. Dot Adams answered the door and looked surprised to see her standing there.

''Ave yer got a minute?' Ada asked her.

'Yeah, course I 'ave. Come in, luv,' Dot replied.

Ada walked into the spotless parlour and saw that the fire had been banked up with coke. It felt warm and cosy, and she loosened her coat as she sat down in the armchair near the fire.

'It ain't too warm for yer, is it?' Dot asked, easing her large frame into the armchair facing her.

'Nah, it's lovely. These places can be draughty 'oles in the winter,' Ada said.

Dot Adams looked at her visitor expectantly. 'Is there anyfing wrong?'

'Nah, nuffink's wrong,' Ada reassured her. 'As a matter o' fact I wanted ter ask yer somefink, Dot. Does your Danny still do any odd jobs?'

'Yer mean, like fer ovver people?'

'Yeah.'

Dot sighed as she looked around the room. 'Look at the state o' that wallpaper,' she said despondently. 'Gawd knows 'ow long that's bin up now. Must be all of seven years. An' look at the woodwork. One time our Danny would 'ave gone frew this 'ouse like a dose o' salts wiv paint an' paper. Now'days I can't get 'im ter do a fing. So yer see I don't fink 'e'd be up ter doin' odd jobs fer anybody else.'

Ada nodded. 'I was only finkin' it'd be a few bob for 'im if 'e'd agree ter do a bit o' joinerin' fer me.'

'It's good o' yer ter fink of our Danny, an' I could ask 'im when 'e comes in, but I don't fink 'e'd be interested, ter tell yer the trufe, Ada,' Dot said with a wry smile.

Ada started to fasten her coat and Dot stood up. 'I just put the kettle on, if yer got a few minutes ter spare,' she said.

The distant sounds of shunting waggons carried into the quiet room as the two women sat sipping their tea.

''Ave you 'eard that Danny's gonna be an usher at the Old Kent?' Dot queried.

'No, I 'adn't,' Ada replied.

'I don't s'pose 'e'll last there more than a few days at the most,' Dot told her. ''E's gettin' no better, an' when 'e 'as one of 'is turns yer can't budge 'im. 'E justs sits starin' inter space.'

'Ain't there nuffink 'e can take, like drugs or somefink?' Ada asked her.

'Nah, yer see it's pressure, accordin' ter the specialist,' Dot explained. 'What 'appened was, there was a piece o' jagged metal stuck in Danny's 'ead an' it was pressin' on the brain. They 'ad ter put a silver plate in 'is 'ead. You're the only one who knows about this. I ain't told people, 'cos yer know 'ow stupid some of 'em can be. I didn't want 'em askin' Danny questions about it. It wouldn't do any good fer 'im ter keep bein' reminded o' what 'appened.'

'I understand, Dot. I won't breave a word to a soul,' Ada assured her. 'Anyway, 'ave a chat wiv Danny an' see what 'e finks.'

Dot put down her empty cup. 'You've 'eard about Pat Kelly an' 'is missus splittin' up I expect.'

'Yeah, Mary Kelly told me 'erself,' Ada replied. 'It seems ter be the season fer broken marriages. Between me an' you, our Elsie's is on the rocks.'

'I'm not surprised,' Dot told her. 'That Ernie Gates is a right ignorant pig. Ter be honest I was shocked when I saw your Elsie tad got in tow wiv 'im. Ernie Gates 'as got a few enemies round 'ere, too. D'yer remember that set-to 'im an' Pat Kelly 'ad?'

'Do I,' Ada told her, nodding. 'It was over somefink Ernie said about the Carter gel by all accounts. The pair of 'em looked like they'd bin frew a mincer. There was blood everywhere. I fink they'd 'ave killed each ovver if that copper 'adn't come along.'

'Pat Kelly can 'ave a fight, but Ernie Gates is an animal,' Dot went on. 'There's a lot of unfinished business between those two, an' I can see the sparks flyin' again before long, now Pat Kelly's comin' back ter the street.'

38

'Our Kay used ter 'ave a fing about Patrick,' Ada remarked. 'In fact I reckon she still finks a lot of 'im. Mind yer, there was never anyfing in it. She was only a kid when Pat went in the army. I used ter watch 'er face though, whenever 'e was on the scene. She didn't fink I knew. Kids are inclined to underestimate their parents sometimes.'

'D'yer wanna cup more tea?' Dot asked.

'Nah, I'd better be gettin' back. Joe's threatened ter take me up the pub ternight,' Ada said, smiling.

Kay had been thinking of the coming Saturday night out with mixed feelings. She met David at their usual rendezvous, the Bricklayer's Arms, far enough away from Waggoner's Way not to be seen by any of her neighbours. They caught a tram to the Embankment and walked through the fog that was drifting off the Thames into the brightly lit Trafalgar Square. The West End of London had always excited Kay, but on this occasion she felt a little flat inside. David seemed quiet too, and she wondered whether he had had a few words with Alice that morning before he moved out into his flat.

The Odeon cinema in Leicester Square was showing *In The Good Old Summertime*, starring Judy Garland and Van Johnson, and long queues were forming outside the foyer. David smiled at her as he steered her into the theatre and presented his reserved tickets to the solemn-looking usher. Kay was suddenly reminded of Danny Adams and a strange sadness welled up inside her. It should be a happy evening, she told herself. Why should she feel the way she did?

All through the show, David held her hand, occasionally squeezing it gently and rubbing his fingers sensuously along her forearm. She was aware of the aftershave he was wearing, and she saw his white teeth flashing in the darkness as he turned and smiled at her. She must try to pull herself together, she thought. David would be a catch for any girl, and he had told her that he loved her. Kay felt that she loved him too and this was real, not like the love she had carried inside her for Patrick Kelly, knowing in her heart that it would never be. David wanted her, and she realised that she must finally come to terms with the way things were. It was madness to go on saving herself for someone who hardly knew she existed. She was nearing twenty-two and still a virgin, still a child in a harsh world.

They caught the tram back to Bermondsey, and it was as they

walked through the deserted railway arches behind Waggoner's Way that David stopped and pulled her towards him. She was in his arms and her lips moulded to his in a long, ardent kiss. She felt his hands moving along her back and his body pressing against hers; she could feel his rising passion and the heat of his body, and she smelled the sweetness of his smooth chin and the strength in his arms as he almost drove the breath from her aching body.

'I must 'ave yer, Kay,' he gasped. 'Say yer want me. Tell me yer want me ter love yer fully.'

'I do, David, I really do,' she told him.

'Come ter me, termorrer afternoon. Say yer will,' he urged her with a break in his voice.

Kay nodded, her eyes fixed on his as she struggled to find her words. 'I will, David. I promise,' she whispered.

The two young people walked into Hastings Street; in the shadows David kissed her goodnight. Kay moved apart, her hand slipping away from his as she looked into his eyes. David stood there on the corner until she reached her front door, then he walked away towards the Old Kent Road. This would be different, he told himself. This time he would prove himself. He would make love with Kay and satisfy her in the way he had never been able to with Alice. Never again would he have to listen to Alice's taunts and jeers as she mocked his manhood.

Ernie Gates sat in the saloon bar of the Mason's Arms on Saturday evening in urgent conversation with Tommy Bamford, an ex-boxer. The two were somewhat alike in appearance, both heavily built with dark wavy hair, brown eyes and florid complexions, though Bamford's face clearly showed the marks of his earlier trade. He had once fought for the Southern Area light-heavyweight title, only to be beaten on points. It had ended up being Tommy's last fight in the ring, for a few months later he was behind bars, serving five years for grievous bodily harm after a pub brawl in which he almost killed a man much older than himself.

Tommy was leaning forward over the table as he made his point. 'Wiv my record I can't be up front,' he was saying, 'but I'll make sure the right people get involved an' I'll do the necessary. I want ten per cent.'

'That seems fair,' Ernie replied, studying his pint. 'Tell 'em it'll be seven tons o' copper an' lead. Now yer gotta make sure yer tell 'em I ain't in it fer peanuts. I want a fair cut, Tommy. After all, I'm gonna be the one who's gonna end up in the frame if anyfing goes wrong. I reckon that load's come to a couple o' grand, an' it ain't gonna go far if it's split too many ways.'

Tommy rolled his shoulders and moved his head from side to side as though squaring up to an opponent. 'The geezers I'm gonna go an' see play it fair an' square,' he said quickly. 'There'll 'ave ter be a snatcher an' a minder fer starters, but yer'll be put in the picture. The people I'm finkin' of 'ave bin involved in quite a few snatches, an' they know the drill, believe me.'

'I'll take your word fer it,' Ernie said nodding.

'Trust me, son, yer'll get a fair shake, yer got my word,' Tommy told him. 'Before yer get too carried away, though, there's some fings you oughta be made aware of.'

'I'm listenin',' Ernie replied.

'Yer'll 'ave ter take a smack on the chops,' Tommy said with a deadpan face. 'Yer'll be dumped somewhere too, most likely in Eppin' Forest or down in Kent, dependin' where the load's gonna be placed. They'll tie yer to a tree an' yer might be there a few hours before someone spots yer. Don't worry, yer won't be dumped too far from the footpath. Yer'll be near enough fer somebody to 'ear yer shout. Now this bit's very important. The snatch usually takes place when yer pull up at a café fer a cuppa. They'll go fer yer when yer come out after yer break, not before. Now fink about it. They've grabbed yer an' you ain't 'ad time fer a piss. Yer've already swallered a couple o' cups o' tea, then yer tied up fer maybe two hours or even longer. So make sure yer piss yerself while yer tied up.'

'Do what?' Ernie said quickly.

'You 'eard. You're s'posed ter be scared out of yer mind,' Tommy explained. 'Yer've 'ad the load nicked, an' yer've took a smack. They've left yer trussed up in the woods an' yer've got two cups o' tea inside yer. If yer didn't piss yerself the boys in blue would be on ter yer straight away. Now if yer still wanna go frew wiv it, let me know now.'

Ernie's face was serious as he picked up his glass of ale and took a large swig. 'I'm in,' he said, wiping the froth from his mouth with the back of his hand.

Colin Brennen sat reading the Saturday evening paper in the

parlour, and every so often he sniffed loudly. Joe had been trying to doze in the armchair and had been getting increasingly irritated. Finally he sat up straight and glared at his son.

'Colin, do yer 'ave ter keep on sniffin?'

'I fink I got a cold comin',' Colin replied, turning the page and flapping the paper to get it into some sort of order. 'I bin soaked right frew a couple o' times this week walkin' ter work. Still, it's all right fer some.'

Ada was busy cutting a pattern for a dress and she looked at her husband with amusement. Joe allowed himself a smile as he caught her eye and she went back to the awkward job in hand, waiting for his response. Colin was inclined to rib his father in a friendly, oblique sort of way, prompting Joe to respond in his own suitably cutting manner. Colin took after his father in many ways, Ada felt. He had his father's fair complexion and pale blue eyes and he was stockily built. He also had a similar dry humour and attitude.

'They'll liven you up when they get yer in uniform, my boy,' Joe told him. 'If yer start sniffin' on parade they'll treat that as dumb insolence.'

Colin grunted something and chuckled behind his newspaper. He had passed his army medical A1 just before Christmas, and was eagerly awaiting his call-up papers. His job at a boxmaker's in the Old Kent Road was a stop-gap as far as he was concerned, though the piece-rate work had been paying a decent wage since he first went there less than a year ago.

'It's all right fer you ter snort,' Joe went on. 'Wait till the drill sergeant gets you lot on the parade ground. I bet yer'll change yer mind then about goin' in.'

The young man put down the paper and sat up straight in the armchair facing him. ''Ow would you know what it'll be like, Farvver? Yer never bin in the Army,' he said, smirking.

'I've 'eard enough about it ter know,' Joe countered. 'You just wait.'

'I am, an' I can't wait ter get be'ind a wheel. I told the selection officer straight out I wanna go in the Service Corps,' Colin said enthusiastically. 'I said I wanna drive the big stuff like tank transporters so when I come out I can get a job at Pickford's or Warren's. They take machinery all over the country on them great big lorries, and the money's really good. I know somebody who works there as a porter an' 'e earns more in a week than I get in a month.'

'I wouldn't bank on gettin' in the Service Corps,' Joe warned him. 'Yer might get put in the Infantry. A lot do.'

Ada felt a sudden fear for her son as she listened to them talking. The war was over, true, but there were other places in turmoil throughout the world, and young National Servicemen were being sent out to those. Palestine and Borneo were two trouble-spots she had been reading about, and only last week she had seen a bit in the paper about two soldiers getting killed in the Middle East while they were on patrol. 'P'raps yer won't 'ave ter go abroad,' she said, almost to herself.

'I wouldn't wanna spend eighteen months in Aldershot or Catterick,' Colin said quickly. 'I wanna go abroad an' see a bit o' the world. I wouldn't mind the Far East, come ter fink of it.'

Ada tried to concentrate her mind on what she was doing, but the thought of her only son being posted to some faraway place set her worrying and she put down her scissors with a deep sigh. 'I fink I'll put the kettle on,' she said. 'The gels should be comin' in soon.'

Jim Carney walked along the quiet street towards his lodgings, contemplating his next move. The chat with Father O'Brian had been a waste of time, and a lot would depend on the interview with the depot manager this coming Tuesday. Perhaps that would be more fruitful. After all, Preston had known him for a few years now and had never had cause to fault his work. Once he told him it was for a good cause, the manager would no doubt supply him with a decent reference.

Jim reached his front door and let himself in, intending to go straight to his upstairs room, but Sara Brady called out from the parlour.

'Is that you, Jim? Got a minute?'

He walked into the cosy room and immediately noticed the teapot on the kitchen-range hob. 'It's a bloody raw night,' he said, hunching his shoulders as he stared at the pot expectantly.

'There's some tea just made. Fancy a cuppa?' Sara asked, smiling at his craftiness.

'Now yer come ter mention it, I could do wiv one,' he said, sitting down in the armchair and holding his hands out to the fire.

Sara poured the tea and added three spoonfuls of sugar.

'Four please, an' not too much milk,' he prompted.

The landlady sighed in resignation as she added another spoonful to the cup. Jim Carney's eating and drinking habits seem to change with the weather, she thought. 'Jim, I wanted to ask yer if there's anyfing wrong,' she said.

'Nah there's nuffing wrong. Why should yer fink that?' he asked, sipping his tea noisily.

'Well, yer've bin ter see the priest an' yer didn't look very 'appy when yer come back that night,' she remarked. 'I'm not one ter pry, but yer seem worried lately, that's all.'

Jim put his empty cup down and scratched the back of his head vigorously. 'I wanted a reference, that's all,' he told her.

'A reference? What for?' Sara asked, looking puzzled.

'It's ter join a club an' I thought the priest might 'ave give me one,' Jim explained

'But yer don't go ter church.'

'Yeah that's what 'e told me.'

'What sort o' club is it?'

Jim Carney had lodged with the Bradys for a few years now, and he knew that Sara was inclined to gossip. It was one thing taking a ribbing at work, but he had no intention of letting the whole street know his business.

'It's a secret sort o' club an' when I join I'll tell yer all about it,' he said, looking from Sara to the teapot and back again.

'Anuvver cuppa?' she asked.

Jim nodded. 'Yus please. That one went down a treat.'

So far so good, Sara thought. 'I've got a slice o' fruit cake in the cupboard if yer'd care fer a piece,' she said, smiling pleasantly.

'That'd be nice,' he told her.

Sara placed a fresh cup of tea and a thick slice of cherry cake in front of him and then sat down facing him. 'I can understand yer bein' secretive about the club,' she said quietly. 'After all, yer wouldn't want yer business bandied all round the street. But sometimes it does 'elp ter confide in somebody, somebody who would promise ter keep a secret, 'cos they might just be able to 'elp.'

Jim thought about what his landlady had said as he scoffed the fruit cake. Yes, she was right, he decided. He had one month to get the four references needed and she might have some ideas. 'Well, it's like this,' he began.

Chapter Six

On Sunday evenings it was customary for Sara and Stan Brady to visit the Mason's Arms in Dover Lane for a sociable get-together with a few of their friends, but on this particular Sunday evening neither of them felt very sociable. They had had a few words earlier that day, and it concerned their lodger Jim Carney.

'I don't care what yer say, Jim's a decent sort o' bloke an' 'e always pays me on Fridays soon as ever 'e sets foot in the door,' Sara said with conviction. 'Never once 'ave I 'ad ter remind 'im, which is more than yer can say fer that scruffy git Morrison who used ter lodge 'ere.'

'I'm not disputin' that,' Stan said, matching his wife's raised tone of voice. 'What I'm sayin' is, Jim Carney strikes me as bein' a bit touched. I can't seem ter get a word o' sense out of 'im. At least ole Morrison could 'ave a sensible conversation.'

'Yeah, that's all Morrison ever did do, talk,' Sara said quickly, folding her arms over her big bosom and snorting loudly. ''E wasn't too good at talkin' 'imself into a job though, was 'e? The lazy bleeder was more out than in, an' I was never sure when I'd get me rent.'

Stan threw down the paper and glared at his wife. 'The man was ill a lot wiv 'is chest,' he countered. 'When 'e was workin' there was never any trouble over payment.'

'That's as it may be, but I'm tellin' yer I prefer Jim Carney as a lodger,' Sara told him. 'All right, 'e may be a bit eccentric, but 'e's got 'is priorities right. Jim's a worker, an' 'e don't cause us no trouble.'

'Eccentric? Is that what yer call 'im? Scatty's more the word,' Stan growled.

Sara looked hard at her diminutive husband. 'If you took a bit

45

more time gettin' ter know Jim Carney, yer'd understand 'im a little better,' she replied. 'The man's got no one, only us, an' 'e tends ter confide in me. 'E'd confide in you too if yer give 'im a chance.'

'I would, but it's like talkin' ter that fender fer all the sense I get out of 'im,' Stan told her sharply.

'Jim's just a sensitive bloke who tries ter do the right fing by everybody. That's why 'e confided in me about the Jolly Boys,' Sara said with a satisfied smile hovering on her lips. 'Jim wants ter join so 'e can get involved in the charity work they do. 'E's got an 'eart o' gold.'

It was Stan's turn to snort. 'Bloody idiot. Fancy goin' ter see the priest. Carney ain't a Catholic. In fact 'e ain't got any religion, as far as we know.'

'I grant yer it wasn't a sensible move goin' ter see that priest fer a reference,' Sara conceded, 'but I've put 'im right.'

'Oh yer did, did yer?' Stan replied scornfully. 'An' what pearls o' wisdom did yer come out wiv?'

Sara unfolded her arms and leaned forward in her armchair. 'If yer must know, Jim Carney asked me if 'e should go an' see 'is guv'nor about gettin' a reference, an' I told 'im I thought it was a good idea.'

'Lovely, bloody lovely that is,' Stan answered, nodding his head slowly. 'Preston can be a cantankerous ole git at times, an' 'e's gonna be askin' questions. What's gonna 'appen when 'e finds out the idiot's wastin' 'is time wiv a bloody 'are-brained scheme? I tell yer what. It's more than likely Carney's gonna be linin' up down the labour exchange.'

Sara looked abashed. 'Well, I don't fink it's an 'are-brained scheme wantin' to 'elp people,' she replied quietly.

'The blokes are puttin' 'im up to it,' Stan told her angrily. 'The Jolly Boys do bits an' pieces fer charity but they're a closed shop. They don't take new members on. It's just a bloody wind-up.'

Sara went into one of her quiet periods, which meant that she spoke in monosyllables whenever Stan said anything to her, and she was still feeling peeved at the Mason's Arms that evening.

'What'sa matter wiv Sara, Stan?' Charlie Catchpole asked him as the two men lounged at the bar.

'Nuffink as far as I know,' Stan replied. 'Why d'yer ask?'

Charlie gave his neighbour and workmate a knowing smile. He was used to the silent treatment from his own domineering wife, and he had read the signs correctly. 'She looks a bit upset. Fell out, 'ave yer?'

Stan nodded. He knew it was no use trying to deceive Charlie Catchpole. The man was an expert as far as matrimonial discord went. 'We 'ad a few words about that scatty lodger of ours,' he told him.

'Carney's gonna go an' see Preston termorrer by all accounts,' Charlie remarked. 'I warned Errol Baines 'e was goin' a bit too far in windin' Carney up, but you know Bainesy. 'E reckons Preston'll be all right about it, but I don't, some'ow.'

'Nor me,' Stan replied, catching Sara's eye and suddenly realising that the drink he had bought for her was still at his elbow. 'I'll see yer later, Charlie,' he said quickly.

'Was you two talkin' about me?' Sara inquired quickly as Stan put her drink down on the table. 'I saw yer keep lookin' over.'

'As a matter o' fact, Charlie was tellin' me that Carney's goin' ter see Preston about a reference termorrer,' Stan said and, noticing his wife's look of concern, added, 'but I didn't let on I knew.'

'Why did yer keep lookin' over this way then?' Sara asked sharply.

'Charlie's in the dog-'ouse again an' 'e was just sayin' 'e wished 'is missus was like you, that's all,' Stan told her with a ghost of a smile on his face.

Sara picked up her drink and gave him a reluctant smile before casting her eyes away. 'You'd be in the dog-'ouse if you was like Charlie Catchpole,' she reminded him. 'That lazy git won't do an 'and's turn fer 'is missus unless 'e's nagged into it. I wouldn't put up wiv it.'

Stan walked back to where Charlie was standing, thankful that Sara's quiet phase had apparently passed.

Charlie had been having a brief chat with the landlord Arthur Selby and he turned towards Stan quickly as he came back over, smiling to hide his guilty feelings at having been less than charitable about his workmate's miserable-looking wife. 'I was just sayin' to Arfur, it's pretty busy in 'ere ternight,' he said quickly.

Stan Brady nodded. 'I s'pose it's less packed in the saloon bar but I don't feel comfortable in there,' he replied.

'Nah, nor do I,' Charlie told him. 'There's a right crowd gets in there. Full o' bloody spivs an' drones. Joe Brennen used ter go in there all the time, though, till that son-in-law of 'is started usin' the bar. Joe can't stand 'im at any price.'

When they ran out of interesting things to talk about, the two stood sipping their beers in silence, with Charlie Catchpole occasion-ally glancing over to where his wife was sitting with a few of her neighbours. She would soon be beckoning him for a refill and woe betide him if he ignored her summons. Stan Brady on the other hand was staring balefully at the mirror behind the counter. He could see Sara's reflection as she sat chatting with Ada Brennen and Mary Kelly and he was still feeling irritated by her defence of Jim Carney. As far as he was concerned the man was taking advantage of her kindness and generosity by acting the fool. Jim Carney was more shrewd than people gave him credit for, and one day he was going to overstep the mark.

In the saloon bar of the Mason's Arms Tommy Bamford was sitting back in his chair with a smug look on his scarred face as Ernie Gates walked over with a gin and tonic in his hand and sat down with a heavy grunt. 'I've done the business,' Tommy announ-ced briefly in a gruff voice, glancing around the bar with his eyes narrowed.

'What's the score?' Ernie asked, trying not to seem too excited.

'They wanna meet yer soon as yer get back from yer trip,' Tommy told him. 'Provided yer can agree the split, give 'em the necessary info an' a firm date an' time an' it's a goer.'

'I'm back Tuesday night, but it'll be late though,' Ernie said, taking a quick sip of his drink.

''Ow late?'

'Eight, nine. It all depends 'ow quick I get the return load on.'

Tommy Bamford pulled a face and picked up his near-empty glass. 'I'll lay the meet on fer nine firty,' he said, swilling the last of his whisky. 'Be in 'ere waitin'. I won't be comin' though, so it's down ter you.'

''Ow will I know 'em?' Ernie asked.

'They know you, or at least one of 'em does, so just wait till you're approached,' Bamford said with a sly grin.

'They know me?' Ernie echoed.

''S'right.'

'But, 'ow ...?

The old-time boxer stood up and buttoned up his camel-hair

overcoat. 'Don't lose no sleep over it. Just be 'ere,' he said, his face becoming serious. 'I'll be seein' yer, pal.'

Ernie Gates watched with a puzzled frown as the heavily built man disappeared into the foggy street. He suddenly felt his mouth go dry and his stomach tighten. There was no going back now, he realised. Everything would go off like clockwork as long as he kept his head. The police would grill him afterwards and would probably pull out every trick they knew to make him crack, to involve him in the conspiracy, but he was prepared. As Tommy Bamford had told him, 'Open yer mouth ter the law an' yer might just as well cut yer own froat next time yer shave – 'cos if you don't, someone else will . . .'

Earlier that Sunday, Kay Brennen left her house in Waggoner's Way with a deep sigh of relief. Dawn had been a real bitch, she thought. The loan of one pair of silk stockings did not warrant the questions she had plied her with. It was bad enough having to deceive her mother by saying she was going to a workmate's engagement party and might be home late, without her sister's sly remarks. As it happened, her mother had been good about it. There were the usual warnings of course about having too much to drink and being extra careful about who she mixed with, but that was to be expected. Dawn had seen through the deceit, however, and she had been out to learn more. Perhaps it would have been better to tell her the truth, that she was going to meet David at his new home and would be going to bed with him. That would have made her sister sit up and take notice.

The chill air made Kay shiver as she left the street and hurried along Dover Lane, cutting through a narrow alley into the Old Kent Road. David would be expecting her and she had been at pains to look her best. Her long blonde hair was tied at the nape of her neck with a thin black ribbon, and hung down to the waistbelt of her bottle-green, knee-length coat. Her make-up had been put on carefully: just the right amount of colouring round the cheeks, and a delicate touch of pale green eye-shadow that accentuated her naturally long lashes. Pale lipstick and a pair of small glass earrings set it off perfectly, and as Kay hurried on towards the bus stop clutching her patent leather handbag, her high heels sounded loudly on the quiet Sunday afternoon thoroughfare.

When she was comfortably seated on the lower deck of a 53 bus,

Kay soon found herself staring absently out the window. All the questions she had asked herself remained unanswered and she sought to dismiss them. It hardly mattered, she told herself. David had been totally honest from the start, and she had been perfectly at liberty to decline his offer of a night out that very first day when he came to her office. What happened now was with her consent and condonation; she had played the lovesick juvenile for too long. She was a woman now, with the feelings of a woman. She needed to experience love, to savour the passion and fulfilment that until now she had only glimpsed vaguely in her dreams. This evening she would let David take her virginity and make her a real woman.

The bus pulled up opposite the New Cross Garage, and Kay stepped down on to the damp pavement. She hurried along the road and took the first turning on her left, a small street of Victorian houses with short flights of steps leading up to the front doors. Kay saw the name David Mason and the message 'Two rings' as she reached the front door of number 6. Footsteps soon sounded from within, and she smiled as David opened the door.

'I knew you'd come,' he said as he took her hand in his. 'I'll go first. Mind the stairs.'

As soon as they entered his first-floor flat, David took her into his arms and kissed her open mouth. He could smell her perfume, feel the sweetness of her young vibrant body, and taste her full lips. His heart was pounding. 'Let me take yer coat,' he said breathlessly as they moved apart.

Kay looked around and was surprised by the shabbiness of the place. The large room was warmed by a gas fire and lit by a lamp standard in one corner, but there was a distinct smell of dampness and old wallpaper. The table standing in the centre of the room was covered with a lace cloth, and the two matching armchairs had been camouflaged with flowered covers draped untidily over them. The only other piece of furniture, apart from a badly scratched coffee table near one of the chairs, was a long walnut sideboard, its doors figured in quartered veneer. Kay glanced down at the worn carpet square and was immediately filled with compassion for the handsome young man who stood by the room door smiling at her.

'I know it's not much, but it's only a temporary arrangement,' he said quickly.

'No, I fink it's cosy,' Kay replied, trying to sound enthusiastic.

'It needs a woman's touch,' David said as he came towards her.

50

Kay suddenly felt that things were moving too fast and she sat down quickly in one of the armchairs. David loomed over her, his eyes appraising her. 'You look wonderful,' he said hoarsely. 'I was prayin' you'd come this afternoon.'

'I said I would,' Kay replied, clenching a fist impulsively as she felt her nylon snag against the chair.

'Yeah, I know, but you've 'ad time ter fink about it,' David said, reaching down and taking her hands in his.

Kay let herself be pulled up into his arms. She felt his urgency as his lips found hers and she tried to relax, not resisting as he reached his hand under her cardigan and grasped her small firm breast. He was squeezing hard when she wanted him to caress her gently, and kissing her almost in a frenzy, forcing open her lips with his as his breath came in gasps. She had thought he would be restrained and tender, arousing her slowly considering it was her first time, but he seemed to have little control over himself. He was a married man who should have been experienced enough to seduce her delicately, capably, but he was behaving like a young boy faced with the situation for the very first time.

As she pushed him away to catch her breath, David took her by the hand and led her towards the bedroom. She saw how flushed with emotion he was, and his eyes had taken on a glassy look as he turned and swept her up in his arms. She felt herself slipping sideways on to the bed and she smelt mothballs as he leaned over her. He was struggling to lift her tight skirt and she tried to help him with the zip. She could hear him groaning, his voice rising in anger as the passion overtook him. He shuddered violently, and for a moment or two his face took on a look of utter misery, then he sank down over her. She felt his chin resting on her white thigh, his hand gripping her stocking top. He was crying softly, his falling tears wetting her leg. Her anger and frustration were dissolved by David's obvious distress, and she held him, gently patting him like a baby as heavy sobs racked his body.

'There, there. It's all right. It doesn't matter,' she whispered.

'I wanted it ter be so good,' he sobbed, his eyes going up to meet hers as he brushed the tears from his cheeks. 'I've failed yer, just like I . . .'

Kay slipped her hand over his mouth, gently shaking her head. 'We were too eager,' she said softly. 'It'll be better next time. You'll see.'

David slid from the bed and hurried out into the bathroom, and as she stood up and straightened her skirt Kay felt confused and frustrated. David had some sort of problem and it looked as if he needed help to get over it. Should she stand by him and be patient, hoping that he could sort himself out, or should she get out before she got hurt?

He was back now, pale and with sagging shoulders. He was looking at her like a young child who was trying to say how sorry he was but unable to find the words. 'Kay. I feel so awful. I . . .'

She took him by the arms and slowly drew him to her, nestling her head against his chest. 'Don't, David. Don't say anyfing. Just hold me,' she said in little more than a whisper.

Chapter Seven

When Elsie Gates took Billy to the school entrance he seemed reluctant to leave her. Normally he would spot one of his classmates and run off, but this morning he was hanging on to her coat with his head close against her leg. Elsie stroked his fair hair reassuringly and the young lad looked up at her. She could see anxiety reflected in his large blue eyes and her heart felt heavy. She knew that Billy wasn't the sort of lad who was frightened of school, or of bullying children. He was very popular and there were always other youngsters hanging round him. No, there was something else troubling the boy, and Elsie felt she knew what it was.

'Look, there's Jimmy Brody an' Anna comin' along, Billy. Say goodbye ter mummy,' she said, smiling at him.

Billy put his arms round her neck as she kissed him and the young woman's eyes filled with tears.

'Don't be late when I come out o' school, Mummy,' he said.

Elsie swallowed hard. 'Now look, my little bundle o' trouble. I'm always outside waitin', ain't I? I'll be waitin' same as always. Now off yer go. Look, Anna wants ter show yer somefing.'

Billy's face brightened as the pretty little girl came up to him with a shy smile and held out a drawing she had done. She whispered something in his ear and the two of them laughed aloud as they walked in through the school gates together. Elsie watched for Billy to look back and wave, but he was chatting to Jimmy Brody now as well as Anna and he walked straight into the building without turning round.

Elsie felt somewhat relieved as she hurried off to work, but she was sure that young Billy had heard at least part of the row she had had with Ernie the previous night. Their voices had been raised, and at one point she had heard the stairs creak. When she went to Billy's

53

bedroom, the lad appeared to be sleeping, but his breathing was quite rapid rather than shallow and slow like that of a sleeping child. He had more than likely been woken up by their loud arguing and gone to the top of the stairs to listen. He might have heard the angry words she threw at Ernie in her temper. 'I can't stand much more o' this, an' fer two pins I'd run away from the lot of it,' she had shouted.

'Why don't yer then?' Ernie had taunted her. 'Who's gonna miss yer?'

Elsie had sat in the parlour for what seemed like hours, and when she finally went to bed she had lain awake until the dawn light. She realised she must have fallen asleep then, for she never heard her husband get out of bed at six o'clock as usual. She had struggled to rouse herself in time to get Billy off to school, and now as she arrived at Dawson's radio components factory at the end of Dover Lane, she was still thinking about how things were getting steadily worse between her and Ernie. They had not made love for ages now and he always seemed to be chiding her about her coldness towards him, even though he never made any advances. Instead he would sit dozing in the armchair after going to the pub at weekends, and during the week it was little different: he had his tea and then usually nodded off as he sat reading the evening paper. There was little or no conversation between them, no homeliness or common ground any more for them to explore, and Elsie knew that the marriage was crumbling fast. It would have been easier if there was someone else involved, she told herself. At least then there would have been an enemy, someone to target, but the way things were it was like searching for something invisible, like trying to grasp at smoke.

'What yer finkin' about, Elsie?' a voice called out, jerking her away from her thoughts.

'Sorry. I was just . . .'

Albert the foreman smiled indulgently as he looked over from the other side of the workbench. 'We've all gotta pull our weight, lovey. These boxes won't jump inter the wrappin's.'

The rest of the girls along the bench smiled at Elsie's embarrassed reaction. 'It's all right, Albert, our Elsie's bin finkin' about last night,' one of the young women joked.

'I'd like ter dwell on last night,' Albert replied with a wink, 'but I got a packin' department ter run.'

The young woman chuckled as she took another silvered diode valve from its tray in the centre of the wooden bench and expertly wrapped a piece of corrugated paper round it, tucking in the ends in one movement. 'Why? What 'appened last night, Albert?' she said grinning.

'Never you mind. Just get on wiv the packin', will yer,' he told her with a straight face.

Elsie joined in the banter, and for a while her troubles were forgotten. It was a happy firm and the work was clean and varied. The hours suited her, too: she could be on hand for Billy, and the money she earned was a godsend.

Ada Brennen enjoyed her morning break after the family went off to work. Joe was out early this week and the house was quiet; there was time for a cuppa and the morning paper before she started cleaning the house and going shopping in the Old Kent Road. Barbara and Dawn had looked their usual chirpy selves this morning, but she thought Kay had seemed a bit quiet and subdued. It wasn't her time of the month. Maybe she had had a few words with that mysterious boyfriend of hers. Anyway, there was nothing to be done until Kay came home. Then she would try and get her youngest daughter to one side and have a few quiet words in her ear. It was about time she brought her young man home to meet the family.

The knock on the front door roused Ada from her reverie and she was surprised to find Dot Adams on the doorstep. ''Ello, luv. Come in,' she told her. 'I've just topped up the teapot. Fancy a cuppa?'

Dot nodded as she walked into the house. 'I've 'ad a word wiv our Danny,' she said as she settled her large bulk into an armchair. ''E's gonna come round ter see yer when your Joe's 'ome.'

'Oh, I am pleased,' Ada replied as she reached for the teapot. 'Joe's on earlies this week. 'E'll be 'ome around four, so any time after that'll do fine.'

'Ter be honest I didn't 'old out much 'ope when I put it to 'im,' Dot said as she watched Ada pour out the strong tea. 'I just told 'im there was some carpentry needed doin' 'ere if 'e felt up to it. 'E said all right. Mind yer, 'e starts that job at the pictures this evenin'. Gawd knows 'ow long that's gonna last.'

''E'll be fine,' Ada reassured her. 'Will 'e still 'ave time ter call round?'

'Oh yeah. 'E starts at six o'clock an' 'e finishes when they turn out about eleven. Then termorrer 'e's on at one o'clock till Saturday, when 'e's back on lates,' Dot explained. 'They must 'ave seen 'e looked a bit vacant when 'e went fer the job 'cos they've wrote it all down on paper.'

The two neighbours sipped their tea in silence. Eventually Ada put down her empty cup. 'Our Joe's got some tools in the shed,' she said. 'I don't know what condition they're in, though. Knowin' 'im they'll all be rusty, but Danny's welcome ter use 'em if 'e needs to.'

''E's got a lot o' tools of 'is own,' Dot told her. 'I kept 'em oiled and cleaned while 'e was away in the Airforce. Good as new they are. Shame really. 'E used ter be always doin' bits an' pieces fer the neighbours.'

'Well, let's 'ope the few jobs we need doin' will get 'im interested again,' Ada said. 'It'll be good fer 'im. P'raps 'e could earn a decent livin' at carpentry. There's always someone round 'ere needs fings doin'.'

'Let's 'ope so,' Dot sighed, 'but I 'ave ter say Danny don't seem ter be gettin' any better. There's still times when I despair fer 'im. Take the ovver day. I got the tea ready at the usual time so 'e can get into a routine but when I called up to 'is room there was no answer. I even went out searchin' fer 'im in case 'e'd 'ad an accident or somefink. Know where I found 'im? Sittin' on that wall where the static water tank used ter be in Astin's Street. It was almost seven o'clock. Gawd knows 'ow long 'e'd bin sittin' there. I said to 'im, "Danny, yer bleedin' tea's gettin' all burnt up." Couldn't 'ave said a worse fing, could I? I saw 'is face change an' 'e just got down from the wall and walked off. Ten o'clock 'e finally arrived 'ome. I dunno where 'e'd bin, 'e wouldn't say. I don't s'pose 'e knew 'imself.'

'I'm sorry, gel,' Ada sympathised. 'Anyway, yer can just do yer best. Who knows, 'e might suddenly get better. Stranger fings 'ave 'appened.'

'Yeah, that's what I keep tellin' meself,' Dot replied.

'Anuvver cuppa?'

'I won't say no.'

'Nice tea this. It's Brooke Bond's divi.'

'Yeah, I get that too.'

'I save the coupons.'

'Yeah, so do I.'

When Ada returned with fresh cups, Dot said, ''Ere, 'ow's your Elsie?'

'Don't ask,' Ada replied.

'Bad as that, is it?'

'Worse.'

Dot carefully slid the cup across the edge of the saucer to get rid of the drips, and then she took another swig. 'Look, Ada, p'raps I shouldn't be sayin' this,' she said hesitantly, 'but you've a right ter know.'

'Know what?' Ada asked quickly, her face suddenly growing alarmed.

'Well, I was comin' back from the doctor's. I'd bin about me back, an' I saw your Elsie comin' out o' Muvver Dines,' Dot said, looking at Ada with concern.

'I told Elsie not ter get involved wi' that ole cow any more,' Ada said with passion. 'If she's that desperate she should 'ave come ter me an' 'er farvver. We're always 'ere for 'er.'

'I don't s'pose she wanted ter worry yer,' Dot replied.

Ada put down her cup with a bang. 'Last time she went ter that bloody witch she got in right over 'er 'ead,' she said angrily. 'If Ernie 'ad got wise to it the cat would've bin among the pigeons, but as it 'appened my Joe found out an' 'e settled it all up. Trouble is, Muvver Dines preys on people like our Elsie. The bloody interest she charges is scandalous. There should be a law against people like 'er.'

'Desperate people do desperate fings at times,' Dot replied with a sad shake of her head. 'Fer a lot of 'em there's no one else ter turn to.'

'Yeah, but it's not the case wiv our Else. She could 'ave come to us,' Ada went on.

'Don't be 'ard on 'er, Ada, or I'll blame meself fer causin' trouble amongst yer,' Dot implored her. 'I just 'ad ter tell yer.'

'I'm grateful that yer did,' Ada reassured her. 'It's about time that gel o' mine started comin' ter me wiv 'er troubles instead o' goin' ter strangers. Gawd Almighty, Dot, yer know 'ow money-lenders get their claws inter yer. If our Elsie's not careful she's gonna be in debt ter that ole witch fer evermore. It can get so bad yer 'ave ter borrer money ter pay the interest an' it goes on an' on.'

'Don't mind me askin', but that ole man of 'ers is in regular work, ain't 'e?' Dot inquired.

'Yeah an' Elsie's got a part-time job,' Ada replied. 'They should be earnin' enough between 'em ter keep the wolf from the door, but I dunno what Ernie gives 'er fer 'ousekeepin'. 'E's always on the piss. I s'pose that's where most o' the money goes if the trufe's known.'

''E's a nasty git,' Dot said pulling a face. 'I remember that time 'e pasted that poor bleeder who accidentally caught 'is arm in the pub. Me an' Mrs Greenedge were sittin' 'avin' a quiet drink in the Dun Cow when all 'ell broke loose. Ernie Gates got barred from the place an' they took the ovver poor sod up Guy's fer stitches. Someone called the police but it was all over by that time, an' apparently the bloke who got bashed up refused ter press charges. That lucky bastard Gates got away scot-free.'

'Yeah 'e's a violent git,' Ada concurred. 'I tell yer somefink, though. If that no-good bastard lays a finger on our Elsie, my Joe'll sort 'im out once an' fer all.'

Dot picked up the handbag at her feet and stood up. 'Well, Ada, fanks very much fer the tea an' the chat. I 'ope yer didn't fink I was openin' me mouth too much about your Elsie, but I 'ad ter let yer know. It's only right, the way I see it.'

'I'm grateful to yer, luv,' Ada replied. 'At least we can sort it out now.'

As soon as Dot Adams had left, Ada started work. There was much to do and she wanted time to pop round and see her eldest daughter when she got home with Billy.

Jim Carney's shift at the shunting yards finished at two o'clock, and as soon as he had slipped out of his overalls and put on his overcoat, he crossed the tracks and entered the large brick-built offices situated near the main gates. As he climbed the wide staircase to the first floor, one of the office girls came out of the ladies' room and giggled as she saw the chalked sign on the back of Carney's black overcoat.

'I need ter see Mr Preston,' Jim said to the secretary as he popped his head round the door. 'Jim Carney's the name.'

'I'm sorry, but Mr Preston's got someone with him at the moment,' the tall thin lady replied, staring at the grinning figure.

'I'll wait then. Yer see, it's a matter o' great urgency,' Jim told her, repeating what Errol had told him to say.

'In that case I'll find out if Mr Preston can see you when he's free,' the secretary told him.

Jim sat down in the outer office and looked around, whistling tunelessly. Miss Belmont continued typing, occasionally wincing at the non-stop noise coming from the unwelcome visitor.

'It's very important that I see Mr Preston terday,' Jim said suddenly. 'Can't let fings like this get left. Too much at stake.'

'Yes I see,' Miss Belmont replied.

Jim looked at her and smiled. 'Nice typewriter that,' he said. 'Electric, ain't it?'

'Yes, it is.'

'D'yer like bein' a secretary?' he asked her.

'Yes, I do.'

'I like my job.'

'I'm glad.'

'Yeah, it ain't the easiest o' jobs, but I like it.'

'I'm glad.'

'There's a lot ter be said fer workin' out in the open.'

'I suppose you're right.'

'Wouldn't you like ter work out in the open?'

Miss Belmont took off her glasses and rubbed her hand over her eyes, mumbling something under her breath. 'I couldn't very well sit typing important letters on a loading bank, now could I?' she said sarcastically.

'Nah, I s'pose yer right,' Jim replied with a wide grin.

The typewriter started clicking away once more, and Jim tapped his feet as he began whistling again. 'I s'pose yer do fousands o' those letters a day, don't yer?' he asked after a few moments.

'Yes, when I don't get disturbed,' Miss Belmont replied acidly.

'Busy man, ole Preston.'

'Yes, Mr Preston is a very busy man,' she said, the acid tone still very apparent.

'I'm kept pretty busy too.'

'Yes, I expect you are.'

'Mind yer, I could still find the time ter be a Jolly Boy.'

'Well, good for you,' the secretary replied, getting ready to scream.

The inner office door opened and a distinguished-looking man came out, followed by Gerry Preston who waved a cheerful goodbye. Jim Carney stood up quickly, and before Miss Belmont had time to say anything, he coughed loudly. 'Carney's the name, guv,' he said, grinning widely.

'Mr Carney wanted to see you on a matter of importance, Mr Preston,' the secretary said quickly, with one eyebrow raised.

The depot manager winced at the inference, knowing through experience that a raised eyebrow from Miss Belmont spelt trouble of some sort. 'Come in, er, Mr . . .'

'Carney's the name, loadin's me game,' Jim said, holding out his hand.

Preston turned without shaking it and led the way into his office. 'What can I do for you, Mr Carney?' he asked rather wearily, seating himself behind his desk.

'Look, I know yer pretty busy, 'cos Miss What's-'er-name said so, so I won't beat about the bush. Yer see, there's a crowd o' blokes – well, it's not a crowd really, more like a small group – an' they meet every fortnight, or is it a week? Anyway, what I'd like ter do is ter get in wiv this group, but I can't, 'cos they don't take in outsiders, not that I'm an outsider really, after all I work fer the railway just like they do, but they're very particular who they let in. Now me an' ole Bainesy was talkin' the ovver day an' 'e—'

'Stop!'

Jim looked abashed as the depot manager glared at him. 'Sorry, Guv. I just—'

'Stop it right there,' Preston implored him, pressing his hands against his temples in an effort to shut out the buzzing noise. 'I'm extremely busy and I've got no time to listen to a life history. Now please get to the point. What do you want from me?'

'Well, ter put it into a nutshell, I wanna be a Jolly Boy,' Jim said, grinning.

'Don't we all,' Preston replied, his voice sounding desperate.

'Yer don't understand,' Jim told him. 'Now, like I was tellin' yer. This group—'

'For God's sake! Not an annual address, just a brief answer, please.'

'Well, yer see—'

'No! Please no!'

'I only want a reference from yer, that's all,' Jim said, spreading his hands wide and looking aggrieved.

Gerry Preston had been told about the strange character who worked on the loading bank, but he had never thought for a moment that one day he would be almost driven out of his mind by him. 'Miss Belmont!' he called out.

The tall, anxious-looking woman hurried in.

'Miss Belmont. Type this man out a reference, before I go completely mad,' Preston groaned.

'But what do I put?' the secretary asked, raising her eyebrow.

'Ask him. He'll tell you. Oh, and cancel my other engagements for the day, will you? I think I might go home. I'm starting to get a headache.'

Chapter Eight

Kay Brennen had spent the whole of Monday in a state of limbo. Her workmates at the office had tried to make conversation and had soon realised that all was not well. One or two of her close friends were aware of Kay's friendship with David Mason, and had assumed by her uncharacteristically quiet behaviour that it was going through a bad patch, though they were unable to wheedle any information from her.

'I reckon she must be 'avin' trouble wiv David's wife,' one remarked when out of Kay's earshot.

'Nah I fink she's overdue,' the other girl ventured with a knowing look.

'It can't be that. She's not actually slept wiv the feller yet,' the first typist replied. 'She told me 'erself.'

'Well, whatever it is I 'ope she gets it sorted out soon. It's so unlike 'er ter be this quiet,' the second girl added.

Kay was actually feeling a little less depressed as she walked home that evening through the cold winter gloom. The air was bracing after the stuffy office, and she had time to reflect on the awful Sunday just past. David obviously had a problem, and from what she had learned from the medical book Barbara had loaned her, it was called premature ejaculation. The book said that it was a problem mainly associated with young men who were sexually inexperienced, and she wondered what was causing it in David's case. After all, although he said he had been living a celibate life for the past two years, he was married and had been for some time. Maybe it was something she should have done, or had not done, which triggered it off.

As she neared home the doubts and fears were still nagging her. What if David's marriage had broken down because of his problem?

Maybe he had not been able to have a full physical relationship with his wife, and that had caused her illness. Whatever the cause the problem could be remedied, according to the book. The article had gone on to say that premature ejaculation was often a complaint of the mind rather than the body, and when the cause was identified it ceased to be a problem. That was all very well, but how was she expected to get to the bottom of it, if that was the case?

The more she pondered, the more Kay came to realise that she could not just walk away from David, even though his behaviour that Sunday afternoon had shocked and disappointed her. She had gone willingly to him, expecting and wanting him to take her virginity and make her a full woman, but instead she had been left feeling flat and depressed. He needed her more than ever now, and the look on his face when he came out of the bedroom had told her everything. She would stand by him and give him her love. She would be patient, and not allow herself to get angry or frustrated when they were next in his flat.

As Kay walked into the house she realised immediately by the worried look on her mother's face that something was wrong. Barbara too was looking worried, and before she had time to ask questions, her mother pulled her to one side. 'I've been over ter see Elsie. She's got 'erself in a right mess,' Ada told her.

'What sort o' mess?' Kay asked anxiously.

'Dot Adams called round terday about 'er Danny doin' some work fer us, an' she mentioned that she'd seen Elsie comin' out o' Muvver Dines.'

'Oh no, not that ole witch,' Kay replied with a sigh. 'I bet Dad's upset.'

'Yeah 'e's just stormed out of 'ere ter get the evenin' paper,' Ada told her. 'The air was blue. Apparently yer sister needed some money fer Billy's clothes an' she was frightened to ask Ernie fer any extra.'

'But Billy's 'is child too. Surely 'e couldn't be that tight-fisted,' Kay said angrily.

'That's Ernie all over,' Ada replied bitterly. ''E can go an' spend pounds in the pub, but when it comes to 'is own flesh an' blood 'e's found wantin'. Why Elsie ever got in tow wiv that no-good whoreson I'll never know,' Ada growled. 'I told 'er straight ter tell 'im what she's 'ad ter do an' let 'im pay off the debt. I also told 'er ter get a full-time job. I said I'd look after the lad willingly. 'E's not

63

a minute's trouble. After all, it'd only be a trip ter the school an' back.'

'What did Elsie say?' Kay asked.

'She said it wouldn't be fair ter me, an' anyway Billy might fret.'

'But that's stupid,' Kay said quickly. 'Billy loves yer, Mum. 'E wouldn't fret while you was lookin' after 'im, an' besides, it'd only be till Elsie got 'ome from work.'

'That's what I told 'er, but yer know what Elsie's like,' Ada went on. 'She's like the rest of yer. You've all got that stubborn streak. I reckon yer must 'ave got it from yer farvver. Yer certainly didn't get it from me.'

The front door sounded and Ada suddenly pulled a face. 'That's Colin an' I fergot ter tell yer. There's a letter come fer 'im second post. It's marked OHMS.'

'Callin'-up papers?'

'Yeah.'

Colin walked into the parlour and immediately noticed the women's troubled faces. 'What's wrong wiv you lot?' he asked, looking from one to the other.

'It's our Else,' Kay said quickly.

'She's gone an' got 'erself in debt wiv that Muvver Dines,' Ada cut in. 'We'll tell yer all about it later. In the meantime there's a letter come fer you.'

'Me papers?!' Colin replied excitedly.

'It looks like it. Open it,' Ada said as she took the buff envelope from her apron pocket.

Colin tore the letter open and his face dropped. 'Bloody Royal Signals. They've put me in the Royal Signals,' he groaned. 'Catterick, too. I've 'eard that's a right shit-'ole.'

''Ere, watch yer language,' Ada scolded him. 'We don't want no dockers' talk in this 'ouse.'

'Dockers' talk?' Colin laughed. 'They ain't the only ones who can swear. Yer wanna 'ear the lads at the factory. It'd make yer 'air curl what they come out wiv.'

'Well, I don't want curly 'air, fank you very much,' Ada said sharply.

'When d'yer go in?' Barbara asked.

'Thursday the sixteenth o' Feb,' Colin replied.

'Now what's all this about Catterick?' Dawn chipped in.

Colin slumped down in the one vacant chair and folded his arms. 'My mate Dave went in the Armoured Corps an' 'e was stationed at Catterick,' he began. 'Dave reckons that Catterick's the worst place of all ter be stationed. 'E said it was bitter cold up there last winter, an' the blokes all 'ad ter go out diggin' motors out o' the drifts. An' that wasn't all.'

'Is there more?' Dawn asked with a smile.

'Oh yes, there's more,' Colin said with a sage look of disdain on his youthful face. 'Most o' the regular soldiers who train the National Servicemen are nutters. They're put there 'cos they're troublemakers. Most of 'em 'ave bin right frew the war an' they make life really 'ard fer the likes of us. Dave reckons that—'

'All right, that's enough about Dave,' Barbara said quickly, noticing the worried look on her mother's face. 'That Dave sounds like 'e's tryin' ter wind you up. I know a few fellers who trained at Catterick an' they reckon it wasn't too bad at all.'

'Well, we'll 'ave ter wait an' see then, won't we?' Colin growled.

Joe Brennen walked in carrying the *Evening News*. 'Was it yer papers?' he asked Colin.

'Yeah, Dad. The Royal Signals, would yer believe? On the sixteenth o' Feb.'

'They've got big lorries that carry all the signal equipment. P'raps you'll get a chance ter drive those,' Joe said encouragingly.

'You know somefing, Dad. Fer a bloke who's never bin in the Army, yer know a lot about it,' Colin told him scornfully.

'Right you lot, I'm gonna serve up in ten minutes, so get yerselves cleaned up right away,' Ada ordered.

Joe Mezzo closed up his shop and looked through into the back storeroom to make sure that Maria had gone upstairs to their flat before he picked up the phone. ''Ello, is that you, Tony? Tony, I got a bit o' business ter put your way. Yeah, that's right. Call round at seven. No, on second thoughts make it 'alf-seven. I wanna go over it wiv yer. Can yer get 'old o' Nick Zanti an' Mick the 'Ammer? Good. Now, don't let on. Just say Joe Mezzo wants a meet. Yeah, bring 'em along wiv yer. No, yer dumbo, not the shop, Maria would go crazy if she saw you lot walk in. We'll meet at the Dun Cow. Yeah 'alf-seven. See yer there.'

After he put the phone down, Joe did a quick calculation then hurried up to the flat.

65

'Who yer bin talkin' to?' Maria asked, giving him a suspicious look.

'I was checkin' on Tony ter see if 'e's available fer the card school ternight,' Joe replied casually.

'Why, what's the matter wiv Tony? 'E always goes along,' Maria said, probing.

Joe sighed irritably. 'Do I 'ave ter give yer a run-down on all me pals' medical problems as well? Tony's bin a bit, you know ...'

'No, I don't know,' Maria replied.

'Well I'll tell yer then,' Joe said. 'Tony Mancini ain't married, as yer know. Now, Tony decided 'e wanted a woman fer the night, so 'e picks up this likely-lookin' bird in the gamblin' club 'e uses up West. Two days later 'e starts gettin' problems.'

'What sort o' problems?' Maria cut in.

'You know. Men's problems.'

'I dunno what yer mean.'

'Tony finds 'e's got some grief wiv 'is one-eyed python.'

'Joe. Will yer stop talkin' in riddles?' Maria implored him.

'Look. Tony got some trouble wiv 'is plonker.'

'What sort o' trouble?'

'Razor-blade trouble.'

'Holy Mary, give me strength,' Maria sighed. 'What yer talkin' about now?'

'Every time Tony goes fer a slash it's like 'e's pissin' razor blades. Now do you understand, woman?'

'Couldn't yer say Tony's caught a dose?'

'All right. Tony banged a wrong 'un.'

'Serves 'im right. Tony should only bang nice girls,' Maria said with feeling as she walked out of the room.

Chief Superintendent Roger Cranley sat back in his chair and flipped through a file while he waited. Cranley had taken up his new post at Dockhead with some reservations; the station had got itself a bad name over the past couple of years, and he was determined to make changes.

A light tap on the office door made the superintendent drop the file into an open drawer. 'Enter.'

Detective Sergeant William Moody walked in and nodded. 'You sent fer me, Guv.'

'Take a seat, Sergeant,' Cranley told him. 'I've sent for you because I want your assessment of the patch you cover.'

'Well, it's pretty quiet at the moment, sir,' Moody answered. 'We're watchin' a few shops in the area suspected of black market-eerin', an' there's bin a flutter wiv the Malts, but apart from that all's quiet.'

'Flutter? Enlighten me.'

'Well, sir, there's always someone ready ter fill a vacuum, as you'll understand, an' it seems as though the Malts are movin' in.'

'Gambling?'

'Privately, but they give us no trouble on that score,' Moody replied. 'It's more down ter nickin'. The feelers are out over the Shad Thames ware'ouse job an' the ovver job at Chambers Wharf. Word 'as it that the Malts could 'ave bin involved. I can't say more than that at the present time though.'

'Is there a name or names?' Cranley asked.

'A group o' Malts meet once a week at the Dun Cow in the Old Kent Road,' Moody told him. 'They sit drinkin' an' playin' pontoon. It's only fer shillin's, but my contact reckons the business is done there. Joe Mezzo, Tony Mancini, Nick Zanti an' Mick the Hammer. Mezzo runs a grocery shop on the corner of Hastings Street. 'E's clean. Nick Zanti's got convictions fer gamblin' an' Mick the Hammer's bin done fer GBH. They're small-time but they seem to 'ave ambitions accordin' ter my snout.'

'Well, let's see if we can contain this little group, Sergeant. Oh, and by the way. Let me see your file on the warehouse break-ins will you? Tomorrow will do.'

Danny Adams felt a little conspicuous in his uniform as he stood outside the Old Kent picture house. The hat was too big and he had had to line it with paper. The coat felt heavy and it was a bit long, he thought. He had been encouraged by the man at the labour exchange to take the job, and he was going to try hard to make a go of it, for his mother's sake. He had been a worry to her, he knew, but she had to understand he wasn't lazy. It was only a matter of time before he found the right work. His headaches still troubled him at times and he found it hard to concentrate. He would improve with time, he felt sure, and then he would be able to hold down the right kind of job.

The last film performance was under way, and it was only a

matter of making sure that no one sneaked in without paying, and then moving the ropes as soon as he heard the National Anthem being played to let the customers out of the theatre. It was easy enough, provided he didn't forget his tasks.

''Ere, mister. Who's that?' a voice asked him.

Danny looked down to see a dirty little face staring up at him. The little boy was pointing to a poster of a film star on a side wall. 'That's Tyrone Power,' Danny replied, smiling.

''Ere, an' who's that?' the lad asked, walking over to the glass case that displayed scenes from the current film.

'That's John Wayne an' that's Randolph Scott,' Danny said amiably.

'Fanks, mister. You ain't like the last man. 'E was a miserable ole sod. Wouldn't tell us nuffink, 'e wouldn't.'

Danny smiled at the lad and put a hand on his shoulder. 'You better be off 'ome. It's gettin' late,' he said.

The boy gave him a saucy grin. 'Our muvver don't mind us bein' out late when Uncle George comes round. They like ter be on their own so they can talk.'

Suddenly out the corner of his eye, Danny caught sight of the line of young children slipping into the cinema foyer, and realised that the lad was merely distracting him while his mates slipped into the cinema unobserved. They would no doubt open the exit door from the inside to let their confederate in. He had done the same thing himself when he was a lad. 'Oi, you lot! Out yer go!' he called out loudly.

It was too late. The lads had slipped into the steeply sloping corridor which led up to the rear of the theatre, and would now be making themselves comfortable to enjoy the main feature.

'Right, you little scarab. I'll remember you,' Danny said, shaking his fist at the grinning lad who had slipped out of arm's reach.

'Shut up, ole rotten 'at,' the urchin called out.

'I'll give you rotten 'at,' Danny shouted back, following the youngster outside.

'You touch me an' I'll bring me Uncle George round. 'E'll give yer a black eye or even two,' the lad called out, grinning from ear to ear.

Danny realised that he wasn't going to reach the nimble young boy and he turned towards the foyer. 'All right, so yer mates got in, but you ain't,' he told him.

'I've already seen it twice. It ain't much good anyway,' came the reply.

Danny Adams stepped back into the foyer out of the cold night air just in time to see the manager escorting four scruffy little lads out of the corridor.

'Next time I'll fetch the police. Is that understood?' he was growling at them.

The lads nodded dutifully until they were outside and then they shouted out in unison, 'Get yer 'air cut, Dummy.'

The bald-headed manager turned towards Danny, his face reddening with anger. 'It's not my job to police the theatre, Adams,' he stormed. 'That's your job. All right, I know it's your first night, but if you can't keep those little guttersnipes out, then I'm afraid you'll have to go. Is that understood?'

Danny bit back an angry reply and nodded instead.

'Now, after the last of the audience has left I want you to sweep up the foyer and the corridors,' the manager ordered. 'If the job's done properly it should only take you half an hour. I want a first-class job done, mind.'

Danny could feel the pounding headache returning and he gave his boss a vacant stare.

'You do understand what I'm saying, don't you?' the manager asked.

Danny slowly removed his hat and put it down at his feet, then to the manager's utter amazement he suddenly jumped on it. 'Poke yer poxy job. I'm goin' 'ome,' he told him.

When he had recovered sufficiently, the manager ran out of the foyer and called out to the disappearing figure, 'Oi, you! Bring that coat back!'

Chapter Nine

As soon as his shift finished on Tuesday afternoon, Joe Brennen made his excuses to Charlie Catchpole and Bill Cosgrove and hurried home. Normally he would have gone into the railway club for a pint and a game of darts before leaving, but today Joe had other things on his mind.

When he got home, Ada had a pot of tea standing on the kitchen range and she was doing her ironing. 'Sit yerself down an' drink this,' she said, picking up the teapot with the ironing pad. 'There's time. That ole cow ain't goin' nowhere.'

Joe crouched down at the cupboard in the corner of the parlour and grunted as he took out a tin money-box. 'Bloody junk in there,' he moaned. 'It's a job ter find anyfing in this 'ouse.'

Ada ignored the comment. Joe was always touchy when he was worried, and the less said the sooner mended was her motto at such times. ''Ere you are, luv.'

Joe sat down in the armchair and sipped his tea. 'I'll be able ter make the 'oliday money up wiv a bit of overtime,' he said, glancing at the money-box on the table. 'There'll be plenty of it comin' up once the weavver brightens up a bit.'

Ada nodded. 'We 'ave ter put fings in their right order, Joe. An 'oliday's a luxury. We can't stand by an' see our Elsie goin' down 'ill.'

'I wouldn't mind if that bastard was fair to 'er,' Joe said angrily. 'There was no need fer our Else ter get in this state, if 'e'd played fair by 'er. I'll be 'avin' a word or two wiv 'im before long, mark my words.'

'Now don't you go makin' fings worse by interferin',' Ada warned him. 'She's the one who'll suffer.'

Joe finished his tea and counted ten one-pound notes from the tin box. 'I'll get round there right away,' he said, replacing the box in the cupboard.

The damp January air was turning into thick fog, and Joe pulled up the collar of his hip-length railway coat as he walked quickly out of Waggoner's Way into Dover Lane. He reached the row of houses which stretched from the Mason's Arms to the end of the turning, and stopped at number 12. The place looked shabby, with paint peeling from the window-frames and front door. The lace curtains looked as if they had been up for some considerable time too, and Joe pulled a face as he knocked on the door. He was suddenly aware that he was being watched, and as he stepped back a pace he saw a face peering at him from the window.

The front door creaked open slightly and a fishy smell reached his nostrils.

'What yer want?' a croaky voice called out.

'I've come ter pay some money,' he answered abruptly.

'I ain't seen you before.'

'It's fer Elsie Gates.'

The door shut and Joe could hear a chain being removed.

'Yer better come in,' the old lady said as she finally pulled the door fully open.

Joe glanced at the gaunt, lined face of Mother Dines as he entered the dark passageway, and he caught his breath as the smell of fish grew stronger.

'Go in there,' the old woman said, pointing to a side room. 'I won't be a minute, I've gotta see 'ow me dinner's doin'.'

As Joe walked into the dark, gloomy room, he heard her grumbling and a mumbled reply, then she shuffled back into the room. He watched as the old lady slumped down into her armchair and reached for a notebook that was lying on the shelf beside her.

'Now let me see. E. Gates. Ah, 'ere we are,' she said pointing to the open book. 'There's ten pounds owin', includin' interest, an' there's anuvver 'alf a crown interest fer no payment this week. That's ten pounds two an' six exactly. What yer payin' off?'

'The lot.'

'All of it?'

'Yeah, ten pounds exactly,' Joe said dropping the notes down on the table.

'What about the 'alf-crown interest?'

71

'That was fer no payment, but I'm payin' it up in full now,' Joe said sharply.

'The payment should 'ave bin yesterday. We're inter next week's payments after Monday,' the old woman said, equally sharply.

Joe was about to argue when he suddenly became aware that someone was standing behind him. He turned quickly and saw a young man leaning against the doorjamb. He was thick-set, his bulk filling the opening, and there was a fixed grin on his wide flat face. 'Everyfing all right, Muvver?' he asked for Joe's benefit.

Mother Dines picked up the ten pound-notes and stood staring down at it for a moment, then she nodded to her son. 'It's all right. The man's paid in full.'

Joe looked hard at the frail old woman and was reminded of a vulture. Her grease-stained black skirt reached down to the floor, and she had a black lace shawl draped over her hunched shoulders. Her dark eyes were two sharp points of yellow light above a long hooked nose, and there were long hairs growing from her chin. She looked unwashed and her raven hair was pulled tightly over her head and fastened in a bun at the nape of her neck. Her hands were long with filthy fingernails, and Joe noticed that she wore a thin wedding ring.

The woman's son shuffled off along the dark passage as Joe turned to go. 'I'd better 'ave a receipt,' he said.

Mother Dines mumbled to herself as she scribbled something down on a piece of lined paper and passed it to him. 'It's not good business payin' in full,' she grumbled.

Joe slipped his hands into his coat pocket. 'I don't want my daughter in debt ter money-lenders,' he told her.

'P'raps it would 'ave bin better if she'd 'ave gone ter you before comin' ter me then,' the old woman replied sarcastically. 'I supply a service fer people who need money an' don't know where else ter turn to. I take a chance wiv people an' I expect ter charge fer it. I'm not a charity.'

Joe ignored the remarks and made for the door. Simon Dines was standing at the foot of the stairs, and Joe glanced at him briefly before letting himself out. As the door shut he heard the chain rattling behind it, and he shook his head as he turned for home.

Ernie Gates changed down into third gear and pressed down on the footbrake as he drove his heavy Leyland lorry down Archway Hill. Below him the lights of the capital loomed out of the gathering fog and he whistled to himself. Luck had been with him that morning. He had managed to get loaded from the Manchester depot early enough to make good time home. Any later and he would no doubt have been caught up in the fog.

Things had worked out very well for Ernie on that particular trip. There had only been a handful of drivers staying at his regular digs in Stockport, and Lily had been able to fuss over him. Her husband was on night-shift at the mill and she had made good use of his absence. That night Ernie had not had to share a room with other truckers, and there had been a cup of tea and biscuits for him before he reluctantly climbed out of Lily's bed early that morning.

As he swung the laden lorry into Holloway Road, Ernie was thinking about his coming meeting that evening. He already knew his work schedule for the rest of the week, and on Friday morning he was to pick up a load of copper and brass fittings from an engineering works in Poplar.

Mrs Greenedge and Mrs Thomas had once been warring parties, but that was long ago now. The reason for their differences had been their children, who were always arguing and fighting. Now, Bet Greenedge's daughter Emily was married to Annie Thomas's eldest son Trevor, and there were three grandchildren for the elderly ladies to dote over. Annie and Bet had become very close, and it was a common sight to see the two of them together. They went arm in arm to the market and to the pub at weekends, and they invariably visited the cinema together.

On Tuesday evening the two women went to the oilshop together. Annie wanted some tin-tacks to keep the oilcloth from rucking up, and Bet decided that it might be a good idea to go along. She felt it was time her lace curtains were washed and she was out of starch.

Basil Cashman, the oilshop owner, groaned to himself as he weighed up the tacks. He welcomed customers, but he knew that when those two came into his shop together they could be there for hours, especially if another inquisitive neighbour came in while the two of them were there. This evening looked like it was going to be one of those times.

''Ello, gel. 'Ow's yer back?' Bet Greenedge asked as Mrs Kelly walked into the shop.

Mary Kelly placed her hand over her right kidney. 'It's a lot better, but I still get twinges now an' then,' she replied.

Annie Thomas laid a hand on Mary's arm. 'You ought ter try that Wintergreen ointment,' she told her. 'It done my back the power o' good.'

'It tends ter burn though,' Bet added.

'Fourpence,' Basil said, laying the wrapped tin-tacks down on the counter.

The women ignored him and Basil retreated in case he was drawn into the conversation.

'I've bin wearin' one o' Tom's woollen vests,' Mary told the other two. 'Yer need somefing extra on in this weavver.'

'Yeah, it's very damp still. It's gonna be a pea-souper ternight if yer ask me,' Bet remarked.

'Trouble is wiv this weavver, yer don't feel like doin' anyfing, do yer?' Annie added.

'Yer got yer tin-tacks anyway,' Basil piped in, praying that the woman would pick them up and go.

Annie fished into her purse for fourpence and laid the coins down on the counter. 'There's somefing else I want, I know there is,' she said, pinching her chin with thumb and forefinger. 'Never mind, I'll fink of it presently.'

Basil picked up the money and backed away mumbling to himself, and the women carried on with their conversation.

''Ere, Mary, did yer know young Danny Adams is workin' up the Old Kent pictures?' Bet asked.

'I 'eard 'e was gonna start there,' Mary replied. 'It's not the job fer a young man like 'im. It's more a job fer an elderly man.'

'That's what I was sayin' to Annie,' Bet told her. 'Me an' Annie went up there last night ter see that cowboy film an' young Danny was there. I could 'ave cried. 'E 'ad a long coat on, touchin' the ground it was, an' dirty? I tell yer, luv, it could 'ave stood up on its own.'

'What about the 'at? Tell 'er about the 'at 'e was wearin',' Annie prompted.

'Well, I tell yer, Mary. Young Danny 'ad this great big 'at on an' it was stuffed wiv paper ter keep it up. There was 'alf a yard o' the *News o' the World* stickin' out the back. Proper sight it was. I wanted ter tell 'im about it but I couldn't. It was so sad ter see 'im. I can't understand why ole Dot Adams let 'im take the job, really I can't.'

Mary Kelly shook her head sadly. 'I s'pose it's easy fer the likes of us ter pass comment,' she replied, 'but yer gotta put yerself in 'er shoes. She's a widow an' Danny's all she's got. She's seen a young strappin' lad ruined by the war. When she's gone, Danny's gonna be left on 'is own, unless 'e can find a nice young lady ter wed. The problem is, who'll 'ave 'im the way 'e is? I fink Dot Adams is tryin' 'er best ter get 'im back ter bein' somefink like normal, an' she ain't gonna do it by mollycoddlin' 'im. All right, the job at the pictures ain't the right sort o' job fer Danny, but at least it's givin' 'im responsibility. The lad needs it. Let's just 'ope 'e sticks it, fer a while at least.'

Basil Cashman was not prone to standing around in his shop listening to the women gossiping, but on this occasion he had, and he agreed with everything Mary Kelly had said. 'What can I get yer, gel?' he said, giving her one of his very rare smiles.

The fog had thickened and there were very few people on the streets as Ernie Gates left his house and crossed the turning. The lights of the Mason's Arms shone out into the gloom, and when he entered the saloon bar he saw it was almost empty. One or two customers sat around, and the landlord was leaning on the counter looking bored.

'Wotcha, Arfur. Bit quiet ternight,' Ernie remarked, taking a ten-shilling note from his pocket and laying it down on the polished surface. 'I'll 'ave a nice pint o' best bitter, an' one fer yerself.'

'Cheers, Ern. Bloody fog's kept 'em all in ternight,' Arthur said, pulling on the beer pump. 'Still, yer can't blame 'em. I'd like ter put me feet up round the fire meself.'

Ernie picked up his pint and walked over to a far table. Arthur Selby was inclined to chat when the pub was quiet, and Ernie wanted time to think. He had to sound knowledgeable about the sort of load he was carrying, otherwise he would most likely not be taken on. Tommy Bamford had been at pains to reassure him that the gang he would be dealing with were fair-minded, but Tommy would say that. He had little to do with the arrangement, except for setting up the meeting and then holding his hand out for his cut. Not bad if you get it, Ernie thought.

At nine-thirty exactly, a dark, well-built young man walked into the saloon bar and went straight to the counter. Ernie watched him as he ordered a large whisky and saw that the stranger was wearing a smart serge suit and expensive leather shoes. The shirt collar was sitting high on his neck, and was most likely made to measure. The silver tie had been knotted with care and his gold wristwatch flashed in the light as he reached out to pick up his drink. His dark wavy hair and swarthy complexion led Ernie to believe that the man was either Italian or Maltese, and he knew that his contact had arrived.

Nick Zanti walked over calmly and sat down facing him 'I understand that you wanted to talk,' he said in perfect English.

'I might do, if somefing can be sorted out,' Ernie replied.

'Oh, I'm sure it can,' the newcomer said, smiling to display white, even teeth. 'You're Ernie Gates and you'd like some assistance to place a load, I understand.'

Ernie nodded and took a swig from his pint. 'Tell me,' he said as he put down the glass, ''ow did yer know me?'

Zanti looked down at his manicured fingernails for a moment, then his dark eyes travelled up to fix on Ernie. 'You've been pointed out, simple as that,' he replied.

Ernie grinned. 'I'm loadin' Friday mornin'. Seven ton o' brass an' copper fittin's. It should come to a nice few quid.'

'I'm sure it will,' Zanti said. 'You'll no doubt be wanting to know the split. We do it four ways, an equal split, and there's no arguing on that score. If that doesn't suit, you say so, and it'll save wasting time.'

'I'm 'appy wiv that,' Ernie said, trying not to appear too keen.

'There's a buyer laid on and he'll pay a good price,' the Maltese went on. 'If you're worried about being cheated, you can be in on the pay-off, it's no trouble. Obviously I wouldn't hazard a guess on the round figure. It all depends on the quality and the type of fittings. What I will say is that there's a demand for quality fittings, what with all the building going on at present.'

'That sounds fair enough ter me,' Ernie said, picking up his pint again. 'What next?'

'I'll need confirmation of pick-up. Time and place. I'll also need your lorry type and registration number. Do you know yet?' Ernie nodded and Zanti leaned forward in his chair. 'Now, if there should be a sudden change of plan we need to know. What you do is call in at Joe Mezzo's shop or give him a ring. He's a cousin of mine. Just say, the shirt's not ready yet, that's all. Say nothing more. Joe doesn't know anything about this. He'll phone me immediately. There's Joe's number in case you need it. Memorise it and then get rid of it.'

Ernie took the book of matches and read the number printed on the inside of the flap. 'Right,' he said.

Nick Zanti looked hard at him. 'Make sure that number's not on you when the police take you in for questioning. It could put you away for a long time. Understood?'

Ernie nodded his head firmly. 'What do I 'ave ter do?' he asked.

Nick Zanti drained his glass and stood up. 'Nothing. Go and get your load and relax. Just don't struggle or my lads will think you've bottled it. Then it could get nasty for you. OK?'

'I'll be seein' yer,' Ernie said as Zanti turned to leave.

'I don't think so. Good luck.'

Ernie Gates watched the man leave and then he went over to the bar.

'Same again?' the landlord asked.

'No, make it a large Scotch,' Ernie said, suddenly realising that he was sweating.

Chapter Ten

The days seemed to drag by for Kay, and on Friday morning she left home for work feeling thankful for the coming weekend. She had met David on Wednesday evening, and they had gone to a little pub at New Cross where they sat chatting until the place closed. They had agreed that he should allow himself time to settle in before Kay went back to the flat with him, and the arrangement seemed to suit David. He looked as if he was ashamed for what had happened, or rather had not happened on that previous Sunday. He was subdued and had not wanted to talk about it. Kay felt a little put out by his reticence, but she had decided to be patient and give him time to pull himself together.

As she turned out of Waggoner's Way, she almost collided with a young man carrying a large suitcase.

'Well, if it ain't young Kay Brennen. It is Kay, isn't it?'

The young woman stepped back a pace and found herself looking up at the tall figure of Pat Kelly. For a moment she just stood staring at him and then finally she managed a smile. 'Yeah, it's Kay. Fancy bumpin' inter you,' she said, feeling her face flushing up.

'Well, it's obvious we were gonna meet sooner or later, considerin' I'm movin' back in the street terday,' Pat told her. 'That's if yer still live in Waggoner's Way.'

'Course I do,' Kay said quickly as she regained her composure.

'Yer could 'ave bin married and moved away though,' the young man said, smiling at her.

Kay smiled back, and suddenly feeling very daring she said, 'I bin waitin' fer you.'

Pat laughed aloud. 'When I left 'ere you was just a pup,' he joked.

'No, I wasn't. I was goin' out wiv a fella,' she said quickly.

Pat put his suitcase down at his feet and rubbed his hands

together. 'Look, I'm just off ter me muvver's. Got time fer a quick cuppa in Sadie's caff? You can tell me all about what's bin 'appenin' round 'ere.'

'I'm sorry, I can't. I'm just off ter work,' Kay told him.

'That's a pity. I was really 'opin' you'd be my welcomin' committee,' he said, pulling a face.

Kay was taken by his disappointed look. 'All right then, but I can't stop too long,' she told him. 'I'll be late as it is.'

Pat Kelly's face brightened, and as he picked up his suitcase he groaned. 'I reckon I've got everyfing but the kitchen sink in 'ere,' he remarked as they set off along Dover Lane.

Kay felt tiny beside the tall, broad-shouldered young man. She looked sideways at him, noticing how his dark wavy hair was brushed back half covering his ears, and how he held his head high. His gait too was just as she remembered, the confident, proud swagger and devil-may-care look. Nothing had changed, she almost sighed to herself. He was still the same infuriating and exciting young man she had loved with every fibre of her childish body. Now though she was a young woman, involved in a relationship with another man, and she would have to be very careful not to give Pat any reason to believe she was available.

'You're not workin' terday?' she queried.

'Nah, I've got a few days off,' he replied.

'Where d'yer work?' Kay asked, suddenly curious.

'You're lookin' at a cable-layer no less,' he said, grinning.

'A cable-layer?' Kay echoed.

'Yeah, I work fer the Electricity Board layin' cables,' he explained. 'As a matter o' fact I'm a ganger in charge of a cable-layin' team. It's a rough tough job but I like it.'

Yeah, you would, Kay thought, imagining him strutting around flexing his muscles and shouting out orders.

They reached Sadie's café at the end of Dover Lane, and Pat pushed his way in and set his suitcase down by the counter. 'Can I stick this out the back fer a few minutes, Sadie?' he asked.

'Yeah, go on, Pat. Two teas is it?' Sadie asked, eyeing Kay.

'Two large, an' stick a couple o' teacakes under the grill will yer, luv,' Pat replied as he humped the case out through the back door.

Sadie gave Kay a humorous look and nodded in the young man's direction. ''E's a right lad that one. 'Ere, 'e ain't nicked that case, 'as 'e?' she grinned.

'No, 'e's movin' 'ouse,' Kay replied with a bashful smile.

The café was full of morning workers and, when they had found a vacant seat in the corner, Pat sipped his tea gratefully. 'This is the first fing past my lips this mornin', truly,' he told her.

Sadie came up with the teacakes. 'Are they both fer you, or is one fer this young lady?' the buxom woman asked.

'Now do I really look like a pig?' Pat said, grinning.

'Ask me later,' Sadie replied as she walked back behind the counter.

Kay had only had a thin slice of toast before she left for work, and the butter-soaked toasted teacake tasted delicious. The mug of tea was hot and sweet, and she sat comfortably listening while Pat Kelly talked.

'I s'pose yer know me an' Eileen 'ave split up. I expect everyone in the street knows by now,' he was saying. Kay nodded, her mouth full of teacake. 'It was good at first but I fink we just grew up suddenly,' he went on. 'There was no one else involved. We just found that we were makin' each ovver miserable. Can yer understand that?'

Kay nodded again and wiped her lips on her handkerchief. 'I fink I can,' she said quietly.

'What about you, Kay? Is there someone special in your life?' he asked.

Her face took on a serious look. 'Yes, there is. Trouble is 'e's married, though 'e's just moved out. 'E's took a flat,' she told him.

'An' you'll be movin' in wiv 'im, I take it.'

'I don't know,' Kay replied quickly, feeling a little put out by his presumption.

'Life can get complicated sometimes, Kay,' he sighed, rolling his eyes to emphasise the point.

The young woman sat listening to him, hardly believing that she was really in Pat Kelly's company. How many times had she dreamed about the two of them chatting together in a moonlit tryst, where he would suddenly look at her in a special way and take her bodily into his arms. He was hardly likely to sweep her into his arms in Sadie's café, but it was still very dreamlike, she thought with a secret sigh.

Workmen were coming and going and still the young man chatted on as though there was all the time in the world. 'I can't believe 'ow grown up yer look. I bet yer've already broke a few 'earts,' he said, smiling.

'Get away,' Kay said quickly.

Pat leaned back and rubbed his stomach. 'I feel better now. Anuvver tea?'

'No, I really must go. I'm very late as it is,' Kay reminded him.

'Look, I can leave that case wiv Sadie fer a while an' I can walk ter work wiv yer. I could even go in an' explain that you was 'elpin' me out in an emergency,' he said, his eyes raised for an answer.

'You really would, wouldn't you,' Kay replied, smiling.

'Sure. Why not?'

'I can manage the excuses, but yer can walk ter work wiv me, if yer really want to,' she told him.

The two young people walked over the Surrey Canal bridge and out into the bustling Old Kent Road. Trams and buses were passing to and fro, and everyone seemed to be hurrying along in the cold morning air. Pat Kelly wanted to know all the news and he plied her with questions. ''Ow's young Danny Adams these days?' he asked.

''E's still the same,' Kay told him.

'Nice feller, Danny. Terrible shame that. What about those sisters o' yours, Barbara an' Dawn? Are they married yet?'

Kay smiled and shook her head. 'Barbara's still wiv Jamie. It's bin four years now but there's no sign of 'em gettin' spliced.'

'What about Dawn?'

'Still playin' the field.'

Pat's face became serious. ''Ow's your Elsie?'

'She's not very 'appy, Pat.'

'I guessed. Ernie Gates?'

''E's a swine.'

The young man's eyes grew distant and Kay noticed the muscles tightening in his jaw. 'I don't need remindin', Kay,' he said in a low voice. 'We 'ad a bit o' business ter take care of once, but we got interrupted. I've no doubt Ernie's gonna be lookin' me up soon as 'e knows I'm back in the street.'

'Don't let 'im get ter yer, Pat. 'E's not worth it,' Kay said with concern.

Pat Kelly turned to face her as they stopped outside the gasworks offices. 'Don't you worry that pretty little 'ead. I can take care o' meself.'

Kay gave him a warm smile as she made to enter the building, and suddenly Pat reached out and took her by the shoulders, his lips gently brushing her cheek. 'See yer around, kid,' he said cheerfully.

Kay turned as she walked through the door. 'Not so much o' the kid,' she called out, giving him one of her best smiles.

'No, you're not a kid any more, that's fer sure,' Pat said aloud to himself as he watched her disappear into the building.

Ernie Gates walked into the transport office in Dockhead that morning and tried to look unconcerned as the yard foreman searched through the collection slips. 'Come on, you dozy git,' he mumbled under his breath.

''Ere we are. Weston's, Poplar. Seven tons o' fittin's,' the foreman said, studying the slip. 'If yer get any 'old-up over there, give us a ring. I've got anuvver collection fer yer at George Payne's this afternoon.'

Ernie nodded and walked out of the office. Ten minutes later he was driving his empty drop-side truck out through the yard gates. The traffic was building up and, as he drove over Tower Bridge, Ernie was beginning to feel nervous. Supposing something went wrong. What if the snatch was bungled? he thought. What could go wrong, though? As long as he kept his head, no one would ever know that he was in on it.

As he swung into Cable Street, a car overtook him; Ernie saw the man sitting next to the driver raise his hand briefly. He deliberately ignored the signal and drove steadily along the dockside street. All he had to do was act normally and do nothing unusual which could raise any suspicion, he reminded himself.

When he pulled up outside the Weston factory, he stepped down from his cab and walked casually into the loading bank office.

'Give us 'alf an hour, mate. We'll call yer soon as we can,' the foreman told him.

Ernie returned to his cab and tried to concentrate on reading the morning paper, but his mind would not relax. He constantly glanced around the wide East End street, but could see nothing of the car. They'll be watching from somewhere, he told himself.

A loader came out into the street and gave Ernie a whistle. It was time to load.

One hour later the laden lorry pulled out of the factory, its load of copper and brass fittings packed into wire cages and securely roped and sheeted. Ernie drove the heavy load carefully back the same way he had come, turning into the West India Dock Road and heading for Tower Bridge. He was beginning to feel apprehensive. There was still no sign of the car, and if the snatch was going to take place it would have to be soon, he fretted.

As he pulled up at a red light opposite the seaman's hostel, a car drew up on his offside. Ernie immediately recognised the passenger as the one who had waved to him in Cable Street. 'Get a cup o' tea an' a sandwich at Bill Maye's,' the man called out as the lights changed.

By the time Ernie had got the lorry moving again, the car was already speeding off. Ahead he could see the line of lorries parked up at Bill Mayes's café, a ramshackle affair set into a dock wall which was little more than a shed with an open counter. It was a good spot to pick, he thought. Everybody stopped at Bill Mayes's. In fact, most lorry drivers swore he sold the best tea and sandwiches in London.

Ernie pulled up behind a laden lorry, allowing enough space for him to drive off without having to back up, and he sauntered over to the café counter trying hard not to look worried. He ordered a large mug of tea and a cheese sandwich and he suddenly realised that his mouth had gone dry. The bread seemed to stick in his throat and he had to wash the sandwich down with gulps of tea.

'They walked out at Millwall this mornin'.'

Ernie turned quickly and saw that the driver was addressing him. 'Oh yeah?' he replied, hoping that he wasn't going to get into a lengthy conversation.

'Second time this week. Trouble wiv the bonuses by all accounts.'

'Oh yeah?'

'I got a load o' tin fruit on. Two bloody trips I've 'ad ter make. Bloody scandalous if you ask me,' the driver was going on. 'I wish us drivers was on bonuses.'

'What poxy use would that be?' another driver piped in. 'We'd end up owin' money, what wiv the bloody time we spend sittin' outside the dock gates.'

'Ter be fair I fink yer gotta look at everyfing in perspective,' someone else butted in. 'You take the amount o' drivers who ain't got a union card. Until we get a closed shop like the dockers, we'll be exploited. If we got organised we'd become the most powerful union in the country, never mind about the docks. If the dockers 'ave got a grievance, let 'em come out. Good luck to 'em, I say.'

Other drivers were joining in the discussion and Ernie took the opportunity to slip away unnoticed.

As he passed the vehicle parked in front of his he was suddenly grabbed by the coat collar and pulled into the gap between the lorries. He hardly had time to see his stocky-looking attacker before a fist thumped into his midriff. He gasped and bent forward.

'Not there! His face!'

A fist crashed into his nose and Ernie saw a flash of light. A warm trickle of blood ran down over his lips and as he blinked he found himself being frog-marched and thrown bodily into a car. His head collided with the door and he lunged back against the seat as the car sped off.

'Bloody 'ell. That was a bit 'eavy-'anded, wasn't it?' he spluttered as he wiped the back of his hand over his bloody nose.

'Leave that face alone. Let the blood dry,' the swarthy man sitting next to him growled.

Ernie sat back and saw that they were driving through the backstreets of Stepney. He wondered where he was bound for. He turned to the dark man next to him. 'You pack a punch, mate,' he said, trying to smile.

'I didn't touch yer,' Tony Mancini replied. 'The geezer drivin' the lorry pasted yer. 'E's in charge o' the physical side o' the business.'

'Where we goin'?' Ernie asked.

'You'll see soon enough,' the Maltese villain said, smiling evilly.

Miss Heather Spiers had never married and had never had any inclination to give up her freedom. She thoroughly enjoyed her current lifestyle, now that she was retired. Heather Spiers had been a civil servant, and some time ago she had been left a comfortable, cottage-type house in rural Essex. When she needed company she called on her man friend, who was also a retired civil servant, and when Heather felt the need for exercise she took her beloved Fifi for a walk in the forest.

The cold damp weather did not trouble Heather. In fact, she felt that the forest looked rather beautiful in winter. There was a crisp carpet of leaves underfoot, and the pollarded hornbeam looked particularly striking at that time of year, she thought. There were other features too for her to admire. A few craggy old oaks, birch, beech and holly all blended in perfectly with the blackberry, broom and gorse. A few fallow deer roamed the leafy glades, and there were rabbits, foxes, badger, squirrels and weasels for Fifi to sniff out. All in all, Heather Spiers could think of no other place which afforded her so much tranquillity, so much peace of mind, until that cold Friday morning when her beloved Pekinese sniffed the air peculiarly and ran off into the brush.

The desk sergeant at Epping Police Station winced as he listened to the phone. 'You say you've found a man tied to a tree in the forest? Oh, I see. Fifi did. Can I have your name, please? Yes, I understand about the man, but if you'd be so good. Right. Heather Spiers, The Firs, Eaves Lane, Epping. Right then Mrs, sorry, Miss Spiers. We'll send a police car right away. Yes, we know the telephone box. Yes, wait there. Yes, I understand you couldn't manage to untie the man. He kicked Fifi. Oh dear, Fifi bit him. Never mind, we'll soon sort it out. Yes, I understand. Fifi got excited. All right, Miss Spiers, we'll be right along.'

Elsie Gates took the plate of meat pie and two veg from the oven and puffed. It was baked up now, and Ernie would most probably throw it at her if she put that in front of him. Where was he, anyway, she wondered? He was nearly always home early on Fridays. He must have stopped off for a pint and got talking. Perhaps he felt there was little at home waiting for him. She could tolerate the way he behaved towards her but he never seemed to have much time for Billy, and that was something she would never forgive him for.

The rat-tat on the front door startled her and she put a hand up to her mouth as she hurried along the passage.

'Mrs Gates?'

'Oh my God!' Elsie gasped on seeing the policeman standing at the door. 'It's Ernie. What's 'appened to 'im?'

'It's all right, Mrs Gates, your husband's OK,' the constable said quickly. 'He's at the station. I'm afraid he's had his lorry stolen and he's making a statement. He should be home soon.'

Elsie walked into the parlour and sat down heavily. Billy came over and stood by her side, aware that something was wrong. 'Is Daddy gonna be all right, Mummy?' he asked in a quiet voice.

'Daddy's gonna be fine, chicken,' she said softly and, to herself, 'it's us I'm worried about.'

Chapter Eleven

Joe Mezzo brought over a round of drinks and set them down on the table in the saloon bar of the Dun Cow. 'I've just 'ad a word wiv the buyer. 'E's very pleased wiv the consignment,' he said, smiling broadly.

'So all in all it was a good day's work,' Tony Mancini said, picking up his drink. 'It went off very sweetly.'

Nick Zanti leaned back in his chair and pulled at his shirt cuffs. It had been a hectic day for him at his scrapyard in Hoxton. The load had been transferred and sent on its way, his trusted workers had been paid their bonuses and, as far as he was concerned, all the loose ends had been tidied up.

Joe Mezzo too had reason to celebrate. He had put up the front money and arranged the sale, managing a nice profit. As for Tony Mancini, he had raked in three hundred pounds for little more than an hour's work, having paid off the driver of the car, a freelance criminal who knew his way around London and could be relied upon to 'borrow' a car and drive anywhere he was told to with no questions asked.

Mick the Hammer walked into the pub and gave the group a big wink as he strolled up to the bar and ordered himself a large gin and tonic. Mick had a Maltese father and Irish mother and had been accepted into the inner circle. He had proved himself more than once when the Maltese gambling community in Cable Street were being harassed by protection gangs. He was a short, powerful man who feared no one on two legs, and he had earned his nickname when he stormed into a mob of villains who had gone to Cable Street looking for trouble.

'Is the motor sorted out, Mick?' Tony Zanti asked him.

'It's burnin' nicely on some wasteground in Peckham right this minute,' Mick said with a grin as he sat down heavily.

'Was that necessary?' Joe Mezzo asked.

Tony nodded. 'Yes, it was. You never know with that crowd at Dockhead nick. I wouldn't put it past them to plant some evidence in the lorry themselves if they thought they could make a killing. You can't get away with such things on a burnt-out shell, now can you?'

Mick sat sipping his gin and tonic. 'Sorry about that this mornin', Tony. I wasn't finkin' straight,' he said apologetically.

'What's that?' Zanti asked quickly.

Tony Mancini playfully thumped Mick on the top of his arm. 'Mick was tryin' ter knock an 'ole in the driver's belly till I reminded 'im it was the face we was after,' he said, grinning.

Joe Mezzo finished his drink and looked round the table. 'You boys won't need remindin' not ter go flashin' money around the manor,' he said with authority. 'I got word that there's new management at Dock'ead nick. Just remember the old sayin', a new broom sweeps clean. They're gonna be out ter win a few prizes, an' if they 'ave reason ter suspect this little caper of ours was a local matter, they'll be like flies round 'orseshit.'

'Why should they?' Zanti queried. 'We did the business over the water and the lorry was dumped in Peckham.'

'What about the driver? 'Ave yer fergot 'e's local?' Joe said quietly.

Nick Zanti smiled confidently. 'We're all strangers to him, except you, Joe, and he can't know you're involved. Anyway, if the law do break him down, what can he tell them? We can all get enough witnesses to say we were elsewhere at the time, can't we?'

Joe Mezzo seemed satisfied and he nodded. 'Just play it cool, that's all I'm sayin',' he told them.

Ernie Gates sat smoking a cigarette in the interview room at Dockhead police station. For almost an hour he had been left alone in the sparsely furnished room, and he guessed that it was part of the ploy. The first thing they would do when they finally came back, he reckoned, was note how many cigarettes he had smoked. They would also tell him that they had arrested someone in connection with the robbery and watch his reaction. Well, there was only one cigarette in the ashtray, and he was controlling his breathing to keep himself calm and steady.

The door suddenly opened and a tall, broad-shouldered detective came in, accompanied by a younger-looking officer who carried a notepad.

'I'm Detective Sergeant Moody, and this is Detective Constable Birkett,' the big man announced as he sat down heavily in the chair facing Ernie. 'Now, I've gone frew your statement very carefully, an' one fing puzzles me,' he said slowly. 'Why didn't they blindfold yer when they bundled yer in the car instead of after they tied yer ter the tree?'

Ernie shrugged his shoulders and put out his cigarette before replying. 'I got a glimpse o' the geezer what give me this,' he said, pointing to his swollen nose, 'so there was no point, was there? Anyway, I couldn't identify the driver. I was sittin' directly be'ind 'im.'

'But you could pick out the ovver man, the man that whacked yer?' Moody asked him.

'Yeah, I'm sure I could.'

'What about when they pulled yer out o' the car?'

'I still couldn't see the driver,' Ernie replied. 'I was told ter walk an' not look round. The driver was right be'ind me all the time.'

'So yer felt it was right ter do as yer was told,' Moody went on. 'Yer didn't try ter make a run fer it. Why?'

Ernie spoke in a measured voice, looking directly at his interrogator. 'I didn't know what the driver was carryin'. It could 'ave bin a gun fer all I knew,' he explained. 'I just reckoned it was better ter do as I was told.'

'You were being sensible to your way of thinking?' the other detective butted in.

'Yeah, if yer like,' Ernie replied. 'I'd already took a bit of a beatin' an' I felt they wouldn't 'esitate ter give me a good kickin', or worse, if I didn't do as they said.'

Moody passed a packet of Senior Service across the table. 'Smoke?' he offered.

Ernie shook his head. 'No fanks, I've just finished one.'

'Do you always stop fer a break when yer've got a valuable load on?' Moody asked.

Ernie looked at the man's large flushed face; it seemed to be full of tiny blue veins. 'I treat all my loads as valuable. I don't know 'ow much they come to,' he said quickly. 'We're s'posed ter stop by law after so long anyway.'

'I'm well aware o' the law,' Moody replied, his voice rising slightly. 'But you wasn't overrunnin' yer time. Why not wait till yer got back in the yard?'

'There's no decent caffs near the yard,' Ernie said, a smile touching his lips. 'Anyway, Bill Mayes's caff is the best around. Everybody stops there if they can.'

Sergeant Moody sat back in his chair and stared at the lorry driver for a few moments. 'I 'ave ter tell yer that we've arrested two suspects this evenin' an' they've screamed,' he said finally. 'You're in this caper up ter yer neck, Gates. Now why don't yer come clean?'

Ernie was prepared for the ploy, and he gave the detective a wide-eyed look of horror. 'Come clean?' he said in a loud voice. 'I'm a law-abidin' lorry driver who's never bin in any trouble whatsoever, an' you're accusin' me o' somefing like this? It's bloody outdacious.'

Moody shifted his position in his chair and leaned forward, his eyes glaring at Ernie. 'I can put you on an ID parade, no trouble,' he said menacingly.

'I'm willin',' Ernie answered with passion. 'I've got nuffing to 'ide.'

The detective changed his tactics. 'Tell me a bit more about that load you was carryin',' he said quietly. 'What d'yer reckon it was werf?'

'I've no idea,' Ernie replied, shrugging his shoulders. 'I know it was brass an' copper fittin's, that's all. Last week I was carryin' machinery. That was valuable too. Prob'ly more than the fittin's.'

'I'm not interested in the machinery. I'm interested in the load you lost by your negligence,' Moody said slowly and aggressively.

'Negligence?'

'Yes, negligence. You stopped fer a cup o' tea an' left a valuable load. Then you allowed yerself ter be bundled into a car wivout puttin' up a fight,' Moody said, his eyes glaring. 'You're a big stocky man, why didn't yer 'ave a go at 'em? A lot o' men 'alf your size would 'ave.'

Ernie Gates shook his head slowly, regaining his composure. 'I beg ter differ,' he said calmly. 'I was punched violently and blinded fer a moment. I tried ter resist but I got anuvver thump in the kidney. I knew it was useless. I could 'ave bin killed there an' then if

89

I'd used any more force ter protect meself. I made those geezers out ter be desperate villains.'

'They're not desperate villains. Not now, Gates,' the detective growled. 'They're sittin' in a cell along the corridor shittin' 'emselves. They've spilled their guts, an' you're implicated. What d'yer say ter that?'

'I'm innocent, an' I don't care if you an' that pal o' yours kick me all round this room. I can't change anyfink, so yer can start gettin' 'eavy right now if yer like,' Ernie said with spirit.

'Don't you get flash wiv me!' Moody shouted, thrusting his face forward inches from Ernie's.

'I'm not bein' flash, I'm just sayin' I've got nuffink to 'ide, that's all,' Ernie answered quietly.

Moody stood up and gave his subordinate a look of resignation, then he glanced down at Ernie. 'You sit tight. I'll be back in a few minutes,' he told him.

As soon as Moody had left the room the other detective sat down facing him. 'I wouldn't try provoking the sergeant, he's a mean character,' he warned. 'If you are implicated, it'll be much better for you to confess now. It'll go a lot easier on you in court. A good brief could even plead that you were forced into it. You could get off with probation.'

Ernie was prepared for the change in approach. The detective was playing the friendly, sympathetic one, trying to win him over. 'Now you listen ter me,' Ernie replied, his voice raised angrily. 'I told that mate o' yours an' I'm tellin' you the same. I ain't involved in anyfink an' I won't be browbeaten. I've got nuffink ter worry about. I'm clean, get it?'

The young detective's face suddenly darkened and, without saying anything, he stood up and abruptly left the room.

Elsie looked at the loudly ticking clock on the mantelshelf for the umpteenth time and breathed heavily. It was eight-thirty, and still Ernie had not come home. She had taken Billy to stay at her family's house in Waggoner's Way, and Kay had walked back with her to keep her company.

''E shouldn't be long now,' Kay said, smiling reassuringly at her older sister.

'I've got a bad feelin' about this,' Elsie replied, hunched up in her armchair beside the gas fire.

90

'Yer mean Ernie might be involved?' Kay said.

Elsie nodded. 'We don't talk much these days, but I noticed 'ow strung up 'e seemed all week. As soon as 'e got back on Tuesday night, 'e went out. 'E said 'e 'ad ter see someone. Ernie never goes out after a trip, an' when 'e did get back 'e was sort of keyed up. I can't put me finger on it, but I reckon it was somefing ter do wiv what's 'appened.'

'Yer could be makin' more out of it, Else,' Kay told her kindly. 'I know 'e's not a saint, but even Ernie wouldn't do anyfing like that, would 'e?'

Elsie smiled cynically. 'You don't know 'im, Kay luv. I live wiv 'im. I wouldn't put it past 'im, ter tell yer the trufe.'

'It's as bad as that then?'

'It's worse, but don't go tellin' Muvver,' Elsie warned her. 'She worries enough as it is.'

'If there's no way back, why don't yer leave 'im?' Kay asked.

'I've bin finkin' o' doin' just that, many times, but I gotta be sensible. Where do I go?' Elsie replied with a deep sigh. 'There's Billy ter consider, too. What life would it be fer 'im wiv us stuck in a furnished room?'

'The two of yer could come back 'ome till yer got yerself sorted out,' Kay suggested. 'We could all muck in. It wouldn't be fer ever.'

Elsie looked at her younger sister fondly. She was so innocent, so naïve, she thought. Life was easy and uncomplicated for her. How could she be expected to understand what it was like to experience a marriage which seemed so good at the beginning change and give way to despair and degradation? How could Kay begin to know what it was like to be rejected and humiliated, to be slapped about for a time and then finally ignored? Her younger sister saw it as merely black or white, good or bad, but the answer to the problem wasn't so simple. She had built a home for Ernie and herself; her energies and love had gone into it. It was too painful to walk out just like that. To give up now would be admitting defeat. There was very little left in her life except her child, it was true, but things might get better one day, if she stuck with it; if she could only convince Ernie that she was there for him, for him and his child, the lad who loved him, despite everything.

Kay was staring at her, aware of the emotion welling up in her sister's eyes, and Elsie hurriedly stood up. 'I'll put the kettle on,' she said quickly.

91

Kay shook her head. 'If I 'ave any more tea it'll be comin' out my ears,' she joked. 'Let's talk.'

'Let's talk about you,' Elsie suggested. 'You must be sick o' my problems.'

'What's to tell?' Kay replied, grinning self-consciously.

'What about your love life?' Elsie asked.

Kay's face suddenly became serious. 'It's complicated at the moment,' she said quietly.

'You can tell me,' Elsie urged. 'It won't go beyond this room.'

Kay sighed. It might be good to unburden herself, she thought. Elsie had always been a good listener, not like Barbara or Dawn, who could both be so infuriating at times with their big-sister advice and loftiness. 'As a matter o' fact, I'm in a difficult sort o' situation,' she confessed.

'Is 'e married?' Elsie asked.

'Right first time,' Kay told her. ''Is name's David an' 'e's separated. 'E's livin' in furnished rooms an', as far as I can tell, the marriage is dead an' buried.'

'Are yer sleepin' wiv 'im?' Elsie asked outright.

Kay was taken aback and shook her head, momentarily dropping her eyes. 'Not exactly,' she replied.

Elsie gave her a comical smile. 'Eivver you are or you ain't,' she said, chuckling.

'We tried ter do it, but it didn't work out,' Kay said, her face colouring a little.

'Are yer still a virgin?'

Kay nodded. 'I wanted to, an' I was really ready fer David ter make love ter me, but somehow 'e couldn't.'

''E couldn't? P'raps 'e was too screwed up. Maybe you both were,' Elsie suggested.

'No, it was more than that,' Kay replied. 'I tried the best I knew ter make it easy for 'im, but 'e just couldn't.'

'Yer mean 'e finished too quick?'

'Yeah.'

'I shouldn't worry too much,' Elsie told her encouragingly. 'It can 'appen. If you listened ter some o' the gels I work wiv you'd be amazed. It's more common than yer'd imagine, but it usually works out all right in the end.'

'Listen ter the expert talkin',' Kay said, grinning to cover her embarrassment.

'Seriously, Kay, I shouldn't lose no sleep over it,' Elsie assured her. 'Once 'e sorts 'imself out, it'll be good, y'know, long as it's not a deep-seated problem.'

'That's what I'm afraid of, ter tell yer the trufe,' Kay said, looking concerned. 'I fink it's bin a problem fer a long while. I got a feelin' it's what soured the marriage in the first place.'

''As 'e told yer as much?' Elsie asked.

'No, but there's somefing in it, I'm sure,' Kay told her.

The elder sister quickly glanced up at the clock again as she shook her head sadly. 'I don't wanna be the one ter put a damp'ner on it, Kay, but yer gotta be careful. Somefing like that could spell disaster. If yer can't manage ter sort it out, then yer've really gotta get out before yer get too involved.'

Kay was thoughtful for a moment and did not say anything.

''Ere, changin' the subject,' Elsie went on. 'Guess who I saw this afternoon. Pat Kelly, no less.'

Kay smiled. 'So did I. This mornin' as I was goin' ter work. In fact, I went ter Sadie's café wiv 'im, would yer believe.'

Elsie looked surprised. 'Yer went ter Sadie's café wiv 'im? What for?'

'Fer a cuppa an' a chat,' Kay replied, looking pleased with herself. 'Pat asked me. 'E looked so disappointed when I told 'im I was already late fer work, I couldn't say no.'

'You're not still carryin' a torch fer 'im, are yer?' Elsie asked.

''Ow did you know I fancied Pat Kelly?' Kay said indignantly.

Elsie laughed. 'Who didn't. Everyone knew. It stood out a mile. Well, are yer?'

'Am I what?'

'Kay, don't act the clown. Are yer?'

The younger woman sighed. 'I've never stopped.'

'That's what I thought,' Elsie said, shaking her head slowly. 'Kay, yer on a loser wiv that one. You know as well as me Pat Kelly's reputation wiv women. If yer get involved wiv 'im, yer'll live ter regret it.'

'I'm not plannin' on gettin' involved, Else. I just 'ad a chat wiv 'im that's all. Besides, I've got a steady fella.'

'Yeah an' 'e's married,' Elsie sighed, still shaking her head.

The noise of a key in the front door lock startled them, and they looked up with surprise as Ernie walked into the room. He nodded briefly to Kay who had risen out of her chair, and then he gave Elsie a brief smile. 'They tried ter put the frighteners in. Yer know what they're like,' he said as he slumped down into a chair.

Kay stared at his battered face for a few moments, then turned to Elsie. 'I'll be off then. I'll see yer later.'

Elsie was full of concern as she stared at her husband. 'You all right?' she asked him.

'I'll live,' he replied sharply.

'Yer tea's all baked up. I'll pop out an' get yer some fish an' chips if yer like,' she offered.

'Yeah, that'll do,' he said, puffing loudly.

'Tell me, Ernie. Yer didn't 'ave nuffink ter do wiv the robbery, did yer?' she asked him.

'Leave us alone, fer Gawd's sake,' he growled. 'I've 'ad enough grillin' fer one day.'

Chapter Twelve

Joe Brennen slowed down his ageing tender as it made contact with the last of the laden waggons, and watched from the footplate as Tom Kelly trotted beside the container which had been set in motion by the impact. As it neared the rest of the coupled waggons, Tom slipped the end of the heavy bar he was carrying into the brake slot and applied the full weight of his body to it, his feet rising off the ground. The waggon slowed down until it made gentle contact with the end waggon, its buffers absorbing the shock comfortably. The nimble brake man quickly slipped into the gap and completed the coupling before slipping off his gloves and shouldering the brake bar.

Tom Kelly climbed down from the footplate and slipped off his cap to scratch his head. 'That's about it, then,' he said as Tom came up to him.

The brake man nodded as he spat out a stream of plug tobacco juice on to the track. 'Yeah, that's about the lot,' he replied. 'Are yer goin' in fer a pint, Joe?' he asked.

Joe licked his lips in reply and the two men set off along the tracks.

Tom was aware that since his operation Joe had eased up on his drinking, but there were still occasions when they chatted over a pint, and on this particular Saturday the brake man felt that his old friend would welcome the chance for a quiet reprieve.

'I wouldn't mind, but fer our Elsie ter get in the clutches o' that ole mare fer the second time,' Joe was saying as they sat in the railway club room. 'I dunno, Tom, it's one fing after anuvver. I told 'er last time ter come ter me or 'er muvver if she got desperate fer a few bob.'

The dapper brake man sipped his pint gratefully. 'I s'pose she didn't wanna worry yer. Yer know what they're like.'

'Yeah, yer right, but it still grates on me,' Joe went on. 'That ole cow charges exorbitant interest. Once yer get on 'er books she's got yer dead ter rights.'

'Muvver Dines is a strange ole mare, an' so's that son of 'ers,' Tom remarked. 'She must be knockin' on seventy if she's a day. Simon Dines must be nearin' forty.'

Joe smiled at his old friend's knowledge of the neighbours, daily updated by his wife Mary, who was an authority on everybody in the community. ''As she only got the one son?' he asked.

'Nah, there's Norman. 'E's the younger o' the two,' Tom told him. 'Yer won't see anyfing of 'im, though. The boy's in the merchant service. Apparently 'e's a radio operator on one o' the big ships that travel back an' forth ter the Far East, so our Mary was tellin' me.'

'Simon was 'overin' by the door when I went in ter settle up,' Joe said. ''E didn't say anyfink, 'e just stood there like a trained 'ouse dog.'

'That about sums 'im up,' Tom replied. 'Mary 'eard that Muvver Dines screams an' shouts at 'im mercilessly at times. She was talkin' ter that Mrs Mitchell who lives next door ter the Dineses an' she said the ole cow won't let 'im move from the 'ouse wivout 'er say-so. D'yer know, fer the past few years the only place Simon's bin goin' is the market on errands fer 'er, an' up the pub fer a pint in the evenin's.'

'Yer mean ter say 'e don't go out ter work?' Joe asked incredulously.

'Nah, 'e's got some sort o' disability pension,' Tom explained. 'I'm not sure what's wrong wiv 'im, but it's ter do wiv 'is eyes, so our Mary was sayin'. 'E mustn't get in sunlight.'

'Sounds like 'e's an albino. They 'ave ter stay in the dark all the time,' Joe remarked.

'Anyway, 'e's still a large lump, an' mean wiv it,' Tom went on. 'Apparently there was some trouble wiv one o' Muvver Dines's customers one night. A bloke come in the worse fer drink an' started swearin' at 'er. Simon clouted 'im an' chucked 'im out 'ead first. I s'pose the boy puts up wiv 'er tantrums knowin' that one day 'e's gonna 'ave all 'er money – an' make no mistake about it, Joe: That ole cow's loaded.'

96

''As she bin on 'er own long?' Joe asked, becoming more curious.

'She's bin widowed this past twenty years,' Tom replied. 'Nice bloke, 'er ole man, accordin' ter Mary. Albert, 'is name was. 'E used ter be a stoker at the bagwash. Got knocked down by a dray as 'e was comin' 'ome from work one evenin'. Tragic it was, but Muvver Dines got a nice lump sum in compensation, an' then there was property too. Apparently Albert owned a couple of 'ouses. They was left to 'im by 'is family. The total settlement came to a tidy sum. That's 'ow she can lend money the way she does. Mind yer, though, she must 'ave earned a fortune 'erself, what wiv the interest she charges.'

Joe drained his glass. 'Fancy a top-up?' he asked.

Tom nodded. 'Yeah, why not?'

With their drinks replenished, the two old friends soon resumed their chat. 'I s'pose our Ada told your Mary about Ernie Gates,' Joe said.

'Yeah. Sounds a bit fishy ter me,' Tom replied.

'I thought the same fing,' Joe remarked. 'Our Elsie's worried sick over it all. I told 'er good riddance if 'e 'as done it an' gets caught, but she don't see it that way. I dunno, I can't understand the gel. Anuvver woman would 'ave pissed off long ago if she'd 'ad ter take what our Elsie's put up wiv.'

'It's down ter loyalty, Joe. Some of 'em can be knocked black an' blue an' they still won't 'ave anyfing said about their ole men,' Tom said, shaking his head. 'It makes yer fink.'

'Loyalty to a no-good whoreson like Ernie Gates?' Joe spluttered. 'I'd slit the bastard's froat if I found out 'e was knockin' 'er about.'

''Ere mind that stomach o' yours,' Tom warned him. 'Yer know 'ow it plays yer up when yer get uptight.'

Joe grinned. 'Yeah, you're right. Let's change the subject. What's the latest on that scatty git Carney?'

'Yer mean ter say you ain't 'eard?' Tom asked.

'What 'ave I missed?'

'It's one down an' three ter go.'

'Yer mean Preston coughed up wiv one?'

''S'right.'

'Bloody 'ell.'

'Accordin' ter Charlie Catchpole, Carney's goin' ter see 'is panel doctor fer the next reference. Errol Baines put 'im up to it as usual,' Tom said, grinning widely.

'Well, if it's Doctor Livermore 'e's goin' to, Carney's in fer a bad time. Livermore can be a right cantankerous ole git at times,' Joe remarked.

'Yeah, especially if 'e finks yer swingin' the lead.'

The two railwaymen drained their glasses and left the club for Waggoner's Way, Tom Kelly breaking off a fresh piece of plug tobacco and Joe consulting his pocket-watch at least twice before they cleared the freight yard.

Charlie Catchpole's information concerning Jim Carney was indeed correct, as was Joe Brennen's assessment of the fiery old doctor, but for the moment Jim Carney sat patiently waiting his turn at the surgery in Hastings Street.

'Now sit still on that chair an' stop pesterin' the gentleman,' Mrs Gorman told her fidgety son. 'Now, Percy, stop it, d'you 'ear me? No, don't put those sticky 'ands on me coat.'

'I wanna wee,' Percy replied.

'Well, yer'll 'ave ter wait,' the harassed mother said sharply.

'Let 'im 'ave a slash in the kerb, I'll save yer place, missus,' Jim offered pleasantly.

'No, 'e's gotta wait like everybody else,' Mrs Gorman told him.

'Wassa matter wiv 'im?' Jim asked her.

'It ain't 'im, it's me who's waitin' ter see the doctor,' she replied.

'Wassa matter wiv yer then?' Jim asked.

Mrs Gorman wanted to see the doctor on a delicate matter, and was not going to describe her ailment to a perfect stranger, even if he did seem friendly. 'It's me ear,' she lied.

'Wassa matter wiv yer ear?' Jim asked her.

'Wax.'

'Aw, I see.'

The child was getting more uncomfortable and he started whining. 'I wanna wee.'

''E doesn't really,' Mrs Gorman told the railwayman. ''E's just sayin' that so I take 'im outside.'

'I wanna wee,' Percy shouted.

Mrs Gorman raised her eyes to the ceiling in despair, which gave Jim the opportunity to pull a face at the child and at the same time make a fist, which had the effect of silencing Percy for a few moments.

98

'I get wax at times,' Jim told Mrs Gorman. 'Makes yer deaf it does.'

'Yes, I know.'

'Tried anyfing fer it?'

Mrs Gorman was beginning to feel quite uncomfortable as she sat stuck in the middle of it. On one side there was her fidgeting child, and on the other a stupid-looking man who insisted on learning all about her medical history, and in front of a packed surgery. 'What d'yer say?' she asked, feigning deafness as a means of escape.

'I said, 'ave yer tried anyfing fer the wax?' Jim shouted.

'No, I'm gonna be syringed,' she told him quickly, hoping it would shut him up.

'You should try sweet oil,' Jim said obligingly. 'Now what yer do is—'

'Mind my place, I'm gonna take Percy fer a wee,' Mrs Gorman interrupted, unable to stand any more of his inane chatter, but the unfortunate mother was spared any further embarrassment by the receptionist calling out Carney's name.

The elderly doctor had had a rather hectic night with a few old friends the previous evening, and was not feeling too disposed to any lengthy conversation with his patients that Saturday morning. He had not bargained for Jim Carney, though.

'Yes?'

Jim sat down and gave the doctor a friendly smile. 'There's not a fing wrong wiv me that I'm aware of,' he began. 'In fact, I'm as fit as a fiddle.'

'Well then, would you mind explaining what you are doing in my surgery?' the doctor said acidly.

''Ave you ever 'eard o' the Jolly Boys?' Jim asked.

'No, I've not.'

'Pity.'

The doctor remembered treating the man sitting before him some time ago for ringing in his ears, and he wondered if it had somehow led to total imbecility. 'I'm very busy, so would you please tell me what you want from me?' he grated.

'Sure. No trouble. I'd like ter be a Jolly Boy.'

'So would I, but unfortunately I don't feel very jolly this morning. Now will you please tell me why you are here or leave me in peace,' the doctor pleaded.

'I'm sorry yer don't feel too good. There's a woman out there I've

99

just bin talkin' to who's got a load o' wax in 'er ears an' it's makin' 'er a bit deaf. She won't be too 'appy yer don't feel too good this mornin' eivver, I shouldn't fink,' Jim rattled on. 'Doctors are s'posed ter feel fit an' well. It's not very comfortin' ter that lady outside when she sees yer not yer ole self.'

Doctor Livermore felt his bile rising. The headache was beginning to thump harder. He drew breath and moved nearer the railwayman. 'Now listen to me, you blithering idiot. Either tell me what you want from me or I'll have you thrown out. Is that clear?'

'Simple,' Jim said, taken aback by what he considered an unfriendly way of carrying on. 'I wanna be a Jolly Boy an' you can give me a reference. Just a few kind words.'

'The only reference I'd supply you with would be an introduction to Colney Hatch as soon as possible,' the doctor snarled. 'Now get out before I have you thrown out. Do you hear?'

'Yeah, I 'ear yer. I ain't got wax in my ears,' Jim said as he stood up and made for the door.

'I wish I had,' Livermore muttered.

As he left the surgery, Jim looked around and saw Mrs Gorman who was cringing in her seat. 'I wouldn't bovver wiv 'im, missus,' he told her. ''E's a bloody idiot. I told 'im about yer ears an' 'e wasn't a bit interested. Go 'ome an' try sweet oil.'

The waiting room returned to normality while Jim walked home feeling deflated. Well, that was a waste of time, he thought. Maybe Errol would come up with something more promising on Monday morning. In the meantime he would have a word with Mrs Brady. She might be able to suggest his next course of action.

As he strolled back into Waggoner's Way, Jim saw the familiar sight of Salvationists selling their own newspaper door to door. He spotted one distinguished soldier of Christ whom he guessed to be the leader of the band and he smiled to himself. 'Er, just a minute,' he called out.

'Yes. How can I help you?' came the pleasant reply.

'Tell me, 'ave you ever 'eard o' the Jolly Boys?' Jim asked him.

Chapter Thirteen

Ada Brennen had waited in vain for Danny Adams to call about the jobs that needed doing in the house, and at last she came to the conclusion that the young man had had second thoughts. Dot had met her in the street the day after her son's disastrous spell as a cinema doorman and had explained what had happened. The young man would be at sixes and sevens at the moment, Ada thought, and the last thing on his mind would be his promise to call round to price up the jobs. It was a try, anyway, she sighed.

Saturday morning was the normal hurried affair of shopping, cleaning and catching up with the various jobs about the place, as well as making numerous pots of tea and having the girls cluttering up the place. Joe's arrival home after his overtime shift did not help matters either. He sat around reading the newspaper, and he and Colin got into a heated discussion about the merits of Millwall and West Ham United football clubs, who were due to meet that afternoon at Upton Park.

'Are you two gonna sit around arguin' all afternoon about football, or are yer gonna give me some 'elp?' Ada growled.

Colin dragged himself out of the chair and spread his hands wide. 'Just tell me, Muvver. What's there ter do?' he asked, grinning.

'Well, you could clean that backyard up fer a start,' Ada said sharply. 'There's all yer farvver's bits an' pieces o' wood layin' around an' the tools as well. It's no good askin' 'im ter do it. 'E'll be snorin' in no time.'

Colin made for the door but Joe stopped him. 'Oi, don't you go movin' those tools o' mine,' he said quickly. 'I know where they all go. I'll be needin' 'em fer those jobs I gotta do.'

'Well yer better get started then,' Ada told him. 'It don't look like Danny Adams is interested in doin' 'em, 'e ain't bin round.'

'We can do 'em in no time. I'm a bit of a dab 'and wiv a saw an' 'ammer,' Colin piped in.

'Oh no you don't,' Joe told him. 'I've seen some of your 'andywork.'

'Please yerself then,' Colin replied lightly. 'I might as well go round an' see a couple o' me mates. We might decide ter go over Upton Park an' cheer the Lions on.'

'Right, that's Colin's Saturday afternoon sorted out. Now what about you, Joe?' Ada said, her hands on her hips.

Her husband gave her a look which she understood to mean he had everything planned.

'Well?'

Joe stretched and picked up the midday edition of the *Star*. 'I'm gonna pop down the corner an' stick a bet on, then I'm gonna come back an' take a nice nap, an' then we'll see about what's ter be done,' he told her firmly.

Ada puffed loudly as she went out into the scullery, knowing that the repair jobs around the house were going to wait at least another week.

'Mum, do yer fink this nail varnish looks a bit tarty?' Dawn asked her.

'I told 'er she looks like a Lisle Street whore,' Barbara said as she lounged against the tall Welsh dresser.

'Yes, it's too bright,' Ada pronounced, 'an' Barbara, I wish you wouldn't use that language, it make yer sound common.'

'Sorry fer speakin',' Barbara said, pulling a face.

Dawn sat staring at her painted fingernails. 'Yeah, yer right, it does look brassy. I'll try that natural varnish.'

'Whose natural varnish?' Barbara queried.

'Sorry, your natural varnish. Yer don't mind, do yer, Barb?' Dawn said, smiling sweetly at her elder sister.

Ada shook her head slowly and walked back into the parlour. Dawn and Barbara worked together as machinists at the Adelphi clothing factory in Tower Bridge Road and they seemed to share everything, from nail varnish to underwear. They were always teasing each other but behind it all there was a very close bond and Ada had long since learned to ignore the arguments and differences between them. She just hoped that their habit of sharing would not suddenly extend to their boyfriends. That would really upset the applecart.

By mid afternoon the house had become quiet and peaceful. Joe sat snoring lightly in his chair, and Kay had gone for a walk to the market at the Blue Anchor. Barbara and Dawn had both slipped out to see their friends, and Colin had not made an appearance since he went off to see his mates. Ada guessed that he had gone over to West Ham, and she took the opportunity of settling down in her chair to read her paperback novel of love and passion in the tropics which she had picked up at the second-hand bookstall.

The knock on the front door startled Ada out of her daydreams, and she reluctantly climbed out of her comfortable chair to discover Danny Adams standing on the threshold.

'Er, I'm sorry, but I was s'posed ter call round,' he said hesitantly. 'I bin pretty busy.'

Ada smiled, knowing that Danny had been anything but busy. She pulled the door wide open. 'Come in, Danny. I'm glad yer called anyway.'

The young man looked a little bemused as he stood in the parlour, not quite knowing what he should do next as he stared down at the recumbent figure of Joe Brennen.

'Take no notice of 'im, lad. 'E's bin on overtime,' Ada said, smiling. 'Take a seat. Would yer care fer a cuppa?'

Danny nodded. 'Yeah, that'd be nice,' he replied.

Ada went into the scullery to put the kettle over the gas ring and when she came back she said, 'Look, while we're waitin' I'll show yer what needs ter be done. It'll save yer sittin' listenin' ter that racket.'

As if hearing the comment in his sleep, Joe moved and grunted loudly.

Danny grinned as he followed Ada up into her bedroom. 'Look, there's this cracked floorboard,' she told him, sliding a square of oilcloth to one side and pulling up the edge of the eiderdown. 'It needs replacin', an' then there's this door. We can never shut it properly. The gels' bedroom door's the same. Oh, an' there's a drawer that needs seein' to. It won't close tight.'

Danny stood looking down at the floorboard for a few moments, and Ada watched his reaction. He looked fit and well and in command of his senses, and he seemed thoughtful, the way a craftsman might look as he assessed a job of work.

'That don't seem too difficult,' he said presently, and he moved over to the door. 'This just needs a few shavin's off it. It won't take long.'

Ada was pleasantly surprised as she looked at him. To hear his mother talk, anyone would think he was a shambling, pathetic shadow of a man who had to be constantly supervised and watched. But to be fair to her, Dot had said that Danny's strange behaviour was spasmodic and triggered off by certain events. This must be one of his better days, Ada thought, and she had the feeling that she would see the other side of Danny before the work was finished, if it ever was. Nevertheless, the young man needed the opportunity to regain his confidence and self-esteem, and she was going to give him that chance. 'Can yer fix it all?' she asked outright.

'No trouble,' he replied.

'Right then. I'll be in durin' the day, so yer can pick yer own time. Now what about payment?' she asked him.

'A couple o' quid should do it,' he told her without hesitating.

'What about the new plank o' wood fer the floorboard though?' she queried.

'I got some wood in the yard. Two quid all in,' Danny told her.

Ada led him into the scullery and bade him sit down while she made the tea. Danny sat staring at the Welsh dresser. 'That's a nice piece o' craftsmanship,' he remarked.

'You like carpentry I take it,' Ada said, filling the teapot with boiling water.

'Yeah, I always like messin' around wiv tools. I'd like a job doin' carpentry fer a livin',' Danny told her.

'Couldn't yer get a job wiv a builder?'

'Nah, yer need credentials ter show yer served an apprenticeship,' he explained.

'What about those ex-Servicemen's courses? Surely you could get on one o' them?' Ada said as she picked up the teapot and filled two large mugs with strong-looking tea.

Danny shrugged his shoulders. 'It's not that simple,' he replied, looking down at his hands. 'I get a bit fergetful since the crash. I can't seem ter take it all in.'

'But yer good wiv tools.'

'Yer gotta know the theory, though, and that's where I fall down,' he said, his face taking on a sad look.

Ada felt she had pressed him too much, and she put the brimming mug down in front of him. 'Well, never mind that. Drink this. 'Elp yerself ter the sugar.'

Danny sipped his tea. 'I s'pose you 'eard about the job at the Old Kent,' he said suddenly.

Ada nodded. 'That wasn't fer you anyway, Danny. Ye're werf a better job than that.'

He smiled sheepishly. 'Yeah, I made a right muck up o' that one. I knew it wasn't the job fer me, but I did it fer me muvver. She's worried about me always bein' in an' out o' jobs. I thought if I could stick it fer at least a few weeks, she wouldn't worry so much. Trouble is, it's these 'eadaches. When they start I get confused. It's like I don't know where I am or what I'm s'posed ter be doin', so I just sit quiet till they pass.'

'Do they last long?' Ada asked.

'They vary. Sometimes it's all day, ovver times they pass off in a matter o' minutes,' he told her.

'I reckon they'll be less frequent as time goes on,' she remarked, trying to reassure him, but Danny shook his head.

'I got a steel plate in me 'ead. It's there fer life,' he replied.

Ada wanted to take him in her arms and cuddle him tightly, the way she used to with her own children when they hurt themselves. He was such a nice, presentable young man, who had gone off to the war voluntarily and had served his country well. He had been a hero, flying on many bombing missions, only to be forgotten, left to fend for himself the best way he could on a pittance of a disability pension. That was how Dot Adams had summed it up, and she was right. How many more young men had come back from the war ruined both physically and mentally and left to their own devices?

'You're spillin' yer tea,' Danny said quickly.

Ada put down her mug and gave him a smile. 'Sorry, I was just finkin',' she said.

Danny drained his mug. 'Well, I'd better be goin',' he told her. 'Will it be all right if I make a start next week?'

'Any time, Danny,' she replied. 'An' don't worry. We're not goin' anywhere. I'll be in.'

That evening, Ernie Gates sat alone in the quiet Mason's Arms waiting. Nick Zanti had arranged to meet him there at eight o'clock sharp, and there were still a few minutes to go. Ernie thought about the detective's parting words as he left the interview room yesterday evening. 'We'll be wantin' ter talk wiv yer again, so don't fink o' goin' anywhere. Enjoy yer freedom, Gates, while yer still can.'

Ernie smiled to himself. They couldn't prove anything, and they were clutching at straws, he thought. As long as he kept his head, and kept his mouth shut, he would be fine. His employers had taken the loss of the load very calmly, considering. They would be well insured anyway, and it wasn't the first load that a local transport firm had had stolen. One thing he would have to do though was not refuse any offered overtime. If the firm thought he was not in need of the extra money it would look bad, and they might well inform the police. He would have to be careful how he handled things at home too. Elsie was saying Billy needed new shoes and clothes for school. If he flashed money around she would know he had been involved in the robbery. She probably had her suspicions, but she could think all she liked. She wouldn't hear the truth from him. He would give her a few pounds for the boy and tell her it came out of his overtime pay.

At eight o'clock exactly, Nick Zanti walked into the pub and ordered a drink. He showed no sign of recognition, but instead sat down at the far end of the bar. Ernie sipped his drink nonchalantly and, after a short while, Zanti got up and walked over to the toilet, his eyes flashing a sign for Ernie to follow him.

Ernie put down his drink and looked around the bar before going out to the gent's. There were no strange faces sitting around, but as he ambled out to join Zanti the landlord glanced over, a thoughtful expression on his face.

'There's three hundred in there,' Zanti said, passing over a long sealed envelope. 'Nice to have done business with you.'

After the Maltese villain had left, Ernie walked back into the bar and sat down. He had one more drink and then strolled casually out into the street, eyed by the curious landlord who turned to Vera, his plump, platinum-blonde wife. 'I wonder what Nick Zanti's game is,' he said. 'Last time 'e come in 'ere 'e went over an' spoke to Ernie Gates. Did yer see what 'appened this time?'

Vera shook her head. 'No, what?'

''E went out ter the closet an' Ernie follered 'im. Then Zanti came out an' left.'

'So what?'

'I dunno. It just seemed a bit mysterious, that's all.'

Vera studied her long fingernails for a few moments. 'Well, whatever they're up to, it's none of our business,' she told him.

Arthur Selby leaned on the counter. 'I was clockin' Ernie Gate's face. It looks like 'e's bin in a punch-up,' he remarked.

Vera turned to face him. 'If yer wanna survive in this game, yer don't spend too much time wonderin' about ovver people's business. I learnt that a long time ago,' she reminded him. 'Nick Zanti's got a bad name an' 'e's one o' those people yer shouldn't wonder about. Less yer know about the likes of 'im, the better.'

Arthur nodded in agreement. There was definitely some funny business going on between Gates and Zanti, but like Vera said: it didn't pay to get too inquisitive.

Pat Kelly was at a loose end. He had re-established himself in the room he used to have, the back bedroom at number 15 Waggoner's Way, the end house, next door to Jack Springer's corner shop newsagent's. There was plenty of space in the family home, now that his two sisters Kathleen and Maureen had both married and moved out, and Pat felt that space was what he needed most. His marriage to Eileen had been a disaster, and they had come to the mutual decision that they should end it. Now, as he sat staring at the old photographs pinned up on his bedroom wall, Pat realised that there were a lot of adjustments he would have to make. Most of his old pals had married, and the girls he used to date now seemed to shy away from him as though he had some infectious disease.

It was turned eight o'clock when Pat Kelly left the house, having decided he would treat himself to a quiet drink in the Mason's Arms. He might possibly bump into one or two of his old mates there, he thought. Failing that, there was always 'Chippy', and he smiled to himself at the memory. Many times he and his pals had ended up drinking at Chippy's, a small riverside pub properly called the Bell. Usually the young men gathered there late on a Saturday night to commiserate with each other over the lack of female talent available, and the unfairness of life in general. The pub had earned its nickname from the landlord, Edward Chipperfield, a crusty individual with a quick wit and an aversion to clocks. Chippy, as he was called, preferred to go by intuition. He closed the pub when he was tired, or else when the last customer left, usually in the early hours. The police tended to turn a blind eye to his flouting of the licensing laws. There was never any trouble there, and very often the policemen themselves enjoyed an off-duty late night at Chippy's.

As he walked towards the Mason's Arms, Pat had a feeling that he was going to end up at Chippy's that night, and as he was smiling at the thought, he came face to face with Ernie Gates.

'Well, well. If it ain't the street's lover-boy,' Ernie sneered. 'I 'eard you were back in the street. Kicked you out, did she?'

Pat bit back an angry reply. Since his bloody set-to with Ernie which had ended inconclusively, he had bided his time, knowing that one day they would finish what they had started. He guessed that Ernie Gates felt the same as he did and was biding his time too.

'No, I wasn't kicked out,' Pat replied calmly, 'not that it's any o' your business.'

'I expect we'll be seein' a bit more of each ovver now then,' Ernie said.

'Yeah, I expect so,' Pat told him.

Ernie sniggered as he started to walk on. 'Yer know where yer can find me if yer fancy yer chances.'

'Yeah, we should sort somefing out pretty soon,' Pat replied, a wry smile touching his lips.

As he entered the Mason's Arms, the young man looked around at the clientele. There were a few familiar faces there but none of his old friends. 'Give us a pint o' bitter, please, Vera,' he asked, leaning his arm on the counter.

Vera Selby knew Pat quite well, and she gave him a big smile as she pulled his pint. 'Yer just missed your ole pal, Gates,' she remarked. 'That would 'ave bin a sight ter see, you an' 'im bumpin' into each ovver in my pub.'

'I just met 'im, as a matter o' fact,' Pat told her. 'Right outside your door.'

'What, no blood on the pavement?' she joked.

Pat laid down a half-crown and picked up his pint. ''Ere's to all the gels, wherever they are,' he said smiling.

'Does that include me?' Vera asked him.

'Yeah, but don't tell that ole man o' yours. Where is 'e by the way?'

The landlady pulled a face. ''E's just gone in the public bar,' she replied. 'I sent 'im in there so I could make eyes at you.'

'You're too much woman fer me to 'andle,' Pat said, smiling.

Vera sighed noisily. 'You always say the nicest fings, Pat. Remind me ter poison Arfur, an' then me an' you can go off ter some exotic place tergevver.'

The young man took a large draught of his ale and licked his lips. 'Well, I can safely say your beer's not changed,' he told her.

''Ow long yer likely ter be around?' Vera asked.

'I dunno, luv,' he replied. 'It all depends.'

'Just stay clear o' that Ernie Gates,' she told him. 'I wouldn't wanna see that 'andsome dial o' yours all bashed up.'

'Don't worry about me, Vera. I can look after meself,' he said, grinning.

Vera was called away to serve another customer, but she glanced back furtively at the young man as he stood alone at the counter. She remembered vividly the previous encounter between Ernie Gates and Pat Kelly and it still made her shudder. Ernie had been drinking heavily and was scathingly running down Kelly, who had returned from the war something of a hero. Ernie was obviously envious of the young Romeo and his confident manner. He had spent the war years driving a lorry for a food manufacturer's, having been granted an exemption from call-up. Vera suspected that it had rankled with him and made him take an instant dislike to the young Pat Kelly, who in her opinion looked like a film star in his uniform.

The customers had held their breath when Pat Kelly walked into the saloon bar with Eileen Carter on his arm, and it was not long before Ernie Gates found something disparaging to say about the Carter girl. Pat threw a punch in defence of his girl's good name and when Gates picked himself up from the floor, the look on his face was terrifying, Vera recalled. The fight spilled out on to the street and into the road, and both men had bloody faces as they fought it out toe to toe. No one had the courage to try separating them, until the local policeman put in an appearance; it was probably thanks to him that they did not finally kill each other.

Pat finished his ale. 'Well, I'm off, Vera. Stay beautiful,' he said grinning.

'An' where are you off to?' she asked.

'I got a date at Chippy's,' he called out.

Vera sighed. 'Lucky her.'

Chapter Fourteen

Jim Carney sat talking with Sara Brady in her neat and tidy parlour. His landlady was feeling a little sorry for the hulking figure as he tried to explain.

'But ole Livermore's me panel doctor an' I didn't expect 'im ter cop the needle, Sara,' he was going on. 'After all, I don't pester 'im as much as some I could mention. Blimey, gel, I ain't bin ter see 'im fer Gawd knows 'ow long, an' when I do 'e almost slings me out on me crust.'

After the heated argument she had had with her husband over their lodger, Sara realised that Stan was right. Jim Carney was being made a fool of. His fixation with joining the Jolly Boys was leading him into all sorts of confrontations. She felt sorry for him and could not bear to tell him outright that he was becoming a laughing-stock. Better if she tried to steer him away from any more trouble, and attempted to talk a bit of sense into him, if that were possible.

'What yer gotta remember, Jim, is that Doctor Livermore's a very busy man, an' it's understandable 'e ain't got time ter go writin' out bloody great references to every Tom, Dick an' 'Arry,' she explained. 'An' let's be sensible. Those Jolly Boys ain't all they're cracked up ter be, if you ask me. All right, they do fings fer charity now an' then, but there's lots the likes o' you could do wivout yer gettin' yerself in all sorts o' trouble tryin' ter join 'em.'

Jim's face dropped. 'Yeah, but the Jolly Boys 'ave got some standin' in the neighbour'ood, gel. They're respected, an' they're always 'avin' those meetin's at the railway club,' he told her. 'It's nice to 'ave some sort of interest outside o' work.'

Sara could see that Jim Carney was really obsessed with joining the élite club, and she tried a different tack. 'Look, yer could knock

yerself out gettin' all those references an' then they might still black-
ball yer,' she pointed out. 'After all, they was all in the 'eavy rescue
durin' the war, accordin' ter what my Stan told me.'

'Yeah, but I was a firewatcher. I done me bit in the war,' Jim said
quickly. 'Surely that counts fer somefing?'

'Well, I dunno who's gonna give yer all those references yer
need,' Sara sighed.

'I only need four an' I've got one already,' Jim reminded her. 'Ole
Preston gave me one wivout too much trouble, an' I fink I can get
anuvver one from that bloke in the Salvation Army who I spoke to
this mornin'.'

'But you ain't in the Salvation Army, Jim.'

'Nah, but I could flog a few o' those newspapers they sell. In fact,
I offered me services,' Jim replied with a sly smile.

'You ain't finkin' o' joinin' that lot as well, are yer?' Sara asked
him with a note of despair in her voice.

'Course not. I'd just 'elp out wiv the newspapers,' he told her.

'I can just imagine you goin' round wiv the *War Cry*. Unless yer in
uniform, people are gonna fink yer nicked the papers,' Sara replied.

'I expect they'd give me a badge or somefink ter show I was
genuine,' Jim persisted.

'I dunno,' Sara sighed. 'It strikes me yer gonna get more than yer
bargained for over this fing yer got about those Jolly Boys.'

Jim would not be shaken. 'Look, gel. I reckon I'll get a reference
from the Salvation Army bloke, an' I've got anuvver trick up me
sleeve,' he told her, tapping his temple with his forefinger.

'Don't tell me, fer Gawd's sake,' she said quickly.

'It's nuffink ter worry about. I'm gonna go an' see the mayor o'
Bermondsey,' Jim said, grinning.

''E won't give yer one,' Sara said dismissively. 'I bet yer won't
even get ter see 'im. The mayor o' Bermondsey's a very busy man.
'E's got all sorts o' functions ter go to. 'E won't 'ave no time ter see
you, that's a dead cert.'

Jim Carney leaned back in his chair and folded his arms. 'We'll
see,' he said with a smile.

Lights were burning late into Saturday night at Dockhead police
station, and the small group of detectives were assessing the
evidence they had gathered concerning the theft of seven tons of
brass and copper fittings.

'Now, what have we got so far?' Chief Superintendent Roger Cranley asked.

Detective Sergeant William Moody opened the thin file in front of his superior. 'When we got ter the lorry it was burnt out, sir, but we managed ter remove what was left of the instrument panel. The speedo 'ad started ter melt but we got a mileage readin'. Now, we checked wiv the firm. Their records show this figure on the clock at the end o' the previous day,' he said, pointing to the open file. 'Wiv this in mind, we did a run in the car from the transport yard ter the collection point at Poplar and then ter Bill Mayes's caff. Then we clocked the mileage from both the tunnel an' Tower Bridge ter Peckham, which only varied by one an' a 'alf miles. So yer see, there's only seven or eight miles unaccounted for, which would be the journey to an' from the drop-off point. Three an' 'alf ter four miles, in fact.'

Cranley stood up and consulted the large wall-map in his office. 'Now, we have to consider whether or not the unaccounted miles were taken up north or south,' he began. 'In other words, was the load transferred within three or four miles of Peckham or Poplar? Any ideas?'

Moody looked confident as he walked over to the map. 'You know my feelin's, sir,' he began. 'Gates is implicated, an' 'e stopped fer a break where 'e was told to. Now, if the gang intended ter transfer the load south o' the river they would've 'ad 'im stop at one o' the pull-ups this side. Why snatch a lorry over the water an' increase the risk o' bein' pulled up comin' over the bridge or frew the tunnel? No. In my estimation the load was dumped over the water.'

Cranley nodded. 'Right then, let's get an area marked out.'

When the circle had been drawn in coloured pencil on the large map, Cranley stood back and stroked his chin thoughtfully. 'The City of London, round to Hoxton in the north and over to East Ham. I think we can discount the City. Any more thoughts, Sergeant?'

'Workin' on my assumption, Gates lined up the robbery wiv local villains, an' my guess is it's the Malts,' he said with conviction.

'Any specific reason, Sergeant?'

'My snout told me there was a gavverin' in the Dun Cow last night, the second one this week,' Moody went on. 'It could 'ave bin a pay-out, although nuffink was seen changin' 'ands. Anuvver

112

thought. The lorry. It was dumped in Peckham. Why Peckham? Well, it was a derelict spot, an' a burnin' lorry in that particular place might not 'ave been noticed right away. Time enough ter turn it into a cinder. But I reckon the lorry bein' dumped south o' the river was meant ter put us off the scent, in their way o' finkin'.'

'Very interesting,' Cranley remarked. 'Sergeant, I want you to get in touch with the Poplar police. Find out if any of those names in the file have connections north of the river.'

Kay had been unable to get Pat Kelly out of her mind since bumping into him on her way to work, and she realised that she had to pull herself together. Pat had been very nice and friendly as they sat chatting together in Sadie's café, but she could tell that he had no designs on her. He still saw her as a child, the daughter of a family who had been friends with his for many years. The trouble with Pat Kelly was that he couldn't see the wood for the trees, she thought. Anyway, it was too late as far as she was concerned. She was seeing a special young man who loved her and wanted her. True it was proving difficult at the moment, but things would soon change for the better.

The bus trundled slowly along the Old Kent Road, and Kay began to get a little anxious. She had arranged to meet David at the little pub they had visited on a previous occasion and she was already late. He might think she had had a change of heart and was not going to meet him, she fretted. Maybe he would not go straight home and instead would go to another pub to drown his sorrows by getting drunk.

When she finally arrived at the Raven in the little backstreet behind New Cross Gate, she saw him immediately sitting hunched over his beer. His face lit up and he stood up as she walked in.

'Am I very late?' she asked him.

David smiled. 'It's all right,' he said. 'I was gettin' worried, though. I thought you might 'ave changed yer mind.'

'I couldn't get me 'air ter go right an' the bus crawled all the way,' she told him.

David took her arm and led her to the bar. 'Usual?'

Kay hesitated. 'I'd like a gin an' lemon, if that's all right,' she replied.

David ordered her drink and a large whisky for himself and then they found a table in a secluded corner.

"Ave yer settled in OK?' Kay asked him.

'Yeah, I went back ter the 'ouse yesterday ter get the rest o' me fings,' he told her.

'Did yer see yer wife?' she asked.

'Yeah, she was there.'

Kay caught the look in his eyes and it troubled her. 'Well?'

David shrugged his shoulders. 'We didn't 'ave a lot ter say to each ovver,' he replied. 'She wanted ter know where I was livin', an' I asked 'er 'ow she was. You know, the usual meanin'less conversation.'

'No regrets?'

'No, none.'

Kay took a sip from her drink. She wanted to feel daring this evening and the gin would help, she told herself.

'David?'

'Yeah?'

'Do yer want me ter come ter your flat ternight?'

He reached out and took her hand in his, holding it tightly in his strong grip. 'I've thought of nuffink else,' he said softly.

Kay watched as David swallowed the contents of his glass in one gulp. He looked nervous, she thought. Most probably as nervous as she herself felt. But it would be good. She would make it good, even though she did not quite understand how she was going to achieve it. She must let him be aware that she wanted him, wanted to be pleasured, not taken roughly and with little thought for her feelings. It had to be good this time. She had waited long enough to experience full, satisfying love, and tonight everything was going to work out just right.

David had gone to the bar for a refill. When he returned he sat down with a look of concern on his handsome face. 'I was watchin' yer while I was at the counter. You looked very deep in thought. Are yer worried?'

'No. Are you?' she replied.

David looked into her eyes. 'I want it ter be right. I wanna make yer really 'appy,' he said in a soft voice.

Kay smiled at him, trying to reassure him, but she could sense the torment he was going through, the fear of failing her. It showed in his eyes. 'Let's drink up an' go,' she said.

David took her hand as they left the pub and they did not speak until they were inside his flat. In the darkness of his sitting room, he took her into his arms and kissed her gently on her open lips. She could feel his breathing becoming faster and she suddenly broke away from his caress as his hands started to stray down her back. She took his hand, gazing into his face as they moved together to the bedroom. The semi darkness encouraged Kay to be bold and she slowly undid her blouse. David stood watching her and, as she slipped off the flimsy silk garment, he moved forward and pulled her to him. She wanted him to undress her slowly and kiss her hard nipples and firm breasts, but he began to fumble. She slid down the zip of her skirt, trying to help him but David stepped back. 'I'll go in the bathroom while you get inter bed,' he said quickly.

Kay stripped and slipped in between the cold sheets, eagerly awaiting him, and excitement welled up inside her, a delicious feeling that made her shiver with expectant pleasure.

David came into the bedroom and slipped into the bed, his hand moving immediately on to her flat belly. She turned towards him, and as their lips met he was caressing her body, stroking her firm breasts, her smooth white thighs, the roundness of her hips. He kissed her neck, her throat and then her breasts. She smelt his aftershave and talcum, and she heard his heavy breathing becoming more a pant as he straightened up and kissed her hard on her lips. Their bodies were now touching from shoulder to toe and she could feel his passion.

'I love you, Kay,' he gasped, reaching his hand between her thighs.

'I love you too,' she whispered.

David groaned as his fingers found her most sensuous spot and she shuddered with pleasure, kissing him with her open mouth. Suddenly he moved on top of her, his hot breath coming in gasps. She closed her eyes and gripped the tops of his arms as she waited for him, eager to feel him, and then she gasped and screwed her hands up into tight fists as she felt the sharp pain of him entering her. He was pressing down on her, his full weight preventing her from moving, and she tried in vain to position herself, to gain some pleasure instead of the pain as he half withdrew then thrust himself into her once more. He shuddered violently and his whole body stiffened.

He had taken her virginity but had left her feeling cheated. She had wanted him to go on, to pleasure her and fulfil her, but instead he had failed her. Kay bit on her lip in anguish and angry tears rose in her eyes as she struggled to turn over on to her side, to get from under his prone body as he lay on top of her, restricting her breathing.

'I wanted you so bad,' he gasped as he rolled on to his side.

'I wanted you too,' she said with emphasis, feeling at that very moment that she wanted to shame him.

David reached out his hand and gently stroked her dishevelled blonde hair. 'I'm sorry if I was rough, darlin',' he whispered. 'I know it wasn't good fer you.'

'You were so 'eavy. I couldn't breavve properly,' she told him, wanting to hurt him for being so clumsy yet at the same time feeling pity for him.

David turned on to his back. 'I'm sorry,' he muttered.

Kay climbed from the bed, suddenly aware that she was bleeding, and she grabbed up her clothes and hurried into the bathroom. A full moon shone into the tiny closet, and as she caught sight of herself in the mirror Kay sighed deeply. The moment should have been one of excitement, one of pure happiness, but the face that stared out at her reflected nothing of such emotion. It looked sad and frightened.

Chapter Fifteen

Joe Brennen folded the *Sunday Mirror* and dropped it at his feet, then he looked around for the *News of the World*. It's always the same, he grumbled to himself. A man don't ask for much on a Sunday. A bit of a rest in the armchair and the chance to catch up on all the news. Fat chance of that in this house, though. One or other of them was always taking the newspapers out of the room.

'You gels took my *News o' the World*?' he called out.

Dawn had taken it out to the scullery to point out to Barbara what she described as a tasty bit of scandal involving a randy old goat and a chorus girl, and the paper had been left on the dresser. Ada had been in her usual hurry to get on with the Sunday lunch and had spread it out on the draining-board to catch the potato peelings.

'I fink it was out 'ere, Dad, but I can't see it now,' Dawn called out, grinning at Barbara.

'Well, it must be somewhere,' he called back, raising his voice a little in irritation.

Ada suddenly winced. 'Dawn. Slip up Jack Springer's an' get yer farvver anuvver *News o' the World*,' she whispered. 'I'm doin' the taters on it.'

Joe came walking out into the scullery. 'I wish people would leave those papers alone,' he growled.

Ada smiled at him. 'Now look, it's no good gettin' yerself all screwed up over a stupid newspaper,' she told him. 'Now go in an' sit down, I'll find it soon as I've finished the veg.'

Dawn was soon back and Ada pointed to the teapot. 'Pour yer farvver out a cuppa, Dawn, I wanna do the greens.'

Barbara was sat at the small table, flipping through *True Romances*, with a leisurely stretch she got up. 'I'll do 'em, Mum,' she volunteered. 'You go in an' put yer feet up.'

Kay came in from the backyard carrying a large wicker basket full of dried washing and Ada glanced at her with concern. Her youngest daughter did not look her usual self, she thought. 'Leave it 'ere, luv, I'll sort it out later,' she said.

Kay put the basket down on the table and took the new electric iron from the dresser cupboard. 'No, I might as well make a start on it,' she said flatly.

Ada nodded. It was no use arguing with her, she decided. When something was troubling Kay, she tended to keep it to herself, unlike Dawn and Barbara who were more inclined to open up when they were feeling worried about anything.

'Is Elsie comin' round fer dinner?' Dawn asked.

'Yeah, she said she would,' Ada told her. 'An' don't you gels go pesterin' 'er about what's 'appened wiv Ernie. She's worried enough as it is. If she wants ter talk about it she will.'

Joe felt into his waistcoat pocket and drew out his silver watch as Ada walked into the parlour. 'What time did our Elsie say she was comin' round?' he asked her.

'Soon as she was ready,' Ada replied, flopping down into the armchair with a thankful sigh. 'I 'eard Barbara say that Jamie's callin' round as well. 'E's bringin' 'er some records.'

'It's gettin' like Waterloo Station 'ere,' Joe said smiling. 'Ain't Dawn's boyfriend callin' as well? It only wants our Colin ter bring a few of 'is mates round an' we could start chargin' tuppence a cup fer tea. We'd do a roarin' trade.'

Ada smiled back at him and then her face became serious. 'I'm a bit concerned about our Kay,' she told him. 'She looks very peeky. I fink it's somefing ter do wiv that fella she's goin' wiv.'

Joe gave her an anxious look. 'Yer don't fink 'e's married, do yer?'

Ada shrugged her shoulders. 'I dunno,' she replied. 'You know Kay. She don't say a lot. I did ask 'er the ovver day when she was gonna bring 'im round an' she just said soon as it was convenient. I didn't press it, she'll only do it when she's good an' ready.'

Joe folded up the newspaper as Dawn came into the room carrying two cups of tea. 'Gordon said 'e might call in this mornin',' she announced, catching the amused look that her parents exchanged. 'Yer don't mind, do yer?'

Joe shook his head emphatically. 'No course not. We'll just wait till Colin comes in wiv 'is crowd an' then we'll put the sign up. Tea

118

bar now open. Tuppence a cup,' he told her, his face breaking into a grin.

The two sipped their tea, vaguely listening to the noisy chatter going on in the scullery, and when they suddenly heard Colin's voice at the front door, Joe put a hand to his head in feigned horror. 'Come in. Bring 'em all in, it's open 'ouse,' he said under his breath.

Colin walked into the room accompanied by two young men his own age. 'This is Pete, an' this is Charlie. They work wiv me,' he announced. 'Pete's got 'is callin'-up papers too. 'E's goin' in the Royal Artillery, ain't yer, Pete?'

The tall thin lad nodded and looked a little embarrassed, but Charlie held out his hand. 'Pleased ter meet yer, Mr Brennen. I ain't eighteen yet,' he said cheerfully.

Joe stood up and shook hands with the confident young man. 'Will you be goin' in the Army too, then?' he asked.

Charlie ran his fingers through his dark curly hair. 'Nah, I'm gonna go in the Navy, if I can,' he replied. 'All my family 'ave bin in the Andrew.'

Colin was getting impatient. 'C'mon, lads, let's go an' sort those fings out,' he said quickly.

Ada turned to Joe as the three of them hurried up to Colin's bedroom. 'They're still only kids, ain't they?' she said, shaking her head sadly. 'It makes yer fink. No sooner are they out o' school than they're puttin' on uniforms.'

'They're young men, Ada,' Joe said quietly. 'We just 'ave ter be fankful the war's over. A lot o' families saw their kids goin' off ter fight in a war. What must they 'ave bin finkin?'

'There's still a lot of unrest in the world though,' Ada reminded him. 'I just worry about our Colin.'

At that moment Billy came bounding into the room, followed by a worried-looking Elsie. Joe scooped the lad up into his arms and began to make a fuss of him, while Ada led her eldest daughter out into the scullery to join her sisters. 'What's the latest?' she asked anxiously.

Kay, Barbara and Dawn all looked at their sister eagerly, and Elsie shrugged her shoulders. 'The police came round for 'im this mornin',' she told them. 'They wanted 'im ter go an' look at some photos. 'E said 'e was goin' straight round the pub afterwards, so I don't know what's 'appened.'

Ada looked at her, dismayed by her appearance. Elsie's normally long fair hair had been cut short and it looked dull and lifeless. Her grey-blue eyes lacked sparkle and she seemed to sag as she stood in the doorway. She had lost weight too.

Dawn got up quickly and offered Elsie her chair, while Barbara picked up the teapot and refilled it from the steaming kettle. Colin had hurried down the stairs to greet his sister, his face eager and solicitous.

'Wotcha, Else. You all right?' he said, noticing her worried look.

''Ello, Colin. Yeah, I'm all right,' she reassured him.

'Ernie ain't givin' yer no grief, is 'e?' Colin asked her, his face taking on a hard expression.

'No. Fings are very quiet as a matter o' fact,' she said, a cynical smile playing on her lips.

''E better not, or 'e'll 'ave me ter deal wiv,' Colin said quickly. 'I'd soon sort 'im out.'

Elsie gave him a warm smile as she felt his upper arm. 'Yeah, I bet yer would,' she joked, knowing that her young brother would stand no chance against her big, violent husband.

Billy had tired of being fussed over by his grandfather and he came bounding out into the scullery to face the usual kisses and cuddles from his aunts.

'Keep 'im away from the oven. I'm gonna look at the meat,' Ada announced.

Joe sat back in his chair and sighed expectantly as the smell of beef and roast potatoes drifted into the parlour. Sunday morning was certainly a time to savour, he thought. All the family were gathered together and there was good food for the table. It was the time for a man to count his blessings, to be able to put his feet up and enjoy the peace and quiet after a hard week's work.

'Joe?'

'Yes, luv?'

'Can yer lay the table?'

'Yes, luv,' he sighed.

'Oh an' Joe?'

'Yes, luv?'

'Can yer come an' take a look at this iron? Kay reckons the element's burnt out.'

Joe sighed in resignation. 'Yeah, so am I.'

Just a street away, at number 12 Dover Lane, Simon Dines was becoming anxious to get to the Eagle in the Old Kent Road where he normally had his Sunday lunch-time drink. It was ten minutes after twelve, and the pubs would be open now. Instead, he was compelled to listen while his ageing mother went on and on about her hard life and the struggle to manage after her husband was killed.

Simon had heard it all so many times and he nodded mechanically as she warmed to the subject. There was more to come and he wished that he could just get up and leave, but that would only have served to aggravate the old lady, now that she was getting to the part about his and his brother's roles in her life.

'Norman was never the dutiful one,' she ranted on. 'Always the selfish one was Norman. Not a bit like you, Simon. You always 'ad consideration fer yer ole muvver. Always a good boy. I remember many a time when I was feelin' poorly. It was you what cared, not that bruvver o' yours. It was you what did the fings around the 'ouse. 'E was always out an' about. I knew 'e would run orf ter sea one day. Always talkin' about the sea 'e was. I don't s'pose 'e's worried one little bit 'ow 'is ole muvver is. I could be in me grave fer all 'e'd know. I made a lot o' sacrifices fer you an' 'im an' what's me fanks? Norman ain't bin near or by fer ages. Still, I got you ter look after me an' don't fink I ain't grateful.'

'It's all right, Ma, I . . .'

'We all get our just deserts in the end an' Norman'll get 'is one day fer the way 'e's treated me,' she interrupted. 'Never mind, when I'm gorn the money'll go ter you. You've bin the one who stood by me, an' don't fink I'll ferget it.'

Simon took down his dark glasses from the mantelshelf, hoping that it would remind his mother that he was ready to leave for the pub, but she continued unheeding. 'I want you ter know that there's quite a bit o' money comin' your way. I bin careful, an' I ain't squandered it. Mind you, I ain't got so much comin' in these days. At one time everybody seemed ter be knockin' at the door fer loans. I can't grumble though. I still get people callin' round who ain't got nobody else ter turn to.'

Simon had heard enough and he put on his glasses. 'Look, Ma, I'm gonna slip up the Eagle fer a pint. I won't be long,' he told her.

Mother Dines pulled a face. 'All right, but make sure you ain't too long. Yer know 'ow I get if yer gone a long while.'

The dutiful son stepped out into the bright sunlight, his weak eyes

121

shielded behind the dark glasses, and he heard the rattle of the heavy chain being fixed into position behind the door.

As he walked swiftly along the turning, Simon Dines was fuming inside. How many times had he been compelled to listen to his mother's rantings? Many of the women around this area had suffered just as much as her – more most likely – but it was a good bet they did not harp on it, he thought. She was just playing on his loyalty, knowing that he would not leave her in the lurch the way Norman had. But Norman had the advantage over him. He had no problem going out and about in bright daylight. He did not have to wear dark glasses and struggle to read the newspapers. Their mother played on his condition. She revelled in the fact that he could not hold a job down and used him like a servant, a trained house dog to protect her night and day. What sort of a life did he have? One or two pints at the pub on Sundays and maybe a pint in the week. He had no friends or acquaintances, except those barflies at the Eagle who were always making snide remarks. There was no woman in his life, and who would be interested in him anyway? He was turned forty, flabby and weak-sighted.

It would be different one day though, he told himself. She wouldn't live for ever. One day the money would be his, all of it, and then he would buy a couple of suits, smart shoes and shirts. He would be able to stay out as long as he liked and maybe he would find a good woman, someone who was not obsessed by good looks. Maybe he could go and see one of those Harley Street specialists he had heard about. Money talked, and it might be possible to get something done about his eyes, even though the hospital had said it was a condition he would have to live with. Wouldn't that be wonderful, he sighed as he saw the sign of the Eagle public house up ahead.

Simon's bad feelings about his ageing mother, and life in general, were running high, but had he been able to see into the dreary parlour that very moment he would have been totally shocked and enraged. Grace Dines was sitting at the table, talking quietly to herself as she pored over the ancient photograph album. ''E still loves 'is ole muvver, don't yer, boy? You was a good boy, Norman. Such a sweet child, an' look at yer now. Yer look so tall an' fine in that uniform. Yer'll be 'ome soon, an' then yer'll come ter see yer ole mum, won't yer? Don't you worry though. I know 'ow busy yer must be. I know yer'll call round when yer can.'

The young man in the photograph was smiling out, standing proud in his white tropical uniform and naval cap, and the old lady touched the print with her bony fingers. 'I've gotta put yer away now,' she said, 'before that lazy good-fer-nuffink bruvver o' yours comes back.'

Chapter Sixteen

Kay had found her sister Elsie to be a good listener, and had jumped at the chance to call round on Monday evening.

'Mum told me Ernie's on a two-day trip, so I thought I'd take yer up on the offer of a chat,' she said as she walked into the front room.

Elsie smiled. 'Let's take yer coat. Fancy a cuppa? Come up an' see Billy first though. I just put 'im ter bed, 'e's dead tired.'

Kay was surprised to see Elsie looking so cheerful and bubbly. It was like she used to be, before her marriage started to go wrong.

'Can Aunt Kay read me a story?' Billy yawned.

'No, Aunt Kay's tired. You go ter sleep like a good little man,' Elsie told him softly.

Kay sat down on the edge of the bed and bent over the child. 'Gimme a big kiss an' I'll read yer a story,' she told him.

Elsie went down into the scullery to put the kettle on, and before it had boiled Kay came down the stairs. ''E's fast asleep,' she said. ''E looks like a little angel layin' there.'

'Yer wouldn't 'ave thought so if yer'd seen 'im terday. 'E's played me up rotten,' Elsie sighed. 'I felt like stranglin' the little sod.'

Kay sat down at the table and watched with an amused smile as her sister fussed around the scullery. 'Yer don't 'ave ter go tidyin' up on the quick just 'cos I've called,' she told her. 'Just make that tea an' let's 'ave a nice chat.'

The wind was rising as the two young women sat sipping their tea in the cosy parlour.

'I called round ter Mum this mornin' after Ernie came 'ome an' told me about the run,' Elsie was saying. ''E was moanin' an' groanin'. 'E reckons they're puttin' on 'im over this robbery business. They've sent 'im ter Cardiff wiv a load o' machinery.'

124

'I'm glad yer suggested I call round,' Kay said. 'I really wanted to 'ave a chat.'

''Ow's fings then?' Elsie asked.

Kay sighed. 'I dunno. I feel all mixed up.'

'I thought yer looked a bit peaky on Sunday when I called round, an' Mum noticed it too,' Elsie told her, 'but I never 'ad a chance ter talk ter yer on yer own.'

'Yeah, she asked if I was all right, but I can't talk ter Mum about it,' Kay replied.

'David, is it?'

'Yeah.'

'Did yer see 'im on Saturday night?'

'Yeah, an' I went back to 'is place,' Kay told her.

'Did anyfing 'appen?'

Kay looked down at her folded hands for a few moments, feeling a little embarrassed. 'Yeah, we finally did it,' she said quietly, 'but it wasn't good. In fact it was bloody terrible.'

'Was 'e rough?' Elsie asked.

'No, I can't say 'e was rough, but 'e wasn't considerate, if yer know what I mean,' Kay replied, looking up with troubled eyes.

'I know what yer mean,' Elsie said quietly. 'Yer lost your virginity an' it was a big disappointment.'

'It was over too quick, almost before it started,' Kay explained.

'I know the feelin',' Elsie said, smiling.

'Was it like that wiv you an' Ernie then?' Kay asked her.

Elsie's smile widened. 'Not wiv Ernie. I lost my virginity on that bombsite in Dover Lane, wiv Bernie Blackmore. Like yer said, it was over before it started.'

Kay looked shocked. 'I would never a guessed you wasn't a virgin when you went ter the altar.'

'There's a lot more ter people than meets the eye, so our muvver ses. She's right too,' Elsie said still smiling.

'I can understand it bein' like that wiv young lads who ain't very experienced, but David's a married man,' Kay told her.

'Well, yeah, but like I said last time we was talkin', it could be a deep-seated problem,' Elsie suggested.

''Ow can we sort it out?' Kay asked her.

'You can't, 'cos it ain't your problem. It's David's, an' 'e's gotta sort it out 'imself,' Elsie said quickly.

Kay stretched out her legs and looked up to the ceiling, feeling that Elsie was right. She could help David by being patient and giving him her support, but at the end of the day there was little more she could do.

Elsie was watching her closely, and after a few seconds she broke the silence. ''Ave yer seen anyfing more o' Pat Kelly?' she inquired.

Kay shook her head. 'Why d'yer ask?'

'I just wondered. I saw 'im on Saturday afternoon. Not ter speak to, but 'e nodded over,' Elsie told her.

'I dunno,' Kay sighed. 'It's strange 'ow fings work out.'

'What d'yer mean?'

'Well, I spent me growin' years lustin' after Pat, an' then when 'e becomes available I'm involved wiv somebody else,' she explained.

'You should consider yerself lucky, Kay,' her sister said sharply. 'Like I told yer already. That fella spells trouble.'

'I wish that sort o' trouble would knock on my door,' Kay said grinning.

Elsie shook her head despairingly. 'Kay, you worry me.'

Her younger sister smiled reassuringly. 'I'll survive. 'Ere, ter change the subject, I gotta tell yer about one o' the gels at work . . .'

True to his word, Jim Carney went along to the Citadel in New Kent Road on Monday evening to meet Major Harrison. The Salvationist had been very busy organising his team when Jim had first approached him, and in an effort to get rid of the man Harrison had suggested that maybe he should call in at the Citadel on Monday to talk further, guessing wrongly that Jim Carney would not bother to attend. The major had underestimated the railwayman's tenacity, and when he saw the gangling figure striding across the large hall, he winced.

''Ello, guv, 'ow's fings?' Jim greeted him. 'Carney's the name, d'yer remember me?'

'Yes, I remember you. Sorry, I can't stop to talk, I'm just off to take charge of a meeting,' the major informed him, hoping it would have the desired effect.

'Right then. I won't keep yer long, if I can 'ave five minutes o' your time,' Jim said, grinning amiably.

The major sighed in resignation. 'I think I can spare five minutes. Come this way.'

Jim sat himself down in the comfortable chair in the small carpeted room and crossed his legs. 'I'm on late shift. Come straight from work as a matter o' fact. I didn't 'ave chance fer a cup o' tea or nuffink. I don't s'pose there's one goin', is there?' he asked.

'No, I'm afraid not,' Harrison replied quickly. 'Now what was it you wanted to see me about?' he asked curtly.

Jim folded his hands and leaned forward in his chair. 'Well, it's like this, guv,' he began. 'I've always felt that one good turn deserves anuvver, so ter speak. It's sort o' like, you scratch my back an' I'll scratch yours. Can you understand what I'm gettin' at?'

The major looked hard at his visitor. 'Frankly, no.'

'Well let me put it anuvver way. I do you a good turn an' you do me one back. Zomper zompers.'

'Zomper zompers?'

'Just a figure o' speech,' Jim informed him.

There was a tap on the door and a bespectacled woman in uniform popped her head in. 'Would you like a cup of tea, Major?' she said sweetly.

'Make that two cups, gel, an' I'll 'ave four spoonfuls o' sugar in mine, if yer don't mind,' Jim cut in before the major had time to answer. 'By the way you ain't got any chocolate biscuits, 'ave yer? Go down a treat wiv a cuppa do chocolate biscuits.'

'No, I'm afraid we haven't any biscuits,' Soldier Brown replied.

'Just two teas,' the major told her, breathing deeply.

Jim Carney uncrossed his legs and started to scratch his chin. 'Like I was sayin, guv. I could do you a favour an' then you could see me all right,' he went on. 'Now I'll be willin' ter flog some o' your papers round the 'ouses, an' you can return the favour, crash bang wallop.'

The major stared intently at his visitor, wondering if he should call the police before the man got violent. These sort usually did. First it was the gibberish and then they tended to flare up. He had seen it before. Maybe it would be better to humour the idiot and then ease him out into the street.

'Now look, Mr, er . . .'

'Carney. Jim Carney.'

'Look, Mr Carney. I don't understand what you require from me,' the worried Salvationist said, shaking his head slowly.

'Only a reference, ole sport,' Jim replied grinning.

'But I don't know you from Adam.'

'Adam who?'

Harrison was getting more and more agitated and he took a deep breath in an effort to control himself. 'I just can't go giving references to complete strangers,' he almost whined.

'But I won't be a stranger, will I?' Jim said quickly. 'After I've knocked out a few 'undred o' those comics o' yours we'll be like good ole pals.'

'Our newspaper is called the *War Cry*, and it is not a comic,' the major said with passion. 'Now I suggest you go and see someone who knows you very well and ask them for a reference.'

'So yer don't wanna 'elp me out? Well, OK. I know where I'm not wanted,' Jim said, looking hurt as he got up to go.

Major Harrison had spent a good part of his life as a Salvationist and he had met many strange characters during that time, but he had to admit that the man in front of him was a one-off. 'Tell me, Mr Carney. What exactly do you want a reference for?' he asked.

'I wanna be a Jolly Boy.'

'A Jolly Boy?'

'Yeah, yer see it's a group o' blokes who do charity work an' they'll let me join if I get references,' Jim explained. 'Me guv'nor at work gave me one, an' I need a few more.'

The major nodded and stroked his chin for a few seconds. The Lord moves in mysterious ways, he thought. Maybe it wasn't such a bad idea after all. The man might prove to be a good worker. Five hundred *War Crys* in five hundred homes would certainly spread the word. 'Right then, Mr Carney. I'll tell you what. You deliver a batch of newspapers and collect subscriptions in a tin I'll provide you with, then we'll see about that reference. How's that sound?'

'Bloody 'andsome, guv, beggin' yer pardon,' Jim said, grinning from ear to ear.

Joe Brennen was on night shift that Monday evening, and he was determined to make the most of his free time. He was due on at ten o'clock and it was only just turned eight. Time for a doze and then a wash and brush up, he thought.

There was a knock on the front door then he heard Ada's voice. 'Yes, of course. Come in, Mr Preston.'

Joe sat bolt upright in his chair as Ada showed the depot manager into the room. It was the first time Preston had ever called round and Joe's surprise was apparent.

'Sorry, Joe. We've got trouble at the yard,' the manager said breathlessly. 'Can you come in right away?'

'Sure fing. I'll just get me coat,' Joe told him quickly.

'What about yer sandwiches an' flask?' Ada asked.

'I'll get somefing in the canteen,' Joe called back as he followed the manager out to the waiting car.

The red glow rising up behind Hastings Street was beginning to light the winter sky, and as the manager drove into the yard he gasped, 'It's gettin' out o' control by the look of it.'

Joe had already been primed on the emergency by Preston as they drove the short distance to the yard, and his face was ashen as he climbed out of the car and joined his workmates who were standing in a group beside the track. Beyond a criss-cross of railway tracks, firemen were battling to control a blazing waggon, the second one from the front in a line of ten which had been coupled up ready to be moved.

Tom Kelly, Charlie Catchpole and Joe's fireman Bill Cosgrove were there, and the whole group gathered round Gerry Preston, all talking at once.

The manager held his hands up for silence and his red face seemed to glow in the light of the flaming waggon. 'Now listen, all of you,' he began in a loud voice. 'That burning waggon and the one in front and behind it all contain drums of cellulose and oil paint. The fire chief's told me that one of the drums of cellulose must have leaked and spilled out on to the track, and the puddle was ignited by a red-hot cinder from the tender. Now we've managed to shunt the waggons right back to the buffers, and as you can see the firemen are damping down the other two waggons to try to contain the blaze.'

'Why can't we uncouple 'em?' Bill Cosgrove cut in quickly. 'The fire's not reached the third one yet. We could uncouple the first three an' pull 'em down the line a way. It'd at least save the rest if we isolated the paint waggons.'

Everyone looked at the manager. Bill's suggestion made sense and it seemed to them all, with the exception of Joe Brennen, that it was the obvious thing to do. Preston glanced quickly at Joe and then looked around his men. 'If we did that we'd have to shunt the blazing waggon past that freight shed and I'm worried about the cargo in there,' he told them. 'One or the other of those adjacent waggons could blow at any minute.'

'But if we don't do somefink the fire could spread along the 'ole line o' waggons,' Tom Kelly said, looking puzzled.

129

'I'm not worried about those waggons. I'm more concerned about the cargo in that shed,' Preston replied. 'It was brought in during the night by military transport ready for loading and transit to Southampton Docks.'

'What is in that shed?' Tom Kelly asked him quickly.

The depot manager looked from one to another and then he drew in a deep breath. 'Ammunition and explosives.'

Chapter Seventeen

A red glow in the night sky above the freight yards brought people out on to the street, and Ada Brennen stood with her daughters at her front door looking very worried.

'I do 'ope yer farvver's all right,' she sighed anxiously. 'It looks like it must be a big fire. Mr Preston looked worried out of 'is life when 'e called round.'

'I expect they'll 'ave ter move the waggons away from the fire wherever it is,' Barbara said, pinching her chin.

'It's prob'ly one o' those big sheds caught light. I do 'ope nobody's bin 'urt,' Ada replied.

Emily Toogood came hurrying up to the Brennens. ''Ere, what d'yer fink? They're movin' the families out o' the 'ouses in Curry Street,' she said breathlessly. 'My sister just come round ter tell me.'

Ada looked even more worried. 'There's a big shed opposite Curry Street. I bet that's the one what caught light,' she told her.

'P'raps they fink it's gonna blow up,' Emily replied. 'There must be somefing very dangerous stored in there. It might even be an atom bomb.'

'I don't fink it's anyfing like that,' Ada said with a smile. 'It could be somefing 'ighly inflammable, though, an' they're frightened it might damage the 'ouses.'

Emily shook her head slowly as she stared up at the glowing night sky. 'It gives me the shivers,' she told her neighbours. 'It's just like the blitz.'

Dot Adams came along, accompanied by Annie Thomas and Bet Greenedge. 'I've just bin talkin' ter Mrs Farrow who lives in Curry Street,' Dot said quickly. 'They've all gotta go ter Monner Road School till the fire's out, all those what live in Curry Street. Tell 'em what you just 'eard, Annie.'

131

The slightly-built Annie Thomas slipped her hands into the sleeves of her coat and looked up and down the street quickly. 'I 'eard that there's a lot of ammunition bin delivered ter the yard durin' the night. Mrs Colman told me. The army brought it in an' 'er ole man got called in on overtime last night to 'elp unload it. The shed's stacked full of it, accordin' to 'im. 'E said there was lorry after lorry drivin' in that yard on Sunday night. Makes yer fink, don't it?'

'Could be anuvver war,' Emily Toogood said fearfully.

'Well, I fink it's all wrong, puttin' dangerous stuff like that near where people live,' Bet Greenedge cut in.

Charlie Catchpole's buxom wife came up to join them. 'They've shut Curry Street right off,' she announced. 'There's ropes across the street. I saw a couple of ambulances drive in the yard. I do 'ope my Charlie's all right.'

Mary Kelly came out of her house and crossed the street. 'Did your Joe get called in early, Ada?' she asked as she reached the group. 'Gerry Preston come round fer our Tom but 'e wasn't in. 'E'd gone round ter see ole Bill Cosgrove about somefink ter do wiv the Jolly boys. I told Preston that Tom was goin' straight on ter work from there. It must be really serious fer Preston ter come round the way 'e did.'

Ada nodded. 'When 'e called round fer Joe 'e looked really worried,' she replied. ''E wouldn't tell me anyfing though. Tell 'er what you 'eard, Annie.'

As folk stood at their front doors, staring up fearfully at the flickering glow in the sky, a loud bang reverberated through the street.

Joe Brennen climbed up into his tender alongside Bill Cosgrove and gave him an anxious look. ''Ow's the pressure, Bill?' he asked him quickly.

The wiry fireman's muscles stood out on his bare arms as he threw another shovel of coal into the firepan. 'It's up nicely, Joe,' he grunted.

'I fink we're gonna need every ounce,' Joe told him as he leaned out of the tender to look along the track.

Up ahead he could see that the fire crews had managed to contain the blazing freight waggon, but their efforts to prevent the fire from spreading to the other two waggons were a little too late. Heat had been building up inside them and smoke was billowing out as the fire took hold. Cosgrove wiped his sweating brow on a piece of cotton waste and laid down his large shovel. 'Those ovver two are gonna go any minute,' he shouted at Joe.

Gerry Preston came hurrying along the track. 'Don't move the tender any nearer, Joe,' he shouted. 'If that last waggon blows it could ignite the shed.'

Joe nodded. He was well aware that there was no more than ten feet between the last waggon and the end of the freight shed. Suddenly the waggon beyond the blazing truck exploded in a ball of flame and firemen were knocked over by the blast. Flaming wood and oil spread along the track and set the fire hoses alight, but fortunately the shed was untouched. The heat was growing, however, and Preston climbed up into the tender alongside Joe. 'I wish I could move the ammo out of that shed, but it's too risky and it'd take too long,' he shouted. 'One spark could well set the whole lot off.'

'We can't just stand 'ere doin' nuffink,' Joe shouted back at him. 'When that end waggon blows it'll set the shed alight. Then it'll be too late.'

'Don't you think I know that?' Preston retorted angrily. 'Have you got any better ideas?'

Joe looked at him for a few moments, at the helplessness and frustration on his florid face. 'There is one fing that might work – but it's a long-shot,' he said, jumping down from the tender.

Preston followed him down but Joe was already hurrying along towards the blaze. 'What yer got in mind?' he bawled out.

'I wanna take a quick look at those buffers,' Joe told him.

Preston suddenly realised what Joe was thinking of; he caught up with the engine driver and grabbed him roughly by the arm. 'It won't work,' he shouted.

Joe did not answer as they skirted the flames and hurried along to the end of the line of waggons. The last one was rammed tightly against the buffers and, after a brief look, Joe walked round to survey the wasteground and the large shed beyond. 'What's in that shed?' he asked quickly.

'It's full of tinned stuff from Crosse and Blackwell's,' the manager replied.

Joe looked back down the track to where his tender was puffing jets of steam as the pressure increased. He could see the firemen hosing down the ammunition shed. 'Look, Gerry, I ain't got time to argue wiv yer. Just give me two empty waggons ter couple up on the front o' my tender, an' get all the spare 'ands ter start loosenin' the soil around these buffers.'

'It won't work, Joe,' Preston said, shaking his head vigorously. 'Just look at these buffers. They're set in a concrete block.'

'All right then, we'll just stand around an' watch the shed go up, shall we?' Joe shouted at him. 'Just set the men ter work.'

The manager looked at his engine driver for a second or two, then he nodded. 'There's empty waggons down by the water tower,' he said quickly.

'Warn the firemen, an' when I give yer two blasts on that whistle, get the men clear,' Joe shouted back as he started off down the track.

Gerry Preston ran across the tracks to where a group of shunters and loaders were standing together. 'Get anything you can and start digging around those buffers,' he told them. 'Quick as you can, or we could all end up being blown sky-high.'

Joe climbed up into the tender, threw over the brake lever and pulled down on the reverse bar. The ancient engine shuddered as its wheels spun on the silver track, and then it started off backwards.

'I'm goin' back ter the branch line, Bill, an' I want yer ter switch the points. I'm gonna couple up two waggons an' take 'em on ter this line,' he shouted above the noise of the thrusting pistons and spurting steam.

Bill knew what his driver was going to attempt and he nodded, his eyes wide with excitement. Suddenly another fireball lit the yard.

'The end waggon's gone up!' he shouted.

Joe merely nodded, his teeth clenched tight as he hung his head out of the tender and pulled on the brake handle. Bill Cosgrove jumped down and ran to the switch lever by the side of the track. 'Right, Joe. Way yer go,' he called out as he bent over and heaved on the heavy lever.

Joe drove the tender forward on to the branch line, then he jumped down himself and helped his fireman to release the two waggons from the spare stock and couple them up to his engine. Joe reversed back on to the straight section of track while Bill switched the points, and as the tender started off towards the blazing waggons, Bill ran forward in an attempt to jump aboard. Joe had his foot raised in the gangway to stop him, and he waved to his fireman as he left him behind. 'Keep yer fingers crossed, Bill,' he shouted out.

Cosgrove stopped running and shook his head slowly as he gathered his breath. He heard the two long blasts on the whistle and he crossed himself. 'Bloody 'ell, Joe. I should be up there wiv you,' he said aloud to himself.

The tender was less than a hundred yards from the blazing end waggon and increasing speed rapidly. Joe gritted his teeth as he took a firm grip on the support rail beside him. He prayed that the other two blazing waggons would be damaged enough to fold up and cushion the impact. If all went well, his tender and the two waggons coupled up in front would have enough power to follow through and push the rest of the waggons through the buffers.

Preston and his makeshift crew of diggers had used bits of wood, iron bars and even their bare hands to scoop away the hard earth and large pebbles from around the concrete block, and they now stood clear as the makeshift battering-ram raced towards the line of waggons.

'If those buffers still 'old, Joe's gonna be burnt alive,' Charlie Catchpole muttered.

'If that boiler goes, 'e'll be boiled alive more like it,' Tom Kelly retorted.

The first impact crushed the blazing waggons like cardboard, and the tender carried on, pushing its own two waggons into the rest. The buffers went down under the rolling stock, torn out from the ground by the force of the main impact. The three leading waggons turned over on to their sides as their wheels left the end of the track and ploughed over the uprooted concrete, coming to rest in a cloud of dust and stones a few feet short of the food shed. The tender jolted to a sudden stop and steam gushed from the damaged boiler as pieces of flying wreckage fractured the external pipes.

''E did it!' Charlie Catchpole shouted out, jumping up and down like an excited schoolboy.

Gerry Preston looked at the tangled wreckage that was still burning and saw that the gap between the fire and the shed had now more than trebled. Disaster had been averted, and he joined the dash as men ran towards the ruined shunting engine.

Tom Kelly was first aboard, followed by the yard manager. They quickly kicked away pieces of glowing coals which had been jolted out of the firepan. They knelt down over the prone figure of Joe Brennen, and Gerry Preston put his ear to the driver's chest. 'He's alive!' he shouted. 'Ease him out gently. Mind his back now, it could be broken. That's right. Keep his legs straight.'

Joe suddenly groaned and opened his eyes. 'I'm all right. Put me down, yer dopy gits,' he growled as he was lowered down on to the track.

'Stay where you are, we'll get an ambulance,' Preston told him.

'No bloody fear. I'm all right, I tell yer,' he insisted. 'I just cracked me 'ead on that bar, that's all.'

'Don't argue,' the manager ordered.

Joe struggled to his feet despite the attempts to restrain him. 'Look, I'm all right, straight. I just wanna nice cuppa an' a sit-down fer a while, that's all,' he told them.

Cold stars looked down from a velvet sky as the last of the fire tenders drove out of the freight yard, their crews blackened and weary after their long efforts to contain the fire. The large corrugated shed containing the boxes of ammunition and explosives had been cooled down with jets of water, and a huge crane had been brought up to clear the track. Teams of loaders stood ready to get the military supplies into waggons once the damaged track had been replaced, and they stood together chatting about the near catastrophe.

In a comfortable office overlooking the yard, Joe Brennen and Gerry Preston stood together holding mugs of steaming tea as they looked down on the activity below.

'I'll have to make a statement to the reporters as soon as the police let them through, but they can wait a little longer,' the manager said to Joe with a grin on his pale face.

Joe looked drawn and weary as he sipped his tea. 'They'll 'ave a field day over this,' he said, eyeing his boss quizzically.

Gerry Preston went over to his desk and removed a green folder from the top drawer. 'This is what they call classified,' he said, throwing it down on the leather desktop. 'I think you've earned the right to see it, but I don't want anything mentioned outside this office. OK?'

Joe nodded and walked over to the desk, and for a few moments he stared down at the folder.

'Open it,' Preston urged him.

Joe picked it up and turned the cover. The first sheet was headed 'War Office' and subtitled 'Troop Movement'. Below were dates and times for transit and embarkation of personnel of the Sixth Armoured Division and their supplies from Southampton aboard the troopship *Empire Fowey*.

Joe looked up at the manager. 'This all looks a bit serious,' he remarked.

Preston nodded slowly. 'That folder was brought to me personally by an under-secretary from the War Office, and I was given a short lesson in Cold War ethics,' he said with a brief smile.

Joe stared at his boss blankly, his fingers reaching into his waistcoat pocket and touching his silver watch. 'Cold War ethics?' he echoed.

'Apparently there's a series of secret talks going on between Nato and the Warsaw Pact countries over reducing tension,' Preston explained. 'Now right in the middle of all this sensitive business the Sixth Armoured are required in the Middle East to police a trouble-spot. I know it all sounds very dramatic, but any large troop movement on either side at this particular time could put the talks into jeopardy. That was how it was explained to me by the courier.'

'So it was all done on the quiet?' Joe cut in.

Preston laughed cynically. 'Army convoys driving through heavily populated areas in the dead of night, with highly dangerous cargoes crated up and marked NAAFI stores. Eggs, handle with care, and so on. That's the strength of it, Joe.'

'An' stored in a shed a few yards away from a residential street,' Joe reminded him.

'I had no choice,' the manager answered. 'Before the load arrived I got a visit from the top brass. That shed was their decision. I had no say in it. I did point out the close proximity of the houses behind the shed, but they said it was all a matter of relativity.'

'Of what?' Joe said quickly.

'In other words, what did risking the lives of a few families mean, compared to preserving the peace?'

The weary engine driver sat down heavily in a chair and sighed. 'So now the fuss is over, all those eggs are gonna be on their way ter Southampton before mornin',' he said drily.

'They'd better be,' Preston replied. 'I've not slept a wink since I was presented with this bloody conundrum last week. Anyway, I'll be supervising the loading.'

Joe stood up and pointed to the folder. 'What yer gonna do wiv that, keep it as a souvenir?' he asked, smiling.

Gerry Preston shook his head. 'As soon as the cargo leaves this yard, I'm to put a match to it. The folder, not the cargo,' he laughed.

Joe consulted his faithful timepiece. 'Well I'd better make the most o' your offer of the rest o' the night off,' he said, making towards the door.

The manager held out his hand. 'That was a brave thing you did tonight and I'll make sure the right people get to hear of it,' he said, shaking Joe's hand firmly.

Joe shrugged off the compliment. As he reached the office door he paused. 'Oh, by the way, before I go, I 'ope you weren't troubled too much by our Jimbo comin' in fer a reference,' he said with a big smile.

Preston shook his head. 'I must admit I was put out a bit,' he replied, 'but tonight when those lads were digging away at the buffers, Jim Carney was right in the thick of it. Most of them were using bits of wood and iron bars but Carney had a pickaxe. God knows where he got it from, but he made all the difference. G'night, Joe.'

Chapter Eighteen

Sergeant William Moody was in a nasty frame of mind as he left Dockhead police station on Tuesday morning to call on Joe Mezzo. It was always the same with the likes of Cranley, he growled to himself. Nothing ever got achieved in the long run when it all had to be done by the book. Here was a golden chance to put the screws on the Malts, and Cranley had to go and block it. He was a chief superintendent, for Christ's sake. He could justify issuing a search warrant. After all, there was a black market flourishing in the area, but what did he do? Come out with the pathetic excuse that there was nothing on Mezzo. That wasn't the point. A liaison with the police north of the river had come up trumps. Hoxton police had said that Nick Zanti owned a scrapyard on their manor, which was one of the areas inside the circle Cranley had drawn on the station wall-map. Zanti's known associates in Bermondsey included Joe Mezzo the shopkeeper, and although Mezzo did not have a police record, he could be made to sweat a little if he thought that he was being tied in with the lorry theft. A bit of pressure brought to bear by searching his shop for black-market goods and a quiet word in his ear about the robbery might prove enough to set the ball rolling. As it was he was going along to interview the Malt with one hand tied behind his back.

Moody turned into Hastings Street and allowed himself a brief smile. This was the turning where he had made his first arrest as a young police constable and he remembered it very well. It had been a Saturday night and the man had been drunk and disorderly, but he'd soon quietened down after a few jabs in the kidneys and a sharp slap across his face. Things had been different in those days, Moody thought. A policeman had people's respect. There was common support for the good old physical approach then, but the war seemed to have changed everything. Nowadays there was an outcry if you so much as laid a finger on anyone, and it was all paperwork and red tape. A policeman's lot was not an easy one these days, though there were still a few loopholes if an officer was smart, thank goodness.

Moody turned into Waggoner's Way and the memories came flooding back. This was another of his beat streets. He recalled having stopped a man in this turning who had something concealed under his coat. It had turned out to be a full smoked gammon. What was the man's name now? Adams. That was it, Jack Adams. Unlike most of the people in this street, Adams had worked in the docks. He had tried to bluff it out at first, but he'd finally admitted to stealing the bacon from his place of work. Old Dyer the magistrate had soon sorted him out. Five pounds or six months was a lenient sentence as far as Harold Dyer went. He detested dockers and usually did not give them an option when they were brought before him. It was prison every time. They're all getting soft these days, even the magistrates, Moody growled to himself.

Joe Mezzo was standing behind his counter when the detective walked into the shop. He showed no surprise when Moody introduced himself.

'Come on out the back, we won't be disturbed there,' he said amiably as he leaned his head through the side door. 'Maria. Come down an' take over, will yer?'

The sergeant followed Joe out into a large room which was stacked high with cartons of tinned goods, tea chests and boxes of eggs. Sides of smoked bacon hung from the hooks in the ceiling and there were numerous bits and pieces of all descriptions piled up. There seemed to be nowhere to sit, but the shopkeeper made room on a stack of tinned peaches. 'I'm sorry I can't offer you a chair. You can see 'ow it is,' he said, smiling.

Moody grunted a reply while his trained eye took in everything in the storeroom. 'There's a lot o' stock 'ere fer a small shop,' he commented craftily.

Mezzo shrugged his shoulders. 'I got a lot o' people registered wiv me,' he replied, sitting himself down on an upturned lemonade crate. 'The nearest market's a tidy walk away.'

Moody nodded. 'I know this area well enough. I did my time on these streets,' he said, a cold look in his dark eyes.

''Ow can I 'elp yer?' Mezzo asked.

'I gotta see all the grocery shopkeepers in this area,' the sergeant began. 'There's bin a spate o' black-market tradin' goin' on round 'ere an' we've nabbed a lorry driver. 'E's give us names an' we're followin' up wiv our inquiries.'

Not a muscle twitched in Joe's face as he eyed the detective. 'It's about time you lads got ter grips wiv those spivs,' he said in a self-righteous manner. 'They make it bad fer the likes of us honest traders.'

'Oh, an' why's that?' Moody asked quickly.

'Well, you take me. I got over two 'undred families on my books an' they all registered wiv me 'cos I give 'em a fair deal,' Mezzo told him. 'They know I don't trade under the counter, but they also know that my prices compare favourably wiv anywhere else. I don't offer 'em an extra ration o' bacon or butter an' charge 'em the bloody earth.'

The detective looked hard at the bulky figure sitting facing him. Mezzo was a cool customer, he thought. It was typical of these Malts. They played the innocent to perfection. 'Tell me, do you 'ave bills an' receipts fer all this stock?' he asked.

Joe smiled and reached behind him without getting up. 'They're all 'ere,' he replied, passing over a large case file. 'I warn yer, though, it'll take yer all night ter go frew that lot. It's your choice.'

Moody waved the file away. 'I didn't come round 'ere ter check up on yer stock,' he said, his voice becoming less matter-of-fact. 'What I really came round for was ter see if you could give me some assistance.'

'Sure, if I can,' Joe replied in a friendly voice.

The sergeant changed his position on the stack of cartons. 'I s'pose you 'eard o' the lorry snatch over in Poplar last week.'

Joe Mezzo shook his head slowly. 'I don't get ter know 'alf of what goes on round 'ere, let alone Poplar. Should I 'ave done?' he replied.

'It was in the papers.'

'I don't get much time fer newspapers.'

Moody smiled briefly. 'The driver comes from round 'ere,' he told him.

'Is that a fact?'

''E only lives round the corner in Dover Lane.'

'I don't get many customers from Dover Lane,' Joe informed him.

Moody stood up. 'I was gonna ask yer fer an opinion on the driver. Y'know, what's 'e like, does 'e drink much, is 'e a customer o' yours.'

Joe smiled patiently. 'Well, at least I answered one question. 'E's not one o' my customers.'

Moody was buttoning up his coat. 'I'll no doubt see yer around,' he said, his eyes narrowing ever so slightly.

Joe led the way out into the shop where Maria was weighing up a pat of butter for Dot Adams.

'See yer around,' Joe said, lifting up the counter flap.

As soon as Sergeant Moody was outside, Maria rounded on her husband. 'What you go an' do now?' she asked anxiously.

'What d'yer mean, what I do?' Joe said innocently.

'That man is a detective,' Maria shouted at him.

''Ow did you know 'e was a tec?' Joe asked her.

'Mrs Adams told me.'

'You know 'im?' Joe asked.

Dot nodded, screwing her mouth up. ''E ain't changed a bit in looks since 'e was a bobby on this beat,' she replied. ''E's still as ugly as ever. Nicked my ole man once 'e did. Nasty bit o' work, so yer better watch yer step wiv that one.'

Joe smiled at her. ''E come round ter check if I'd bin black marketeerin'. As if I would.'

'Course yer wouldn't,' Dot chuckled.

Joe Brennen had enjoyed a long lie-in that morning and he had the day planned. First he would pop into Jack Springer's for his morning paper and maybe pick a few winners. Then he would go over to see Tom Kelly about the extraordinary meeting of the Jolly Boys that coming Saturday evening, and then he would take a quiet nap before his late shift. First, though, he would have a comfortable shave and spruce up before Ada got back from the market.

As he poured boiling water into his shaving mug, Joe heard the front door open.

'Joe. I want yer ter go straight up ter the bedroom an' move that bed over, an' while yer at it take up that square o' lino,' Ada ordered as she stepped into the scullery.

'What's goin' on?' he asked her.

'I've just seen Dot Adams. Danny's comin' over in five minutes ter do that floorboard,' she replied, slipping off her coat.

Joe pulled a face. 'I thought 'e'd forgot us.'

'No, 'e didn't. Dot said 'e's bin busy.'

'All right. I'll 'ave a quick shave first,' Joe said obstinately.

'Get up them stairs an' do like I said,' Ada told him firmly. 'Yer got plenty o' time ter shave afterwards.'

Danny Adams pulled out his canvas tool-bag from under the stairs and checked the contents. The large-tooth rip-saw was sharp enough, he decided. The chisels too had a fine edge on them, though the plane didn't look very good. It had a pitted sole and the blade was blunt. He sorted through and found a claw hammer, screwdriver, a box of nails and a brace and bit. There were enough tools there for what he had to do.

Danny reached into the dark recess once again and found his carborundum stone and a tin of oil. He sat down in the scullery and began to strip down the plane. The young man was feeling good this morning. The headache had left him and he felt confident about tackling the job of work at the Brennens'. Maybe it would lead to some other work, he thought hopefully. He would have to do a good job though. A good craftsman could always find work and word would spread.

Danny worked away at the plane iron for some time, holding it firmly in his hands and moving it back and forth over the lubricated stone. Occasionally he checked the edge and continued until he was satisfied, then he wiped the oil from the stone and replaced it under the stairs. The clock seemed to be racing this morning, he thought, as he quickly threw the plane into the bag, picked up the length of timber that was standing upright in the passage and left the house.

Jack Springer had run his newspaper and tobacconist business on the corner of Waggoner's Way for more than twenty years. He was a tall, lean man in his fifties with thinning grey hair and steely blue eyes. Jack was married to Alma, a short, slight woman in her fiftieth year. The Springers had no children and were devoted to each other. They had a good relationship with their regular customers, and with the small team of youngsters who delivered their morning papers. Jack Springer had been a section leader in the Heavy Rescue Squad during the war and had been decorated for bravery. His other claim to fame was his membership of the Jolly Boys, the only member of that élite band who was not a railwayman.

An extraordinary meeting had been called for that Sunday, and he was already hard at work formulating a few proposals of his own when Joe Brennen walked into his shop.

''Ow do, Joe? You are all right fer Sunday I take it?' he asked.

Joe nodded. 'Yeah, I booked the room at the club an' the word's gone out,' he replied. 'I still gotta contact Maurice, though. We should 'ave a full membership there on Sunday.'

'That's good,' Jack said as he slipped his pencil behind his ear and closed the large paper delivery book.

'I believe we'll be discussin' the charity do,' Joe said as he picked up the *Daily Mirror* and handed over the coppers.

'Yeah, I reckon so,' Jack replied. 'Anyway, what was all this I 'eard about you playin' the silly bugger last night?'

Joe shrugged his shoulders. 'It wasn't nuffink. I was just on 'and at the time. The ovver drivers would 'ave done the same.'

'Yer could 'ave killed yerself from what I 'eard,' Jack went on. 'If that boiler 'ad gone up we'd 'ave bin goin' round wiv the 'at fer your missus an' kids.'

'Kids?' Joe replied grinning. ''Ave you seen 'em all lately?'

Jack smiled. 'I 'ear your lad's got 'is call-up papers.'

'Yeah, 'e's goin' in the Royal Signals,' Joe told him.

'Are the gels all right?'

'Yeah, but I still can't marry 'em off though.'

Jack Springer leaned his elbows on the counter. 'By the way, Joe. That silly git Carney was in 'ere this mornin',' he said. ''E told me 'e 'ad a proposition ter put ter me. 'E wouldn't tell me what it was. 'E said 'e'd come an' see me again when it was all sorted out. Any idea what 'e's up to?'

'Knowin' 'im, no. But if I were you I'd play it carefully,' Joe warned him. 'Carney's ganger's bin primin' 'im up. 'E told 'im there was a chance of 'im joinin' the Jolly Boys if 'e got some references.'

'Well, 'e won't get one from me, that's a dead cert,' Jack said firmly.

'You make sure 'e ain't tryin' ter stitch you up,' Joe replied. ''E's as slippery as a barrel o' snakes.'

'I'll just wait an' see when 'e comes back,' Jack said, straightening up. 'If 'e tries anyfing on I'll send 'im away wiv a flea in 'is ear.'

Joe walked to the door. 'See yer later, Jack.'

Alma came into the front of the shop carrying a large mug of tea. ''Ere you are, luv, get that down yer,' she said cheerfully.

Jack sipped his tea thoughtfully. 'If Jim Carney comes in while I'm out, don't 'ave no truck wiv 'im. Tell 'im ter call back when I'm 'ere,' he warned her.

'Funny you should say that,' Alma replied. 'I just bumped into 'im as I was comin' back from the shops. 'E asked me if I ever read the *War Cry*. I said to 'im, "Why d'yer ask?", an' 'e just give me a crafty look.'

'Was that all 'e said?' Jack asked her.

'No, 'e said somefing about 'im branchin' out in sellin', but I didn't stop ter chat,' Alma told him. 'Once Jim Carney gets chattin' yer can't get away from 'im.'

Jack put down his empty mug. 'Well, just remember what I said if 'e comes in while I'm out.

'What d'yer reckon 'e's up to?' Alma asked.

'Jim Carney wants ter be a Jolly Boy,' Jack said, grinning at her.

Danny knelt down over the floorboards and offered up the piece of timber he had cut to size. It was a good fit, he thought. A few shavings off the edge of the plank and it would set in perfectly. The job had been a little more difficult than he had first envisaged. He had had to prise up a floorboard and cut it back to the joist, but at least the new piece would now sit firmly in the gap.

Danny whistled to himself as he fished into his tool-bag for the metal plane, and as he took it out his face dropped. He had forgotten to put the blade back. It was stupid of him. He had only just sharpened it, he remembered. Why had he not fitted the blade back in?

Danny hurried down the stairs. 'I gotta pop back 'ome fer a minute,' he called out.

'All right, Danny, I'll put the kettle on while yer gone,' Ada called back from the scullery.

The young man hurried across the street and into his house, expecting to find the plane blade on the scullery table, but it wasn't there. He looked under the stairs and found the oil-can but the blade was nowhere to be seen. Danny sat down heavily at the scullery table. He could feel his headache returning and he rested his head in his hand. He must have imagined honing the blade. But then why was it not still set in the plane? Perhaps he took it out intending to sharpen it and left it somewhere, he told himself. The headache was getting worse and he could not think straight. Maybe he should lie down for a while until his head cleared. That was the answer. It would all come back to him.

Joe Brennen left for work with a flea in his ear, and he had to admit to himself that he might possibly have gone over the top about Danny Adams.

'What did I tell yer?' he had grumbled to Ada. 'The lad's just not reliable.'

'P'raps 'e's 'ad ter go an' buy somefink. 'E'll be back,' Ada had said defensively.

'Yeah, an' pigs can fly,' Joe countered.

'Well, it ain't no big fing. We'll just 'ave ter be careful when we go ter bed, that's all,' Ada told him.

'I could 'ave done the bloody job meself in no time,' Joe went on.

'Don't make me laugh, Joe. I bin askin' yer ter get those jobs done till I'm blue in the face. You're all talk,' Ada berated him.

The chastened railwayman left the house just ten minutes before Dot Adams called in. She was worried and eager to speak to her neighbour. 'Didn't 'e finish the job?' she asked.

'It's almost done. 'E's cut the wood an' 'e's only gotta nail it down,' Ada said. ''E 'ad ter go back fer somefing.'

'Yeah, fer a nap. I found 'im up in 'is bedroom fast asleep,' Dot replied sighing.

'It's prob'ly one of 'is 'eadaches,' Ada suggested.

'I dunno,' Dot said despairingly. 'I went back in after 'e'd left ter come over 'ere an' I found 'is tools lyin' all over the place. There was an oil-can left on the table an' a bit of oily newspaper, as well as an 'ammer. I've 'ad ter clear up after 'im.'

Ada took her neighbour by the arm. 'Now look, luv. It's no good you gettin' yerself all screwed up about it,' she said kindly. 'Danny can come back termorrer or the next day ter finish the job. There's no big rush.'

'What about your Joe?' Dot replied. 'I bet 'e ain't none too 'appy about the job only bein' 'alf done.'

Ada waved away her fears. 'I tell yer straight, Dot, our Joe's as good as gold. 'E wasn't the slightest bit put out. 'E said ter me 'e didn't care 'ow long it took Danny ter do the job. 'E knows 'e'll finish it sooner or later.'

'Oh, I am pleased,' Dot told her. 'It was worryin' me. I 'ad ter come over.'

Ada felt a wave of pity flow over her and she motioned Dot Adams towards the armchair, reacting in the way she always did in a crisis, by announcing that she was going to put the kettle on.

Chapter Nineteen

Pat Kelly finished his tea and sat back in the chair with a satisfied smile. 'That was fit fer a king, Ma,' he said.

Mary Kelly picked up his empty plate. 'There's some plain an' syrup if yer got any room,' she told him.

'I fink I could manage it,' he replied, patting his midriff.

Mary hurried out into the scullery and took a suet pudding from the oven. It was lovely to have him home, she thought, although it was sad that the marriage had not worked out. He was a good lad, Pat, never any trouble. It was worrying, though, him going out to the pub every night. It wouldn't do him any good sitting brooding in pubs all the time.

Mary tipped the pudding upside down on a plate and cut a thick slice. Maybe she should get Tom to have a word with him. Pat always listened to his father, although he didn't always take heed. He looked very fit and well at the moment, but he would soon go down the drain if he kept up that drinking. There was nothing she could do about it, though. Nothing anyone could do. Pat would have to sort himself out. Perhaps he'll find himself a nice girl soon, she thought. He never had any trouble in the past. A nice girl would soon straighten him out.

'Why don't yer stop in ternight an' put yer feet up? Yer look a bit tired,' Mary said, hoping.

'Yeah, I might just do that,' Pat said, tucking into the plain and syrup.

Mary busied herself with the dishes. It had been a lonely house at times since the girls had married, especially when Tom was on late shifts. Pat being back home had certainly brightened everything up, and he didn't seem too upset about his marriage breakdown, she thought. The way things were he was probably glad to be out of it.

He hadn't looked happy for the past year. Eileen Carter was not the girl for him. Too moody and obsessive, from what Mary had seen of her. But like Tom had said, it was no good putting the blame entirely on Eileen. Pat himself had to take a share of it. He could be a cowson at times. He had always had a roving eye and Eileen would surely have noticed it. Sad how so many marriages seemed to break up these days, Mary reflected. It didn't happen in her day.

Pat popped his head into the scullery. 'I've changed me mind, Ma. I'm goin' out fer a pint,' he told her. 'I'm just goin' up an' change.'

Kay had felt better after her chat with Elsie, but she still agonised over David. It had been good at first, she remembered as she sat in front of her dressing table. There had been an element of intrigue in those first few dates. How soon things changed, though. David had become morose since the first attempt at making love, and she too had felt depressed and let down. It wasn't as if she could confidently bring her young man home in the way her two sisters did. They would be plying him with questions, all innocent enough, but they would soon suspect that David was a married man by the way he fended them off – and he would. It was his way.

Kay picked up a hairbrush and proceeded to untangle her long blonde hair, her mind full of uncertainties and questions. She knew that she had no one to blame but herself for the position she was in. She could walk out on it right away and there was nothing to stop her, except her own conscience. David needed her, needed to know that she would stand by him until he could pull himself together. It would be hard, though. He was living in a grotty flat, alone with his thoughts, and with his self-esteem at rock bottom. It must be terrible for him, she thought. He was a young, good-looking man with everything going for him, if he could only conquer his inadequacy.

Kay put down the brush and studied herself in the swivel mirror. What did the future hold for her, for the both of them?

'Kay, are you ready?' Barbara called up the stairs.

'Five minutes. I'm just puttin' on me make-up,' Kay called back, realising that she was only half ready.

'Be quick or we'll miss the start,' Dawn shouted.

Kay tried to hurry herself but she did not feel very enthusiastic.

149

The film was a weepy and she would have preferred to see the Technicolor musical at the Trocadera. Dawn and Barbara were adamant that they should go to the Trocette to see the re-issue of *Camille*, however. 'The gels at work said that Greta Garbo played a really good part, an' so did Robert Taylor. All the gels cried buckets,' Barbara had been quick to report.

When Kay came down, her sisters were waiting in the passage looking irritated.

'I dunno why you take so long gettin' ready, Kay. I started after you an' I've bin ready fer ages,' Dawn grumbled.

'Yer didn't 'ave ter wait,' Kay retorted.

'C'mon then, don't let's argue,' Barbara cut in.

The three sisters stepped out of the house into the cold night air and walked towards Hastings Street. As they neared the end of the turning, Pat Kelly was coming out of his place. He smiled in greeting. 'If it ain't the three beautiful Brennen gels. An' where are you lot off to?' he asked.

'The pictures,' Kay replied for the three of them. Dawn and Barbara walked on a few paces, leaving Kay alone with the young man.

'I was finkin' of goin' meself but I wasn't too keen on what was showin' this week,' he told her.

'We're gonna see *Camille*,' Kay replied. 'I don't fink you'd like it though. It's a woman's film.'

'Yeah, I prefer a good western or a good bloodthirsty gangster meself,' Pat told her, casually slipping his hands into his trouser pockets and grinning.

'C'mon, Kay, or we'll be late,' Dawn called out.

'You walk on, I'll catch yer up,' Kay shouted back.

The young man watched the two sisters hurry off and then turned to Kay. 'You don't seem too enthusiastic about the film,' he remarked.

'Not really,' she replied. 'I prefer a good musical.'

'I'm off fer a drink meself,' Pat told her.

'The Mason's?'

'Nah, I'm gonna pop down ter Chippy's place.'

'Where's that?' Kay asked, suddenly curious.

The young man smiled. 'It's a ramshackle little pub down near the river. All us fellas go in there ter cry in our beer,' he replied.

'Oh, I see. It's one o' those men-only pubs,' Kay said, smiling at him.

'Nah not really, but we do tend ter congregate there some nights,' Pat replied.

'We?'

'Yeah, all the dregs o' society. We sit in Chippy's bar an' moan an' groan into our beer an' talk about better days,' he went on, overdoing his downcast look.

'I was given to understand these were the better days,' Kay countered, beginning to enjoy the banter despite the chill wind.

Pat smiled cynically. 'Better fer some.'

'You sound really sorry fer yerself,' Kay told him. 'That don't seem like you. What's 'appened ter the Pat Kelly I used ter admire from afar?'

'You're right,' the young man said quickly. 'I've bin lackin' stimulatin' conversation. We should continue this chat, but not 'ere though.'

'What about at Chippy's?' Kay suggested.

Pat looked surprised. 'What, now?'

'Why not?'

'Wasn't you s'posed ter go an' see *Camille*?'

'It's too late now. It'll already be started, an' I can't bear ter go in after the film starts,' she told him.

'Won't yer sisters be waitin' fer yer?'

Kay shook her head. 'They can't wait ter sit there sniffin' inter their 'ankies. They won't wait.'

'Well, Chippy's it is then,' Pat said, grinning.

The two set off along the quiet turning. Kay was feeling very pleased with herself. It felt good to be walking beside Pat Kelly. If it had happened a few years ago she would have been too nervous to speak. As it was she felt in control of the situation. They were nothing more than neighbours and friends enjoying a quiet chat together, and if they were seen and tongues started to wag, let them.

Pat took Kay's arm as they crossed into Hastings Street, but to her disappointment he let go as they reached the other side of the deserted street and walked along to St James's Road. The wide thoroughfare led over the railway and down to Jamaica Road through a long arch, but it was quiet now after the evening rush. Pat pointed to a narrow turning opposite. 'Chippy's is down there,' he told her. 'The pub's called the Bell, but everyone knows it as Chippy's after the bloke who runs it. 'E's a real character.'

Kay could smell the river mud as they walked along the cobbled street. Ahead she could see the pub sign swinging in the wind, and as they entered the small public bar she felt the heat of the coke fire on her face.

'Well, if it ain't young Kelly lookin' very pleased wiv 'imself, an' wiv good reason,' the landlord said grinning.

'Kay, I want yer ter meet Chippy 'imself,' Pat said as they reached the counter. 'Now I gotta warn yer not ter listen to anyfing this character tells yer.'

Chippy held out his gnarled hand and, as Kay gripped it, she noticed the man's eyes. They were very large, grey and friendly and she smiled. 'Pleased ter meet yer, Chippy.'

'I've bin waitin' fer the opportunity ter meet yer. Pat's told me so much about yer,' he said, grinning.

'The lyin' ole git,' Pat growled. 'Chippy knows I never discuss anyfing wiv 'im. 'E's not ter be trusted.'

Kay felt immediately at ease. The pub was grotty, as Pat had said, and the proprietor was dressed to match. His waistcoat hung open and his grey shirt-sleeves were rolled up over the elbows. He looked badly in need of a shave and his thinning grey hair was dishevelled, but his eyes captivated the young woman and she gave him a warm smile. 'Pat's told me a lot about you too,' she told him.

'All bad, I 'ope,' Chippy replied with a devilish look.

'I'll 'ave a pint o' the usual, Chippy, wivout the conversation, an' a drink fer this young lady,' Pat said, turning to Kay.

She thought for a moment. A gin and tonic might be nice but she wanted to be completely in charge of herself. It would be so easy to forget the way things were and be smitten by the handsome Pat Kelly's charm. 'I'll 'ave a light ale,' she said.

The fire sent out a warm glow as the two young people sat chatting in a secluded corner. A few customers were scattered around the small bar and Chippy was busy holding a lengthy conversation with an elderly docker, while outside the wind got up.

'Tell me about this young man of yours,' Pat said, sipping his drink.

Kay looked down at her hands. 'David's very nice an' 'e wants us ter get married when 'e's free,' she replied.

Pat looked intently into her blue eyes and sensed pain. 'Tell me about you,' he urged her.

'You know all about me. I'm the kid who couldn't take 'er eyes off yer, remember?' she said, smiling.

'No, tell me about the real you. Kay Brennen, the prettiest of the Brennen gels. The one wiv the large sad eyes,' he said quietly.

'They're not sad,' she countered.

'They look sad ter me,' he told her. 'I've made a study of eyes. D'yer know that the eyes reflect the soul?'

'So they say,' Kay replied averting her gaze.

'Look at me, Kay.'

She looked up slowly and met his stare. 'What d'yer see there?' she asked.

'I see trouble, uncertainty, an' I can see vivacity,' he said with a disarming smile.

'It frightens me that you can see right inter me,' Kay replied. 'I couldn't fool you, could I?'

Pat took a sip from his drink. 'If there is anyfing troublin' yer, Kay, I'm a good listener.'

She gave him a warm smile. 'That goes fer me too.'

The young man leaned back in his chair and surveyed the bar. 'So now yer know where all us dead-beats 'ang out,' he said, smiling.

'Yer know, you surprise me,' Kay told him. 'Pat Kelly, the man who could take 'is pick of the gels at one time, an' now 'e's reduced ter callin' 'imself a dead-beat an' feelin' sorry fer 'imself.'

'Yeah, it must seem strange ter you, Kay, but there comes a time in a man's life when 'e's gotta take stock,' he explained. 'There was a time when I could take me pick, as yer rightly said, but then the eligible gels go off an' find 'usbands. They see frew the likes o' me. Then one day I wake up an' find that life's not so much fun any more. In fact, life's a bitch, an' then yer die.'

Kay shivered. 'Stop it, Pat, yer frightenin' me.'

'I'm sorry,' he said quickly. 'What I'm tryin' ter say is that it was all a big joke. I suddenly found that I needed a place o' me own, wiv a wife an' kids, so I married Eileen. I should 'ave known it wouldn't work out. She was possessive ter the point where I couldn't breave wivout 'er bein' there. Me past finally caught up wiv me.'

'So marriage didn't work for yer,' Kay replied.

'It would, wiv the right gel,' he said slowly.

153

'An' you're still lookin?' Kay said.

'Not any more I'm not.'

'So you've given up?'

'No, I don't need ter look any furvver.'

'You've found 'er?'

'Yeah, she's no more than two feet away right this minute,' he said quietly.

'Don't make jokes like that, Pat,' she said in a serious voice.

He looked at her, his large dark eyes gazing into hers. 'I'm in deadly earnest, Kay,' he told her. 'That mornin' when I watched yer walk inter that office it hit me like a brick. The young gel I used ter know 'ad suddenly flowered into a beautiful woman. I couldn't get you out o' me mind, but I knew it was 'opeless. You'd told me that mornin' there was someone in yer life an' you looked like you were in love. I 'ad ter laugh at the stupidity of it all. There 'e was, Pat Kelly, the man who could step out wiv whoever at one time, an' then she comes along. The one gel who sets 'is 'eart racin', an' she's out o' reach.'

Kay stared down at her near-empty glass. 'I 'ad no idea yer felt that way, Pat,' she replied, her cheeks flushed with emotion.

He smiled briefly. 'Like I said, life's a bitch.'

She nodded. 'I remember one night durin' the war,' she began. 'It was just before the invasion. I was in the railway club an' you were there talkin' to everybody an' lookin' like a film star in yer uniform. Well, that night I could 'ave died. I really wanted to. Yer never gave me more than a smile, an' I was madly in love wiv yer. I was all of fifteen. I swore that I'd keep meself fer you, an' one day you'd know just 'ow much I loved yer. It was gonna be just like the films. You'd sweep me up in yer arms an' carry me off. Then I realised one day that life really is a bitch – the day someone told me that you an' Eileen Carter 'ad got engaged.'

Pat Kelly had been listening intently to what she was saying and his eyes were large and sad. 'I know you're in love wiv someone else, Kay, but I won't stop lovin' yer,' he told her, his voice faltering.

She drained her glass and set it down on the table. 'I fink I'd better go,' she said quietly.

Pat nodded. 'Yeah, maybe you're right.'

The two young people walked slowly back to Waggoner's Way through the empty cold streets, both dwelling on the evening they

154

had shared. Kay felt drained and unhappy, and the man beside her was experiencing utter misery. They hardly spoke, both shocked into silence by each other's revelations. When they reached their street, Pat stood and watched her cross to her house. She turned and lifted her hand in a brief wave and then she was gone.

Chapter Twenty

Late on Wednesday morning, Danny Adams called at number 8 looking very sheepish. 'Sorry I couldn't get back yesterday,' he said as Ada stood back to let him in. 'I got delayed wiv a few fings.'

'It's all right, Danny, I left the bedroom ready for yer,' Ada replied.

The young man hurried up the stairs and removed the sharpened plane iron from his back pocket, whistling to himself as he quickly fitted it into the plane. Meanwhile Ada put the kettle on and busied herself with sorting out the washing. She heard a scraping sound and then hammering. Ten minutes later Danny came down into the scullery looking pleased with himself. 'Well, it's done. Wanna take a look?' he asked.

Ada followed him back up into the bedroom and stood admiring his work. 'That's really professional, Danny,' she said smiling. 'It didn't take yer long.'

He smiled back. 'What else was it yer wanted done?'

'Well, there's this bedroom door,' she pointed out. 'It won't close prop'ly, an' then there's the drawer in the gels' room I was tellin' yer about.'

Danny pushed the door closed and stood scratching his head. 'It'll need a bit off the bottom an' the side. It's swollen wiv the dampness,' he told her.

'Can yer manage it?' she asked.

'Yeah, it's no problem. I'll need ter take it off the 'inges though.'

Ada nodded. 'Right then, I'll go an' make us a cuppa an' leave yer to it.'

Danny set to work confidently. It had been very reassuring to find out that he really had sharpened the plane iron after all, and the nagging from his mother about leaving things lying around had not

156

unduly troubled him. She had produced the plane iron from the dresser drawer and gone on about it being as sharp as a razor and she could have cut herself on it. His calmness had probably made her feel even more irritated, but Danny was not worried. He was feeling in control of himself this morning and there was work to do.

The door refitted, and the dressing-table drawer repaired with a few short nails where the joints had sprung, Danny was in a self-assured frame of mind, and when he answered Ada's summons to come down for his tea the young man was smiling. 'Well, that's that. Was there anyfing else needed doin'?' he asked her.

'Well, there is one fing,' Ada replied. 'The weavverboard on the front door. It was all rotted, so my Joe took it off. 'E promised ter fit me anuvver one but 'e ain't got round to it. Is there any chance o' you doin' it, Danny?'

He nodded. 'Yeah sure. I'll see if I've got anyfing suitable in me backyard. There's a load o' wood out there,' he told her.

Ada reached for her purse. 'What's the damage?'

Danny waved his hand in a dismissive gesture. 'Leave it till I've done the front door, Ada. I can do it this afternoon, if it's all right wiv you?'

Ada nodded. 'Come round any time yer like. I'm usually always in.'

Danny got up and pointed to the tool-bag. 'Can I leave that 'ere fer the time bein'?' he asked her.

'Yeah, course yer can. I'll just put it under the stairs,' she replied.

Ada stood at her front door watching the young man striding away and she suddenly caught sight of Elsie coming along. She saw her daughter wave a greeting to Danny as she passed by on the other side of the turning. As the girl drew near, Ada grew worried. Something was wrong, she could tell. Elsie looked troubled and it was unusual for her not to be at work this time of day.

'Anyfing wrong, luv?' Ada asked her as she closed the door and followed her into the parlour.

'The police called round this mornin' just after Ernie left fer work,' Elsie replied. ''E's gotta go ter Dock'ead police station as soon as 'e gets 'ome.'

'Did they say what for?' Ada asked.

'Nah, they won't let on, will they?' Elsie replied with a deep sigh as she eased herself down into the armchair. 'Farvver at work?'

'Nah, 'e's on late shift. 'E's gone ter see someone about that charity do that's comin' up,' Ada told her. 'I bet that frightened yer this mornin', didn't it? Police knockin' on the door is enough ter frighten anybody. I bet they're convinced 'e was involved in that business.'

'Yeah I'm sure they are,' Elsie agreed. 'Mind you, the way 'e's bin actin' lately, I fink so too.'

Ada shook her head slowly. 'I dunno, it's all worry, what wiv one fing an' anuvver.'

'It's no use you gettin' upset about it,' Elsie countered quickly. 'It's my worry, not yours.'

Ada gave her daughter a hard look. 'Now listen, Elsie. What worries you worries us. We've always bin a close-knit family. Cut one of us an' we all bleed.'

Elsie nodded. 'I'm sorry, Mum, but I don't like you takin' on my worries. Yer got enough o' yer own ter contend wiv.'

Ada smiled briefly and reached for the teapot. 'Anyway, why ain't you at work terday?' she inquired.

Her daughter looked down at her clasped hands for a few moments. 'I was feelin' a bit sick an' dizzy this mornin' when I took Billy ter school, so I took the day off,' she replied.

'Yer not . . .'

'Nah, there's no chance o' that,' Elsie cut in. 'I dunno, I fink it's all the worry lately. It's just got ter me, that's all.'

'Well, yer can't be made ter feel guilty fer what Ernie does,' Ada told her sharply. 'If 'e was involved, the police'll find out sooner or later an' yer gotta be prepared fer it. All the tongues are sure ter start waggin' an' it won't be easy. You take ole Mrs Colly. Remember when 'er ole man got done fer nickin' that stuff at the wharf? Six months 'e got an' the shame of it nearly killed 'er. Ill fer weeks she was wiv 'er nerves. She went like a deal board too. She couldn't eat or face goin' out o' the 'ouse. Terrible time she 'ad.'

'Fanks fer remindin' me, Mum,' Elsie said with sarcasm in her voice. 'I came round 'ere fer a bit o' cheerin' up an' yer've made me feel more depressed than ever.'

'I'm sorry, luv, but I just wanted yer ter know the score,' Ada said quietly as she handed her daughter a cup of tea.

Elsie sipped it in silence for a while, soon becoming aware that her mother was studying her closely. 'I'm not the slightest bit worried about meself,' she said, seeking to reassure her. 'I'm worried fer Ernie.'

'The way fings are between you two it's a wonder yer bovver,' Ada remarked.

Elsie sighed deeply. 'Whatever 'e is, an' whatever 'e's done still don't alter the fact that 'e's my 'usband,' she replied. 'I know I've said a lot o' fings, but when somefing like this 'appens yer gotta ferget all what's gone on an' give 'em yer support. You would if it was Dad.'

'Yeah, but there's a big difference,' Ada was quick to remind her. 'Yer farvver's a good man. 'E don't go out boozin' every night an' 'e don't keep me short o' money. What's more 'is first concern is you kids, an' that's more than I can say fer that no-good 'usband o' yours.'

Elsie nodded. 'I know yer right. I know Ernie was involved in the robbery, an' I know that sooner or later they're gonna come fer 'im, but when they do 'e's gonna need me an' I've gotta be there fer 'im, despite everyfing.'

Ada sighed sadly. She knew there was nothing more she could say to change her mind. Elsie was determined to do it her way and there would be no shifting her. She decided to change the subject. ''Ere, while yer 'ere, can yer give us an 'and wiv changin' the curtains in our bedroom?' she asked her. 'Danny Adams 'as just fixed the floorboard an' that door an' I wanna spruce the room up a bit while I got the chance.'

Elsie followed her mother up the stairs and when she saw the repairs she seemed surprised. ''E's made a good job o' that floorboard,' she remarked.

'Try the door,' Ada said. 'Danny fixed that as well.'

Elsie tested it and nodded appreciatively. 'Yeah, it shuts easily. I'll 'ave ter get 'im ter do a few jobs fer me,' she said, grinning. 'There's a lot needs seein' to, an' Ernie can do anyfing wiv an 'ammer 'cept knock a nail in.'

'Well, if yer really serious, why not 'ave 'im call round?' Ada suggested as she climbed up on to a chair and unclipped the curtain pole. 'I'll tell 'im if yer like, or you could go an' see 'im yerself.'

'I might do that,' Elsie replied.

''Ere, take these, will yer?' Ada said, passing down the curtains.

Elsie helped her mother replace the grimy lace with a freshly starched piece and then together they hung and adjusted the heavy brown velvet curtaining, tying back the drapes with wide yellow ribbon.

'Word's goin' round that yer farvver might be gettin' some sort o' recognition fer what 'e did durin' that fire at the freight yards,' Ada said as they were enjoying their third cup of tea.

'I fink it's right too,' Elsie said firmly. 'Dad could 'ave bin killed or badly scalded doin' what 'e did. Fancy storin' ammunition in a shed right next ter people's 'ouses. I fink it's scandalous.'

'They've tried ter keep it secret but it's leaked out,' Ada told her. 'Everybody's talkin' about it. I bet it'll be in all the papers before long.'

They sipped their tea in silence for a while, then Ada decided she would take the opportunity to mention her worries about her youngest daughter. 'It was nice you an' Kay findin' the time to 'ave a quiet chat,' she began tentatively.

Elsie was immediately put on her guard. 'Yeah, we don't get much chance ter chat tergevver these days,' she replied.

Ada took the bull by the horns. 'I'm worried sick over that gel,' she said bluntly. 'She's so secretive. I can see there's somefing wrong an' I'm pretty sure it's ter do wiv that bloke she's goin' wiv, but every time I try ter get 'er ter talk she shuts up like a clam.'

'I shouldn't worry, Mum. Kay's got it all under control,' Elsie told her.

'Yer know what I fink? I fink 'e's a married man,' Ada prompted.

Elsie shrugged her shoulders and pulled a face, which told Ada that she was on the right track.

'I don't fink it's right fer gels ter shut their parents out o' their lives the way Kay tries ter do,' she went on. 'If the man is married she should tell us. We wouldn't condemn 'er out of 'and. It'd be nice if she'd bring 'im 'ome an' introduce 'im like Barbara an' Dawn do wiv their blokes. It keeps everyfing out in the open that way.'

Elsie had no desire to get into a deep discussion about her sister's affair. She put down her empty teacup. 'Kay wouldn't do anyfing silly, Mum,' she said reassuringly. 'Just leave it an' don't worry. As soon as she knows it's serious she'll bring 'im 'ome ter meet you an' Dad. Anyway it could all fizzle out.'

Ada nodded. 'Yeah! I s'pose yer right,' she replied, almost to herself.

Elsie got up to leave. 'I better get movin', there's a stack of ironin' waitin' for me. I'll try an' pop in termorrer sometime ter let yer know what 'appens wiv Ernie,' she said.

Ada nodded. 'Yer wanna be careful about takin' any extra money off 'im, 'cos you'll be implicated if 'e is involved.'

Elsie smiled cynically. 'Muvver, I've 'ad ter remind 'im a dozen times about givin' me some extra money fer Billy's clothes. Ernie's not likely ter shower me wiv gifts.'

Ada watched at her front door until her eldest daughter was out of sight. It was so sad the way things had turned out for her, she thought. It was as though Ernie Gates had wrung all the vitality and sparkle from her. Elsie had remained loyal to him where another girl would have left him long ago. What was going to happen to her? Would it all end in sorrow and heartache?

Jim Carney wanted to keep his options open, and when he called in at the Citadel in New Kent Road on Tuesday morning to see Major Harrison, he was disappointed.

'I'm sorry but the major's had to go out on business,' he was informed.

Jim looked at Soldier Mary with a pained expression on his face. 'I came round this mornin' especially ter see 'im,' he replied. 'I'm on lates, yer see, an' it's very important we get fings movin'.'

'I'll be able to pass on a message if you wish,' the bespectacled soldier of Christ told him.

'Right'o. Just tell 'im that Jim Carney's settin' up a contact who might be able ter knock out a few fousand o' your newspapers on commission. It'll mean divin' down the ole collection boxes but I might be able ter swing a good deal: say, fifty-fifty. Now can yer remember all that?'

The Salvationist nodded and smiled. 'I'll tell Major Harrison as soon as I see him,' she replied.

Jim gave her a wide grin. 'Right then. I'll try ter call back later in the week,' he told her. 'All the best. Keep up the good work, an' stay out o' dodgy pubs.'

As the clatter of Carney's heavy boots faded, the major peered out of his office window. 'I do feel guilty, but I couldn't face the man, not this morning,' he said in a tired voice as his secretary came back in.

When Soldier Mary delivered the message, Major Harrison sat down at his desk with a sigh. 'I think I made a big mistake in entertaining Mr Crash Bang Wallop in the first place,' he told her.

161

'When he comes back I could tell him you've been transferred,' the secretary suggested.

'No, I must see this through,' Harrison replied, looking at Soldier Mary but seeing in his mind only the grinning face of Jim Carney armed with a tin-opener and standing over a table stacked up with filled collection boxes. 'Get thee behind me, Satan,' he mumbled.

'I beg your pardon?' said the shocked secretary.

'I'm very sorry, I was somewhere else,' Harrison replied quickly.

Jack Springer groaned aloud as he saw the hopeful candidate approaching his shop. 'Alma, there's trouble on the way,' he called out. 'If I get tied up wiv this character, come in an' say I'm wanted on the phone, will yer?'

'Wotcha, Jack me ole mate. 'Ow's tricks,' Jim said pleasantly.

'Not so bad, Jim. 'Ow are you?'

'Mustn't grumble.'

'What can I do yer for?'

Jim Carney folded his arms. 'I got a proposition for yer,' he said, grinning widely.

'Oh, an' what's that then?'

''Ow'd yer like ter make a nice few bob sellin' newspapers?'

'What d'yer fink these are, apples an' pears?' Jack replied sarcastically.

'Nah, I mean free newspapers,' Jim told him, his grin growing even more wide.

'Now 'ow the bloody 'ell am I gonna earn a nice few bob sellin' free newspapers?' Jack growled.

'Simple,' Jim told him. 'I bring yer a bundle o' *War Cry*s an' stick 'em next ter those. Now when the customers come in yer just tell 'em to 'elp themselves, an' when they pick one up yer rattle the collection box, just like the Salvation Army people do when they go round the pubs. People always shove a few coppers in those collection boxes. I tell yer, mate, that box is gonna be chock-a-block before yer know it.'

'An' 'ow's that gonna benefit me?' Jack asked.

'Well, it's like this,' Jim explained. 'Yer give it ter me. I take it ter the Salvation Army people, they count it out an' yer get five bob in the pound commission.'

'An' why are you gettin' involved in all this?' Jack asked suspiciously.

'I'm doin' this fer the Salvation Army,' Jim said, looking almost holy.

'Tell me somefink,' Jack asked him. ''Ave you got permission ter do this?'

'Course I 'ave,' Jim replied with conviction. 'I just gotta tie up a few loose ends, that's all. Once I've sorted out the details it'll be zomper zompers.'

'An' 'ow many o' these papers am I s'posed ter take?' the weary shopowner asked.

'Oh, I dunno. About six or seven 'undred,' Jim said casually.

'Six or seven 'undred!' Jack shouted. 'Yer gotta be mad. 'Ow many customers d'yer fink I've got? I doubt if I could knock out 'undred a week.'

'Give 'em two or three each. Tell 'em ter pass 'em on ter their friends,' Jim replied.

'An' where the bloody 'ell d'yer fink I'm gonna store seven 'undred newspapers?' Jack growled.

'Couldn't yer keep 'em upstairs or somefink? Yer could always put 'em under the bed or somefink.'

'No, I couldn't, an' what's more I ain't gonna take 'em. Not seven 'undred, not six 'undred, an' not even one 'undred.'

'But it's fer the Salvation Army.'

'I don't care if it's fer Fred Karno's Army,' Jack shouted. 'You listen ter me. If yer so keen on sellin' the *War Cry*, why don't yer go round door-knockin'. Now piss orf, Jim, before I get really mad.'

A thoroughly deflated Jim Carney walked along Hastings Street with his hands thrust deep into his trouser pockets. All he wanted was just a few lousy references, and in the process of getting one solitary one he'd succeeded in upsetting half of Bermondsey. There must be someone with a bit of clout who knew him well enough to supply him with one, he thought. Maybe he should go and see the mayor. Mrs Brady had reckoned it wasn't a good idea when he'd first suggested it to her, and she had said that the mayor didn't give personal references, but how did she know? After all, Jim Carney's name would be found on the roll of wartime firewatchers. He had even put an incendiary out when it fell on the town-hall roof and was threatening to burn the building down. Yes, he would go to see the mayor.

Chapter Twenty-one

The cold wintry weather was back with a vengeance, and February was threatening to be the coldest month so far. Winds from the north whipped through the backstreets and snow clouds massed, blotting out the evening stars. Folk tended to remain beside their banked-up fires as much as possible during the bitterly cold spell, and as Kay Brennen lowered her head against the chill gusts she questioned her own sanity in going out on such a night. Even Colin had advised her against it, and he was always loath to stop at home during the evening. She could not explain to him or the other members of her family the reason for venturing out on such a night: deep down inside her there was the nagging, inexplicable feeling that something was terribly wrong.

It had been a miserable two weeks. David had been quiet and moody; only once had he shown any inclination to take her back to his flat, and on that occasion they merely sat and talked. She had hoped that he would bring his problem out into the open, try to explain just how he was feeling and help her understand him a little better, but instead he still seemed to be obsessed with his marriage, trying to justify walking out on his wife. Kay recalled how he had sat hunched and pale-faced, drained of vitality and sense of purpose, so alien to the David she had come to know, as he went on about how they had failed to reach out to each other when their marriage first began to sour. They had pursued their own interests and seemed to grow apart slowly, hardly noticing the change in each other over the seven years they were together, but the weakened bond had finally snapped and there was little left to hold the marriage together.

Kay recalled how she had wanted to scream out at him, desperate to know if his failure to love her fully had also been the underlying cause of his marriage break-up. She had wanted to let him know that she was there for him now and would try to understand, if he would only open his heart to her, give her some clue which would make her aware of the reason behind his inadequacy. She had held back, however, hoping that if she just listened and gently urged him on he would finally unburden himself, but it was in vain. He had seemed strangely different that night at the flat, and even his early kiss had lacked any passion. She had left him with a goodnight peck, hardly a brush of lips, and she walked the full journey home, feeling utterly miserable but more determined than ever to drag him screaming if necessary from the darkness which was threatening to engulf him.

Now, as she left the bus at New Cross and walked the short distance to David's flat, Kay was becoming more and more anxious. She was half expecting to find him sprawled across his bed, fully clothed and with an empty tablet bottle clutched in his lifeless hand. She must pull herself together. It was David's black depression reacting on her, she told herself, colouring and charging her imagination and making her torture herself with all sorts of bizarre and tragic spectacles.

As she walked into the small turning, Kay suddenly stopped in her tracks, rooted to the spot as though her legs had turned to stone. There, just a few yards in front of her and walking down the few steps from David's front door, was Alice, his wife. She was wearing a heavy black coat with a grey fur collar, but her face was clearly visible in the light from a nearby streetlamp as she turned at the bottom of the steps and came towards her. They had never met, but David had once shown her a snap of him and Alice together, and Kay knew that she was not mistaken. She found her legs and moved on, passing the woman without a glance.

Kay continued walking, hardly daring to look round till a fair distance had been put between them. What did it all mean? she asked herself. She turned and walked slowly back to David's flat and paused at the foot of the few steps leading to his front door. Gone was the anxiety, and in its place cold anger. He had been trying to tell her, that awful night at his flat; placing the blame on his own shoulders for the failure of his marriage, and steeling her for the inevitable. She would hear it all now. How he was full of remorse, and had to sacrifice his own happiness, their happiness together, in an effort to atone for the heartache he had inflicted on his devoted wife.

Almost without realising it, Kay reached the front door and pressed on the bell. The young man stood hollow-eyed, his face drained of colour, and he stood back without a word as Kay walked into the dreary passage. She turned to face him as he quietly closed the door. 'I just saw Alice leavin',' she said in a voice she hardly recognised.

He nodded. 'Come upstairs, Kay, it's warmer up there,' he said flatly.

She followed him up the steep carpeted stairs and into his sitting room. A gas fire warmed the place and one small table-lamp lit the dreary surroundings. She sat down, her eyes never leaving him as he moved another chair to one side of the fire.

'I know yer must be wonderin' what the 'ell's goin' on,' he said quietly, 'but I can explain.'

'You owe me that at least,' Kay said sharply.

'Alice wrote ter me last week askin' me ter sign the tenancy over to 'er an' I 'ad arranged ter go round last night,' David began, 'but I came down wiv this 'eavy cold. I fink it's the flu. I couldn't get in touch an' she thought I'd forgotten ter call. Anyway, she came round ter get it sorted out.'

'But 'ow did she know your address in the first place?' Kay asked. 'Yer told me yer didn't let on where yer was stayin'.'

David looked down at the worn carpet. 'I wrote to 'er before. There was somefing I 'ad ter get sorted out,' he said hesitantly.

Kay held back her boiling anger. 'Look at me, David,' she replied coldly. 'You're lyin'. She's bin comin' 'ere. Tell me the trufe. Allow me that at least.'

Slowly his head came up until his eyes met hers. 'I didn't wanna say anyfing. I knew 'ow it'd 'urt yer,' he said quietly. 'Yes, she's bin a few times. Alice wants us ter try again. She realised she made a mistake gettin' involved wiv someone else. It's not worked out.'

Kay's eyes filled with angry tears and she bit on her lip in an effort to keep control. 'So you buttered me up, 'opin' I'd understand,' she almost sobbed. 'You were preparin' me fer the time when you could find the courage ter finish it between us. An' there was I, stupid me. I listened to yer, David. I listened an' encouraged yer ter go on, 'opin' yer'd unburden yerself about everyfing, about us, an' why yer failed ter love me the way I wanted yer to. Maybe I would 'ave understood if yer'd only tried to explain. I would 'ave even waited

166

till it was right, no matter 'ow long it took, but no. You couldn't do it, could yer?'

David let his eyes travel about the grotty room, waiting while Kay composed herself. 'Yer don't understand, an' I take full blame,' he said finally. 'Yes, I 'ave failed yer, an' I knew I couldn't satisfy yer, but it's a long-time problem, somefing I could never talk about. I couldn't talk about it wiv Alice an' it cost me my marriage. I couldn't talk about it wiv you, even though I love yer. I tried to, though, believe me I did, but I couldn't find the words to explain what was wrong wiv me. When you left that night I wanted to end it all. I thought of the un'appiness I'd caused Alice, and now you, an' I knew that I could never 'old on ter yer. You would 'ave become like Alice in time: bitter an' resentful. I saw suicide as the only way out for me. It would 'ave bin the end o' the torment I was sufferin', but then Alice called. It was as though she knew that I was ready to end it all. I was at my lowest ebb an' there she was, talkin' as though everyfing was right between us. There was no animosity, no anger left in 'er, an' she made me feel that, fer all my failin's, I was still a man, 'er man.'

Kay was shocked by his candour, and she felt at a loss. 'So you intend ter try again wiv Alice?' she asked him in a quiet voice.

'I don't know, I honestly don't, Kay,' he replied. 'I feel right now though that I can overcome my problem. I've come to accept that it's not a physical fing. It's in me mind, an' I know that it'll all work out, now that I've finally found the courage ter face it 'ead-on.'

'Do yer still love Alice?' Kay asked him bluntly.

'Yes, I still love 'er, but not in the way I love you,' he told her. 'My love fer Alice is gentle an' warm an' reassurin', like bein' in a cosy room on a cold night, but my love fer you is wild an' excitin'. I wanna feel the rain an' reach out ter the lightnin'. I've never experienced such feelin's before, an' that's why it's all the more terrible that I can't love yer in the way you need an' deserve ter be loved.'

Kay stood up and pulled her coat tightly round her slim figure. 'I fink we both need time on our own, David,' she said quietly, without any anger in her voice.

'You're right, Kay,' he replied. 'I just want yer ter know though that, whatever 'appens, whatever decisions we come to, I'll never stop lovin' yer.'

Kay left the flat and walked home through the cold biting wind, thoughts chasing each other inside her head, and when she finally got home and walked into the parlour, Colin was there. He was ready for bed, a mug of cocoa held in his fist.

'They've all gone up already,' he said smiling. ''Ere, yer better 'ave this. Yer look frozen.'

Kay took a quick sip and put the mug down on the table while she slipped off her coat. Then, as Colin made for the scullery she placed her hand on his forearm and kissed him tenderly on the cheek.

'What was that in aid of?' he said, grinning.

'I dunno. I just felt like it,' she replied, returning his smile.

Ernie Gates had come to realise that the police were scratching around without much to go on, and their constant harassment was designed to make him break. No doubt they felt that he would seek out his cohorts for some reassurance and in so doing point a finger in the right direction. Well, they were going to be unlucky. He could take all the snide remarks and innuendoes they liked, he wasn't going to panic. He guessed that they had informants on the streets who had been alerted. Any unusual behaviour on his part would inevitably get back to Sergeant Moody and his team. All he had to do to stay in the clear was act perfectly normal. The proceeds from the lorry theft were safely stashed away, and he had been careful to chase the overtime and bonus loads in the way he always had. Any deviation from the norm would be viewed with suspicion.

Ernie let himself into his flat and sat down by the fire to warm his hands after the short walk from the Mason's Arms. Elsie had been ironing in the scullery and she came in carrying the filled teapot.

'D'yer wanna cuppa?' she asked him.

Ernie looked up and nodded. 'It's like Siberia out there,' he said, his eyes moving over Elsie's slim body as she poured the tea. She could feel him looking at her and she knew that he would be wanting to make love that night. It was the way it went with him, she sighed to herself. There were long periods when he totally ignored her and was snoring by the time she got to bed, and then there were a few times when he suddenly found the urge. Usually it was after his trip north, and she had got to wondering about this. It was possible that he had a fancy woman up there somewhere and after going with her his sexual appetite was aroused. The thought of him making love and all the while imagining it was with his other woman filled Elsie with disgust, and she had at first found it very difficult to gain any

168

pleasure from him. Then she told herself that it was all in her mind and Ernie's need for her came from sleeping alone in a cold bed. She had needs too, and she was prepared to accept his advances and allow him to make love to her, grabbing what little she could, while she could.

'I expect they'll be callin' again soon,' Ernie said as he took the brimming mug of tea from her.

Elsie shrugged her shoulders. 'If yer innocent they can't make yer say ovverwise, can they?' she said acidly.

'What d'yer mean, if I'm innocent?' Ernie replied sharply. 'Yer know I didn't 'ave anyfing ter do wiv it.'

Elsie sat down facing him and studied his wide fleshy face while he sipped his tea. Continuous drinking had left its mark on his complexion and there were reddish-blue patches on his cheeks and nose. His weight had increased too. As she stared at him he suddenly smiled mirthlessly.

'I bet yer still ain't sure about me, are yer?' he said.

'When I first asked yer about it yer nearly jumped down me froat so I just left it,' she replied quickly.

'S'posin' I told yer I did set it up, what would yer say?' he asked her.

Elsie leaned forward in her chair, her eyes widening slightly. 'Look, Ern, I'm yer wife, an' I'd stick by yer, but if yer can't confide in me there's nuffink I can do about it,' she replied.

Ernie put down his mug and leaned back in the chair. 'I didn't 'ave anyfing ter do wiv it,' he told her, his eyes shifting under her stare. 'The trouble is there's a lot o' loads gettin' nicked lately an' the law always fink the drivers are in on it. They'll keep pesterin' me till they finally realise that they're barkin' up the wrong tree. So there's no need fer you ter be worried. I've got nuffink ter fear.'

Elsie had seen the sudden movement of his eyes and it told her everything. He was as guilty as they came. 'I'm not worried,' she said quickly. 'I knew yer didn't 'ave anyfing ter do wiv it all along.'

Ernie seemed satisfied and he gave her a lecherous look. 'What about an early night?'

Elsie nodded and gave him a brief smile. It would be what he deserved if she refused him, but it had been so long since he had shown any interest in her and her body ached for love.

The fire at the railway freight yard had been taken up by the

169

newspapers, and Joe Brennen had rated a mention, but he was eventually made aware of the reason why his heroic action in averting a disaster had not been fully reported.

'I had to make out a full report and present it to the bigwigs,' Gerry Preston said, leaning back in his comfortable desk chair and clasping his hands together. 'The under-secretary from the War Office was there and he explained that, owing to the secrecy of the troop movements and how it involved us, news coverage has been censored. Personally I feel that you've been given a raw deal. What you did that night deserved a medal, and I told them so.'

Joe sat facing his depot manager with a grin on his face. 'There's no need ter feel upset, Gerry,' he replied. 'I only did what any o' the ovver shunter drivers would 'ave done. I ain't lookin' fer any recognition.'

Preston nodded. 'That may be so, but it was you who prevented the fire from reaching that shed. I still get nightmares over what could have happened,' he went on. 'Between me and you, Joe, I think someone's head's going to roll over this. It was a big mistake to allow explosive cargo to be stored here, and whoever sanctioned it is in big trouble. You just imagine the powers-that-be trying to censor the press if that shed had gone up. All hell would have broken loose. Anyway, I have to tell you that you will be getting a personal letter of thanks from the chairman of the Southern Railway. At least it'll be something to show the grandchildren.'

Joe smiled and took out his faithful timepiece. 'That letter will do nicely,' he replied, glancing briefly at the figured dial.

Preston took the hint. 'Well, I'd better not keep you, Joe.'

The engine driver stood up and adjusted his waistcoat. 'As a matter o' fact I'm takin' the family out ternight fer a drink,' he said smiling. 'Our Colin's goin' in the army termorrer.'

Chapter Twenty-two

The impassioned Jim Carney had long since failed to heed sensible advice, and as a result he had invariably found himself in trying situations of one form or another. But Jim was a very determined man, and his earnest desire to join what he considered to be a very prestigious group had clouded his thinking and closed his ears. So far he had managed to obtain only one reference, and he was aware how time was moving on. The Jolly Boys would soon be involved in their annual charity work, as soon as the weather broke, and Jim desperately wanted to be part of it. He could see it now: a large photo of him in the local newspapers, and below, an urgent request to all good members of the community to respond to the latest appeal from the Jolly Boys.

Jim strolled purposefully along Spa Road and entered the council offices. 'I'd like ter see the lord mayor, please,' he told the doorman.

The man had heard that one before. 'Yeah so would I, but yer gotta get yer place early or yer miss the 'ole show,' he replied.

'When will I be able ter see 'im?' Jim asked.

'I should reckon about the first week o' November,' the doorman told him, 'or is it the second?'

'November? That's bloody outrageous!' Jim stormed. 'I might let you know I 'elped save this town 'all durin' the war. A bloody great incendiary dropped on the roof one night an' if it wasn't fer me actin' sharply the 'ole place would 'ave burnt down.'

The doorman had often been accosted by members of the community who were unsure of their requirements, and like all responsible council representatives he strived to put them at ease and steer them in the right direction. The character he was

171

confronted with this morning, however, was a special case to say the least, and it looked as though it was going to be tricky.

'Now let me get this right. You did say it was the lord mayor yer wished ter see?' he queried.

'Yeah that's right. 'E is 'ere, ain't 'e?'

'No, I'm afraid the lord mayor resides at the Mansion 'Ouse over the City,' the doorman explained.

Jim looked relieved. 'Nah, I didn't mean that one. I mean the mayor o' Bermondsey.'

'Oh, I see,' the doorman said, smiling indulgently. ''E's not a lord mayor. Our mayor's just an everyday, common-or-garden mayor. But yer can't see 'im.'

'An' why not?' Jim asked quickly.

''Cos 'e's off sick.'

'Wassa matter wiv 'im?'

'I dunno, 'e ain't took me into 'is confidence. Could be anyfink.'

Jim Carney scratched his head in frustration. 'Now look 'ere, mate. I ain't got time ter play silly buggers,' he said angrily. 'I gotta get ter see the mayor. I need ter get fings sorted out pretty quickly or I'm never gonna be a Jolly Boy.'

'No, yer bloody well won't wiv that attitude,' the doorman told him firmly. 'I can't 'elp it if the mayor's off sick.'

'Ain't 'e got no 'elpers, like an assistant mayor or somefink?' Jim asked.

'As a matter o' fact there is a deputy mayor.'

''E'll do. Which way do I go?'

''E's off sick too.'

'Well, who the bloody 'ell's 'oldin' the fort?'

'Councillor Shergold.'

'Point me to 'im.'

'It's an 'er.'

'Well, point me to 'er then.'

'Nah, I can't do that.'

'Why the bloody 'ell not?'

The doorman took a deep breath. 'Now look, ole mate. I'm only the doorman an' I ain't got the authority ter let every Tom, Dick or 'Arry who comes bargin' in 'ere go an' see councillors wivout appointments. Yer've all gotta 'ave appointments. It's the way the system works.'

'Sod the system. I ain't got time ter make appointments,' Jim growled.

The doorman took another deep breath. 'It ain't such a big fing. Yer just fill in a form. It don't take five minutes an' then yer get a reply frew the post.'

'Bloody charmin'. I should 'ave done that when the town 'all was in danger o' burnin' down,' Jim told him sharply. 'Just a minute. A bomb on the roof yer say? Well, just fill in this form an' I'll try an' fix a visit.'

'There's no need ter get shirty,' the doorman replied.

Jim tried to calm himself down a little and he smiled at his antagonist. 'Now look, ole sport. I know yer gotta be careful who yer let in, but this is urgent,' he said quietly. 'Can't yer just look in on Councillor Sherwood an' say that Jim Carney would like ter see 'er fer five minutes?'

'It's Councillor Shergold, an' no I can't.'

Jim finally realised that he was getting nowhere fast and it was useless arguing any further. 'I should 'ave let the bloody place burn down,' he mumbled as he turned and made for the door.

The doorman gave a huge sigh of relief and set about polishing up the door-plate, watched by the disappointed railwayman who was retying his bootlace on the bottom of the steps. A van pulled up and when the driver leaned out of his cab holding a delivery sheet the doorman walked down the steps to answer his query, unaware that the resourceful Jim Carney was taking the opportunity to slip back into the town hall.

'Can yer point me in the direction of Councillor Shergold's office, please?' he asked a woman clerk.

'Top of the stairs, second door on the right.'

Jim hurried up the wide marble staircase and tapped lightly on the appropriate door.

'Enter.'

'Councillor Shergold?'

'Nice to meet you. Please take a seat. I'll be two minutes,' the large bespectacled woman told him, smiling broadly as she held out her hand.

Jim was not sure whether he was expected to kiss it or shake it, but he settled for the latter, and then watched closely as the councillor left her desk and proceeded to rummage through a cupboard in one corner of the large office.

'Ah, here we are,' she said, coming back to the desk and placing a large-boned corset down on the top. 'You can see where the material has split and the bone is sticking out. It's been pressing into my back so I had to take the thing off. I hope you can fix it pretty quickly. I'm in absolute agony without it.'

Jim stared down at the corset and scratched his head, not knowing what to say. 'Yeah, I can see the problem but I need a reference,' he mumbled finally.

Councillor Shergold stared at him blankly for a moment and then suddenly smiled. 'Oh, I see what you mean. Just a moment, it should be in this drawer. Ah yes, here we are. "Crossways surgical appliances. One boned corset. Reference number 345784." Is that what you need?'

It was Jim's turn to look blank. 'I can't do anyfing about them stays, luv,' he told her eventually.

'But I've only had them less than two months. Your firm assured me that they were guaranteed for two years at least,' she moaned.

'If yer take my advice yer'll send 'em back an' tell 'em they're a load of ole rubbish,' Jim urged her. 'The 'ospital gave me a pair o' them once when I cricked me back. I couldn't get on wiv 'em. Bleedin' fings were stickin' in me an' I couldn't bend. Bloody rubbish if you ask me.'

The councillor looked at him in horror, suddenly aware that she had made a terrible mistake. 'You're ... You're not from Crossways?'

'Nah. I come from Waggoner's Way. Jim Carney's the name.'

'Then what in heaven's name are you doing here?' she asked him.

'I just told yer. I need a reference,' he explained. 'Yer see, I was one o' the borough firewatchers durin' the war an' I tell yer now, gel, if it wasn't fer me you wouldn't 'ave a town 'all. A bloody great incendiary bomb dropped on the roof an' I was the one who put it out. So I fink one good turn deserves anuvver, don't you?'

'You mean you want me to give you a reference?'

'Yeah, 'cos I'm tryin' ter be a Jolly Boy.'

'A Jolly Boy?'

'S'right. I need four references,' Jim went on. 'I got one from me employer an' then I tried the Salvation Army. No, tell a lie. I tried me panel doctor first, but 'e reckoned I was round the twist. Anyway, the major bloke at the Sally Army was gonna give us one but I couldn't flog the papers for 'im. Well, I could 'ave done, if it wasn't fer that miserable ole git Jack Springer. 'E wouldn't stick 'em on 'is counter. Some people just won't put themselves out. Now me, I'd 'elp out where I could. I'd even 'ave a go at those stays if I thought I could mend 'em, but they look past it ter me. Best ter send 'em back an' get yer money refunded.'

Councillor Shergold had gone pale and she flopped down in her chair wearily. 'I knew it. I just knew it,' she groaned. 'I shouldn't have volunteered to stand in for the mayor.'

'Yer do look a bit peaky,' Jim told her. 'If I were you I'd take a few days off yerself. Get somebody ter stand in for yer. It seems ter be the normal fing 'ere. I reckon there's a bug goin' round.'

There was a gentle tap on the door and a young woman put her head round. 'This is Mr Bernard from Crossways to see you, Councillor,' she announced. 'I'm afraid he got lost in the building.'

Jim realised that he wasn't going to get his reference and decided it was time to make an exit. He backed towards the door and, as the surgical appliances man came into the room, he pointed to the corset. 'I'd chuck that bloody fing in the bin an' give 'er 'er money back if I was you,' he told him. 'The poor cow ain't 'ad it five minutes an' it's all split.'

'I beg your pardon,' Mr Bernard gasped, a look of outrage on his thin face.

'Granted,' Jim replied as he walked out.

The cold weather had kept the social activities of the Waggoner's folk down to a minimum but Annie Thomas and Bet Greenedge still found time to meet at their usual locations.

'I saw Mrs Adams yesterday,' Annie said as the two old friends stood in Basil Cashman's oil shop. 'She was pleased about 'er Danny. 'E's got a job.'

'That's nice. Where?' Bet asked.

'At the baths in Spa Road.'

'That's nice fer 'im.'

'As long as 'e don't go scaldin' 'em all,' Annie joked. 'Yer know 'ow fergetful Danny can be.'

Basil Cashman was in one of his anti-social moods and he grunted loudly. 'That'll be one an' ninepence.'

Bet ignored him. 'Mind you, Dot Adams was sayin' 'e's bin gettin' back ter doin' a bit o' carpentry on the side. It could be the makin' o'

175

the lad. 'E was really a dab 'and at it before the war. 'E put me a new door on once.'

'Yeah, I know. 'E done quite a bit o' work in the turnin',' Annie agreed. 'Like yer say, it could be the makin' of 'im.'

'Look, I know yer ain't got no 'omes ter go to, but I 'ave, so if yer quite finished pullin' yer neighbours ter pieces I'd like ter lock up an' piss orf 'ome,' Basil told them in no uncertain terms.

''Ere's yer one an' ninepence,' Bet said. 'Bloody ole misery.'

Outside the shop they were joined by Emily Toogood from number 12. ''Ello gels. What a bloody perisher,' she said, pulling her coat up around her ears. ''Eard the latest?'

'No,' they chorused.

'Charlie Catchpole's pissed orf.'

'Yer don't say!'

'I jus' seen Ivy Catchpole comin' from the paper shop,' Emily went on. 'She looked really upset, an' when I asked 'er what was wrong she burst out cryin'. Apparently 'er Charlie finished 'is tea an' got 'is bits an' pieces ready fer the late shift an' then calmly told 'er that 'e wouldn't be comin' back.'

'What's all that about then?' Bet asked.

'Well, accordin' to Ivy 'e reckons she's bin naggin' 'im narrer an' 'e's 'ad enough of it,' Emily told her. 'Mind you, she does go on at 'im, but she won't admit it. As a matter o' fact I asked 'er if she'd bin leadin' off at 'im lately an' she said it was only over the time 'e spends on that committee of 'is.'

'The Jolly Boys?'

'Yeah. They've started 'avin' meetin's fer their annual charity do.'

'Well, as far as I'm concerned, Ivy Catchpole should fink 'erself lucky she's got a bloke like Charlie,' Annie cut in. ''E does a lot fer 'er. Yer see 'im doin' the front step every Saturday, as well as the winders. I fink she puts on 'im.'

Bet nodded and turned her back against the gusting wind. 'Yer don't fink Charlie's got anuvver woman, do yer?' she asked.

'What, Charlie? No chance. 'E finks the world of Ivy. 'E's just doin' it ter frighten 'er, I should fink,' Emily replied.

The three set off along the turning as the first flakes of snow drifted down from a grey sky. Smoke rose up from chimney-pots as folk banked up their fires, and at number 8 a young man was making his last preparations before embarking on what he thought was to be a big adventure.

176

Chapter Twenty-three

Colin Brennen caught a number 63 bus in the Old Kent Road and settled back in his seat on the upper deck. He wore a single-breasted overcoat with the collar pulled up around his ears, and between his feet was a small brown attaché case containing his toiletries and a packet of sandwiches his mother had made for him.

Colin smiled to himself as he recalled the fuss that morning. Barbara was always the first one ready for work, and she had given him a big cuddle before she left, along with a few words of advice. Dawn had shed a few tears as he had expected, but Kay had smiled cheerfully and joked with him about not upsetting the sergeant-major. His father was on late shift and would normally have had a lie-in, but he too was up early to see him off with a firm handshake and a reassuring wink. His mother had embarrassed him by hugging him tightly and wetting his shirt collar with a few tears as she reminded him to eat properly and look after himself.

It was all to be expected, he thought as he idly watched the snowflakes swirling past the window. He was the youngest of the family and they had always been inclined to fuss over him. Well, all that was over now. He was going to put on the King's uniform, and if need be fight for his country. Maybe he would be sent to Germany, or even the Far East. He might even have the misfortune to be sent to some depot in England – that would be terrible. Anyway, there was no use worrying now. Better to get the training over and take it from there, he told himself.

The young man could see the river traffic as the bus crossed Blackfriar's Bridge, and he took out a Player's Weight from a crumpled packet and lit it. His family would be shocked to know that he had started smoking, he thought with a smile, but he was a man now and quite able to please himself what he did or did not do.

The bus continued along the cold winter streets, passing Fleet Street and the Smithfield meat market. Almost before Colin realised it he had arrived at King's Cross Station. He jumped down from the bus and hurried into the station forecourt. There seemed to be lots of young men carrying suitcases, all hurrying in the same direction, and one young man caught Colin's eye. He was short and frail-looking and he wore a long overcoat which reached down almost to his heavy boots. His short hair was sticking up from the top of his head, and his pale thin face had a worried expression.

'Straight on, son. Just show yer warrant at the barrier,' the elderly porter instructed him.

Colin stepped out alongside the young man and gave him a friendly smile. 'Catterick?' he asked.

The young man nodded. 'I wonder what it's gonna be like,' he said, giving Colin an anxious glance.

'It should be a lark, once the first few days are over,' Colin replied, grinning.

The young man's face remained serious. 'I 'eard it's the worst place of all,' he said as he changed his rather large suitcase over from one hand to the other. 'I didn't wanna join up. I got a good job.'

They had reached the barrier and, as they were waved through, Colin turned to his new-found companion. 'What d'yer work at?' he asked.

'I'm a sausage-maker at Liptons,' the young man said proudly.

'I worked in a sawmill meself,' Colin said, smiling.

They found an empty carriage and settled down in their seats.

'I might try ter get out on medical grounds,' the young man said.

Colin sighed to himself. It was going to be a long journey to Yorkshire, and if he was not careful it looked as if he would be suffering from extreme depression by the time he got there. 'I don't fink yer got much chance o' that,' he replied. 'I should reckon they're up to all the dodges.'

'I got a weak chest. I get out o' breath quickly an' I can't run very far,' the young man told him.

'There can't be much wrong wiv yer or yer wouldn't 'ave passed the medical,' Colin replied. 'Anyway, they'll soon build yer up.'

Suddenly hurrying footsteps sounded on the platform and three young men crowded into the compartment.

'Soddin' 'ell, I stepped in a lump o' dogshit,' one groaned as he flopped down in the seat.

'Bloody porter told me the wrong platform,' another moaned.

The third young man sat upright in his seat and pulled his cuffs down below his smart suit with a flourish. His long dark hair was wavy and brushed back over his ears, and his grey tie was neatly knotted over a pale blue shirt with cut-away collar. 'I tell yer now, if they come the old acid wiv me I'm gonna cut up rough,' he said, rolling his shoulders. 'I ain't 'avin' no jumped-up sergeant speak ter me like I'm a bit o' shit.'

Colin smiled and studied the other two newcomers. They were both of average build with pale, city faces and fair hair.

'I'm goin' in the Signals. Where are you lot bound for?' the dark-haired one asked.

The fair-haired young man who was still trying to scrape his shoe clean took out a small buff-coloured envelope and glanced at it. 'Royal Signals, Verdun Lines, Catterick Camp. That's what it ses 'ere.'

'That's where I'm bound for,' Colin said.

'Me too.'

'An' me.'

Everyone looked at the other conscript in the long overcoat and the dark-haired young man leaned forward in his seat. 'What about you, uncle? Where they stickin' you?'

The thin young man smiled nervously. 'Verdun Lines, same as you.'

'Well, as it looks like we're gonna be in the same mob, my name's Colin Brennen an' I'm from Bermondsey.'

'I'm Pete Willis an' I come from Stepney.'

'Mick Jackson, from Peckham.'

The smartly dressed young man rolled his shoulders again. 'Ken Moseley, Poplar.'

Once again all eyes went over to the thin young man. 'You got a moniker, uncle?' Ken asked.

'I'm Stanley Upjohn an' I live in Camberwell,' he replied.

The whistle sounded and the train began to move out of the station. Snowflakes rushed past the carriage window as the call-up

179

special picked up speed; soon the occupants were looking out on backs of houses and grimy factories.

'I bet we'll all be glad ter see this again after a month of yes-sir, no-sir, three-bags-full-sir,' Pete remarked.

'I'm gonna tell 'em ter be careful wiv the ole barnet,' Ken said, running his fingers through his thick dark hair. 'Those army barbers nearly scalp yer, so I 'eard.'

Stanley sat with a gloomy expression on his thin face. He seemed to be an object of curiosity to the young man from Poplar. 'What's your view of it all, uncle?' Ken asked him.

'I never wanted ter go in the army. I got a wife an' child ter fink of,' he replied.

'You married? Cor, bloody blimey!' Ken blurted out. 'Bit young ter be spliced an' wiv a kid too, ain't yer?'

'I'm twenty-one. I got a deferment,' Stanley told him.

Mick Jackson studied his dirty shoe for a few seconds. 'I thought I got a bird up the duff once,' he said, smiling comically. 'Four months gone she was before I found out this geezer 'ad it in fer us. Was I pleased? I was gettin' ready fer a pile o' shitty napkins an' sleepless nights.'

'Never go anywhere wivout yer overcoats, that's my motto,' Ken remarked, tapping his hip pocket for effect.

'I was over 'Ackney Marshes one night an' this woman come up ter me,' Pete Willis said. 'Cor, she was ugly. In fact, I nearly jumped wiv fright when she poked 'er 'ead out o' the bushes. She looked like Frankenstein's ole woman. "Like a good time?" she said. Well I looked at 'er fer a few seconds an' then I walked off. She was that ugly. After a few yards I stopped an' turned back. Yer know 'ow it is at times. I was a bit randy an' I'd just got the elbow from me bird. I thought ter meself, yer don't look at the mantelpiece when yer pokin' the fire. Anyway, I walked up ter these bushes an' I ses, "All right, 'ow much?" This ole prosser popped 'er 'ead out o' the bushes an' ses, "Wait yer turn." She was actually on the job, would yer believe?'

'What did you do?' Ken asked.

Pete's eyes sparkled. 'I shouted out to 'er "'Ow much?" an' she pokes 'er mooey out o' the bushes an' ses, "A dollar." So I ses, "Make it 'alf a quid an' yer can 'ave me." Cor, yer should 'ave 'eard the language. She raved off alarmin'. Then this ole geezer pops 'is 'ead out o' the bushes an' calls me everyfing from a pig to a dog.

"Shut up you dirty ole git," I said, an' out 'e comes wavin' 'is walkin'-stick an' 'oldin' 'is strides up. I tell yer lads I 'ad ter scarper on the quick or 'e'd 'ave cracked me skull open.'

Everyone in the carriage was grinning at Pete's story, with the exception of Stanley Upjohn, who looked positively disgusted. His expression was not lost on Ken, who seemed to have taken an immediate dislike to him.

'I fink that was really funny, don't you, uncle?' he said.

Stanley suddenly turned to face him. 'My name's Stanley, not uncle,' he said in a loud voice. 'And for your information, I did not fink that was very funny. Now if yer don't mind, I'd like ter be left alone.'

Ken looked a little abashed. 'Sorry fer you, then, pal. It was only a joke.'

The young conscripts settled down to the long journey, each wrapped up in his own thoughts. Ken and Pete were already starting to doze off. Colin studied the strange young man sitting in the corner seat for a while, wondering what personal torment he was going through, being forced into the army and deprived of his wife and child. He was going to suffer more than the rest, Colin told himself.

It was already dusk when the train finally slowed down on its approach to Richmond Station, having been diverted from the main line on to the track which ran through the Yorkshire Moors. Colin roused himself and saw that his companions were already awake and looking apprehensive.

'I s'pose we'll 'ave ter get a bus ter the camp,' Pete remarked.

'Nah, they'll send a lorry I should fink,' Mick said, yawning widely.

As the train pulled into the tiny station, all hell seemed to break loose. Loudhailers shouted out instructions as weary young men clambered down stiffly from the carriages and stared at a line of military policemen.

'At the double! Come on, you load o' crap! Get yer fingers out,' the red-caps sneered.

Colin hurried along beside his new friends, shocked at the reception they were getting. Suddenly he groaned aloud. Stanley Upjohn's case had spilled on to the platform. As the young man crouched down to repack it, he was grabbed by the scruff of the neck. 'Get yer fat arse in that truck,' a bullet-headed military policeman screamed at him.

Stanley was almost in tears as he quickly grabbed up his gaping case, and as he was bundled off Ken Moseley stopped to pick up the bits and pieces still lying on the platform.

'Don't you understand English, dumbo?' a red-cap shouted in his ear.

The young man from Poplar stood up with the clothes clasped in his hand and faced the soldier hovering over him. 'What's the 'urry, pal. Yer got four weeks ter bawl an' shout,' he said calmly.

For a moment it looked as though the red-cap was going to explode, but instead he waved Ken on. 'In that truck, spiv,' he growled.

Colin hurried along beside Ken, who was cursing under his breath; they found themselves being almost kicked into the rear of the army lorry.

''Ere's yer nightshirt, uncle,' Ken called out, tossing a few pieces of clothing to an ashen-faced Stanley.

'I'm much obliged,' he managed to croak.

The lorry drove through the snow-covered countryside with its cargo of apprehensive young rookies, fresh from their homes and families: some away from home for the first time, others looking forward to the challenge and excitement, and all shocked by their initial introduction to military service. They were cold, tired and hungry, looking forward to a hot meal and a bed to sleep away their weariness, but if they had known what was still awaiting them at Verdun Lines Catterick camp they would have jumped from the vehicle *en masse* and took their chances on the bleak and bitter moors.

The truck drove into the barracks and pulled up outside a large brick building. Other trucks arrived and suddenly there was a hush as everyone looked out from the backs of the lorries at their home for the next four weeks.

'Right, you load of pigswill. Out! Out now!' a booming voice rang out.

Men jumped down from the trucks to see a surprisingly slightly built sergeant-major with a heavyweight voice facing them. Behind him stood the squadron leaders, sergeants, corporals and lance-corporals, all wearing rows of campaign ribbons. Colin stood alongside his friends and waited for the barrage of abuse which he felt sure was coming, but instead the leaders moved forward and began to section men off into groups. From then on everything seemed a mad, dashing manoeuvre from one shed to another as they were kitted out.

'Boot size?'

'Nine an' a 'alf, Sir.'

'Address me as Corporal, lad. 'Ere's a size ten. Grow into 'em.'

'Shirt, vest, pants, army issue, one of each for the use of.'

'I ain't got no mess tins, sir.'

'Too late now. Borrow yer mate's.'

'I ain't got no knife an' fork, Sergeant.'

'God gave yer eight fingers an' two thumbs. Be satisfied.'

Finally the squads of recruits were shown to their dormitory at the double, where they were given a demonstration in how to make a bed, army-style. Worse was to follow as they were all doubled down to the sheds once more to collect their equipment: small packs, large packs, ammunition pouches and straps, bayonets and scabbards, water bottles and waterproof capes.

Back in the dormitory with their supplies lying all over the beds, the by now exhausted recruits watched another demonstration, this time of kitting up. The sergeant smiled like an indulgent parent as his reluctant model, a tall lad from Shropshire, stood adorned in full kit.

'That's how it should be done, my lucky lads,' he said in a quiet voice. 'This webbing has to be blancoed regularly, so when I show you where the NAAFI is you'll all purchase one block of Blanco. Now you'll no doubt be glad to know that it's supper-time. We all like sausage and mash, I take it?'

'Yeah, smashin', Sarge,' one bright young man replied.

'Shut up, you little worm!' boomed the sergeant. 'Speak when you're spoken to! Right now, follow me, at the double.'

At eleven o'clock on a bitter February night, an exhausted number 16 Squadron climbed thankfully into their beds and listened to the camp bugler sounding 'lights out'. Colin stared up at the shadowy ceiling from his hard pillow and thought about his family back home. He was too tired to worry about what was ahead of him and his friends, but he was glad that they had all managed to stay together in 16 Squadron. He thought about Stanley Upjohn who was in the next bed, and he recalled the courageous act of Ken Moseley, who had confronted the bullying red-cap to salvage Stanley's clothes. There were sure to be hard days ahead, but Colin Brennen was determined to make his family proud of him. When they saw him next he would be a trained soldier. Tiredness overcame him, and his last conscious memory that night was of Signalman Stanley Upjohn sobbing into his pillow.

Chapter Twenty-four

The Brennen girls had gathered in their bedroom on Saturday afternoon for a chat and they had been joined by Elsie, who usually called in after shopping. They found the bedroom to be the only place in the house where they could talk together with some privacy, especially when their father was sprawled out asleep in the parlour and their mother was doing the ironing in the scullery. Barbara had been looking forward to the get-together, for she was impatient to announce that she and Jamie had finally named the day. She waited for the right moment to spring the surprise, but as she sat listening to Dawn's tale of woe, she was beginning to feel a little deflated.

'I was really sure that we were gettin' there, but it's all changed this last few weeks,' she sighed. 'I told 'im straight, I wasn't goin' ter play second fiddle to 'is rugby. I mean ter say, Saturday night is special. We should be goin' out tergevver.'

'Well, yer would be,' Barbara replied as she rolled over on the bed and propped her chin on her elbow.

Dawn gave her a hard look. 'I mean on our own, not ter those stupid club socials,' she moaned. 'Who wants ter sit listenin' ter dirty songs and 'ow they beat the ovver team. It's dead borin'. Trouble is, Gordon's firm are rugby mad. They're in some sort o' league, an' it's all about prestige. As far as I'm concerned it's all a load o' nonsense. I told Gordon it was eivver me or rugby.'

'An' what die 'e say?' Elsie asked.

'Rugby,' Dawn said with another big sigh.

'I fink yer bein' a bit unreasonable,' Barbara told her. 'From what yer said, Gordon's got a good position in that firm an' it's only ter be expected 'e'd wanna put 'imself forward. 'E probably sees it as a step on the road ter promotion.'

'Put 'imself forward?' Dawn said in disgust. 'Gordon puts 'imself forward on the field every Saturday an' 'e's beginnin' ter look the worse fer wear. 'E's already 'ad one of 'is teef knocked out, an' last week 'e broke 'is nose, not ter mention all the black eyes an' bruises. I'm frightened ter get near 'im at times.'

'So is it all off then?' Elsie asked her.

'Yup. 'E knows where I live if 'e changes 'is mind, but I ain't gonna sit around waitin' fer 'im,' Dawn said firmly.

Kay was sitting on the bed with her back resting against the wall and she guessed that it would be her turn next.

''Ow's you an' David?' Barbara asked, right on cue.

'I dunno,' she said dismissively. 'I don't fink it's goin' anywhere.'

Elsie gave her a quick look. She had been taken into her younger sister's confidence and had been expecting to hear that it was all over.

'Yer gotta be sure before it gets too serious,' Barbara said. 'Take me an' Jamie. We've bin goin' tergevver now fer the past four years an' there were times when me an' 'im was on the point o' splittin' up, but I'm glad ter say we've got it all sorted out now.'

'That ole muvver of 'is ain't kicked the bucket, 'as she?' Dawn asked grinning.

'No, but she's finally decided she wants ter go in that ole people's 'ome in Dulwich,' Barbara replied. 'Some of 'er ole friends are there an' Jamie's agreed.'

'So it looks like we'll be 'avin' a weddin' in the family soon then,' Dawn said with a sideways glance at Elsie.

'Yes. We've named the day,' Barbara declared triumphantly.

'Well, come on, don't keep us in suspense,' Dawn said quickly.

'The first Saturday in November,' Barbara announced with a smile.

'Cor, that'll be nice,' Elsie said. 'Armistice week. We can all 'ave poppies pinned on us.'

'Couldn't yer make it any earlier?' Dawn asked. 'It's a long while ter wait.'

'Nah, we got a lot o' savin' ter do yet,' Barbara told her. 'Then there's Jamie's muvver. She's gotta be settled down in the ole people's 'ome before'and.'

Dawn got up from her seat at the dressing table and picked up the tea-tray. 'Pass yer empty cups over an' I'll fetch us a fresh cuppa,' she said.

Barbara volunteered to give her a hand; as soon as the two left the room, Elsie turned to Kay. 'I 'ope yer've not got yerself in a three-way stretch,' she said quietly.

'Yer mean wiv Pat Kelly?'

'The same.'

Kay shook her head. 'There's nuffink goin' on wiv me an' Pat,' she replied.

'No, but 'e's back on the scene an' available,' Elsie hinted.

Kay gave her a wry smile. 'As a matter o' fact, David's the one who's bein' pulled in different directions, not me. 'Is wife's back on the scene.'

'Then yer gotta be very careful,' Elsie warned her. 'It'll be you who loses out in the end.'

Kay slid her legs off the bed and leaned forward, her arms resting on her knees. 'It's all soured between me an' David,' she went on. 'We both agreed not ter see each ovver fer a while. Personally I feel that 'e'll end up back wiv 'is wife.'

'Do yer still love 'im?' Elsie asked.

'I thought I did, but now I don't feel anyfing. It's like I'm numb inside,' Kay said, sighing deeply.

'I can understand 'ow yer feel,' Elsie replied. 'We 'ave ter tell ourselves that fings are sometimes done fer the best, although it's small comfort when yer 'eart feels like it's bin torn out.'

Footsteps sounded on the stairs and Barbara came in carrying four cups and saucers on a tray, followed by Dawn who held a filled teapot. 'This is just like when we were kids,' Barbara grinned. 'Remember those secret tea parties we used to 'ave up 'ere?'

'By the way, Danny Adams is gonna fix my street door,' Elsie said, with a quick glance at Kay.

'Will 'e remember where yer live?' Dawn said jokingly.

Elsie was not amused. 'Yer know what really gets ter me? Everybody round 'ere seems ter fink Danny Adams is some sort o' nut-case,' she said irritably.

'I didn't mean anyfing. I was only jokin',' Dawn quickly replied.

'Yeah, I know yer was, but that's the impression it gives,' Elsie told her. 'Danny's no different to anyone else, 'cept 'e's a bit fergetful at times. I fink 'e's a smashin' bloke.'

'Danny likes you too,' Dawn remarked, trying to make amends. 'I remember 'ow 'e was always 'angin' round you when we were all kids on the street. Ter be honest I fancied 'im meself, but 'e only 'ad eyes fer you.'

'I was that bit older. 'E just looked on me like 'e would a big sister,' Elsie replied, smiling. 'Anyway, 'e's comin' round next week ter mend my front door, an' I only 'ope it's when Ernie's not there.'

'Why's that?' Kay asked.

''Cos Ernie tends ter take the piss out of 'im, that's why.'

'That's terrible.'

'That's Ernie – unfortunately,' Elsie said sighing.

It had been a busy day for Joe Mezzo and now, as the customers dwindled and the wintry sun dropped behind the rooftops, he went into the storeroom behind his grocery shop and sat puffing on a large cigar. PC Albert Fuller would be on his way back to the station after his stint on the beat and he had promised to call in. Albert was a rare commodity, Joe felt. He was the sort of beat policeman who should be respected. Joe knew that Albert had no time for the crooked members of his profession, and was saddened that Dockhead Police Station seemed to have more than its share. He had said as much when he called in a few days ago for his parcel of lean back bacon.

Joe's thoughts were interrupted by Maria who popped her head round the door. 'Should I mark Mrs Greenedge's ration book, Joe?' she asked.

'Nah, it's OK. Tell 'er next week,' Joe replied with a sly smile.

Maria was soon back. 'Mrs Greenedge wants ter know if there's any red salmon goin'.'

Joe shook his head. 'Tell 'er I'm waitin' fer some, but not ter let on to anybody.'

Maria gave him a withering look. She knew that her husband was up to his ears in the black market, although he thought he was being clever in denying it to her. Who did he think she was, some silly woman who would not have the sense to see what was going on under her very nose? It was only rarely that he marked his customers' ration books, and where did all the extra supplies come from? She would have had something to say about it, but for the fact that Joe was very supportive to her family back home in Valletta. There were always a few pounds put away, and she herself wanted for nothing. He was a good man, generous to a fault, but he did have that irritating habit of excluding her from his risky wheeling and dealing.

Joe sat puffing on his cigar, his thoughts centred on two hundred cases of red salmon which were already earmarked for his confederates over the water. A few cases spread here and there would soon take care of the consignment, but it had to be completed over the weekend. On Monday morning the driver would walk into the transport office at Cornfield's Wharf and state that he could not find his laden lorry. The distribution centre for National Restaurants too would soon be wondering why their delivery had not been made. Perhaps he had better check with Nick Zanti. He should have it all set up by now.

PC Albert Fuller walked into the storeroom and greeted his old friend as he sat down wearily on a stack of cases containing black-market tinned fruit. 'I'll be glad ter get this day over, Joe,' he sighed. 'I 'ad an ole lady who got locked out of 'er 'ouse, an' then a bloody dog got run over in St James's Road. If that wasn't enough I 'ad a drunk pissin' up against a front door in Dover Lane. The ole woman came out an' went off alarmin'. She was 'oldin' a carvin' knife an' threatenin' ter cut 'is fundamentals off. What a day.'

'Never mind, Albert, 'ere's yer bacon,' Joe said, handing him the rashers neatly wrapped in greaseproof paper. 'What's the latest?'

PC Fuller shook his head slowly. 'Word 'as it that Moody's took a verbal pastin' from the super over that load o' brass fittin's that was nicked over Poplar,' he replied.

'What's that gotta do wiv Dock'ead nick?' Joe asked.

'The transport firm that lost the load is only round the corner from the nick an' the driver comes from Dover Lane,' Fuller explained.

'Oh, I see. So they reckon it was a put-up job,' Joe replied.

'Yeah, they've bin grillin' the driver, but it's all come ter nuffink,' Fuller told him.

''Ave they got any idea who was be'ind it?' Joe asked casually.

PC Fuller looked at his bundle of fresh rashers and felt loath to go on. To answer might well put his future handouts in jeopardy. 'Well, I dunno, but there's talk of some o' your countrymen bein' involved,' the constable said hesitantly. 'But I wouldn't pay no attention ter rumours, 'cos that's all they are.'

Joe puffed on his cigar. 'I 'ad a visit from Sergeant Moody the ovver day,' he replied. ''E wanted ter know if I'd bin approached about buyin' black-market stuff. I told 'im I wouldn't entertain it at any price, an' 'e seemed satisfied I was tellin' 'im the trufe.'

Fuller looked a little guilty. 'I got called in as well,' he said.

189

'Moody asked me about the shops on this manor, an' 'e mentioned yours.'

'Oh, an' what did 'e 'ave ter say?' Joe asked him.

'Only if I thought you were mixed up in the goin's-on round 'ere.'

'I 'ope yer put 'im straight.'

'No sweat, Joe. I told 'im you was as straight as a die.'

'That was good of yer, Albert.'

'Well it's the trufe, ain't it?'

'Sure fing, mate. Like I told the sergeant 'imself.'

Fuller looked down at his clasped hands for a few moments and then his eyes came up to meet Joe's. 'Look, Joe,' he said quietly. 'You an' I 'ave bin good mates fer a good few years now, an' I gotta warn yer. Moody's after stampin' down on the dealin's round 'ere an' 'e'll tread on anyone an' everyone ter get a result. Now, I know you ain't involved in anyfing shady, but be careful who yer seen wiv. Mud sticks. Just watch yerself.'

'I'll do that, Albert, but there's nuffink fer you ter concern yerself wiv,' Joe told him, his mind working overtime. 'Trouble is, I'm in the dark. I go out once a week fer a game o' cards, an' sometimes Maria invites a few friends round fer a drink an' a meal, but ovver than that I don't see anybody.'

Albert Fuller felt that Joe was being either very cagey or very naïve. 'I'm only a beat bobby, Joe,' he replied. 'I only get to 'ear bits an' pieces of what the plainclothes lot are up to, but I can tell yer that those card pals o' yours are bein' watched, an' what's more they're bein' linked wiv nickin' the lorry as well as that ware'ouse break-in at Shad Thames a few months ago: so be warned.'

Joe stubbed out his cigar and held out his hand as Fuller stood up. 'I'll be careful, pal, an' fanks fer everyfing,' he said, smiling.

Albert Fuller patted his breast pocket. 'Well, fanks fer the rashers, Joe. I'll be seein' yer.'

As soon as the policeman had left, Joe picked up the phone. 'That you, Nick? Now listen. About the goldfish. Save a few fer me, but I can't keep 'em in my pond. Yeah, that's right. I'm expectin' the bloke in soon ter do a spring-clean. Nah, it's just a routine visit. We'll all be gettin' one round 'ere.'

Maria had brought Joe in a cup of tea and heard the conversation. 'Goldfish? What yer mean goldfish? We can't keep goldfish in a flat,' she went on at him. 'An' what's this about gettin' someone in ter do the spring-clean. Don't I always keep the place nice an' clean? What d'yer wanna spring-cleaner for, an' in winter as well?'

Joe looked at his wife benignly as she stormed on. She was a good woman, the best, but there were certain things she could not be told, for her benefit. She was deeply religious and went in fear of the church, so for her piece of mind, if nothing else, Joe had to play a shrewd hand. 'Now listen,' he began. 'Yer know 'ow Nick gets worried about that woman of 'is. She ain't sensible like you, Maria. She can't keep this shut,' his fingers going quickly up to his mouth. 'So when I talk ter Nick we use the Costra code.'

'What's the Costra code?'

'It's like backslang.'

'What's backslang?'

Joe puffed loudly. 'It's jumbled talk. Like words meanin' somefing else.'

'Like when I say no an' mean yes?'

'You got it.'

Maria nodded. 'So what does goldfish mean?'

'Salmon, my little sugar plum, salmon.'

'Just as long as it's not that black-market stuff,' she warned.

Charlie Catchpole had decided that enough was enough in any language, and he had finally plucked up the courage to tell Ivy he was leaving her. He hadn't expected her to react in the way she did and it knocked him off balance. Charlie had quite expected to be knocked off balance, with a well-directed backhander from his buxom wife, but instead she flopped down in her chair and snivelled. Charlie could never abide a woman snivelling; he stood for a few moments wondering what he should do.

'Ain't I bin a good wife? Ain't I always 'ad yer meals ready when yer come in?' Ivy asked him as she dabbed at her eyes with her handkerchief.

'That's not why I'm leavin' yer,' Charlie said angrily. 'I'm goin' 'cos yer don't give me a minute's peace. Joe Brennen an' Tom Kelly can sit an' read the papers, an' they can take a nap when they feel like it, but not me. "Charlie, do the winders." "Charlie, do the front step." It's Charlie this, Charlie that. I'm just about fed up wiv it, so I'm orf.'

'Where yer gonna go?' Ivy asked him anxiously.

191

'I dunno. I might stop at the men's 'ostel in Tower Bridge Road. They got clean beds,' he told her.

'None o' them places are very clean, an' who's gonna do yer washin' an' ironin?' she sobbed.

'I'll pay somebody.'

'You ain't got a fancy woman, 'ave yer?'

'No, I ain't. But I bin tempted, the way you've bin goin' on at me lately,' Charlie growled.

'I 'ave ter keep the place clean an' tidy, that's why I get on ter yer, Charlie.'

'Well, in future you can do the bloody winders yerself, and that poxy doorstep,' Charlie shouted. 'I'm just about sick of it. Even me mates are talkin'. The ovver day, one of 'em walked past the door when I was doin' that step an' 'e asked me where me apron was. I've 'ad enough I tell yer.'

Charlie Catchpole stormed out of the house in a huff to begin his late shift, but by the time he reached the railway yard he had calmed down somewhat. Sleeping at the men's hostel was not a very pleasant prospect, he thought, but Ivy needed to be taught a lesson. She was making him a laughing-stock amongst his friends. What was more she was getting fat and idle while he sweated over the chores. A man needed some respect when he was providing the means.

Charlie was still turning everything over in his mind when the first of the laden waggons came rumbling down the line. Normally he would have been ready and waiting, and with his usual skill and agility he would have applied the brake at the precise moment to bring the waggon to a halt just as its spring-loaded buffers connected with the waggon in front. On this occasion, however, the troubled shunter was slow off the mark. He ran alongside the moving waggon and slipped his brake bar into the socket a few seconds too late. The impact was absorbed by the buffers but it was still powerful enough to jolt the half-dozen or so waggons which had already been coupled up.

'Oi, you dozy git!' an irate fellow shunter called out. 'I was between the waggons. Yer could 'ave done me an injury.'

Charlie looked crestfallen and quickly waved his hand in an apology. He had spent many years at the freight yard and knew as well as anyone how important it was to concentrate on what he was doing. Men working there trusted their mates' ability and any lack of concentration could cause serious injury or worse. He took a deep breath and exhaled slowly in an effort to pull himself together. Be careful, he told himself.

At ten o'clock the shunters, loaders and engine drivers congregated in the canteen for their supper break, and when Joe Brennen walked in with Tom Kelly they were met at the door by a grim-faced Charlie Catchpole.

'Me an' Ivy's 'ad a bust-up,' he said simply.

'Oh yeah?' Tom said grinning. 'An' what was it this time?'

'Nah, I'm serious. I walked out on 'er.'

'I fink 'e means it,' Joe said, looking at Tom.

'Too bloody true,' Charlie growled. 'I've 'ad enough. In future she can put the bloody apron on.'

The two old friends watched as Charlie stormed off, then they found a quiet corner to eat their sandwiches and sup their tea.

''Ave you 'eard from young Colin yet, Joe?'

'Nah not yet. I don't s'pose 'e's 'ad the time. 'Ow's Pat gettin' on?'

'I dunno,' Tom replied, shaking his head. ''E seemed quite all right at first but this last week 'e's bin very moody. It's unlike 'im.'

'Yer don't fink 'e's 'ad second thoughts about the bust-up, do yer?' Joe asked.

'Nah, I don't fink so. 'E's bin knockin' back the ole beer a bit lately. I don't fink that's 'elped.'

The men started to drift out from the canteen into the cold night air, and when Joe climbed up on to his tender alongside Bill Cosgrove he saw Charlie Catchpole leaning on his brake bar beside the track. 'I'm gonna start shuntin' the food waggons, Chas. Watch out for 'em,' he called out.

Work got under way once more and the noise of compressed steam, buffeting, clanking waggons and iron wheels on steel track echoed out into the backstreets. Laden freight trucks were moved from loading points to various positions along the track, and from the apparent chaos of frenzied activity, freight trains were made up ready for the night journey south. The railwaymen had worked hard that night, and were coupling up the last few waggons for the Brighton line when a shout went out, 'Get somebody down 'ere quick! It's Charlie. I fink 'e's 'ad it.'

Chapter Twenty-five

Ivy Catchpole had never even considered that Charlie would take it on himself to walk out on her. After all, there weren't many wives who looked after a man the way she did, she told herself. All right, she had insisted on him helping out about the place, but it was only fair that a man should share the burden of running a home. It had been different when the girls were at home, but they had all married and moved away. There was just her and Charlie now, and he should have been glad to help out. Instead he had decided to leave her after all those years together. He must be having a brainstorm. Never mind, just wait till he woke up in the night with the bugs biting. He'd soon wish he was back in his warm bed with someone to cuddle.

Ivy pottered about the house, trying to take her mind off her troubles. Better change the bed, she thought. When Charlie decided he'd had enough of that doss-house, he'd come back with his tail between his legs, and he'd appreciate getting in between clean sheets. Might be an idea to do the front step tomorrow as well. He would see then that she wasn't reliant on him for everything. The neighbours would be a problem. By the morning everyone in the turning would know that Charlie had left her. Still, she would hold her head up and not let them see she was worried.

The epilogue ended and Ivy turned off the wireless. Normally the preacher's late-night broadcast gave her comfort, but tonight he had been going on about compassion and togetherness; silly old fool, she thought as she made herself a cup of cocoa to take to bed with her.

The loud knock startled her and she hurried to answer the door, putting on a bright face to let Charlie know he was welcome back.

'I'm sorry, Ivy, but Charlie's 'ad an accident,' Joe told her quietly.

'Oh my Gawd!' Ivy gasped, her hand going up to her face. 'What's 'appened?! Is 'e 'urt bad?!' The look on Joe's face made her heart start to pound.

'They've took 'im ter Guy's, luv,' he told her. 'Charlie was found beside the track. 'E was unconscious.'

Ivy grabbed her coat from behind the front door. 'I'm on me way,' she blurted out, her face ashen.

'Ada said she'll go wiv yer,' Joe told her. 'She's all ready.'

The two women hurried out into the Old Kent Road hoping to catch a late-night tram, but the thoroughfare looked deserted. Ada held on to Ivy's arm as the two of them walked quickly past the shuttered shops and pubs, feeling the ground beneath them growing slippery with night frost.

'I never meant ter make 'im feel bad. I can't understand why 'e would wanna do it,' Ivy said, choking back tears.

'Do what?' Ada asked her.

'I thought yer might 'ave 'eard from the neighbours about Charlie leavin' me,' Ivy replied.

'When?'

'Ternight, just before 'e left fer work. 'E told me 'e wasn't comin' back.'

'I don't fink 'e'd mean it, luv. 'E was most prob'ly in a temper,' Ada said reassuringly.

'Oh, 'e meant it all right.'

'Well, don't worry about it now, gel,' Ada said in a kind voice.

''E could be dead by the time we get there,' Ivy said breathlessly.

The yellow-brick building loomed out of the gathering mist, and when the two anxious women hurried up to the reception desk in casualty they were met by Tom Kelly.

'I came in the ambulance wiv Charlie,' he told them. 'The doctor's wiv 'im now.'

'What 'appened?' Ivy gasped.

'We don't know, luv,' Tom said quietly. 'One o' the lads found 'im lyin' by the side o' the line. It could 'ave bin an 'eart attack or a stroke. There was no sign of injury, apart from a bruise on 'is cheek. 'E would 'ave done that fallin'.'

Tom led the way along a wide white corridor to a wooden bench outside a frosted-glass panelled door. Ivy sat and stared down at her feet, her hands clenched tightly in her lap and Ada sat close to her, not wanting to intrude into her troubled thoughts. Tom Kelly stood a few yards away, idly watching the activity at the far end of the corridor. After what seemed like an eternity to Ivy, the door opened and a serious-faced young doctor came out.

'Mrs Catchpole?' he said, looking at each of the two women who had jumped up quickly.

'I'm Mrs Catchpole,' Ivy replied.

'Your husband's either taken a knock which rendered him unconscious or he fainted, which would account for the bruising on his face,' the doctor told her. 'I don't think it was a heart attack, but we won't know for sure until we do tests. He's regained consciousness but he's very groggy, as you would imagine.'

'Could it 'ave bin a stroke?' Ivy asked him.

'I wouldn't have thought so, but we can't be sure yet. As I said, we'll do some tests and then I'll be able to let you know,' the doctor went on. 'Your husband doesn't seem to know what happened, but it might come back to him once he has rested up. He'll be taken up to a ward as soon as we can get a porter.'

'Can I see 'im?' Ivy asked.

'Yes, you can, but not for long. Mr Catchpole needs to get some rest.'

Ivy went into the room and caught her breath as she saw Charlie propped up on a bench in the corner. His face was the colour of the sheet he had over him, and she could see the angry purple bruise on his right cheek. ''Ow yer feelin', luv?' she said softly.

'Not so bad,' he replied in little more than a whisper. 'I don't know 'ow I got 'ere. One minute I was swingin' on the brake bar then it all went black.'

'Well, yer gotta rest, so the doctor said,' she told him. 'I've bin told not ter stay long.'

Charlie smiled wanly. 'I might 'ave brought this on meself, gel,' he said. 'I couldn't stop finkin' about what I'd said ter yer before I left ternight.'

'It's all right. I've changed the bed an' there's nice clean sheets on. I've also changed the curtains in the parlour. I'm gonna do the winders termorrer, an'—'

'Now don't get all soppy,' Charlie said as he saw the tears start to fall. 'I'll do 'em for yer. I don't care what the blokes say. Sod 'em all.'

'There's gonna be some changes made from now on, luv. I'm

gonna do more work around the 'ouse an' you're gonna take it easy. I've bin a bad wife ter yer. I can see it now.'

'Now don't you be so silly. Yer the best gel a feller could wish for. I just ain't appreciated yer up till now,' Charlie said softly.

Ivy dabbed at her eyes, then she bent down and gave him a gentle kiss on his bruised cheek. 'I better get goin' before they chuck me out,' she told him. 'I'll come in termorrer at visitin' time. Now try ter get some rest.'

As she reached the door, Charlie raised his hand. 'By the way, can yer iron me apron, luv?' he said, grinning widely.

The cold bleak days had not unduly troubled Pat Kelly. The labour of cable-laying was hard and demanding, but he had a good gang to work with. They were running a tight schedule, and when he seemed a little more gruff than usual or a little less inclined to share a joke, his gang put it down to the pressure he was under from the management to complete on time. A few of the men who knew something of his personal life did not think his sometimes hard-handedness and gruffness had anything to do with the break-up of his marriage. They knew their ganger to be a Jack-the-lad who was no doubt having a great time with the girls now that he was fancy-free.

When the picks, shovels, drills and cable-drawing ropes had been stowed away for the night, and the gang sent home, Pat Kelly felt the dark mist of depression begin to close down on him. He had a choice to make after finishing his tea and flicking through the evening paper. It was either a night spent round the fire listening to the wireless, or a stroll to one of the local pubs. The alternative would be a night at the cinema, but he never felt comfortable sitting alone in the pictures. He had tried sitting at home during the bitter cold weather, but the wireless tended to send him off to sleep and when it was time for bed he lay twisting and turning for half the night. A few drinks helped to dull the depression and allowed him to sleep soundly, although the morning-after feeling was invariably something he had to work through.

The wind near the river felt extra cold, and Pat dug his hands deeper into his overcoat pocket as he walked into the narrow lane and saw the welcoming light from Chippy's pub illuminating the wet cobblestones. It was the first time he had gone to that particular pub since the night he took Kay Brennen along with him and he smiled sadly to himself as he saw her in his mind. She had captivated him with her sorrowful expression and wistful smile and he remembered how he had felt for her. She had been just a child when he went into the Army, and she had still seemed a child when he returned home, but the recent few years of his courtship and marriage had seen her blossom into a beautiful, desirable young woman. He had been smitten by her innocence and her delicate beauty and he could not get her out of his mind.

'Well, if it ain't our ole mate, Patrick me lad,' Chippy said grinning. 'An' 'ow the bloody 'ell are yer?'

Pat shrugged his broad shoulders as he slapped a ten-shilling note down on the wet counter. 'I'm cold, miserable an' thirsty, pal, so what yer gonna do about it?' he replied.

Chippy pulled down on the beer pump and watched the dark frothy brew rise up slowly in the pint glass. 'Well, this is sure ter quench the thirst, an' that fire over there is banked up enough ter take the ache out o' yer bones, but the miseries are somefing else. Maybe a chat'll 'elp ter raise yer spirits. Now what do we talk about? The current general feelin' is that a third world war is inevitable in the not too distant future, an' wiv that in mind the construction of atomic shelters fer the general public is goin' ahead at a brisk pace. If that's too gloomy a topic fer discussion, 'ow about the current climate in the Far East?'

Pat picked up his pint and took a long draught. 'Go on.'

'Well, it seems there's trouble brewin' along the thirty-eighth parallel, an' in India the separatists are 'ard at work,' Chippy went on. 'The Middle East is like a tickin' time-bomb, an' if yer want more, take the population explosion. By the year nineteen-'undred-an'-frozen-ter-death, the world's population will 'ave trebled. 'Ow we gonna feed 'em all? That's the burnin' question.'

'Fanks, Chippy, yer've raised me spirits no end,' Pat said, smiling.

The ragged-looking landlord leaned forward over the counter and stroked his two-day growth of stubble. 'Seriously, pal, it don't do ter dwell, whether it be on current affairs, world problems or the prolongation o' the species. Better ter drown the 'ole bloody lot in God's own brew. Yes, my friend, God's brew. When 'e made the earth, 'e 'ad a load on 'is plate, what wiv finkin' about the green fields an' the runnin' rivers, but wiv all what 'e 'ad on 'is mind 'e never fergot ter put the 'ops in Kent. Now, I'll ask yer a simple question. What ovver use can yer fink of fer 'ops, ovver than fer brewin'? No, yer can't. I tell yer somefing else too. If the Lord God come down on earth terday, 'e'd knock off preachin' fer a spell an' 'e'd go an' sample a nice pint o' bitter.'

'Well, if 'e does, I 'ope 'e don't come in 'ere, Chippy.' Pat was grinning. 'Wiv your chat, yer'd drive 'im straight back wiv the multitudes.'

The scruffy landlord walked away to serve an elderly man who stood at the counter biting on the broken stem of his clay pipe. 'There we are, Nobby. Now take it steady. I don't wanna 'ave ter be carryin' you 'ome again,' he said, passing over a pint of ale.

The old man broke into a chuckle which brought on a fit of coughing, which in turn caused his face to flush scarlet. 'Yer'll be the bloody finish o' me one day,' he said when he regained his composure.

'Yer'll be the finish of yerself if yer don't take that cough medicine I've just given yer,' Chippy told him.

Pat finished his pint and then pushed the empty glass across the counter. 'Fill it, Chippy. One fer yerself an' one fer Nobby.'

The old man raised his half-empty glass. 'Gawd bless yer, son,' he said, smiling.

Pat walked over to the fire with his fresh pint and sat contemplating the tiny, flickering blue flames coming from the banked-up coke. In the background he could hear Nobby talking to another elderly man.

'Nah, yer wrong, Bert. It was the Russians who got ter Berlin first. That's why we never got ter put old 'Itler on trial.'

''Itler committed suicide,' Bert replied.

'Oh no 'e never. The Russkies done 'im in, stan's ter reason. 'Itler never 'ad the bottle ter top 'imself. They done it for 'im.'

'P'raps yer right,' Bert went on, 'but the Russkies would never 'ave got ter Berlin first if ole General Patten 'ad 'ad 'is way. 'E wanted ter cross the Rhine an' go 'ell-fer-leavver ter Berlin. 'E would 'ave done it, too, if ole Churchill 'adn't stopped 'im. Too risky 'e said. Churchill was worried about the casualties.'

Pat smiled sadly to himself as he listened to the old men discussing the war, and his thoughts drifted back to an isolated airfield the night before D-Day. They were discussing casualties then, and the officer commanding had had a few words to say on the subject. He had reminded his blacked-up and kitted-out paratroopers that casualties could be kept to a minimum if the surprise element worked. The battalion had orders to drop over Normandy during the night, secure two bridges and hold them till they were relieved by the invading forces the next day.

Pat recalled the thoughts running through his mind in the aircraft that night as it winged its way across the channel. Eighty per cent casualties were to be expected in such a dangerous mission, he had heard said, but he discounted it. He was young and full of himself. He would survive, and if not then he would die fighting and take a few of the enemy with him. Brave thoughts, but soon he was to understand just what war was all about. He remembered the red light going on and the men all standing and doing their last-minute checks as they hooked up to the static line. Green on, and they were off, tumbling out of the plane into space, down, down, until the reassuring jerk on the harness as the chute billowed. For a few precious seconds it was peaceful, a sense of euphoria as he floated down from the starlit night sky. Then all hell broke loose. Flares lit up the drifting paratroops and small-arms fire opened up. Some men were killed before they reached the ground, and the lucky ones braced themselves for the shock of landing. It was like a terrible nightmare: the flares, bullets flying, and mortars shrieking towards them. Men were screaming and dying in the headlong rush to take the bridge.

Pat's glass was empty once more; when he walked over to the counter for a refill he discovered that his hands were shaking. They had been shaking that night too, and he remembered the loud clatter of his sten gun as he raked the bridge office with fire. His sergeant fell as he ran alongside, and two other paras fell, but somehow Pat reached the bridge office without a scratch. The German sentry who suddenly appeared in front of him seemed as startled as he was, and for a fraction of a second their eyes met. The German must have been out of ammunition, for he swung the butt of his rifle and gasped loudly as the eight-inch commando knife went into his chest up to the hilt.

'Pat? Pat, you all right?'

The young man steadied himself and saw that the empty glass he had been holding was shattered. 'Yeah, I'm OK. Sorry, I must 'ave slipped,' he said quickly.

'Yer've cut yerself. 'Ang on, I'll get me medical box,' Chippy said, hurrying into the back room.

When the inch-long cut had been cleaned with iodine and pinched together with thin strips of sticking plaster, Chippy applied a bandage. 'There we are,' he grinned. 'Florence Nightingale couldn't 'ave done better.'

Pat stood at the bar studying his fresh glass, alone with his troubled thoughts. He had tried to put the incident on that bridge to the back of his mind and forget it, but it kept coming back. It was one incident of many that he wished to God had never happened, but war was total, brutal and terrible. The memories of battle would always be there, rearing up to haunt and torment the survivors. He thought he had come to terms with what he had done, but tonight the image of that young soldier he had killed rose up like a phoenix to torture him. Why?

'I should go 'ome if I were you, Pat. Yer look like yer need the sleep.'

The young man nodded. 'Yeah, I fink yer right. One more, an' then I'm off.'

'Don't say I didn't warn yer,' Chippy told him as he refilled the glass.

Margie Dolan pulled her fur collar up around her ears and stepped out smartly, her high heels echoing on the cobblestones. She had had two punters that evening, and that was enough for any working girl as far as she was concerned. She had had it all planned: a nice soak in the bath, and then she would slip in between the sheets and dream of meeting the perfect customer. He would be very wealthy and adore her to death. He would insist that she gave up the game and kept her body for his pleasure only. He would not be too demanding but he would lavish her with expensive gifts. A holiday in Bournemouth at a smart hotel. A new fur coat from Harrods, and other luxuries too. It would all come her way, in her dream at least.

Margie had run the bath and suddenly realised that she was out of cigarettes. Chippy's was sure to be open, and as she hurried along the cold street she smiled to herself. She was forty and already getting fat. Her hair was losing its lustre and the bags under her eyes were not a pretty sight to behold. Never mind, she still had her loyal punters, and they put a few perks her way.

''Ello, Margie luv. 'Ow's commerce?' the landlord asked her as she walked up to the counter puffing loudly.

'So-so. Give us a large brandy an' a packet o' Capstan full strength, darlin',' she told him.

Chippy glanced over towards the fire as he raised a brandy bowl to the optic and saw that Pat Kelly had fallen asleep. ''E's bin fightin' the demons ternight,' he said sadly.

'Is that Pat Kelly?' Margie asked.

'Yeah, that's 'im. I'm frightened 'e's gonna topple off that chair an' land up in the fire.'

'Woman trouble?'

'No less.'

''E looks like 'e should be 'ome an' in bed,' Margie remarked as she took a sip from her brandy.

''E's got a fair ole walk back. I dunno if 'e's gonna make it,' Chippy said.

'Can't yer call a cab?' she asked.

'Nah, they won't take drunks,' he reminded her.

'Bloody shame. 'E could 'ave an accident goin' 'ome, the state 'e's in,' Margie sighed.

'Margie.'

'Yeah?'

'I was just finkin'.'

'Yeah?'

'I wonder if . . .'

'No, Chippy. No, I couldn't. I've got a good reputation ter consider.'

'But . . .'

'No buts. I said no an' I mean no.'

'Yeah, yer right. I shouldn't 'ave asked,' Chippy said solemnly. 'I reckon the air'll sober 'im up a bit. I reckon so, don't you?'

'Yeah, course it will.'

'Still, yer never know when they're like that.'

Margie finished her drink and looked hard at the scruffy landlord. 'All right, you win. I'll put 'is 'ead on a piller. It'll cost yer though,' she said smiling.

'Name yer price.'

'One large brandy.'

'Good as done.'

Pat Kelly did not resist as Margie and Chippy helped him to his feet, and he gave the prostitute a crooked smile as she led him out into the cold night air.

'Come on, Pat, yer doin' fine.'

'I . . . I dunno what came over me,' he mumbled.

'Yer tired, Pat. Yer'll be right as ninepence in the mornin'.'

As she leaned the drunken young man against the wall and fished into her handbag for her front door key Margie saw the righteous Mrs Peabody peering through her lace curtains opposite.

'It's all right, lovey,' she called out. 'I found 'im in the gutter. I'm only chargin' 'im 'alf price.'

Chapter Twenty-six

Danny Adams had started work at the municipal baths in Spa Road, and he soon settled into the routine. The head attendant, Len Thompson, had taken him under his wing and given him a few pointers which helped to make the job easier. It was pleasant to work inside during the cold spell, Danny thought, and he considered himself quite smart in his white trousers and short-sleeved shirt, which was all he needed to wear in the hot, steamy atmosphere. His job was to fill the large baths, mop out the cubicles and collect all the used towels. He had often used the baths himself, and was familiar with the procedure. Customers bought a bath ticket at the reception window and were able to pay for an extra towel and a small cake of soap, as well as a sachet of hair shampoo. Many customers brought their own soap, preferring it to the hard bath-house variety, which did not provide a very good lather, and Len was quick to point out the implications to the new recruit.

'Collect the soap if they leave it, an' store it in a tin box,' he said, smiling slyly. 'Yer can earn a few bob a week by givin' the customers your soap when they complain about that rubbishy stuff they've bin given. Yer'll find that they tend ter give yer a tip if yer look after 'em. Anuvver fing too,' he went on. 'Watch the towels after they're finished wiv. Some are werf dryin' off yerself. Keep 'em 'andy in a cupboard. Yer'll often get asked fer an extra towel.'

Danny thanked him and started off enthusiastically. He made sure that the baths were properly swilled and cleaned between each customer, and he endeavoured to be on hand for the usual requests for more hot water, and a decent bit of soap.

The first week went well, and as he was required to work all day on Saturday, Danny was given Thursday off. He was feeling fine and the headaches were not troubling him, so he decided to use his free time to fix Elsie Gates's front door. It was not much of a job. A few shavings off the edge and bottom allowed it to shut cleanly, and he adjusted the lock setting to make it easier to use the key. Elsie had seemed pleased when he told her it would be five shillings and she had given him an extra half-crown.

Danny sat thinking about Elsie during a quiet spell late on Saturday afternoon. He had always liked her, and he remembered how she used to find time for him when they were all kids on the street. He had been concerned to see how sad she looked and how dowdy she had become. She had a nice figure and a pretty face, and her fair hair had always been well groomed. Now, though, she wore it pulled back in a ribbon, and did not seem to bother with make-up. Her shoulders too were rounded, and she looked tired and careworn.

'More 'ot water in number seven, please, mate,' a voice called out.

Danny had not realised that number seven cubicle was being used, and guessed that one of the other attendants had let the man in while he was on tea-break. He turned on the hot water valve outside the cubicle, and heard the water start to gush, then the customer's voice again.

'Fanks, mate. Ain't got any decent soap, 'ave yer? This stuff ain't no good.'

Danny found a tablet of partly used Palmolive soap in his tin and slid it under the door.

'That's better,' the occupant called out. 'I'll smell like Peter the Pouff wiv this.'

Danny smiled to himself and leaned against the cubicle while he waited for the man to call out when the bath water was hot enough.

Len Thompson walked into the section and nodded a greeting. 'Got a minute, Danny?' he asked. 'I want yer ter mop those end cubicles out when yer get a chance. Lofty's gone fer a tea-break an' left 'em.'

Danny followed his supervisor along the gangway, wanting to look willing. 'Yeah, no trouble,' he said.

''Ow yer findin' it 'ere?' Len asked him.

'I like it. I like bein' left alone ter get on wiv a job,' Danny replied with a smile.

'Well, you stick wiv it an' after a few weeks we'll see about givin' yer a spell in the steam rooms,' Len told him. 'It's a bit sticky in there, as you'd imagine, but the wages are better an' the tips are good.'

Back in number seven cubicle, the occupant was beginning to feel that the temperature was just about right. 'OK, mate. Fanks,' he called out, and then, 'All right, that'll do. Turn it off, mate. Bloody 'ell, it's gettin' 'ot!'

Danny decided to get started with the mopping. Suddenly he caught his breath as he remembered leaving the hot water running in number seven. He dashed back to hear the man cursing in the cubicle, and then the door opened to reveal a perspiring Jim Carney with a towel wrapped around his middle.

'I feel like a bleedin' lobster,' he growled. 'Didn't you 'ear me call out?'

Danny knew the railwayman by sight and by name, although he had never before spoken to him. 'I'm sorry, Jim. I got called away.'

'You should be sorry. I could 'ave bin scalded,' Jim told him. 'I've 'alf a mind ter report this. It ain't safe to 'ave a bleedin' barf lately, what wiv one fing an' anuvver.'

'I said I'm sorry,' Danny replied quietly. 'I didn't do it on purpose.'

'That's not the point,' Carney went on. 'Do you realise I could 'ave 'ad a serious injury?'

Danny felt himself getting tense as he listened to the moaning, and a pain started up suddenly at the base of his skull.

'Now what's all the trouble?' Len asked as he came up.

'This bleedin' clown tried ter scald me,' Jim raved.

The supervisor faced him squarely. 'Right, sir. When you're dressed I'll sort it all out. Just knock on the office door on yer way out. Yer know where I mean?'

Jim nodded and then gave Danny a blinding look as he closed the cubicle door.

'I'm very sorry,' Danny said beginning to feel distressed. 'I ... I ...'

'Just leave it ter me,' Len said quickly as he walked off.

Ten minutes later, Jim Carney was seated in the supervisor's office, looking as though he had been lying in the sun. 'I wanna take this all the way,' he said firmly. 'I ain't one ter complain, but there's a limit.'

Len nodded. 'Right, Mr Carney. Now, I should warn yer that ter press fer damages against Bermondsey Borough Council Baths yer gotta get medical evidence ter support it. It'll mean the council doctor takin' a look at yer, an' 'e may suggest a skinoptomy.'

'A what?' Jim asked quickly.

'A skinoptomy. What it means is they take a slice o' skin off yer,' Len explained. 'They take about a four-inch square piece off the top o' yer leg. It don't 'urt – well, not all that much.'

'What the bloody 'ell for?' a shocked Jim Carney asked.

'Well, yer see they gotta test it ter see if yer've bin boiled. I mean ter say anyone could come in 'ere wiv a bit o' sunburn an' blame it on the 'ot water, now couldn't they?'

'What, in the depths o' winter?' Jim said sarcastically.

'Yeah, but in the summer they could, so that's why they do these tests,' Len told him. 'Oh, an' one more fing while we're talkin'. Yer won't be able ter use these baths again. Well, not till it's all sorted out.'

'Why not?'

'Well, if yer claimin' negligence, yer wouldn't wanna put yerself in danger again, now would yer? It's like gettin' knocked down an' then standin' in the middle o' the road again,' Len said.

'So bang goes me weekly barf.'

'You could always go over ter Poplar. They've got a good municipal baths,' Len told him.

Jim was beginning to wonder whether he had been a little hasty in complaining. 'I don't wanna make no fuss, but I could 'ave got boiled alive,' he said.

'Well, it's up ter you, but if yer do wanna take this furvver there's a ten-page questionnaire ter fill in,' Len warned him. 'I know it sounds a bit dauntin', but it 'as ter be done. I could 'elp yer if yer like. Come round on Monday an' we can go frew it. It'll only take us a couple of hours. Oh, by the way, 'ave yer ever 'ad a test fer epilepsy?'

'No, why?'

'If yer an epileptic yer not s'posed ter come in 'ere wivout a certificate. So if yer do decide ter proceed, I'll get yer an epilepsy testin' form an' yer take it ter the testin' centre at Barkin'.'

'Barkin'?'

'I fink it's Barkin', or maybe it's Dagenham, I'm not sure. Anyway, they just do some tests. It shouldn't cost yer much, a couple o' quid I should fink.'

'Ere, ferget it,' Jim said, getting up quickly. 'I can't piss-ball about wiv tests an' form-fillin'.'

'I wish yer'd 'ave told me sooner,' Len replied, putting on a stern look. 'That poor chap outside was really worried about yer, an' 'e was only tryin' ter do 'is job. Somefing like this could ruin 'im fer life.'

Jim Carney looked concerned. 'Don't worry, I'll 'ave a word wiv 'im on the way out,' he said reassuringly.

'Well, I fink that's big of yer,' Len told him smiling.

Jim stood up. 'We're both men o' the world.'

The baths supervisor waited until he was sure the placated customer was off the premises before calling Danny into his office. 'Don't worry, son, we got it all sorted out,' he told him.

'Fanks, Len. I thought I was out on me ear fer a while,' Danny said gratefully.

'Nah. Jim Carney's bin comin' in 'ere fer 'is barf as long as I can remember,' Len explained. ''E's always moanin' about somefing or the ovver. 'E was never gonna make it 'ard fer yer.'

'Well, fanks anyway,' Danny said, looking relieved.

'That's all right, son. Yer better get off 'ome.'

At five o'clock, Len locked up the office and then checked the cubicles before leaving the baths. It had been a satisfying day on the whole, he thought as he walked home through the murky back-streets. He had promised the manager of the labour exchange that he would keep an eye on Danny Adams after finding out from him a little of the young man's case-history. Len had a vested interest anyway. His own son had flown in Lancasters with the RAF during the war, and he had returned home unscathed.

Grace Dines was in a bad mood as she stirred away at the pot of greens. They were all getting a little too comfortable in the neighbourhood now, she told herself resentfully. At one time she could expect at least six or seven callers during the day, each of them desperate to borrow a few pounds. Now she was lucky if she got more than five or six callers a week. Maybe she should send that lazy, good-for-nothing son of hers out to work. His eyes were not nearly as bad as he made them out to be. He could find his way to the pub every night. Norman wouldn't have stood by and let her struggle to make ends meet. He would have been earning his keep and not forcing her to dig into her life savings.

The old lady added another pinch of soda to the greens and then she checked the potatoes with a fork. They were breaking up in the water nicely. Simon wasn't too keen on mashed potatoes, greens and pork sausages, but he would have to put up with it. He would be more at home with roast beef and Yorkshire pudding, but her teeth and jaws would not stand the chewing.

''Ow long's dinner gonna be?' Simon asked as he walked into the steamy scullery.

'About twenty minutes,' the old lady replied, giving him a quick look. 'While yer waitin' yer might as well take a look at that front door chain. It don't look too secure ter me. I don't want anybody bargin' in 'ere while you're up the pub.'

'Yeah, all right,' Simon sighed.

Grace Dines opened the door of the oven and pulled out the sizzling sausages. They were nearly ready, she decided. There was time to put everything away before she served up the meal.

'This screw-eye is a bit loose. It's the wood it's in. It's rotted,' Simon told her as he walked back into the scullery.

'I guessed as much,' the old lady said. 'You keep an eye on those greens an' watch they don't boil over while I lock up.'

Simon peered into the large pot with distaste and saw the yellowing greens swirling about in the water. The potatoes didn't look too good either. He sighed, knowing that in a few minutes he would be sitting down to a plate of slopped-up, almost inedible rubbish. She couldn't even cook sausages properly. They would most likely be underdone. It wouldn't be so bad if she'd let him have sauce with it, but she didn't allow it in the house. It would have been a good painkiller, since it was painful trying to eat her cooking.

The old lady hurried into the parlour and slipped off the string loop with the key on it, then she gathered up the small money-box and notebook which were lying on the corner of the table and put them into the sideboard drawer. Finally she locked the drawer and slipped the key string back over her head. It was a ritual which took place about that time every night after Simon had slipped the heavy chain across the front door.

As she went back into the scullery, Grace Dines felt the key with her hand to reassure herself that it was safe under the bodice of her long black cotton dress. She had to be careful. Simon had a nasty habit of nosing about in drawers and cupboards, and he must never be given the opportunity of going into that particular drawer. Apart from the money and her policies, there was the amended will which had been drawn up by her solicitor only a few months ago.

Simon was sitting at the small table reading an old newspaper, and Grace gave him a withering look. 'The gas 'as gone out under the greens,' she remarked. 'Yer just sat there an' watched 'em boil over.'

'No, I never, I turned 'em out. They're almost boiled away,' he told her sharply.

The old lady served up the meal while her son watched with a look of disgust on his face. Much more of this pigswill and I'll be a gastric ulcer case, he thought to himself.

'What yer gonna do about that door?' she asked him as they sat down to their meal.

'I'll 'ave ter get somebody ter fix it. It'll need a new piece o' wood in the frame,' Simon told her.

'Well, yer better not leave it too long. I gotta be sure I'm safe while you're gallivantin' about up the pub,' Grace Dines growled.

Her much-maligned son gave her a look that spoke volumes. Sitting in the Red Lion with a pint at his elbow in company with a few old men could hardly be described as gallivanting. She was getting worse as she got older. It was quite likely she would end up dying without making a will, or she might take it into her head to leave all her money to the RSPCA; not that she was an animal-lover, but just to spite him. Pity he couldn't get hold of that key she kept round her neck. All her private stuff was in that locked drawer.

At nine o'clock, Simon left the house and heard the chain go across the door, then his mother's croaky voice, 'Don't be too long.'

Simon gave a deep sigh of frustration. 'I'll swing fer 'er one day,' he muttered aloud.

Pat Kelly had managed to get back to his old self after the night spent in Margie Dolan's bed. He had woken up very early and spent some time trying to remember where he was, and it was only when his host came in with a cup of sweet tea that he vaguely recalled her holding on to his arm as they walked through the dark, cold street. Margie was wearing a flowing cotton robe over a flimsy nightdress and she smiled indulgently.

'You gave me trouble last night,' she told him.

'I didn't, did I?' he asked her as he sat up in bed and winced at the pain in his head.

'Didn't what?'

'I didn't take liberties, did I?'

'Well, yer didn't take kindly ter me takin' yer strides off. I expect yer thought I was gonna rape yer,' Margie said grinning.

Pat looked at the pillow beside him and then at the buxom blonde. 'Where did you sleep?' he asked her.

'That's where I park the punters,' she said. 'I slept in the next room. That room is out o' bounds.'

Pat drank his tea and dressed quickly. 'I don't s'pose yer got a razor? No, course yer wouldn't,' he said, smiling sheepishly.

Margie left the room and came back carrying a large towel. ''Ere you are. Barfroom's first on the left,' she told him. 'Yer'll find a razor and shavin' soap in the cabinet over the sink.'

Pat washed and shaved, then patted his smooth face with cold water. He felt much better when he finally walked into the scullery and found Margie frying eggs and bacon.

'Get this down yer, Pat,' she told him. 'Yer look awful.'

At seven o'clock, Pat slipped on his coat and took Margie by the shoulders. 'Look, luv, don't fink I don't appreciate what yer did fer me last night, an' this mornin',' he told her. 'We'll 'ave a drink tergevver in Chippy's one night. An' if you ever need anyfing, just let me know.'

Margie went up on her toes and kissed the tall young man on the cheek. 'I'll remember to,' she said. 'Now get goin' or yer'll be late fer work.'

She sat down heavily as the front door slammed shut. If only she were a few years younger and a bit less plump, she sighed, the rest of the girls wouldn't stand a chance with him.

Chapter Twenty-seven

The fifth annual meeting of the Jolly Boys was convened in the railway club on Saturday night, the only night the freight yard was closed and all the members were available. Walter Smith chaired the meeting, his huge bulk and deep voice giving him a commanding presence. Walter worked in the freight office and was one year away from retirement. On his right was Maurice Woodley, the secretary. Maurice was in his fifties, a tall, thin individual who had been awarded the British Empire Medal for his wartime service in the Heavy Rescue Squad. Joe Brennen, the current treasurer, sat on the chairman's left, his hands clasped over the accounts book.

Five other members sat around the large polished table: Tom Kelly, Bill Cosgrove, Alec Bromfield, a short, stocky man with ginger hair who worked on track maintenance, Jack Springer the newsagent, and Charlie Catchpole, who had only been discharged from hospital that morning. The diminutive Charlie still looked a little pale and subdued, but he had insisted on attending the meeting, despite Ivy's plea for him to rest up.

Walter Smith opened the meeting by welcoming Charlie back into the fold, and the indestructible shunter decided to take the opportunity of reporting to the committee on his current matrimonial situation.

'I s'pose you all know that me an' Ivy 'ad a bust-up last week an' I decided ter piss orf. Well, I can tell yer now that my ole dutch come round ter my way o' finkin', so I'm givin' it anuvver go.'

'Good fer you, Chas, an' 'ow's the barnet?' Walter asked.

'Not too bad,' Charlie told him. 'I 'ad a bit o' concussion, so they told me.'

''Ow the bloody 'ell did it 'appen?' Alec Bromfield asked him.

Charlie smiled self-consciously. 'I wasn't concentratin' on what I was doin' an' I got a whack on the crust.'

''Ow did yer manage that?' Alec persisted.

'I dunno, do I?' Charlie replied irritably. 'All I know was, I was chasin' after the waggon an' I remember trippin' over a sleeper. The next fing I know I'm propped up in bed in Guy's. I reckon I cracked me 'ead on the line.'

'Yer frightened the bleedin' life out o' me,' Alec went on. 'I thought yer was dead when I looked down at yer.'

'Look, I fink we should postpone the court of inquiry over Charlie's barnet an' get down ter the business in 'and,' Walter said in his deep voice.

'Go on then, Walter,' Charlie told him.

The chairman gave the little shunter a hard look and then proceeded. 'Now, as you are all aware, every year since we formed the Jolly Boys in '45 we've 'eld a community get-tergevver an' this year'll be no different,' he began. 'The first item on the agenda is ter decide what we should do wiv the money we'll raise. Last year it went ter the Railwaymen's Orphans' Fund when we raised the grand total of one 'undred an' fifty-five quid. This year we've got two proposals on the table so we've got a decision ter make. On one side we've got two deservin' cases, Mrs Comfrey an' Mrs Robbins, both railway widows an' both strugglin' ter make ends meet, an' on the ovver side we've got the Railwaymen's Sick Fund. I'd like ter call on our secretary ter give yer the update. Maurice?'

The secretary coughed to clear his throat and then looked round the table. 'Gentlemen, I gotta report the sad news that Mrs Robbins died a few weeks ago,' he began, 'but Mrs Comfrey is still alive, I'm pleased ter say, though she's livin' on 'ard times. I went round ter see 'er a few weeks ago an' she's not a well woman. She suffers from bronchitis an' she's got no family ter turn to. I gave 'er a grant of five pounds from our emergency fund, which I 'ave ter tell yer now stands at twenty-seven pounds, fifteen shillin's an' tuppence.'

'What's the financial position of the Railwaymen's Sick Fund?' Joe asked him.

'Not too brassy, I 'ave ter tell yer,' Maurice replied. 'the Sick Fund committee was lookin' fer a few bob from us this year.'

Bill Cosgrove put his hand up. 'I'd like ter say somefing,' he said

213

and, taking his cue from the chairman's gesture, 'the Sick Fund's a godsend, we all know. It puts a few bob in our members' pockets when they're long-term sick, but we 'ave ter remember that they do get sick benefit. Unfortunately, though, Mrs Comfrey's strugglin' along on just a widow's pension, so I propose we donate the proceeds of our annual do ter the Sick Fund, but keep an agreed sum back fer Mrs Comfrey.'

'Anyone else wanna say anyfing before we take a vote?' Walter asked, looking around the table. 'Right then, all in favour o' the proposal on the table . . .'

The response was unanimous and Bill Cosgrove looked particularly pleased. 'Forty years 'er ole man worked 'ere,' he said. 'We done the right fing, lads.'

'The next item on the agenda is the community social, an' I'm now gonna throw the meetin' open fer discussion,' Walter informed them. 'Just remember the bar closes at ten o'clock so let's get started.'

Ada Brennen was feeling a little isolated as she got the Sunday lunch ready. Joe was now preoccupied with the preparations for the annual community social, and the girls were not very talkative or forthcoming about their affairs of the heart. Kay was like a bear with a sore head, she thought, and she had been non-committal about going out that evening. Dawn too had been evasive when asked about Gordon, and Ada turned to Barbara, imagining that she would want to talk about her future marriage. 'I expect yer'll be lookin' out fer a place ter live now you an' Jamie 'ave made yer minds up,' she prompted.

'I expect so,' was the unenthusiastic reply.

''Ave yer thought about yer weddin' dress an' the bridesmaids' outfits?' Ada went on.

'Not really, Mum. There's plenty o' time yet.'

Ada shifted her attention to Elsie, who had now become a regular visitor on Sundays. ''Ow's fings wiv you an' Ernie lately?' she asked her.

Elsie shrugged her shoulders. 'Just about the same,' she replied.

Barbara took a clean tablecloth from the dresser drawer. 'I'll lay the table,' she offered.

'Yer'd better wait fer a while, young Billy's drawin' in there. Leave 'im while 'e's quiet,' Ada told her.

Barbara went up to her room, soon to be followed by her elder sister, and Ada began to think there was a conspiracy of silence directed against her. At one time they would all have been eager to discuss their problems. She sighed as she sliced up a large cabbage.

Up in the bedroom, the Brennen girls were discussing their aggrieved mother.

'She was askin' me about Gordon, but I didn't say too much, yer know 'ow she worries over every little fing,' Dawn told her sisters.

'Is there any chance yer'll get back wiv 'im?' Barbara asked her.

'Certainly not,' Dawn replied with passion. 'I told 'im straight about 'ow I was feelin'. As far as I'm concerned 'e can go an' take a runnin' jump.'

Elsie nodded. 'That's the way ter do it, gel. I wish I'd bin a bit more sensible.'

'I wouldn't take a load o' bloody nonsense from any feller,' Dawn responded pointedly. 'Gordon 'ad ter be told. I wasn't gonna play second fiddle ter rugby or anyfing else. Start the way yer mean ter go on, that's my motto.'

They heard a knock on the front door and then voices.

'It's probably a Jehovah's Witness. They're always comin' round on Sundays,' Dawn remarked.

''Ere, did I ever tell yer about that Jehovah's Witness who knocked on my friend-at-work's door?' Barbara asked.

Down in the scullery, a rather battered-looking young man sat talking to Ada. 'Dawn doesn't expect me, but I had to come round, Mrs Brennen,' he said. 'We've had a bit of a tiff, you see. I wonder if you could let her know I called.'

Ada looked at his bruised face. 'Where did yer get that black eye?' she asked him.

'Playing rugby yesterday,' he replied.

'D'yer play every week?' Ada inquired.

'Yes, I love it. I've got a trial with a big club,' Gordon told her, smiling.

'An' what was the tiff over, if I'm permitted to ask? Was it ter do wiv you playin' rugby?' Ada prompted.

'Yes, I'm afraid so. How did you guess?' the young man asked her.

'Just a muvver's intuition,' Ada said, smiling.

Gordon looked a little embarrassed. 'I think Dawn feels I'm more interested in rugby than her,' he said.

Ada studied the young man. His face looked flushed with good health and he had a charming smile, she thought. He was well spoken and his manner too was pleasant, and she found herself warming to him. 'I thought that might be the case. So I s'pose my daughter gave you an ultimatum?'

'I'm afraid so.'

'Will you take a bit of advice from me, son?'

'Surely.'

'Don't let Dawn dictate to yer. Tell 'er straight if she wants yer she's gotta accept yer the way you are.'

Gordon nodded and threw his shoulders back. 'You're right. I will,' he said firmly.

Ada walked out into the passage. 'Dawn?'

'Yeah?'

'Come down, there's someone ter see yer.'

The young woman hurried down the stairs and her face flushed bright red when she saw Gordon sitting at the scullery table. 'What 'ave yer done ter yer eye?' she asked him with concern.

'Never mind about that,' Gordon replied sharply. 'You and I need to talk. Get your coat.'

Dawn looked shocked, and she complied without hesitation. Gordon stepped out of the scullery looking very serious, and he turned to give Ada a big wink.

Sergeant Moody felt he had gained a minor victory at least in persuading his chief to grant him a search warrant, and as he stepped out from Dockhead Police Station along with Detective Constable Birkett he had a good idea that he was hoping to find what he was looking for. The raid over the weekend on Cornfield's Wharfage had netted the villains a valuable cargo of tinned salmon. It had been a clean job with not as much as a fingerprint to go on, and the detective was feeling more than a little angry that criminals were becoming increasingly ambitious on his manor. They're getting smart, Moody growled to himself as he crossed into St James's Road. Like the lorry hijack at Poplar it was an inside job, he felt sure. The robbers obviously knew the layout and where to find the keys of the articulated lorry. He was convinced that the Bermondsey Maltese faction were behind both jobs, and he had been quick to make his feelings known when he was called into the super's office that morning to make his report.

The backstreets were comparatively quiet after the morning rush to work, and as the two policemen walked quickly through Waggoner's Way they were spotted by Dot Adams who was standing at her front door talking to Annie Thomas.

'I wonder what that no-good git's doin' round 'ere,' she said.

Annie followed Dot's eyes. 'Who is it?' she asked her.

'They're both tecs. That big one's Bill Moody. 'E was the one who nicked my ole man a few years ago,' Dot told her.

The two women watched as the policemen entered the grocery shop and Dot pulled a face. 'Yer can bet yer life they ain't gone in there ter buy their groceries, that's fer sure,' she remarked.

Joe Mezzo was busy stacking tins of condensed milk on a shelf when the detectives walked in. He looked up and nodded casually.

'Mr Mezzo. You remember me, an' this is Detective Birkett. We've got a warrant ter search yer premises,' Moody said sternly.

'Oh yeah, an' what d'yer expect ter find?' Joe asked, smiling calmly.

The two detectives looked around the shop and Birkett pulled out a notebook from his inside pocket. Moody gestured towards to the counter flap and the grocer raised it with an exasperated sigh.

'What's goin' on 'ere?' Maria asked as she came in from the back room.

'They've got a search warrant,' Joe told her, raising his eyes to the ceiling theatrically.

'What do they expect ter find?' Maria asked him, looking shocked.

'That's what I just asked 'em,' Joe replied.

'Pity they don't spend more time on important fings,' she said loudly.

The two policemen set about examining the cases of tinned fruit, shoulder hams and sultanas which were stacked around the store room. Joe took out a box-file and set it down on a case.

'There's the receipts and authorisation forms from the Ministry o' Food,' he told them, leaving them to it.

After a while, Moody turned to his subordinate. 'There's nuffink 'ere,' he said darkly.

The detective constable shook his head. 'Should we check the stock against the receipts?' he suggested.

Moody gave him a hard look. 'I can't waste time goin' frew that lot,' he growled. 'C'mon, let's get back ter the station.'

As they walked back into the front of the shop, Joe gave them a friendly smile. 'Find what ye're lookin' for?' he asked.

Moody gave him a brief glance and led the way out into the street, passing two women who were making their way to the shop.

'That's the one I was tellin' yer about,' Dot said to Annie as they walked by the policemen.

'What, the fat ugly one?' Annie replied with a straight face.

Moody's jaw tightened in anger as he heard the comment, but his subordinate's face remained impassive as they walked away down the narrow street.

Simon Dines put on his dark glasses and left the house with a pair of shoes under his arm. Even with his eyes shaded he felt the bright glare, and he cursed his infirmity as he stepped into Sammy Dinsford's shop. 'I want these soled an' 'eeled,' he said.

Sammy examined the shoes briefly and nodded. 'They're pretty worn down. I'll 'ave ter stitch the soles on, all right?'

The young man nodded. 'Yeah, that's OK.'

The cobbler scribbled on a card and tore it in half, handing one piece to his customer and putting the other half into one of the shoes. 'They should be ready by Friday,' he told him.

Simon took off his glasses and rubbed his eyes with a grubby handkerchief. 'Do yer know where Danny Adams lives?' he asked. 'I was told 'e does a bit o' carpentry.'

'Yeah, I believe 'e does. 'E lives just across the street. Number Seven,' Sammy replied.

'I gotta get the ole lady's door-chain fixed, yer see,' Simon told him. 'She's bin naggin' me narrer about it.'

''Ow is she?' Sammy asked. 'I ain't seen 'er about lately.'

'Nah, she don't get out much. She feels the cold,' Simon replied.

Sammy slipped a boot on to the last and clamped it with a strip of webbing. 'Danny's workin' terday but 'is muvver'll be in,' he said.

'I'll pop over there,' Simon told him. 'Me muvver wants the job done soon as possible. She's frightened of someone breakin' in while I'm not there.'

Like most of the locals, Sammy was aware that Mother Dines was a moneylender and he had heard tell of the large amount of money she kept in the house. He had also heard about how she totally dominated her son and had turned him into an object of ridicule.

The young man looked worried and the cobbler felt sad for him. 'I don't s'pose yer get out much yerself though, do yer?' he asked.

'Only up the pub fer a pint or two now an' then,' Simon told him.

'Ain't yer got a lady friend?'

Simon shook his head. 'Nah, I couldn't take anyone 'ome, the way fings are,' he replied. 'Me muvver relies on me yer see, 'er not bein' too well.'

Sammy picked up his sharp cobbler's knife and proceeded to trim the leather sole, watched vacantly by the young man who seemed in no hurry to leave the shop.

'I s'pect yer kept busy,' Simon said.

'Yeah, there's always boots an' shoes needin' repairin',' Sammy replied.

'Well, I'd better get over there,' the young man said, still intrigued by the deft hands of the cobbler as he worked on the leather.

Sammy put down his knife and picked up a flat rasp. 'Danny'll do yer a good job,' he said as he felt the rough edge of the leather with the tips of his fingers.

'I'd do the job meself but me eyes ain't too good an' I ain't got no tools,' Simon told him.

Sammy nodded and set about smoothing the edge of the leather. 'Yer don't go out ter work then?' he asked.

Simon shook his head solemnly. 'I'm registered disabled.'

'Oh, I see.'

The young man pushed his dark glasses up on to the bridge of his nose and walked to the door. 'I'll be seein' yer,' he said.

Sammy slowly shook his head as he watched the young man cross the street and then he set to work once more.

Chapter Twenty-eight

The letter from David was short and to the point, and after reading it for the second time, Kay tore it up and threw it into the fire. She had known in her heart that it was all over between them since the night she saw Alice walking down those steps. She had seen the change in David, and she knew then that it could never work for them. The affair had been brief and exciting at first, and she had convinced herself that she was in love with him; now though, she realised that she had been fooling herself. Seeing Pat Kelly again had made her look at everything in a different light. Pat had told her of his feelings towards her and it had both shocked and excited her. He had always been the man of her dreams, but she had never dared to believe that he felt the way he did towards her.

Kay undressed quickly in the cold bedroom and slipped between the clean sheets, her feet seeking out the hot-water bottle. Pat Kelly had been avoiding her, she knew. He had passed her by on the other side of the street only a few days ago, pretending not to have noticed her, and then there was the evening she and Dawn were going to the cinema. Pat had stepped out of Jack Springer's corner shop and turned into Hastings Street to avoid her. It was so obvious, and it left her feeling desolate. She wanted him to speak to her, to ask her how things were going, and she would then be able to make him aware that she was his for the asking.

The young woman turned on to her side, her head resting on the soft pillow, and suddenly she felt panic. Pat Kelly was not the sort of man to be on his own for long. He would soon form another attachment, it was the way he was, and there was nothing she could do about it, apart from openly touting herself. It was a ridiculous situation, she sighed. Pat was living directly opposite, in a small street, but he might just as well have been hundreds of miles away for all she had seen of him.

Kay turned on to her back and stared up at the white ceiling. There had to be a way of getting to meet him very soon face to face, she told herself. If she waited for a chance meeting it could be too late. It might already be too late. Pat might be seeing someone this very moment. Perhaps she should knock at his door and confront him. But what could she say? And what would he think of her? No, it was out of the question. She would have to be a little more inventive.

Kay heard footsteps on the stairs and she turned on to her side once more. Barbara and Dawn were coming to bed and she did not feel disposed to chat with them, not tonight.

Signalman Colin Brennen sealed the envelope and slipped it into his bedside locker just as 'lights out' sounded. He knew that his family would be eagerly awaiting his first letter home, and they would be getting worried by now. It had been impossible to find a few spare minutes until this evening, and as he slipped into the uncomfortable camp bed, Colin realised that his upper arm had swollen considerably. The whole training squad had had their smallpox vaccinations that afternoon and they were all feeling the effects. Their sergeant had told them grudgingly that they were allowed twenty-four hours excused duty after the jabs, and Colin could see why. Most of the young men were flushed and running a temperature and he himself felt nauseous and shivery.

As he eased his swollen arm into a more comfortable position, Colin allowed himself a brief smile. His letter home was just a pack of lies. He had said that he was enjoying the training and the sergeant was a good sort, the food was good and he was putting on weight. What if he had told the truth? All movement was conducted at the double, between drilling on the barrack square for hours on end and the torturous spell in the gymnasium. The sergeant and his corporals were an ignorant, foul-mouthed, bullying lot and he would be glad to see the back of them. As for the food, it was only fit for pigs, and they would most probably have turned their noses up at it, especially the boiled liver and the synthetic potatoes. Colin felt sure that the inoculations had been administered with blunt needles, and that was after the victims had been forced to queue up stripped to the waist outside the medical hut in the freezing cold.

Colin winced as he tried to change his position in the bed. There was more to tell, but it would have worried his family sick. He could have written about the importance the training staff placed on winning the drill competition. It could mean promotion for them, though it was little glory for the drill squad, and torment and sheer misery were inflicted on the odd man out, the recruit who found it difficult to adapt to the hard training, to coordinate his movements and carry a rifle at the right slant.

The unfortunate young man in the next bed was the one on the receiving end in number 16 Squad. 'Signalman Upjohn, you look like a pregnant kipper! Pull yer stomach in! Stick yer chest out! You're a disgrace ter the human race! What are yer?!'

The rest of the recruits smiled to themselves at first, only too glad that they were being spared the brunt of the bullying, but then it became more and more apparent to them all that Signalman Upjohn was a hopeless misfit. He was never going to become a trained soldier. He found it difficult to keep up and the drill sergeant screamed endless obscenities at him as the unfortunate conscript marched out of step with his right arm and leg going forward together. The sergeant could see his promotion going up in smoke and his course of action was clear.

Colin glanced at the pathetic young man lying exhausted in the next bed and was filled with concern for him, as were the rest of the squad. Signalman Upjohn was being systematically broken in spirit. He was being mercilessly badgered, bullied, and made to feel utterly useless. In less than two weeks the young man had become pale and gaunt, and he appeared to have gone into a shell, refusing to speak to anyone other than to answer the sadistic sergeant. Someone, all of the squad in fact, should speak up for him, Colin knew, but no one dared, and as he waited for sleep to overtake him, the young man from Waggoner's Way heard Signalman Upjohn crying into his pillow.

Danny Adams decided that he would make the most of his rest day, and early that morning he gathered his tools together and set off along the street. He was particularly pleased that since he had started work at the baths his headaches had been less frequent. There had been one day, however, when he felt the all-too-familiar pounding in his temple, and then the stiffening at the base of his skull. He remembered getting confused: he had had to go into an unused bath cubicle until the pain subsided. Len had been sympathetic when he discovered him sitting there and he had let him rest in his office out of sight for a while.

''Ello, Danny. C'mon in,' Elsie said, giving him a cheerful smile. 'I didn't know if yer could make it terday.'

Danny set his bag down and took the seat Elsie offered him. 'I remembered yer tellin' me you was off work this week, so I thought I might as well get on wiv those ovver jobs yer wanted done,' he told her.

The young woman picked up the teapot from the hob and filled two large mugs with strong tea. ''Ow's the job at the baths comin' on?' she asked him.

Danny's dark eyes widened. 'I like it, Else,' he told her enthusiastically. 'The supervisor's a nice bloke an' 'e knows about me 'eadaches.'

'Are they still troublin' yer a lot?' she asked him.

'Not so much lately,' he replied. 'I get bad days, but I can manage. I just 'ave to.'

Elsie passed him a mug of tea then sat down facing him. 'What about these carpentry jobs you're doin', Danny? Does it 'elp?' she asked.

The young man nodded. 'Yeah, it does,' he replied. 'I don't like sittin' around the place wiv nuffink ter do. It gives me too much time ter fink.'

Elsie crossed her legs and adjusted her skirt around her knees. 'D'yer get depressed when yer've got time on yer 'ands, Danny?'

He took a sip from the mug. 'Sometimes when I'm sittin' around I get ter finkin' about the war an' that night we raided Bremen,' he told her. 'The aircraft was all shot up an' we were limpin' 'ome. I can feel meself gettin' all screwed up inside as I fink about it. It all comes back very clear. I remember the skipper tellin' us all ter brace ourselves fer a crash-landin', an' then I must 'ave blacked out. The next fing I can remember is seein' the flames. They were all around me an' I couldn't move. I fully expected ter be roasted alive – an' I would 'ave bin, if that farmer 'adn't pulled me from the wreckage. I was the only one of the crew ter survive. The navigator was the same age as me, an' the co-pilot wasn't much older.' Danny took another swig from his mug. 'D'yer know, though, Else, there are times when I wonder whevver it would 'ave bin better if I'd 'ave perished wiv the rest.'

'Why ever should yer fink that?' Elsie asked in a shocked voice.

Danny looked down at his feet for a few moments. 'What use am I to anybody?' he went on. 'I worry the life out o' me muvver the way I am, an' what's there ter look forward to fer me? I can't bring meself to ask a gel out, an' anyway, the gels round 'ere who know me fink I'm a bit loopy.'

Elsie leaned forward and rested her hand on his forearm. 'Listen, Danny. Yer mum's concerned for yer, of course, but she's got yer back from the war an' that's all she wanted. As fer the gels, if I was available I'd go out wiv yer. Any nice gel would.'

'Would you really 'ave gone out wiv me?' he asked, his eyes briefly holding hers.

'You bet yer life,' Elsie said, smiling.

'I always used ter look up ter yer when we were kids,' Danny told her. 'I fink I was in love wiv yer at the time.'

The young woman got up and turned away from him to hide her embarrassment as she put her empty mug down on the table. 'I sometimes wish I could turn the clock back,' she said.

'Don't we all?' he replied, getting up and reaching for his bag.

Elsie felt a sudden urge to take him to her, hold him close and shut out the world, the way she would with her young son when he woke up fearful after a bad dream. Instead, she turned and gave him a warm smile. 'It's nice 'avin' a quiet chat,' she said.

'It's nice chattin' ter you too, Else, but I'd better set ter work,' he told her.

The young woman busied herself about the house while Danny began the job of removing the yard door. She could hear him working away and she hummed happily to herself. It was nice to be paid the compliment, she thought with a secret smile, and as she changed the pillowcases in her bedroom, Elsie stole a glance at herself in the dressing-table mirror. She made the bed, and then just as she was gathering up the discarded sheets, she heard the lorry pull up outside and she frowned. Ernie was not going to be too pleased about Danny working in the house, she thought to herself as she hurried down the stairs.

'It's bloody cold in 'ere,' he moaned as he came in the parlour.

'Danny Adams is mendin' the yard door,' she told him curtly.

Ernie pulled a face. 'I'm only 'ome fer a few minutes. I gotta go ter Manchester again,' he told her. 'They're comin' the ole soldier wiv me since I lost that load.'

224

'Well, why don't yer look around fer anuvver job?' she suggested.

'Don't fink I ain't tried,' he said sharply. 'Anyway, I'll get me overnight bag an' 'ave a quick cuppa, then I'll 'ave ter be off.'

While Elsie waited for the water to boil, Ernie packed his bag quickly and then walked out into the scullery. 'What's all this?' he asked.

Danny looked surprised at seeing him. 'I've 'ad ter take the door off the 'inges,' he replied. 'They're rusted, an' the bottom o' the door's swollen. I gotta take a few shavin's off before I can put the new weavver-board on.'

Ernie looked at the young man with a smirk on his wide flat face. 'Oh, I see. I'm glad yer told me,' he said with sarcasm.

Danny's felt the muscles in his face tensing. He could sense the hostility of the man and he resented being ridiculed. 'P'raps I should 'ave left it fer you ter do,' he countered.

Ernie's features stiffened. 'Yeah, p'raps yer should,' he growled. 'I didn't know she was gettin' you in ter do the back door. I don't like ter be left in the dark about fings.'

Danny fought hard to control his rising emotions. He had been on the receiving end of Ernie's sarcastic jibes on more than one occasion. 'That's your problem. I just bin asked ter do a job o' work, that's all,' he replied quickly.

Ernie took a step forward and put his face close to Danny's. 'Don't start gettin' flash wiv me, Dopey, or I might take it badly,' he snarled.

The younger man felt his head starting to pound and he gritted his teeth. 'Don't you go callin' me dopey,' he said loudly.

Suddenly Elsie rushed into the scullery and grabbed Ernie's arm. 'What's the matter wiv you?' she shouted at him. 'Can't you ever be civil to anyone? Danny's only doin' the job I asked 'im ter do. I bin askin' you ter do it fer ages.'

Ernie pulled his arm away quickly. 'Yer might 'ave told me what yer intended ter do,' he said sharply. 'Anyway, get 'im to 'urry up. It's like a bloody ice-box in this 'ouse.'

Elsie waited until her husband had left the scullery, then she turned to the young man, her face still flushed with anger. 'I'm sorry, Danny. 'E's just a pig,' she said disgustedly.

Danny smiled and shrugged his shoulders. 'It's all right,' he told her. 'I know what 'e's like.' He picked up his plane. 'I won't be long.'

'Take yer time. Don't rush on Ernie's account,' Elsie replied.

Errol Baines had been puzzled by Jim Carney's recent quietness, and he decided that it was about time he quizzed him. ''Ow you bin gettin' on wiv that application?' he asked him as his team broke off for tea.

'What application?'

'You know. The Jolly Boys application.'

'Oh, that one.'

'Well?'

'I've 'ad a bit of a kickback,' Jim confessed.

'Bloody 'ell, Jim, 'ow long's it take ter get a few references?' Errol went on.

Jim Carney looked peeved. 'It ain't that easy,' he replied irritably. 'Yer jus' can't go askin' anybody. Me doctor wouldn't oblige an' the bloke from the Sally Army let me down as well. I even tried the mayor, but 'e was off sick.'

''Ow comes yer tried the mayor?' one of the men asked.

''Cos I was in the firewatchers durin' the war, that's why,' Jim told him sharply.

'Oh, I see,' the railwayman replied, stifling a grin. ''Ave yer thought about goin' ter see our guv'nor?'

Jim gave him a disdainful look. 'I've already got a reference from Gerry Preston,' he told him brusquely.

''Ow many more d'yer need?' the man pressed him.

'Four in all.'

''Ere, I was just finkin',' Errol cut in. 'Why don't I give yer a reference? After all, I am the ganger.'

Jim's face brightened. 'Would yer really, Errol? I'd be grateful if yer did.'

'No worry. I'll do it ternight,' the ganger told him.

'Yeah, but yer'll 'ave ter tell the trufe,' one of the men said. 'It might go against 'im.'

'I work as bleedin' 'ard as you do, Nobby. I ain't got nuffing ter fear,' Jim retorted.

''E's only jokin',' Errol assured him. 'I'll write it out ternight. In the meantime, why don't yer 'ave a word wiv Charlie Catchpole. 'E knows yer tryin' ter join the Jolly Boys. Ask 'im if they'll accept two references instead o' four.'

'D'yer fink they would?'

'I don't see why not.'

Jim went back to work in a happy frame of mind, unaware that Errol and his cronies were plotting once more.

Chapter Twenty-nine

Joe Mezzo had learned life's lessons the hard way, and he soon realised that Sergeant Moody was attempting to put the frighteners on with the search warrant. He heeded the warning but was determined that no corrupt policeman was going to get the better of him. It had taken him years of hard work and shady dealings to get where he was, and he was not about to throw it all away.

''Ello, Nick. I've 'ad the spring clean. I'll take five, an' look after anuvver twenty while the weavver's unreliable. Got me?'

The reply was favourable and Joe put the phone down and smiled to himself. Now it was time to take some of the pressure off, he told himself, his smile broadening.

Early on Monday afternoon, a totter drove his horse and cart into Waggoner's Way and pulled up in the turning, his loud, unintelligible call bringing no response, until Emily Toogood looked out of her front door.

'Oi, you! D'yer take ole wringers?' she called out.

'Not terday, missus,' he replied.

Emily looked bewildered. 'What's the matter wiv terday?' she pressed him.

'Nuffink, 'cept it's bloody cold,' he told her.

'Why won't yer take me ole wringer then?'

'I'd like to, missus, but it's me back.'

'Wassa matter wiv yer back?'

'I've ricked it.'

'So yer can't take me wringer.'

''S'right, unless you can 'ump it out an' put it on the cart.'

'Go sod yerself,' Emily said emphatically as she slammed her front door shut.

After a short while the totter moved his horse and cart up

228

to the end of the turning and sat for a few minutes smoking a cigarette.

'Oi, mate. I got some ole pots an' pans stuck in me tin barf what's got an 'ole in it,' Sara Brady called out.

The totter turned and cursed under his breath. 'Sorry, missus, I can't take no more terday,' he told her.

'Why not, there's still room on yer cart.'

'I know that, but it's me ole grey mare, yer see. She's took a turn fer the worse an' it'll be touch an' go whevver she pulls this lot 'ome. I'm takin' 'er ter see the vet this afternoon.'

'Poor fing,' Sara said, walking over to the bored animal. 'It don't look too good.'

'Don't get too near, missus. She gets a bit shirty when she ain't feelin' too good,' the totter warned her. 'I wouldn't like 'er ter kick out at yer.'

Sara went back into her house and returned with a spongy apple. ''Ere we are, you eat this,' she said, offering the apple on the palm of her hand.

The animal looked at it for a few moments as though making its mind up, then it snapped it up.

'Fanks, missus, I'd better get 'er 'ome now,' the agitated totter told her.

Sara went into her house and watched through the curtains. She saw the cart move off and turn the corner, only to stop outside Joe Mezzo's shop. 'The poor fing's really queer,' she told her husband.

Stanley Brady looked up from the paper. 'Yeah?'

Sara ignored him and hurried out into the street again. 'Is she all right?' she asked anxiously.

The totter swore under his breath. 'Yeah, it's a bit o' wind. She'll be all right in a few minutes,' he said.

The totter smoked another cigarette, then once he was sure the street was clear he jumped down and went into the shop. A few minutes later he was on his way out of Hastings Street, having delivered five cases of tinned salmon concealed under a large rug.

At the other end of Waggoner's Way, Basil Cashman the oil-shop proprietor hummed to himself as he wrapped up a block of hearthstone the following afternoon. 'There we are. Anyfing else?'

Annie Thomas pinched her chin. 'Give us a tin o' Brasso an' a bundle o' wood,' she told him.

'Nice day terday,' Basil said pleasantly.

'It's bloody cold,' Annie replied, pulling her coat collar up around her ears.

'Fresh, though. Better than all that fog we've bin 'avin',' Basil went on.

Annie turned to Bet Greenedge. ''E ain't bin on the turps, 'as 'e?' she mumbled.

Basil ignored the aside. 'Is that all?'

'Yeah, that'll do fer now. C'mon, Bet, let's get 'ome, my feet are killin' me,' Annie sighed.

The oil-shop owner watched them leave, then he picked up the phone. ''Ello. Dock'ead Police Station? I wanna report some dodgy goin's-on. No, I can't give yer me name an' address. Just pay Mezzo's grocery shop a visit. It's on the corner of Waggoner's Way an' 'Astin's Street. 'E's knockin' out tins o' black-market salmon by all accounts.'

Margie Dolan sat down painfully on the edge of her bed and studied her bruised face in the dressing-table mirror. She saw the purple area growing round her left eye and she noticed how swollen her lips were. Her ribs felt tender when she touched them and her whole body ached. It would be a week at least before she could go back to work, she sighed.

The knock on the door startled her and she pulled her dressing robe around her plump body as she got up from the bed.

'Who is it?' she called out.

'It's me, Chippy.'

'Just a minute.'

The publican hummed tunelessly as he waited, then when Margie eased the door open he cursed aloud. 'I guessed it,' he said quickly as he saw her bruised face.

'It'll mend,' she said with an attempt at a smile.

'Ain't yer gonna invite me in?' Chippy asked her.

'It's a bit awkward right now,' she replied.

''E's not 'ere now, is 'e?'

'No but . . .'

'But nuffink. Now c'mon, let me in,' Chippy said firmly. 'I know the score. I've bin told 'e's back.'

The big blonde sighed as she stepped back to let him in. 'Who told yer?' she asked.

230

'Never mind who told me. 'E's back on the manor an' you ain't bin seen fer a week. It didn't need a Sherlock 'Olmes ter figure it out,' Chippy said with a cynical smile.

''E got out last week an' 'e come straight round. Someone must 'ave kept 'im informed while 'e was banged up. I told 'im 'e wasn't welcome an' 'e gave me this,' Margie said, pointing to her eye.

'Vic Dolan ain't changed none after bein' put away fer five years,' Chippy remarked. ''E was always a nasty bastard.'

Margie nodded and held her ribs as she followed him into her comfortable parlour. 'Yer might as well sit down an' I'll put the kettle on,' she told him.

Chippy produced a flat silver flask from inside his coat. 'This might be better. It's five-star brandy,' he grinned.

Margie took two small glasses from the sideboard and sat down heavily as Chippy poured out a large measure in each.

'There yer go,' he said, handing her a filled glass. 'Now are yer gonna tell me the full story, or am I ter guess?'

'There's not much ter tell really,' Margie replied. 'Vic told me 'e was gonna be my pimp, an' when I told 'im ter piss off 'e really let fly. I got kicked all round the room, an' then when 'e calmed down 'e 'ad the cheek ter tell me 'e still loved me, would yer believe?'

'Yer mustn't let 'im stay, Marge. 'E'll end up killin' yer,' Chippy said with concern.

'There's nuffink I can do about it, luv. If I get shirty 'e *will* kill me,' Margie replied, her eyes filling with tears.

'Now don't upset yerself,' Chippy said quickly. 'Drink that down. There's anuvver one 'ere. I got a few docker pals who'll soon sort Vic Dolan out.'

'I don't want you ter get involved, is that clear?' Margie said firmly. 'I'll 'andle this my way.'

'Yeah, like takin' a right beatin' whenever that bastard feels the need,' the publican growled.

'Chippy, I mean it. Just let me sort it out,' she told him.

'Well, 'e better not whack yer again or I'll put the boys on 'im,' he said with passion.

Margie drained her drink and Chippy took the glass from her. She watched as he carefully tipped the flask and noticed how his hand shook.

'Fanks fer the concern, Chippy,' she said quietly.

'It's all right, gel. I gotta look after me friends, don't I?'

231

She smiled and suddenly winced as a sharp pain pierced her rib cage. 'Don't you ever eat?' she asked him.

'Yeah, course I do. I 'ad a nice pie an' mash yesterday,' he told her.

'An' what about terday?'

'I ain't felt 'ungry terday. I'll get a bite back at the pub.'

'Who's lookin' after the pub?' Margie asked.

'Brendan McClusky.'

'Christ! 'E'll drink all the profits.'

'Nah, 'e's on the waggon. Doctor's orders.'

'Who told yer, Brendan?'

Chippy smiled. 'I know I'm never gonna get rich runnin' the Bell, but I got a good crowd o' mates there, Marge.'

'You're the best, luv,' she told him. 'I really appreciate yer callin' but yer better be goin' before Vic gets back. 'E's gone dog-racin' an' 'e might leave early.'

Chippy left the house and walked unsteadily back to his riverside pub. I'd better have a word with Tubby Wallis and Mick Mollison, he thought to himself. They both have a bar bill to settle.

Sergeant Moody jumped into the police car and grinned evilly at his subordinate. 'I'll nail that bastard Malt this time,' he growled.

Detective Constable Birkett did not feel so optimistic, but he smiled nevertheless. He considered himself to be a straight copper doing a worthwhile job, and the likes of Moody irked him. If he was honest with himself he had to admit that on this occasion he hoped his sergeant was going to be disappointed.

The car sped over the railway bridge and turned into Dover Lane. Moody sat forward in the back seat impatiently. 'Turn right 'ere an' pull up at the end,' he ordered the driver.

Joe Mezzo looked shocked as the policemen hurried into his shop.

'I'm actin' on information received,' Moody said as he lifted the counter flap and went into the back of the shop.

'Where's yer warrant?' Joe asked.

'Show 'im the warrant,' Moody growled to Birkett.

Joe looked at the paper then followed the detectives into the storeroom. 'What yer lookin' for?' he asked.

Moody gave him a hard look and carried on moving the cases about. 'Got a case opener?' he asked.

Joe handed him a crowbar. ''Elp yerself,' he said sarcastically.

The policemen prised open a plain case and discovered it contained display cards. Another plain case revealed tins of shoe and metal polish. Suddenly Sergeant Moody's face brightened as he reached behind a stack of tinned fruit and pulled out a large case marked 'Sockeye Red Salmon'. He wedged the edge of the crowbar into the side of the case and pressed down. The lid squeaked open and the two detectives looked down on a number of scale weights packed in straw.

'They're old ones waitin' ter be picked up by the weights an' measures people,' Joe told the officers. 'I won't use dodgy weights in my shop. Honest Joe, that's me.'

Moody looked furious as he threw down the crowbar and stood with his hands on his hips. 'I wanna see the shelves,' he said sharply.

Maria was serving Emily Toogood and she tutted loudly as the policemen began pulling tins from the shelves.

'What they lookin' for, salmon?' Emily said, grinning.

Moody gave her a blinding look then turned to Birkett. 'That's it. Wait outside,' he ordered.

Joe caught the detective's eye and led him back into the storeroom. 'Satisfied?' he asked.

'We were given a tip-off by phone,' Moody replied.

'Yeah, it figures,' Joe told him.

'What d'yer mean?'

'They're takin' the piss, whoever they are,' Joe went on. 'Yeah, there's salmon on sale round 'ere, but I ain't got any. Whoever it is they're keepin' you blokes tied up on false alarms till they knock it all out. By the way, I'll be callin' in the nick termorrer sometime ter make a formal complaint. I'm gonna ask your guv'nor 'ow many more times I can expect ter be turned over. I'm also gonna ask 'im if it's a vendetta against the law-abidin' Maltese people who live in Bermondsey. We'll see what 'e 'as ter say about it. Now, if yer've finished, I'll be obliged if yer'll piss off an' let me get on wiv my business.'

Moody's face was a dark mask as he stormed out of the shop, and had he been looking he would have seen the ghost of a smile on the face of his subordinate.

Basil Cashman watched the police car leave the street and then he picked up the phone. 'All right, Joe? Yeah that'll be very nice. Nah, I'm sure. 'Alf a dozen tins'll do nicely.'

233

Back at the grocer's shop Joe took a row of tinned fruit down from a shelf and then eased out the back board. Behind it was a row of tins containing Sockeye red salmon.

'Maria, stick these tins in a carrier bag an' drop 'em in ter Basil before 'e closes, will yer?' Joe said, smiling with satisfaction.

'Is that the lot?' Maria asked him.

'Yep,' he replied. 'We sold four cases by twelve o'clock terday.'

Chapter Thirty

Grace Dines sat reading the evening paper, her metal-rimmed glasses perched on the end of her nose and her head held back to focus on the print. Occasionally she would look up at Simon who sat nodding in the armchair facing her. The fire burned low in the range and white ash overflowed from the firepan and spilled out on to the grey hearth. The grubby, threadbare carpet was in need of a thorough sweeping and the curtains were overdue for a wash but the old lady was determined not to lift a finger while her lazy son spent his days lolling around the place or dozing in the armchair. She had asked him to clean out the fire, blacklead the range and whiten the hearth that morning, but he had just lit the fire and sat over it grumbling about the cold. Maybe if he showed some willingness and did a bit more about the place she would change the curtains and tidy up a bit. The way things were, though, he seemed quite prepared to live in filth, so why should she bother?

'Wake up, Simon, 'e'll be 'ere soon,' she called over to him.

The young man sat up in the chair and rubbed his large hand over his face. 'What time is it?' he asked her.

Grace gave him a cold stare and he twisted his head to glance up at the ornate clock in the centre of the mantelshelf.

'It's no good lookin' at that. You ain't wound it up,' she told him.

The sleepy young man got up and turned on the wireless. 'It's gettin' dark out,' he mumbled.

'It's after six. Put that clock on fer a quarter past,' she told him.

Light music drifted into the room as Simon took a key from beside the clock and opened the glass face.

'Wind it up prop'ly. Yer never wind it up prop'ly,' she moaned at

235

him. 'It's s'posed ter be a seven-day clock an' it never goes more than a couple o' days.'

Simon gritted his teeth as he turned the key against the spring. One of these days he would take the clock and throw it through the window, he told himself. The thing lost over an hour a day and it only seemed to chime when it felt like it. Everything was breaking down in this house. The doors didn't shut properly, the ceiling paper was beginning to come away and the paintwork was peeling everywhere. She knew painting affected his eyes and yet she kept on about him doing the place up. She had the money to get a decorator in, but instead she was prepared to live in a hovel. Why should he put himself out while she was so obstinate and stingy?

'That's not enough. The bloody fing won't last more than a day or two. Wind it right up,' the old lady grumbled at him.

'If I overwind it the bloody fing won't go at all,' he replied irritably.

Grace puffed and threw down her newspaper. 'When yer gonna clean that grate? It's a disgrace.'

'I'll do it termorrer,' he told her.

'I got people comin' in 'ere an' Gawd knows what they must fink when they see the state o' this place,' she went on. 'I must be the talk o' the street.'

Simon walked out of the room to put the kettle on and the old lady sat fiddling with the key hanging round her neck as she looked about the grotty parlour. 'It wouldn't take 'im long ter put a coat o' whitewash on that ceilin',' she said aloud to herself.

The young man heard his ageing mother mumbling and he sighed. Norman had done the right thing in joining the Navy, he told himself. If it hadn't been for his eyes, he would have gone too. Unfortunately he couldn't leave his mother now that she was so old and decrepit.

'Why ain't 'e called?' Grace shouted out.

'I dunno, do I?' Simon called back.

'It's gettin' on fer 'alf-six.'

''E said after six.'

'People should 'ave a bit more consideration,' Grace went on. 'If they say a time they should stick to it. It wasn't the same in my day. I dunno what the world's comin' to.'

''E should be 'ere any minute,' Simon told her.

'While yer out there, put the water on fer the greens, an' turn the taters on,' she called out.

Ten minutes later Simon showed Danny Adams into the parlour to face the old lady's wrath.

'Yer late.'

'Sorry, luv.'

'It's no good bein' sorry after.'

Danny stood holding his bag and feeling like a naughty school-boy. 'Anyway I'm 'ere, so can yer tell me what yer want done?' he said in a pleasant voice.

'Didn't yer get the full message? I want that street door fixed,' Grace told him sharply.

'Yeah, I know, but what exactly d'yer want doin' ter the street door?'

'Show 'im what needs doin', Simon,' the old lady said, dismissing the part-time carpenter with a wave of her bony hand.

Danny put his bag down in the passage and watched as Simon pulled the heavy chain across the door and slipped the last link over a thick hook.

'The ole lady's frightened this won't 'old if someone pushes on the door,' Simon explained.

Danny glanced at the doorjamb and saw that the wood was rotten. 'Yeah, I can see,' he replied. 'It needs a new piece of 'ardwood set in ter make it really safe.'

'Can yer do it?' Simon asked him.

'Yeah, it shouldn't take too long,' Danny replied.

'What'll it cost?'

Danny pulled at his chin for a few moments. 'The wood's gonna cost two an' a tanner. Call it twelve an' six,' he said.

Simon left Danny standing in the passage while he consulted his mother. ''E reckons twelve an' a tanner.'

'That's a bit dear.'

''E said the wood'll cost two an' a tanner.'

'Why should I pay fer the wood? There's plenty o' wood on the bombsites.'

Simon puffed loudly. 'Well yer better tell 'im yerself.'

Danny could hear the conversation and he picked up his bag. 'Look, if yer wanna go scroungin' fer wood, make sure it's 'ardwood, an' make sure it ain't full o' woodworm,' he said loudly.

'Oh, all right. Tell 'im ter do it. Find out when,' Grace Dines growled.

'When can yer do it?' Simon asked him as he walked back into the dark passage.

'It'll 'ave ter be me next day off.'

'When's that?'

'Next Thursday.'

''E said next Thursday,' Simon called out.

'Can't 'e do it before?'

Simon looked at Danny who shook his head firmly.

'No, not till next Thursday.'

'I s'pose it'll 'ave ter do,' the old lady grumbled.

'What yer say?' Simon shouted.

'You deaf? I said all right.'

Danny reached for the door catch. 'I'll be 'ere about nine, all right?'

Simon nodded. 'I'll see yer then,' he replied, closing the door and slipping the large chain across.

'Put that chain on,' his mother shouted out.

'It's done.'

'What yer say?'

'I said I've done it,' Simon shouted out.

'What yer shoutin' for? I can 'ear yer, I ain't deaf.'

Pat Kelly slipped out of the house and set off along the quiet street. It had become a regular routine now, and as he turned into Dover Lane and saw the lights shining out from the Mason's Arms he sighed dejectedly. He didn't really need a pint, he told himself, but at least he could chat to people at the pub. It was preferable to sitting at home with his mother fussing over him all the time.

Vera Selby the landlady smiled at him as he walked into the public bar. 'Wotcha, Pat. 'Ow's tricks?'

'Not so good. All work an' no play,' he told her, forcing a smile.

'You an' me could play, if it wasn't fer that man o' mine,' Vera replied, winking. ''E won't give me any time off.'

Pat ordered a pint of bitter and stood at the counter sipping it. The evening was young and he knew that he would have to pace himself. The last time he drank too much he had found himself in a strange bed. Fortunately Chippy and Margie Dolan had taken care of him then, but it could have worked out quite differently, he realised.

Vera was eyeing him. 'There's bin a lot o' tecs sniffin' round 'ere lately,' she told him quietly. 'We've 'ad 'em in 'ere twice this week. I fink it's ter do wiv that ware'ouse job in Shad Thames.'

'You ain't started sellin' salmon, 'ave yer?' Pat asked with a grin.

Vera leaned forward on the counter. 'They was askin' if we'd 'eard any talk. Arfur spoke to 'em. I just kept out o' the way,' she went on. 'Trouble is, in this business you're obliged ter cooperate wiv the police or they can make it awkward. Mind yer, though, Arfur's pretty cute. Yer gotta be, or yer get a bad name wiv the villains. It's a case of 'eads they win, tails we lose.'

Pat Kelly sipped his drink, nodding dutifully while Vera rambled on. He was glad when the regular customers started arriving. Vera was a nice sort, he thought, but she did go on a bit.

''Ello, Pat, I ain't seen yer fer ages. 'Ow yer doin?'

The young man turned to see Charlie Catchpole standing beside him. 'Not so bad, Chas. What about you?' he replied.

Charlie shook his head. 'I bin under the weavver. Did yer farvver tell yer what 'appened ter me?' he asked.

Pat nodded. 'I see yer've recovered.'

'I still get a bit dizzy now an' then, but they said it'll wear off in time,' Charlie told him.

Pat drained his glass and called Vera over. 'Same again, luv, an' one fer Chas.'

Charlie declined the drink with a wave of his hand. 'I gotta be careful. My ole dutch don't like me 'avin' too much ter drink since me accident,' he said. 'She's only finkin' o' me. She's a good 'un.'

Pat smiled indulgently. Very soon the pub would fill up and he would inevitably be drawn into banal conversation. At least at Chippy's he could sit alone if he felt like it. 'Well, I'd better be off, I'm meetin' someone,' he told Charlie as he put down his empty glass.

'Sure yer won't 'ave one wiv me?' Charlie asked him.

'Anuvver time, Chas. Be seein' yer then. See yer, Vera.'

As soon as Pat Kelly left the pub, Vera came up to the shunter. 'It's a bloody shame about 'im, the way 'e's let 'imself go,' she said, shaking her head slowly. 'Alec over there saw Pat the ovver night in the Bell. Pissed out of 'is brains, 'e was. A prosser took 'im 'ome wiv 'er, accordin' to Alec.'

'Yeah, it's a bloody shame right enough,' Charlie replied. 'Is ole man's worried sick about 'im. Tom Kelly was talkin' ter me about it only the ovver day.'

Vera was called away to serve a customer and when she returned Charlie pulled out a book of raffle tickets from his coat pocket. 'By the way, luv, can yer do a few o' these fer us?' he asked. 'There's the list o' prizes. It's fer the community get-tergevver.'

The landlady nodded. 'Tom Kelly's already give us some, but I'll take those anyway,' she replied. 'We're donatin' a barrel o' best ale.'

'Vera, you're a love,' Charlie said, grinning.

Jim Carney was handed a sealed envelope by Errol Baines as the gang sat together at their tea-break, and he made to open it.

'No, yer can't do that,' Errol said quickly. 'All decent references 'ave gotta be sealed up, or people could fink yer comin' the ole soldier an' writin' 'em yerself.'

Jim nodded as he put the envelope into his coat pocket. 'I'm really grateful, Errol. I've only gotta get two more, unless I see Charlie Catchpole. If 'e ses it's all right, then it's only one.'

'' Ave yer thought any more about who else ter see fer one?' Errol asked him as casually as he could.

'Yeah, but I'm stumped ter tell yer the trufe,' Jim replied. 'It ain't easy ter get people ter stand for yer.'

'I got an idea, but yer might not wanna do it,' Errol told him.

'I'll try anyfing,' Jim said quickly.

'Well, I was finkin'. It's only a suggestion, though.'

'Yeah, go on.'

'Nah, yer might not fink it's werf it.'

'Try me,' Jim said impatiently.

'Well, all right. But it's only a suggestion.'

Jim Carney started hopping about as though he was standing barefoot on a hotplate. 'C'mon fer Gawd's sake, Errol.'

'Why don't yer try an' contact the chairman o' the Civil Defence Remembrance Committee?' the ganger suggested.

'The who?' Jim said with a puzzled look on his large face.

'You 'eard,' Errol said quickly. 'I 'appen ter know the chairman an' I reckon 'e's a decent bloke. 'E'll 'ave yer name on 'is books, you bein' a firefighter durin' the war.'

'Cor, fanks, Errol. 'Ow do I get ter see 'im?'

'Yer don't.'

'But . . .'

'Now listen carefully,' the ganger cut in. 'First yer phone a number. Yer can use a phone, can't yer?'

'Course I can. D'yer fink I'm stupid or somefink?' Jim said quickly.

'Right then. Just ask ter speak ter Mr Sprat,' Errol went on. 'When 'e answers, just tell 'im briefly what yer want from 'im. 'Is first name's Jack, by the way. Now 'e's bound to ask yer a few questions, but I don't see any problem. If 'e takes ter yer 'e'll give yer a reference, I'm sure of it.'

'What d'yer mean, if 'e takes ter me?'

'Yer know what I mean. Like bein' straight wiv 'im,' Errol explained. 'Don't try an' pull the wool over 'is eyes, 'cos 'e won't take kindly ter that.'

'I really appreciate this,' Jim told him as the gang got ready to resume work.

'Well, don't yer want the telephone number then?' Errol asked, giving Jim a look of dismay.

'Yeah, sorry, Errol,' he said, grinning sheepishly. 'I gotta 'ave that, ain't I?'

The ganger fished into his trouser pocket and pulled out a screwed-up slip of paper. 'There's one fing, though,' he warned. 'Yer can only contact this bloke at a certain time. I've made a note on the paper as well as 'is name. It's gotta be termorrer night at nine sharp.'

Jim went back to work whistling happily. The other members of the loading gang had smiles on their faces too. They all felt that it was going to be hilarious at the Samson on Saturday night.

Chapter Thirty-one

Pat Kelly could see that something was wrong the minute he walked into Chippy's riverside pub. The landlord was engaged in a heated argument with a heavily built man, watched by a few old men who listened from a safe distance.

'An' I'm tellin' you ter keep yer poxy nose out o' my affairs,' the big man shouted as he leaned over the counter.

Chippy stood his ground. 'That gel's a friend o' mine an' I got the right ter call in on 'er any time I like,' he replied in his normal voice.

'Well, I'm tellin' yer now that yer not welcome, so keep away or I'll be back an' sort you out,' the stranger told him, banging his clenched fist down on the counter.

'Don't you go threatenin' me, ole son,' Chippy replied. 'I saw the state o' that gel after you'd finished wiv 'er. If it'd bin left ter me I'd 'ave put the police on ter yer, but as it 'appened, Margie wouldn't 'ave it.'

Pat Kelly had stood back from the counter listening, but as soon as he heard the girl's name mentioned he stepped forward. 'What's the trouble, Chippy?' he asked quietly.

The big stranger turned and glared at him. 'It's none o' your business, son, so keep out of it,' he said menacingly.

Pat leaned his arm on the counter and glanced at Chippy. 'Are you talkin' about Margie Dolan?' he asked, his eyes narrowing.

Chippy nodded. 'This is Margie's ex-'usband,' he replied, nodding towards the big man. ''E's took umbrage at me poppin' round ter see 'ow she was.'

'Too bloody right I did,' the man growled.

'I 'eard yer just say 'e gave Margie a good 'idin',' Pat said quickly, the colour draining from his face as he looked at the landlord.

'I told yer ter keep out o' this,' the big man snarled.

Pat Kelly stood up straight, placing his feet apart to balance himself carefully. 'Margie's a good friend ter me, so I'm makin' it my business,' he said in a harsh voice. 'I'll tell yer somefing else, pal. I don't go a lot on blokes who beat up women, an' I don't like anyone threatenin' my mates. So why don't yer piss off out while yer in front.'

Suddenly Vic Dolan let fly with a left-hand punch that came up from his side. Pat could not fully avoid it and he caught a glancing blow on his chin. Dolan threw a looping right-hand punch to the side of Pat's head and brought his knee up quickly. Pat caught his leg and straightened up, sending his attacker reeling backwards. The young man's vision was blurred from the second blow, and he heard Chippy shout out something. Dolan had picked up an empty beer mug from a nearby table and was coming towards him slowly. Suddenly he brought the mug down sharply on the edge of the counter and broken glass flew about. As Pat's vision cleared he could see that Dolan was holding a jagged piece of the mug in his hand.

'I'll cut yer ter pieces, you interferin' bastard,' he growled.

Pat Kelly backed away slowly, keeping a safe distance.

'What yer gotta say fer yerself now?' Dolan snarled as he thrust the glass forward menacingly.

Pat backed away still further, his hand searching behind him for something to protect himself with. Dolan suddenly leapt forward and then staggered to his knees as Pat swung a heavy chair which came crashing down on Dolan's head. A thin trickle of blood started to run down the side of his face as he stared up at the young man. 'I'm gonna tear you apart,' he growled.

'All right, that'll do,' Chippy called out, feeling safer behind the counter.

Dolan ignored him and scrambled to his feet, felled again by Pat's swinging right hand. This time he found it difficult to rise and he shook his head from side to side as he crouched on all fours. Pat was amazed to see that his attacker was still conscious, and he drew a deep breath as he drew his right arm back. As Dolan rose up from the floor Pat's blow smashed into his left temple and he fell forward.

Chippy clambered over the counter and looked down at the prone figure of Vic Dolan. 'Bloody 'ell, Pat, I thought 'e was gonna slice you up,' he said breathlessly.

The young man rubbed his bruised knuckles and smiled self-consciously, aware that the elderly customers were staring at him.

'It's no more than the cowardly git deserves,' one said, looking down at Dolan.

'That was a nice right-'ander, son,' another old man remarked as he came over with a clay pipe held between his first two fingers.

'We better get 'im outside. I don't want 'im in 'ere when 'e wakes up,' Chippy said.

Dolan was dragged face down from the public bar and propped up against the wall outside, his knees drawn up against his chest to support his weight. He started to groan and his eyes flickered open. Pat Kelly bent down and grabbed his chin in his hand. 'Listen, pal,' he told him. 'I'm gonna spell it out ter yer. Go near Margie again an' yer answer ter me. If you lay a finger on 'er I'll come lookin'. Understood?'

Dolan nodded, his eyes rolling as he tried to pull himself together.

'C'mon, Pat, let's get a drink,' Chippy said, putting his hand on the young man's arm.

'You go back inside, Chippy. I'll be in later,' he replied. 'I'm gonna call on Margie. She needs ter be warned.'

The muffled sound of a river tug carried through the cobbled street as Vic Dolan painfully dragged himself to his feet. He leaned against the wall outside the pub till his head had cleared a little, then he staggered off, making for the seamen's club in Rotherhithe. With a bit of luck he would find Benny Carter there. Benny's boys did not come cheap, but they were good and they could be relied on to do a thorough job.

Kay put down her empty teacup and eased back in her chair. 'Ter be honest, Else, I'm not concerned about what Pat Kelly gets up to,' she said sharply. 'What's 'appened between me an' David is a separate issue. It was 'is decision ter call it off, not mine. I might 'ave tried ter make it work, given the chance.'

Elsie reached into the hearth and took up the teapot. 'Give us yer cup,' she said, eyeing her younger sister indulgently. 'Yer said yer might 'ave tried ter make it work, Kay. That tells me somefing.'

'Like what?'

'It tells me that you do care about what Pat Kelly gets up to,' Elsie replied.

''Ow d'yer make that out?' Kay asked as she took the fresh cup.

Elsie gave her a wise look. 'Look, Kay. Would you 'ave taken David's letter so calmly if Pat Kelly 'adn't come back on the scene? I don't fink so. The reason I told yer about the rumours flyin' around concernin' Pat was 'cos I'm worried for yer. I don't wanna see yer get 'urt any more. I'm not stupid. I see the look on yer face every time that feller's name's mentioned. Be honest wiv me, Kay. If Pat Kelly asked yer out termorrer, would yer turn 'im down?'

The younger woman lowered her eyes. 'Yeah, I would,' she answered.

Elsie smiled affectionately. 'No yer wouldn't. Yer've always loved 'im, right from a kid. I just 'ad ter tell yer what's bein' said about Pat before you an' 'im got tergevver.'

'What makes yer fink we'll get tergevver?' Kay asked her.

'Credit me wiv a bit of intelligence, luv,' Elsie told her. 'Yer told me earlier that Pat's in love wiv yer. It's a stone certainty you two are gonna get tergevver sooner or later. Look at the way fings are. There's Pat gettin' pissed every night an' endin' up wiv ole toms, if the rumours are true, an' there's you moonin' about all doe-eyed. Yer gonna come face ter face wiv 'im sooner or later. Yer both live in the same street, fer Chrissake. It don't want much workin' out, does it?'

'You're a shrewd cow, Elsie,' her sister said smiling.

'I'm nuffing o' the sort,' Elsie told her. 'It's just common sense. Anyway, it's your life. Just be careful, an' don't pay too much attention ter what's bein' said. Yer know 'ow fings tend ter get blown out of all proportion.'

Kay gave her elder sister a warm smile. 'I'll be careful, Else.'

Errol Baines sat drinking with a few of his loading team in the Samson on Saturday evening. As they sipped their pints the men's eyes kept straying to the large clock behind the counter.

''E won't bovver ter ring,' one of the loaders remarked.

'Don't you be so sure,' another replied. 'Jim Carney's stupid enough ter fall fer anyfing.'

Errol had already informed the publican that a Mr Jack Sprat was expecting a call and he had positioned himself in a seat beside the counter ready.

'It's after nine. 'E won't ring now,' the first loader said.

Errol picked up his pint and took a long draught. ''E'll ring,' he told his men confidently.

245

At ten minutes past nine the phone rang. 'Who? I see. Just a minute, I'll see if 'e's about,' the landlord said, placing the phone on the counter next to Errol and handing him the receiver.

''Ello. Yes, I'm Mr Sprat. No, you can't call me Jack, not just yet. After all, I don't know yer from Adam,' the ganger replied in a deep voice.

The rest of the men gathered close to the phone, straining to hear as Errol turned the earpiece slightly for their benefit.

'I see. You need a reference. Well, I'm sure we can oblige an ole Civil Defence volunteer, providin' we can clarify that you did do a number of hours firewatchin' durin' the blitz,' Errol went on, grinning at his mates. 'Yes, I'm quite sure you're not lyin', but we do 'ave ter check these fings thoroughly. Can I take yer name an' address? Mr Barmy of Thirteen Waggoner's Way, Bermondsey. Sorry, Mr Carney. Is that wiv two e's? Oh, right. Well, I'll do a check right away, Mr Barney. Just 'old the line fer a minute. Sorry? Mr Carney.'

The loaders grinned at each other as Errol hummed loudly into the phone for a few seconds and then the ganger waved at them to be quiet.

'Right now, I've got a Mr Barnes an' a Mr Brand, but there doesn't seem ter be a Mr Barney on the roll of honour. Oh, of course. Yes I'm sorry. It's Mr Carney. Yes I've got that.' There were a further few seconds of silent mirth, then Errol continued. 'I've found it, Mr Carney. Yes 'ere we are. J. Carney of Thirteen Waggoner's Way. It ses 'ere ... Oh dear. Oh dear, oh dear. Well, I'm sorry Mr Barney, sorry, Carney, I'm afraid I won't be able ter supply a reference. Well, I'll tell yer why not. It ses 'ere in black an' white that you got a D an' D. Yes, I'll tell yer what a D an' D is. It's a dishonourable discharge. The report ses that you got it fer fallin' asleep on duty, whereby allowin' the Belton Tannery ter burn ter the ground. What's more, it ses 'ere that you failed ter keep the fire buckets filled an' that the controller took the necessary steps to 'ave you chucked out o' the Civil Defence 'cos you were responsible fer more damage ter the area than the German Airforce. Well, that's what it ses 'ere. Now look, Mr Barney, sorry, Carney. I can only go by what's bin written down 'ere. If yer wanna contest it, I suggest yer get yerself a few character references an' demand ter see someone who could get the record put straight.'

The audience of loaders were finding it hard not to laugh out

246

loud, especially when Errol winced at the torrent coming down the line.

'Look, I can't 'ear yer if yer keep screamin' down the phone, Mr Barney, sorry, Carney. Yes, I can tell yer who you should see. Go directly ter the mayor. Yes, I'm listenin'. Yes, you can call me Jack, it's all right now. I see. Right, Mr Carney, I'll do what I can. Can I ring yer back? Oh, I see. Well, can you phone me back in an hour? You can? Splendid. Cheerio, Mr Barney.'

'One o' these days yer gonna get your comeuppance, Bainesy,' the landlord told him with a grin on his face.

Errol chuckled as he looked around at his team. 'I'll make it all right, don't worry,' he told them.

Jim Carney came out of the phone-box in Hastings Street deep in thought. Someone had been on to that Civil Defence bloke, and it didn't need much working out who it was. Although all the gang knew he was going to ring the man, it was Errol Baines who had given him the phone number. It had to be him, Jim growled to himself.

As he stepped into the house, Sara Brady called out from the parlour. 'Did yer talk ter the man?' she asked.

'Yeah, but I gotta ring back in an hour,' he replied, popping his head round the door.

'I've just made a pot o' tea, Jim, if yer'd care fer one,' she told him.

'Fanks, luv, I won't be a minute, I've just gotta slip upstairs,' he said.

Sara sighed sadly as she poured out two cups of strong tea and laced them both with heaped spoonfuls of sugar. It was a shame the way they plagued that man with their stupid tricks, she thought. Errol Baines and his cronies would go too far one of these days. The whole gang were like a lot of school kids.

'Just what I could do wiv,' Jim said as he walked into the parlour.

Sara handed him the cup of tea and watched him closely as he sipped it thoughtfully. 'Are you all right?' she asked him.

'Yeah, I just feel a bit fed up,' he replied.

'It's all that runnin' around yer doin' after those references. I dunno why yer bovver,' Sara remarked.

'Nah, nor do I,' Jim said quietly, taking an envelope from his coat pocket and handing it to his landlady.

'What's this?' she said.

'Read it.'

Sara slipped on her glasses and read the letter aloud.

To whom it may concern.

Jim Carney has been working for the Southern Railway for fifteen years, and in that time he has proved to be a lazy good-for-nothing, a bad timekeeper, and a disrupting influence. As his ganger, I have no hesitation in saying that I would not recommend him for anything.

Errol Baines.

'That's terrible,' she said angrily. 'The man ought ter be 'orse-whipped.'

Jim gave her a weary smile. 'It's not that terrible. Errol Baines knew I'd open the letter out o' curiosity,' he told her. ''E'll give me a decent one, you'll see.'

'An' what about that phone call yer just made, Jim? I'll bet yer a pound to a pinch o' shit that was Baines at the ovver end o' the line,' Sara said with passion.

'There's no way o' knowin',' Jim said, shrugging his shoulders.

Sara sipped her tea for a while and then a smile slowly appeared on her face. 'I got an idea,' she said.

'Yeah?' Jim replied unenthusiastically, staring at the tea leaves in the bottom of his cup.

Errol leaned back on the counter, his hands clasped over his ample stomach. 'Carney'll be ringin' in a few minutes,' he said, smiling smugly. 'I wonder if 'e's read that reference I gave 'im.'

'If 'e 'as, you're in trouble,' one of the men told him.

'Nah, Jim ain't no problem,' Errol replied. 'I'll just tell 'im it was a joke an' I was gonna write 'im out a pukka one that 'e'd be pleased wiv.'

At ten o'clock precisely the phone rang in the Samson public bar.

'Mr Sprat, it's fer you,' the landlord said, handing him the receiver.

The loading team watched and waited, and they suddenly saw all the colour drain from Errol Baines's face. His eyes seemed to bulge in their sockets and he was trembling noticeably as he placed the receiver back on its stand.

248

'What is it, Errol?' they asked him.

'It was a woman's voice. She said Jim can't come ter the phone any more,' Errol said in a husky voice.

'What d'yer mean?'

Errol's eyes looked glassy and he gave a shuddering sigh. 'Jim Carney's just put 'is 'ead in the gas oven.'

Chapter Thirty-two

Mary Kelly dabbed at her eyes as she sat in Ada's tidy parlour on Saturday night. 'I wouldn't mind so much if it was just the drink, but it's the shame of knowin' our Pat's usin' them sort o' women,' she said tearfully.

Ada nodded sympathetically, though she felt a little irritated. Since he was little more than a teenager, Pat Kelly had used women like they were toys for him to discard whenever he got tired of them. To hear Mary going on, anyone would have thought it was all right for her son to use women just as long as they weren't prostitutes.

Tom Kelly looked at his old friend Joe and caught his eye, and they got up and left the women chatting to each other.

'She's naturally upset,' Tom said, 'but what can yer do? Pat's a grown man. I don't fink our Mary can accept it.'

'I s'pose it don't 'elp 'im comin' back ter live wiv yer. Women won't let their kids grow up sometimes,' Joe told him. 'I'm sure it'll work out all right in the end. Pat'll sort 'imself out.'

Tom nodded and watched while Joe filled two glasses from a flagon of ale. Mary had been tearful all day and he had suggested to her that they visit the Brennens. Ada could be relied upon to comfort her and cheer her up and it gave him a chance to chat about ideas for the community get-together.

'What upset Mary more than anyfing was the way she found out,' Tom went on. 'Charlie 'eard it in the Mason's an' 'e told 'is ole woman. She told Emily Toogood an' before yer could say Jack Robinson it was all round the street. Our Mary got stopped by Annie Thomas as she was comin' back from doin' the shoppin'. She come in cryin'. I thought she'd 'ad an accident.'

Joe handed him a brimming glass of beer. 'Never mind, Tom, get that down yer,' he said smiling.

Back in the parlour, Ada was consoling her friend. 'Look, Mary, your Pat ain't a child any more. 'E'll pull 'imself tergevver soon enough. After all, 'e's bin frew it wiv that Eileen Carter. I never reckoned they'd make a go of it, though I couldn't really say anyfing to yer.'

Mary nodded. 'Yeah, I s'pose I'm makin' too much of it, but I can't 'elp it,' she said, tears beginning to flow again.

Ada patted her shoulder as she got up to refill the teacups. 'Our Kay was upset when she 'eard about it,' she said casually. 'She always liked Pat, yer know. She used ter colour up every time 'is name was mentioned. Babs an' Dawn used ter tease ter rotten about 'im.'

'I wish 'e'd find a nice gel like your Kay, Ada. It's what 'e needs,' Mary sighed.

'It's strange the way fings work out at times,' Ada went on. 'You take our Else. She was mad about that git Gates. We tried ter tell 'er, but no, she wouldn't listen. Ernie Gates 'as treated 'er like a dish-rag ever since young Billy was born. Mind you, 'e was always a piss-artist, but they seemed ter get on all right till Billy come along. You know what I fink? I reckon it's eivver Ernie don't believe 'e's the farvver, or 'e didn't want kids in the first place.'

Mary nodded her head slowly. 'Yer might be right about 'im not wantin' kids,' she replied. 'Men are very selfish at times.'

Ada passed over a fresh cup of tea. ''Ave yer seen anyfing o' Dot Adams's boy?' she asked.

'Yeah I saw 'im only the ovver day,' Mary told her. 'I thought 'e looked very well.'

'Danny's doin' a bit o' spare-time carpentry. 'E done a nice job o' work on our floorboard, an' the room doors,' Ada said, sipping her tea.

'I was talkin' ter Dot the ovver day,' Mary said. 'She told me Danny still gets those 'eadaches now an' then, but not so much. P'raps they'll go altergevver in good time.'

'I fink that job at the baths 'elps,' Ada remarked. ''E seems ter like it, accordin' ter Dot.'

Edward Chipperfield had married young and soon realised his mistake. From being a successful hotel manager in the West Country, Chippy had trod a downhill path, and years later he finally settled for peace and quiet amongst the rivermen of Bermondsey.

251

Dockers, stevedores and lightermen were his regular customers and they had all heard the story many times of the scruffy landlord's downfall. They had seen the tatty photograph album which he sometimes brought out when he was in a nostalgic mood, with the snaps of an immaculately dressed hotel manager and a beautiful, smiling young woman, who had stolen Chippy's heart – and his bankroll, if he was to be believed.

The landlord of the riverside pub had made many good friends amongst the rivermen and there were tales a-plenty of how he had served free drinks and put a few bob their way when the men were 'out on the cobbles'. Such things were not forgotten, and when the freighters were queuing up to berth and it was one mad rush to turn them round, and the men earned well, they remembered the kindness shown to them by the rumpled Chippy.

'Just the bloke I wanna see,' Chippy said as Big Mick Mollison walked into the bar.

'Now 'ang on a minute, Chippy,' Mick told him. 'I bin down the dogs ternight an' I'm cleaned out, 'cept fer the price of a pint.'

The landlord looked at the man's big flushed face and smiled. 'I ain't callin' yer in, Mick,' he said. 'I'm just glad ter see yer, that's all.'

Mick put down a handful of coppers on the counter. 'That should do fer a pint o' bitter,' he said, grinning comically.

'Pick yer money up, son, it ain't needed ternight.'

'You backed a few winners, 'ave yer?' Mick asked him.

'Nah, I'm just glad yer showed up. Is Tubby due in?'

Mick Mollison's eyes narrowed slightly. 'What's it all about?' he asked.

'I'll tell yer when Tubby gets 'ere,' Chippy said.

Ten minutes later the portly figure of Tubby Wallis rolled up to the counter and he bellowed out for a pint of bitter. 'C'mon, Chippy, I'm croaked,' he said, his booming laugh filling the bar.

Chippy was a shrewd operator and he knew very well that a full belly brought contentment. Tubby and Mick both owed him a favour, and loath as he was to remind them, he knew he had no choice.

'Mick?'

'Yeah?'

'Get Tubby, will yer?'

'Sure fing.'

'Lofty?'

'Yeah?'

'Look after the bar fer a few minutes, I gotta talk ter these pair o' piss-artists,' Chippy told the lighterman who stood all of four feet eleven in his working boots.

Pat Kelly had been shocked on seeing Margie Dolan. She had been too frightened to let him in, and for a few minutes they stood chatting at her front door. Margie told him that she had managed to get the lock changed but still feared for her safety. Vic Dolan had just come out of prison and was determined to move in, even though she had told him in no uncertain terms that he wasn't wanted there. Margie was quick to let Pat know that Vic would be out for revenge and that he knew a lot of nasty people.

Pat dwelt on Margie's warning as he walked purposefully through the dark byways. The riverside streets were badly lit and deserted after dark, and there were a dozen or more places for someone to lie in wait, he knew full well, but it was a matter of pride. If he did not show his face in the area, word would get back to Vic Dolan and he might decide to ask a few questions. It was better to face up to the danger and walk tall, he decided, rather than hide like a hunted animal, never knowing when retribution might come.

The moon was fitful on Saturday night, with fleeting rain-clouds blanketing the stars as the young man stepped into the narrow cobbled lane that led to the Bell. Up ahead he saw the light from Chippy's pub shining out on the wet cobbles. He glanced about him. If he were to be set upon it was more likely to be around this spot, he reckoned.

A cat scurried out from a dark doorway, quickly followed by another, and Pat breathed out hard. He must be getting past it, he thought with a brief smile. There was a time when he would have enjoyed a violent set-to, just for the hell of it, but he was older now and he had been through a war. Injury and death had become intimates, surrounding him and crowding into his dreams: it had changed him, would have changed anybody. Maybe he should have a pint or two and then get home while he could still walk a straight line. A bellyful of booze would be a liability if it did come to a punch-up.

The tug on the back of his neck was violent and sudden, and as Pat staggered to keep his feet he twisted sideways trying to protect his head. The blow came down sharply on his collarbone, numbing his arm, and he found himself being dragged into a dark archway. The man holding him round the neck smelt of beer, and Pat retched as a knee came up and caught him full in the crotch. It was a bad match, he remembered thinking. Three against one.

'Vic Dolan sends 'is compliments,' beery breath growled.

Pat tried to butt him but the hand round his throat was like a clamp, slowly choking the life out of him. His arms were pinioned and he tried to kick out, but a searing pain in the pit of his stomach took away his legs and he slumped down in the attacker's grip. A fist caught him in the kidney and another full in the face, and a red haze grew in front of his eyes. This was it, a voice in his head was saying. Trapped and slaughtered in a dockside alley, outnumbered and without even seeing the faces of his attackers clearly.

Another blow to the side of his ribs took every bit of breath from his body, and Pat knew he was as good as finished. He had nothing to fight back with and the man behind him was throttling him harder. Another blow to the side of his head was quickly followed by another in his face, and he tasted his own blood. A bottomless pit was opening beneath him and he made one last desperate effort to fight back. He tried to arch himself like a spring to come back at them sharply, but a violent blow smashed into the pit of his stomach. All hope was gone, and as he began to choke on his blood he felt cold fear as he heard the metallic click of a flick-knife.

'Keep 'im still,' a voice growled.

Pat's hair was yanked back and he gritted his teeth, waiting for his attackers to cut him up. It was hopeless. His head was pulled back till his neck was stretched taut, then he felt the edge of the knife against his throat.

The last thing Pat Kelly remembered that night was being borne away. He could not speak and he felt as though his head was separated from his body. So this was to be his end, he thought. The cold river on a dark lonely night, his voice-box slashed so he couldn't call out. Would Margie Dolan remember him? Yes, she would be there at the Limehouse mortuary, her face pale and bruised and a small handkerchief held up to her mouth as she looked down on the bloated, river-whitened corpse.

Solly Weitzman had lived in Bermondsey since the pre-war Mosley riots. He had found good friends and comradeship there. He ran a newspaper stand in Jamaica Road, and after a long day at his pitch he invariably went into Chippy's for a tot of rum and a few rounds of stimulating conversation. Every night at the same time, come wind, rain or shine, Solly walked the riverside cobbled street to park himself on a barstool and provoke Chippy into a friendly row.

Tonight it was to be the future of Israel and the prospects of peace with its Arab neighbours. Solly had followed the subject closely and he had his own thoughts on the matter. Chippy would no doubt be cussed as usual, but this time he was prepared for battle.

The noises frightened Solly and he edged away from the dark archway, his small, crêpe-soled feet featherlike on the hard cobbles. He passed unnoticed and unheard, but he had glanced into the gloom just long enough to recognise the bloody face of the man who had fought over a woman a few nights ago. Solly hurried on, his eyes darting left and right like a frightened animal, and when he reached Chippy's pub he was shaking from head to foot.

Pat woke up and blinked at the strong light shining in his eyes. He could feel pressure on his forehead and he heard voices.

'He should be in hospital.'

'No. I'll take care of 'im.'

'Give him these every three hours. The cold compresses must be applied until the swelling goes down. I'll call in again tomorrow morning. Goodnight.'

'Pat? It's me, Margie Dolan. Don't try ter move.'

'What ... Where am I?'

'Don't talk now. Just lie still.'

Pat Kelly tried to open his eyes again but the light was too bright. He could smell disinfectant and then he felt a gentle warmth and saw a vague shape as the figure bent over him.

'You've 'ad a bad time but you're safe now,' the voice said softly.

Pat let his body go limp and he sighed deeply as the pain began to grow more distant.

'You're gonna sleep now. I won't be far away.'

The young man felt his body being lifted again, but this time it was as though he was rising on a cushion of air, and he did not try to resist.

Mick Mollison and Tubby Wallis stepped quickly into the back room and washed their hands at the grubby stone sink. Mick had a bruise above his eye and he felt sure that his knuckles were broken. Tubby was unscathed, except for a slight scuff mark on the side of his face and he grinned at the landlord. 'They won't be troublin' anybody fer some time,' he said. 'I reckon I broke one geezer's jaw wiv me daisy roots an' I'm sure Mick's clobbered one real bad. One geezer run off like a scared rabbit an' left the ovvers to it. Anyway, me an' Mick sorted 'em out, didn't we, pal?'

'An' only just in time by the look of it,' Chippy replied.

'The young bloke didn't 'ave a chance wiv them geezers,' Mick said. 'Me an' Tubby were more their weight.'

The thankful landlord took out a bottle of his best brandy from a cupboard and poured three large measures. ''Ere's ter two true friends; the only kind,' he said, raising his glass.

Chapter Thirty-three

Errol Baines had spent a sleepless night riddled with guilt, and on Sunday morning he was up early. His long-suffering wife Molly had grown accustomed to his habit of playing the practical joker, and she had become fed up with warning him that one day he would go too far. He had invariably laughed away her fears, but on this particular Sunday morning he was not laughing.

'Look, luv, I know yer feel terrible about what's 'appened, but yer shouldn't blame yerself too much,' she said kindly, her initial anger tempered by Errol's obvious distress. 'Jim Carney was a strange man, an' like yer said, 'e thrived on you an' yer mates jokin' wiv 'im. What 'e did was on the cards. If it 'adn't bin one fing it'd be somefink else. Yer said yerself all the blokes took the piss out of 'im. You wasn't the only one.'

Errol toyed with his slice of toast. 'Yeah, but it was me who done it. I'll never get over this, I'm sure I won't,' he groaned.

Molly had to let him see that she had been right all along. 'I did warn yer, didn't I?' she told him. ''Ow many times did I warn yer?'

Errol stared down at the plate and pushed it away. 'I can't eat anyfing,' he said. 'I feel sick.'

'Look, why don't yer get shaved an' go an' get yer paper,' Molly advised him. 'Go on, the walk'll do yer good.'

'I dunno,' he moaned. 'I can't face goin' inter that street after what's 'appened.'

'Well, don't go ter Springer's shop, go ter the ovver one in Dover Lane,' she replied.

'D'yer fink Jim told anybody about what was goin' on?' he asked her.

Molly shrugged her wide shoulders. 'I dunno. 'E must 'ave told that woman who phoned you up last night.'

257

'Yeah, but 'e might 'ave left a suicide note askin' 'er ter phone the number wivout sayin' why,' Errol suggested, lifting his eyes from the table.

'Well, yer'll soon find out,' Molly told him with a deep sigh. 'If this woman does know the full story, she's most likely tellin' everybody about it right this minute.'

Errol leaned forward in his chair and dropped his head into his hands. 'They'll all be pointin' fingers every time they see me in the street,' he groaned. 'I can just see it now. "There 'e goes. That's the evil git who sent Jim Carney to 'is grave." They'll make my life a misery. They'll 'ound me, Molly.'

Molly was tempted to remind her distraught husband that he had hounded Jim Carney for goodness knows how long and was now reaping the crop he had sown, but she thought better of it. The way he was acting right now there might well be another suicide in the area very shortly if she wasn't careful. 'The best way ter face it is 'ead on,' she told him. 'Let people see that you can 'old yer 'ead up, despite everyfing. They'll come ter realise that Jim Carney couldn't 'ave bin right in the 'ead an' it was on the cards that 'e'd top 'imself some time or anuvver.'

'Yeah, you're right, Molly. I'm gonna go ter Jack Springer's fer me paper, an' if anyone ses anyfing I'll just say that me an' Jim Carney were great friends an' I feel as sick about it as anybody,' Errol said fervently.

Sara Brady sat discussing the 'suicide' with her husband Stan, and he was finding it hard to contain himself.

'Dear, oh dear,' he choked, wiping the tears from his eyes. 'I can just see Errol's face when you got on that phone. I bet 'e was in a right state. Still, it serves 'im right. 'E's bin goin' a bit too strong an' now it's backfired on 'im.'

Sara looked suddenly frightened. 'Yer don't fink 'e'll do anyfing silly 'imself, do yer?' she asked him.

Stan started giggling again, and after a fit of coughing he looked up at his wife with watering eyes. 'Sara, you're killin' me,' he spluttered. 'I can see the 'eadlines now in all the papers. "Double suicide over practical joke." It's goin' from bad ter worse.'

'It's all right you laughin' about it,' she growled at him.

Stan got up and put on his coat, still trying to contain himself. 'If Errol comes round ter give 'is condolences, tell 'im that Jim'll most prob'ly come back to 'aunt 'im,' he told her with his eyes rolling suggestively.

Errol Baines walked hesitantly into Waggoner's Way and saw that everything looked quite normal for a Sunday morning. A few women were chatting at their front doors and children played in the street. The shrimp and winkle man had just pushed his laden barrow into the turning, and big Joe Mezzo was standing outside his shop chatting to an old lady. Nothing looked amiss.

Errol walked on and exchanged nods with two of the women, and he breathed a bit more easily. He knew that Jim Carney lodged at number 13, two houses away from the paper shop, and as he drew level he jumped with shock. Stan Brady had almost bumped into him as he came out of the house and he was wiping his eyes with a handkerchief.

''Ello, Errol. Shame about ole Jim,' he said reverently. 'Would yer care ter see 'im?'

Errol nodded and shuffled his feet uncomfortably. 'I'll be back in five minutes, Stan,' he told him.

After buying his paper, Errol hurried along to the florist shop at the end of Hastings Street and bought a spray of winter pansies. It was the least he could do, he thought. It would show a bit of respect. Funny that Jack Springer hadn't said anything about Jim Carney though. He must have heard the news, considering it had happened only two doors away.

When he got back to the Brady house, Errol stood hesitating. What could he say to them? They would know how he had taken the rise out of their lodger – well, Stan would if not Sara, him working at the freight yard. Well, he had to face it sooner or later, he told himself. Better get it over with.

Sara answered the door and she looked quite normal, Errol thought. That was the way it was with some women, he reflected as he followed her into the passage. They seemed able to remain calm when relatives and friends called at such times.

'Go in, Errol,' Sara told him.

He stepped into the parlour, his face set and his lips compressed as he prepared to see his victim washed and laid out ready for the undertaker.

'Oh my Gawd!' he gasped, as he saw Jim Carney sitting at the table dipping a finger of bread into a soft-boiled egg.

''Ello, Errol. 'Ow yer doin?' Jim asked him.

The ganger staggered forward and dropped into a chair. 'I-I thought . . . You're s'posed ter be dead!' he stuttered.

'Those flowers fer me?' Jim asked, grinning broadly at him as he saw his ashen face.

Errol looked down at the pansies he had dropped on the table and then his eyes went up to Sara. 'It was you who phoned me,' he said. 'You was in on it. You put 'im up to it.'

'Yeah, that's right,' Sara said boldly. 'Yer've just 'ad a taste o' yer own medicine. It don't taste very nice, does it?'

Errol leaned forward on the table, his hand over his forehead. 'You're right, luv. I did ask for it. What can I say?'

'P'raps yer could start by sayin' yer sorry,' she told him firmly.

Jim Carney wiped his mouth on the back of his hand and picked up his mug of tea. 'It's all right, Errol. I ain't 'oldin' no grudges, even though yer gave me a right poxy reference,' he told him.

Errol smiled sheepishly. 'I knew yer'd open the letter, that's why I put what I did. I got the real reference indoors. Yer can read it if yer like before I seal it. It's a good 'un, Jim.'

'Nah, you can seal it if yer like. I trust yer,' Jim replied.

'After what 'e done ter you?' Sara said quickly.

'It's all right, Sara. Me an' Errol are good pals really,' Jim told her, winking at his ganger. ''E looks after me at work, don't yer, Errol?'

''E better do so from now on,' Sara said sharply. 'If there's any more trouble I'll 'ave somefink ter say ter that guv'nor o' yours.'

Errol stood up looking very chastened. 'Well, I'd better be off,' he said. ,

'Fanks again fer the flowers,' Jim said, grinning as Errol went out.

Vic Dolan had made sure he was nowhere in the vicinity when his hired thugs waylaid Pat Kelly. He had paid the three of them ten pounds each and Benny Carter was due to be paid off once the job was done. Benny had assured him that the men would make a good job of it and he should stay clear until the next morning, then call in at the club around lunch-time to settle up.

Dolan was feeling pleased with himself as he walked along Jamaica Road that Sunday. He had not spent five years in Wandsworth Prison only to be told who he could and could not see. Margie was his wife once, no matter how she felt about him now. She was going to work for him and she had better get used to the idea, he told himself. Once he had settled in there he could get a few more girls working for him, and if there was any trouble he had Benny and his boys to turn to. All in all, things could work out very nicely.

As he walked into the seamen's club, Vic saw Benny Carter polishing the counter. He waved a greeting. The club owner beckoned him over.

'There was a bit o' trouble wiv the job last night,' he told him.

'Didn't they get 'im?' Vic asked quickly.

'Yeah, they done 'im, but they couldn't finish the job. Kelly must 'ave 'ad somebody lookin' out fer 'im,' Benny explained. 'The boys got set on before they could dump 'im in the river.'

'I wanted a good job done on 'im, Benny. I paid good money,' Vic said sharply.

'Look, Vic they gave Kelly a good workin'-over an' I don't fink 'e's gonna trouble yer again,' Benny replied. 'The boys are out the back. Why don't yer go an' 'ave a chat wiv 'em. When yer see 'em you'll realise they earned their money last night.'

When Vic Dolan walked into the back room he understood what Benny meant. Two heavily built men sat at a table eating a late breakfast. One was having trouble chewing his food. His face was black and blue. The other had a large plaster over one eye and his ear was caked in dried blood. His lips were swollen and he held a hand to his ribs as he ate.

'I understand there was a spot o' trouble last night,' Dolan said as he sat down at the table.

'We got jumped ourselves,' the first man told him. 'Our pal was lucky. 'E pissed off, but we didn't get the chance. Those geezers outweighed us by a couple o' stone apiece. They could 'andle 'emselves pretty well too.'

'So it seems,' Dolan said, looking from one to the other. 'What about Kelly? Did yer manage ter do a good job on 'im?'

'Yeah, we sorted 'im out. 'E ain't gonna be bovverin' yer again, yer can bank on it,' the second man said, wincing as he took a deep breath.

Dolan fished into his pocket and took out two five-pound notes. 'There's a little bonus fer yer trouble,' he told them as he laid the money down on the table. 'I'll keep in touch. I might be needin' yer services again in the near future.'

The two men did not seem too enthusiastic as they pocketed the notes. 'We'd need at least twenty-five apiece if it was anyfing like last night's turn-out,' one said.

'Nah, this won't even be strenuous,' Dolan assured them. 'We'll talk later. All the best.'

When he walked back into the bar, Benny took him to one side. 'One o' the boys took this off o' Kelly,' he said, dropping a brown leather wallet on the counter. 'There was only two quid in it an' they've kept that, but I told 'em not ter get rid o' the wallet till you've seen it.'

Dolan picked it up and opened it. It was empty, apart from a photograph of a pretty young woman with long fair hair and large blue eyes. The villain studied it for a few seconds then he threw the wallet back down on to the counter. 'Yer can chuck it,' he said.

Chapter Thirty-four

The Brennen family began their Sunday as they had always done. Ada got up quite early and boiled the kettle. Joe took his cup of tea and biscuits in bed, and the girls stretched out comfortably, enjoying a leisurely lie-in especially as the weather looked rather threatening.

Joe dressed, shaved and drank another cup of tea before strolling along the turning to Jack Springer's newsagent's for his *News of the World*. Ada sat in the scullery, her arms folded while Barbara took out the rollers and combed out the tight curls. It was a little luxury that she enjoyed before the ritual of cooking the Sunday meal and baking a fruit cake for tea.

Usually Dawn was the last to emerge from the bedroom, but on this particular Sunday she was up early. 'Gordon's comin' round soon. We're goin' ter Greenwich,' she announced.

Kay came down into the scullery with her towelling dressing-gown wrapped tightly around her, and stood with her back resting against the dresser as she sipped a cup of tea pensively. Barbara glanced up at her occasionally as she ran a large, wide-toothed comb through her mother's tangled hair.

'You look a bit thoughtful this mornin', Kay,' she said finally.

'I was just finkin' about our Colin, as a matter o' fact,' Kay replied. ''E said in the letter 'e'll be gettin' a forty-eight-hour pass next week. I was wonderin' about 'avin' a little party for 'im.'

'That's a nice idea,' Ada said. 'We could invite the Kellys an' the Catchpoles, an' maybe the Springers. Yer farvver would like that. We've not 'ad a good party fer ages.'

'I could bring Jamie an' I'm sure Dawn would want Gordon ter come now that they seem more close,' Barbara added.

Ada smiled happily to herself as she recalled the Saturday night

263

parties when all the neighbours dropped in and Emily Toogood played the piano. 'I could invite Emily,' she said. 'I'd 'ave ter get someone in ter tune the joanna though. It ain't bin played fer years.'

Barbara and Kay exchanged disapproving glances. 'We ain't gonna 'ave a sing-song party are we, Mum?' Barbara asked her. 'We've got the record player an' we've got loads o' records.'

Dawn came into the scullery and took a quick look at herself in the small mirror standing on the dresser. 'Is my lipstick too bright?' she asked.

'Yeah, it is a bit,' Ada told her.

'What about me eyes?'

'They look all right ter me,' Barbara said.

'I look a right mess this mornin',' Dawn sighed.

'Yer've not seen Gordon yet. 'E was playin' yesterday, wasn't 'e?' Kay asked her.

Dawn nodded as she wiped the tip of her little finger round the corner of her mouth and then turned away from the mirror. 'I do 'ope 'e's not damaged 'is face again,' she puffed.

'Just as long as it's not anyfing else 'e's damaged,' Barbara said, grinning.

Ada gave her a sharp look as she got up to view her hair in the mirror. 'That looks better. D'yer fink I should 'ave a colour rinse?' she asked.

They heard the front door go and then Elsie walked into the scullery looking worried.

'You're early, Elsie. Anyfing wrong?' Ada asked her.

Elsie glanced at each of them in turn, then she fixed her eyes on Kay. 'A woman called round just now,' she said hesitantly. 'She said 'er name was Margie Dolan an' she told me Pat Kelly's got into a bit o' trouble an' 'e wants ter see you, Kay.'

'Me?' Kay replied, looking noticeably shocked.

'Yeah, 'e sent this woman wiv the message.'

'Where is 'e? What's 'appened to 'im?' Kay asked her quickly.

'Apparently 'e got beat up last night outside a pub in Dock'ead,' Elsie told her. ''E's stayin' at this woman's place. I got the address 'ere.'

'What about Pat's mum an' dad? They should be told,' Ada said.

'That's what I said ter this woman, but she said Pat don't want 'em ter know.'

264

'That's all very well, but they're bound ter be worried over 'im not goin' 'ome last night,' Ada remarked. 'Mary Kelly was 'eartbroken over Pat when she come round ter see me the ovver day.'

'Well, that's the message, Mum. What can we do?' Elsie replied, shrugging her shoulders.

Kay reached for her coat. 'I'd better go straight away,' she said.

'Want me ter come wiv yer?' Barbara volunteered.

'No, I'd better go on me own,' Kay replied. 'I'll try not ter be too long.'

As soon as Kay had left the house, Elsie turned to her mother. 'That woman who called. I fink she's on the game.'

'She could be the one Pat's s'posed to 'ave bin seein',' she suggested.

'Quite likely,' Elsie said nodding. 'She seemed brassy an' 'er face was all made up. She was quite nice though.'

'I wonder what Pat wants ter see our Kay for?' Ada asked her daughters.

''E's in love wiv 'er, Mum,' Elsie said bluntly.

Ada looked a little startled. 'I know Kay's 'ad a crush on 'im ever since she was a teenager, but I never knew 'e felt the same way about 'er,' she replied.

Elsie took her coat off and sat down at the small table. 'Yer know it's all off wiv Kay an' David?' she queried.

'Yeah, she got a letter from 'im,' Ada said. 'I'm glad, ter tell yer the trufe. I'm sure 'e was a married man.'

''E was, but don't tell Kay I said so fer Gawd's sake,' Elsie said quickly.

Ada shook her head slowly. 'I dunno. It's one shock after anuvver.'

'It wasn't really a shock, Mum. You guessed it right,' Barbara told her.

Joe walked in with the Sunday paper tucked under his arm. 'Are you runnin' the street down as usual?' he asked, grinning. 'I dunno why I bovver ter buy this paper. I can get as many juicy bits o' scandal just listenin' ter you lot.'

The morning mist was lifting as Kay hurried through the quiet Sunday streets. She heard the solemn toll of the St James's church bells as she drew near. She puzzled over why Pat wanted to see her. Maybe something terrible had happened to him and he was hoping

265

she could break the news to his family. Perhaps he was going to die and wanted her to hear his last words, she imagined fearfully.

By the time Kay reached Jamaica Road she had worked herself into a state of panic and she realised that she was breathing rapidly. She must try to stay calm, she told herself. It might only be that he had minor injuries and had decided to stay at the woman's house for the night. What of her? Kay found herself wondering. Was she the street woman who Pat had supposedly been seeing?

The young woman turned into a backstreet and quickly consulted the slip of paper on which a crude map had been sketched. Finally she turned into Cotton Lane and knocked at number 7.

'I'm Kay Brennen,' she told the big blonde woman who opened the door.

'C'mon in, luv,' Margie said, giving her a smile. 'Before yer see 'im, me an' you need to 'ave a chat.'

Kay sat down on a comfortable armchair and looked about the small room. It was tastefully furnished and the draperies looked expensive. She could smell perfume, and as Margie came nearer and sat down facing her, the scent was almost overpowering.

'Tell me first off, are you Pat's gel?' Margie asked.

Kay shook her head. 'We're just neighbours,' she replied.

'But yer'd like it ter be more?' Margie said, smiling.

Kay nodded. 'Can I see 'im now?' she asked.

Margie leaned forward and touched the young woman lightly on the forearm. 'There's no rush, luv, 'e's sleepin',' she replied. 'I'm gonna wake 'im up fer 'is tablet in a few minutes. In the meantime we should talk.'

Kay studied the big blonde. She could see what looked like bruising under her heavy make-up. The woman would be in her forties, she guessed. She was heavy around the hips and her ankles looked swollen, but she had a confident air about her and her smile was charming. It was probably one of the things about her that had captivated Pat Kelly, she thought.

'Ter begin wiv, Pat 'appens ter be 'ere because my place was 'andy,' Margie told her. 'Me an' 'im ain't lovers or anyfing like that. We're just good friends. The reason Pat got jumped on last night was because, a few nights ago, 'im an' my ex-ole man Vic got ter blows over Vic beatin' me up. Pat was incensed about it, an' when my ole man went inter Chippy's an' started shoutin' the odds, it all blew up. Vic got a few of 'is cronies ter waylay Pat an' they would 'ave killed 'im, I've no doubt, if it 'adn't bin fer a couple o' Chippy's docker friends. They sorted Vic's blokes out, then they carried Pat back 'ere an' I sent fer the doctor.'

''Ow bad is 'e?' Kay asked her.

'Apart from a broken nose, a few loose teef and bad bruisin', 'e's OK,' Margie told her. 'The doctor reckons there might be some cracked ribs so 'e's bandaged 'im up. That's about it, really.'

''Ave yer got any idea why 'e should wanna see me?' Kay asked.

'Apart from the fact that 'e's crazy about yer, I can't fink of any reason,' Margie said, smiling.

'Can I see 'im now?' Kay asked anxiously.

'Yeah, why not?'

Margie led the way into the bedroom. As Kay saw the young man lying propped up on pillows, she gasped. His face was almost unrecognisable.

'I'll leave you two alone. Call me if Pat wants anyfing,' Margie said and, seeing Kay's indecision, 'go on, wake 'im up. Like I said, 'e's due fer a tablet soon.'

Kay sat down beside the bed and reached out her hand to touch Pat gently on the forehead. He stirred and opened his eyes.

'I'm glad you could come,' he said croakily. 'I didn't know if yer would.'

'I 'ad to, Pat. When they said you'd bin in a bit o' trouble I feared the worst,' Kay told him.

The young man tried to move his arm but winced with pain; he let it rest on top of the bedclothes. 'I was lucky last night,' he said. 'They were tryin' ter finish me.'

'Margie told me all about it,' Kay said quietly.

'I wanted ter see yer, Kay,' he whispered through swollen lips. 'I sent Margie ter yer sister Elsie 'cos I knew she could be trusted ter be discreet. I didn't want Margie bargin' in on you an' alertin' yer mum an' dad. They would 'ave told my parents an' I don't want 'em worried.'

'Don't yer fink they're worried already, you not goin' 'ome last night?' Kay reminded him.

'Yeah, but they'll suspect I was wiv somebody,' he told her.

'It figures,' Kay said, smiling. 'Word 'as got about.'

'Yer gotta understand that there's nuffink between me an' Margie,' he said earnestly.

'Why should it concern me?' Kay asked him. 'You're free. You're entitled ter go wiv who yer like.'

'It concerns me,' Pat replied quickly. 'I love yer, Kay, an' I want yer ter know it. All right, I know there's someone else in yer life at the moment, but from what yer've told me an' from what I can gavver, it might not be permanent. I wanna be there for yer, just in case.'

Kay looked at his bruised face and reached out her hand and touched his forehead once more. 'There's no one else, Pat,' she said softly. 'Me an' David 'ave decided it wouldn't work. 'E's gone back wiv 'is wife, an' I've spent my days an' nights prayin' that you an' me would bump into each ovver, just so I'd be able ter tell yer.'

Pat closed his eyes for a few moments and sighed deeply. 'I've not 'ad yer out o' me mind since that mornin' I walked ter work wiv yer,' he told her.

'You're never far from my mind, Pat,' she whispered.

His hand moved slowly over the bedclothes and Kay took it in hers. 'I love yer, Pat. I've always loved yer, ever since I was a kid,' she whispered. 'I wanted ter die when the rumours started flyin' round about you an' those women.'

'Like Margie?' he replied.

She nodded and he smiled painfully. 'Friends don't come no better than Margie,' he said.

Margie Dolan came into the bedroom carrying a tumbler of water. She bent over the bed. 'C'mon, cry baby, take this,' she said smiling, and then looking at Kay she said, 'did you ever see such a carry-on when a feller 'as ter take a pill?'

When they were alone once more, Kay bent over and kissed him gently on the lips. 'What do I tell yer parents?' she asked him.

He sighed. 'I s'pose the pretence is over. Tell 'em the trufe, Kay, but do it gently, please.'

She nodded. 'That goes wivout sayin', but I'm also gonna tell 'em about me an' you. I want everyone ter know it,' she said with a big smile.

Joe Mezzo sat alone in the comfortable flat above his shop on Sunday lunch-time and waited for his visitor to arrive. It was opportune that Maria had decided to call in on one of her friends that morning, he thought. Maria did incline to worry over every little thing, and the less she knew about his shady dealings the better it was for her.

Joe poured himself another whisky and settled down to listen to the wireless, and as the strains of a full orchestra drifted through the room he considered his future. Sergeant Moody was no doubt feeling very angry at what had been a disappointing raid on the shop. On top of that, the visit he had paid to Moody's boss had been like rubbing salt on his wounds. Chief Superintendent Roger Cranley had been very courteous and had gone so far as to apologise for the inconvenience caused to him.

Joe smiled to himself as he sat thinking about the visit. He had been at pains to assert that the Maltese population of Bermondsey were a pillar of society, and many of them had fought and died for this country. It was sad to think that uninformed people like Moody assumed every Maltese was crooked. Sure there were a minority who shamed the rest, but that was the case with every nationality. Cranley had felt compelled to agree and the two men shook hands warmly with a passing shot from Joe.

'If ever I 'ear of any under'and dealin's in my neighbour'ood, Superintendent, you'll be the first ter know.'

At one o'clock Mick Mollison arrived and introduced himself. Joe led him into the room and bade him sit down. 'Fancy a drink?' he said, pointing to the bottles on the sideboard.

The big docker pointed to the whisky. 'That'll do fine, Mr Mezzo,' he replied.

Joe poured out two large measures and then passed one over to his visitor. 'Me friends call me Joe,' he said, smiling. 'Nick Zanti phoned me about your problem. 'E told me you've bin of assistance to us an' we might be able ter return a favour.'

Mick Mollison eased back in the armchair. 'Nick's a pal o' mine an' I managed ter put some info 'is way,' he replied.

Joe nodded slowly. 'Yeah, I know. Nick told me the inside information you gave 'im concernin' the salmon business was spot on and you were ter be trusted,' he went on. 'I believe 'im, ovverwise you wouldn't be sittin' 'ere now. Anyway, ter the business in 'and. I understand you an' a pal came ter Pat Kelly's assistance an' there may be a come-back. As a matter o' fact I know the Kelly family. Mary Kelly's a customer o' mine an' I like ter look after my customers in any way I can.'

Mick sipped his whisky and pulled a face. 'I recognised one o' those geezers we pulled off o' Pat Kelly,' he said. ''E's a nasty git an' 'e drinks in the seamen's club in Rovverhithe. I'm not concerned fer meself, but I got a wife an' kids ter fink about. They could be in the firin' line if this geezer an' 'is pals come callin'.'

'I know where the seamen's club is,' Joe replied. 'Leave it wiv me. I'll get a couple o' friends o' mine ter make a few discreet inquiries an' then I'll get back ter Nick Zanti. We'll no doubt be able ter sort somefing out. If you phone Nick termorrer evenin' 'e should be able ter put yer mind at rest. 'Ow's that?'

Mick Mollison swallowed his drink and got up. 'I really appreciate it, Joe,' he said, holding out his hand. 'Best o' luck ter yer.'

Kay Brennen felt as though she was walking on a cloud as she hurried back home on Sunday lunch-time. It all seemed so unreal. Pat Kelly and her, together at last. Tongues would wag now, she thought, but it didn't matter. Nothing mattered, as long as they were together.

The family had gathered in the parlour, eager to hear just what had happened, and Kay was prevailed upon to explain in detail, but she delayed saying anything about the two of them until she was sure they would all be agreeable.

'Pat Kelly's always bin a reckless fella an' it's just like 'im ter react the way 'e did,' Ada said.

Elsie had an idea that her younger sister was biding her time. 'I don't fink 'e's 'alf as bad as people make 'im out ter be,' she remarked. 'I didn't believe fer a minute 'e was involved wiv prostitutes, not in that way. I mean, take that what's-'er-name who used ter live in number Nine. She was on the game an' she used ter chat wiv all the fellers round 'ere.'

'Yeah, she was always chattin' ter you, wasn't she, Dad?' Dawn reminded him.

'Yer mean Sadie Somers,' Joe replied. 'She was just a neighbour as far as I was concerned. She was a good-'earted gel. Look 'ow she used ter run errands fer the ole people.'

Kay was encouraged by what Elsie and her father had said. 'That's what Margie Dolan's like, accordin' ter Pat,' she went on. 'She chats wiv all the neighbours, except one or two, an' she jokes wiv all the fellers, but she don't solicit 'em.'

Elsie felt for her younger sister. They had become very close of late, and she wanted to help her bring everything out into the open.

270

'What about the future?' she said tentatively. 'D'yer fink you an' Pat might get tergevver? After all, 'e did wanna see yer. Margie Dolan told me 'e finks a lot of yer.'

Kay was aware that everyone's eyes were on her and she flushed up. 'Pat did ask me ter walk out wiv 'im, once 'e's better,' she replied as casually as possible.

'I s'pose yer could do a lot worse,' Joe told her. 'The boy comes from a nice family. Me an' Tom Kelly 'ave bin mates fer years.'

Barbara and Dawn both looked pleased with the news, but Ada's face registered concern.

'Yer shouldn't lose sight o' the fact that Pat Kelly's bin a real womaniser,' she remarked. 'All right, 'e might 'ave changed, but yer need ter be very careful, Kay. I wouldn't wanna see anuvver mismatch in this family. It's bad enough wiv one.'

Elsie and her sisters exchanged humorous glances.

'Yer can't compare Pat wiv Ernie,' Barbara cut in. 'I fink Pat Kelly'd make a real good 'usband, as long as 'e's not given too much rope.'

'As long as 'e's bein' watched, yer mean?' Ada replied.

'What I mean is, don't go givin' the man cause ter start castin' 'is eye,' Barbara explained.

Joe chuckled as he looked at Ada. 'They're all experts, ain't they?' he said derisively.

The matriarch nodded her head slowly. 'Yeah, they're all full o' good intentions.'

Kay felt that the first hurdle was over. She now had the task of going to see Pat's parents to tell them what had happened to him, and she was feeling strangely apprehensive as she slipped her coat back on.

Ada walked to the front door with her. 'Are yer sure you're all right, or would yer like me ter go wiv yer?' she asked.

'No, I'd sooner go on me own, Mum,' Kay told her with an affectionate smile. 'I'm not lookin' forward to it though.'

Ada took her daughter by the arm. 'I fink Mary an' Tom Kelly'll be very pleased to 'ear that you two are gonna get tergevver,' she said quietly.

Kay suddenly hugged her mother tightly. 'I'm so 'appy,' she sighed.

'Yeah, I know,' Ada said, patting her back gently. 'Yer've always loved that lad, 'aven't yer?'

271

Chapter Thirty-five

Benny Carter looked up from the counter as two well-dressed men sauntered into his seamen's club early on Sunday evening.

'Mr Carter? Mr Benny Carter?'

'Yeah, that's me,' Benny said, putting down the glass he was polishing. 'What's the pleasure, lads?'

The two men looked around the grotty clubroom with distaste and then the shorter of the two smiled. 'We're just errand boys, sad to say. We've been told to make you aware that you've transgressed,' he said quietly.

'I've what?'

'Sinned, Benny boy.'

The club owner leaned forward over the counter. 'Now why don't yer come ter the point?' he said, anger colouring his voice.

'Very well then,' the short man replied, matching his stare. 'A good friend of a friend of yours got beaten up last night, and your friend is saddened that you've taken it upon yourself to go into the contract business without first consulting him.'

Benny gave them a puzzled look. 'I don't know what you're talkin' about,' he replied quickly.

'Yes you do,' the man told him. 'Let me clarify it. You get your booze and cigarettes from a specific source, and I happen to know that you're very satisfied with the arrangement, considering it's a time of shortages. Your supplier is very satisfied too with the arrangement. He likes to feel that his customers are his friends. In fact, he only deals with people he looks upon as friends. Now do you savvy?'

'Yer mean that the bloke who yer say got sorted out last night is a friend o' my supplier?' Benny queried.

'Prezactly.'

'Look, there was a geezer came in 'ere the ovver night who was in fear of 'is life an' 'e asked me if I knew anyone who'd sort it out for 'im,' Benny said quickly. 'All I did was point 'im in the right direction. I didn't earn out of it.'

'That's beside the point,' the visitor replied. 'You aided and abetted a felony. Against us – forget the police. Now unless we get names of the parties involved, we'll have to assume that you do not value friendships.'

The taller of the two callers broke his silence. 'What it also means is that you're goin' ter take a premature retirement,' he said with quiet menace.

Benny felt the sweat forming on his forehead. 'Those three geezers ain't seamen. They just frequent the club,' he replied in desperation.

'Names please, Benny.'

The club owner sagged visibly as he leaned nearer the two visitors and mumbled.

'Thank you, Mr Carter,' the shorter man said. 'I'm sure that you won't be disappointed. Your friend will be pleased with the cooperation you've shown. By the way, he'll most probably be telling you about some new commodities coming on to the market very soon. Very profitable by all accounts. Goodnight, Mr Carter.'

Grace Dines had waited impatiently for her son Simon to make his regular trip to the pub that evening, and when he finally left the house, the old lady put on the heavy chain, made herself a cup of strong tea and then sat back down in front of the fire. She took out her silver snuffbox and tapped her fingers on the lid as she looked down at the unopened letter on her lap. It was postmarked Capetown, and Grace smiled to herself. Norman would have received the letter she had sent to the shipping line's office in Capetown a month ago and this was his reply.

Grace had felt it necessary to write to him and make him aware of her wishes. She had told him in the letter that she was in the winter of her life and not a well woman, and she wanted him and not Simon to have her life savings when she passed away. She had gone on to say that she knew him to be a careful, thrifty lad, not totally irresponsible like his older brother. She knew he would make better use of the money and could be trusted to make some sort of provision for Simon.

Norman would know where to find the money. He knew that she did not trust banks and would have kept all the money securely hidden in the house, and he would know just where to look. It had been a secret between them both since Norman was a puny child, bullied by his older brother. She had shown him the secret place where he could hide his toys and his treasured possessions. Now, the secret place contained not toys but a large sum of money which she had amassed over the years.

The old lady took a pinch of snuff and wiped her watery eyes on her black apron, then she settled down to reading Norman's letter. He told her that he had received the one sent to him and he understood her wishes. She could rely on him to look after Simon, and he knew where to find the money. The six-page letter went on to describe his travels, telling of warm moonlit nights in the faraway ocean, of temples and lush gardens where waterfalls cascaded down over huge rocks, where tropical birds screeched, monkeys chattered in the trees and the rain fell in sheets for days. He described idyllic mornings on board ship far out at sea, where the sun rose up like a giant red globe and flying fishes played. It was a lovely picture he painted, the old lady sighed. How long was it now that he'd been away? Two years? More like three, she decided. Yes, nearer three. He would be home in a few weeks and this time he would call on her for sure.

Grace Dines got up from her armchair and took the key from around her neck to unlock the sideboard drawer. She took out the tattered photograph album, carried it over to the table and drew up a chair. It was nice to look at those old snaps, especially the ones Norman sent her from Port Said, she thought with a smile. He was younger then, his first trip as ship's radio operator. He looked lean and tanned. He would be much heavier now and his beard would make him look older. Yes, he would surely come to see her this time, especially after getting her letter.

The old lady browsed through the pages for some time, then she sighed with fatigue as she took the album back to its resting place in the drawer, along with Norman's letter. She locked them away, slipped the string back over her head and tucked the key into her bodice. Simon would be in soon and then she would be able to go to bed.

At nine o'clock on Sunday night the Maltese confederates gathered in a small restaurant in Shoreditch owned by a cousin of Nick Zanti. They dined on mussels, crab salad and caraway seed-cake and the meal was washed down with Chianti; then, as coffee and brandy were being served, the two awaited men arrived. Cigar and cigarette smoke spiralled up from the table as the group discussed in lowered voices the business in hand.

'We can pick them all up in no time at all, but it should be as soon as possible,' Zanti said. 'We need to stamp on this before it gets out of hand.'

Joe Mezzo nodded in agreement as he tapped the ash from his Sumatran cigar. 'That's right. We need fings ter settle down fer a spell,' he said. 'The last fing we need is street battles at this time. If someone gets found in an alley wiv their froat cut then the boys in blue'll start swarmin' all over the place. That's not very conducive fer business.'

Mick the Hammer sipped his coffee, the cup almost hidden in the crook of his hand. 'When do we grab 'em?' he asked.

'I'd say first fing termorrer,' Joe replied.

'I suggest we use the old Commer van. It's closed in and secure,' Zanti said, pulling on his shirt cuffs.

'What's it ter be, the frighteners?' Tony Mancini asked the others.

'I should fink so,' Joe said, nodding. 'Like we've agreed, we don't wanna leave bodies layin' around. It tends ter give a place a bad name.'

Their smiles were restrained, and Nick Zanti stroked his chin. 'We'll use the factory. Tony, are you and Mick going to preside?'

'I wouldn't miss this one,' Tony replied with an evil grin.

'What about you, Mick?'

'Likewise.'

'Right then, let's sort out the details an' call it a night,' Joe said. 'Maria's told me I'm neglectin' 'er lately.'

Pat Kelly moved the tea-tray to one side and eased himself on to the edge of the bed, gritting his teeth as a sharp pain stabbed at his lower ribs. The room started to swim and he rested where he was until his head cleared a little. He was determined to be out of Margie's house as soon as possible; she was in enough trouble as it was without Vic Dolan discovering that she was looking after the man his thugs had tried to kill.

The young man stood up, holding on to the bedhead for support.

It didn't seem too bad, he thought. He would be able to walk the short distance to Chippy's pub and get him to phone for a cab.

'An' what d'yer fink you're doin'?' Margie asked in a firm voice as she came into the bedroom.

'I can't stay 'ere, luv. It's too risky for yer,' Pat told her.

The big blonde woman held his arms and gently pushed him into a sitting position on the bed. 'I decide when you're ready ter get up, not you,' she told him. 'In any case, the doctor's callin' round soon. 'E wants ter take anuvver look at yer.'

Pat tried to protest but she cut him short. 'Now get back inter bed, an' stop worryin',' she said. 'There's no need. I've changed the lock on the front door an' Vic won't be stupid enough ter try an' barge in. I know 'im well enough, I married the bastard, remember?'

'That's all very well, but yer gotta leave the 'ouse sooner or later,' Pat pointed out. 'What's ter stop 'im givin' yer anuvver pastin'?'

Margie grinned. 'Let me show yer somefing,' she said, hurrying from the room and returning with her handbag. 'If Vic tried ter touch me I'd give 'im a taste o' this.' She pulled out a metal comb which had been filed down to about halfway along its ridge. 'If 'e lays a finger on me I'll open 'is face. 'E won't be 'urtin' me ever again.'

Pat saw her determined look as she fingered the sharp edge. 'Where did yer get that?' he asked curiously.

'One o' me regular punters gave it ter me. Us street gels need a bit o' protection,' she reminded him. 'I only wish I could 'ave got ter me 'andbag when Vic set about me last time. I would 'ave killed 'im fer sure.'

Pat reached out and took her by the shoulders as he saw her starting to tremble. 'Are you all right, Marge?' he asked her.

'Yeah, it's OK. I just get all screwed up when I fink about that evil git,' she replied.

'Why d'yer do it?' he asked.

'Do what?'

'Earn yer livin' on the streets.'

Margie sat down on the bed next to him and rested her clasped hands in her lap. 'It's a long story. You wouldn't be interested,' she told him.

'Why don't yer try me?' he replied.

Margie sighed and was silent for a few moments, then she looked up at him, her large blue eyes fixing him intently. 'I was nineteen when I first got married. Not ter Vic. Vic was my second ole man,' she explained. 'Jimmy was a lovely lad. 'E was Irish an' I was madly in love wiv 'im. We 'ad one fantastic year tergevver.'

'What 'appened?' Pat prompted her.

'One day Jimmy came in lookin' white as a sheet,' she went on. 'I'll never ferget that day. 'E was 'oldin' 'is stomach an' then 'e started vomitin'. I didn't know what ter do, I was little more than a kid. Anyway, it seemed ter wear off a bit an' then the pain came back wiv a vengeance. I got the doctor in an' they rushed 'im ter the 'ospital. It was appendicitis. We'd left it too long an' it'd burst. Jimmy died the next day from peritonitis. I was devastated. I just can't tell yer 'ow I felt. The next week I found out that I was pregnant. I lost the baby. I miscarried.'

Pat reached out and squeezed her hands in his. 'That's terrible,' he said softly.

Margie sighed and then carried on. 'I was workin' in the Bryant an' May match factory over at Stratford at the time, an' it was the gels there who got me frew those early days. It was awful. I took a long time ter get over Jimmy an' I 'ad no desire ter marry again. I was only twenty, yer gotta remember. Anyway, I finally pulled meself tergevver an' I started goin' out wiv a couple o' the gels I'd befriended where I lived at the time, over in Stepney. They always seemed to 'ave money ter spend an' I was too green at the time ter realise. They were goin' wiv seamen. They used ter meet 'em in the pubs by the docks. They must 'ave thought I wanted ter be the same as them, so they took me out to a pub one night. I got a bit tipsy an' before I knew it the fellers 'ad arrived. I don't remember much about that night, 'cept that I ended up in bed wiv one of 'em. The next mornin' when I woke up the feller was gone, but 'e'd left a pound note on the washstand. The trufe dawned on me then an' I lay there cryin' me eyes out. But as I say, I was very young then an' times was 'ard. It was easier the second time, an' after that it was just like an ordinary job, 'cept I earned more in one night on the game than I could 'ave done workin' fer two weeks at the factory.'

'When did Vic come on the scene?' Pat asked her.

'The war was on an' 'e was a merchant seaman,' Margie told him. 'We all felt sorry fer those lads. They were gettin' clobbered every time they set sail. Vic was different in those days. I gotta be honest, 'e was good fun ter be wiv an' 'e got ter be one o' my regulars.

Durin' the winter o' '42, Vic's ship was sunk. 'E was one o' the lucky ones. They were rescued after two days an' nights in an open boat. Vic was certified medically unfit after that an' 'e got a job wiv a buildin' firm. That's when we got married. 'E was a changed man an' 'e started gettin' involved wiv the spivs an' black-market villains. They finally caught 'im an' 'e got two years. It would 'ave bin more except fer 'is war record. After 'e came out o' prison fings started ter go wrong between us an' 'e started knockin' me about, so I left 'im. Just after the war was over we decided ter try again but nuffing 'ad changed, so I put in fer a divorce. While it was all goin' frew, Vic got done fer ware'ouse breakin' an' 'e got five years. That's about it,' Margie concluded. 'Now 'e's back on the scene an' 'e wants ter put 'is feet under my table. This time though 'e wants ter be me pimp. I don't work that way, Pat. Anyway, me an' 'im are finished fer good. It was over between us a long time ago. Trouble is, Vic won't accept it.'

The young man looked at Margie with sad eyes. 'Wouldn't yer like ter get out o' the game while yer still got yer looks?' he asked her.

'Yer a kind man, Pat, an' fanks fer the compliment, but no, I'd sooner do what I'm doin' than sweat fer eight or nine hours a day in some poxy factory.'

'I should get 'ome,' he told her, attempting to get up, but Margie placed her hand firmly on his arm.

'Oh no you don't. Get back inter bed,' she ordered him. 'I'm gonna give yer a nice shave. Yer young lady friend's callin' later an' I don't want yer lookin' like somefing the cat's dragged in, do I?'

Chapter Thirty-six

Monday morning dawned wet and dreary, and as the factory hooters sounded and the morning rush began, a plain, blue-painted van drew up outside a lodging-house in Dockhead. The driver jumped down and went inside, leaving his colleague sitting in the passenger seat. He was soon back. ''E'll be out in a few minutes,' he said, standing beside the passenger door.

Vic Dolan came out five minutes later and frowned as he reached the man standing beside the van. 'It's a bit early fer Benny ter be up, ain't it?' he queried.

'Yeah, but 'e's got a problem an' 'e wants ter see yer urgent,' the man explained.

Vic climbed in between the two men and the van set off.

'I thought we was goin' straight ter Benny's,' Vic said, beginning to feel a little suspicious.

'Sorry, pal, but we gotta do a little detour. We gotta pick up anuvver geezer,' the driver told him.

The van drove through the busy morning streets and finally stopped at a tenement block off the Tower Bridge Road. 'I won't be a minute,' the driver told his colleague.

Vic Dolan watched the man hurry into the block and then he turned to the other passenger. 'What's goin' on?' he asked him quickly.

He merely shrugged his shoulders and Dolan began to panic. 'I wanna stretch me legs,' he said.

The man turned to him and smiled evilly. 'Stay where you are, pal. This ain't a peashooter in me coat pocket,' he growled.

Dolan turned grey as he looked down at the unmistakable bulge in his overcoat. 'Where we goin'?' he asked fearfully.

'We're gonna take a little trip, an' while we're at it, don't be tempted ter try an' grab this gun,' the man warned him. 'I get a bit nervous at times, an' if yer make a sudden move I'll be forced ter blow yer ugly guts all over the seat. This is a service revolver by the way, an' it'll cut yer in 'alf from this distance.'

The driver came out of the building, followed by two men who looked like they had just got out of bed. He opened the back doors of the van and told them to jump in, then before he got into the cab he padlocked the doors.

'What's it all about then?' one of them called out.

'Nuffink ter worry about,' the driver told him.

The van drove along Tower Bridge Road and turned left at the Bricklayer's Arms.

'This is a funny way ter go,' the man in the back of the van remarked.

'We gotta pick up yer pal,' he was told.

The two men looked at each other. They had seen nothing of Spiv Norris since he ran away from the fight on Saturday night. Looking over the driver's shoulder they saw that they had turned into a narrow backstreet, and when the van pulled up sharply they stared at Dolan.

''Ere, d'yer know what this is all about?' one of them said.

Dolan felt the muzzle of the revolver pressed into his side. 'Nah, I'm as much in the dark as you are,' he replied, his eyes flickering up at the hard-looking man with black wavy hair who sat next to him.

The driver went into a block of flats and glanced at the number-board before running up a flight of stone stairs.

'Tell Spiv Norris that Benny wants 'im, urgent,' he told the fat young woman who stood looking dumbly at him.

'Tell 'im yerself,' she growled and made to close the door.

He put his foot against the opening and shoved hard. 'Now look, darlin', I ain't got time ter piss-ball about. So be a good gel an' get Spiv, or I'll clock yer one, OK?'

She suddenly looked scared. 'I ain't seen 'ide nor 'air of 'im since Saturday afternoon,' she told him. 'That's the Gawd's honest trufe.'

The driver fished into his pocket and took out a ten-shilling note. 'Now I want you ter do me a favour. Will yer?' he asked her.

The woman's eyes widened when she saw the note. 'Yeah, sure,' she replied.

'Tell Spiv that 'e better stay low. Tell 'im that the ovver two are gettin' the concrete treatment. Now can yer remember that?'

The woman grabbed the ten-shilling note and backed away from the door, her eyes popping. 'Yeah, I can remember. I'll tell 'im, when I see 'im,' she croaked.

The van moved off once more and this time it went directly along the Tower Bridge Road towards the high stone bridge. The dark man next to Vic Dolan leaned over the back of the seat and pulled out his gun, staring at the two men in the back. 'Now, I want you two ter sit back against that door,' he scowled at them. 'If eivver of yer tries ter move terwards me I'll put a bullet in this geezer's 'ead first, then I'll put you two out o' yer misery, is that understood?'

The two nodded quickly as they slid to the door, terrified by the revolver waved in their faces. Dolan sat passive. He had come to realise that he had upset the wrong people and his only chance was to cooperate the best way he could. He decided not to try and grapple for the gun. The men looked like professionals and they were both powerfully built. Better if he played it cool, he told himself.

The van was moving steadily along Cable Street which ran alongside the river. Suddenly it turned sharply into a narrow street and stopped. The driver said something to a man in overalls who stood lounging by a pair of gates and then he drove the van through into the small yard. When Dolan stole a glance in the side mirror he saw the overalled man shutting the gates behind them. He began to feel really frightened. He sat perfectly still as the driver got out and spoke for a couple of minutes to a well-dressed man of about his own age.

Finally the door of the van was unlocked and the three unwilling passengers were paraded in the yard. The well-dressed man came up and smiled casually.

'We'll try not to keep you very long. It's just a friendly chat,' he said, then he turned to the driver and his colleague. 'Go and get a bite to eat, lads.'

The three men were led into a large room and motioned to sit on a pile of sacks. 'Someone will be with you in a few minutes,' they were told.

Dolan looked around. The room was large and appeared to be used for packing. Empty cases and cartons were stacked up against the far wall, and there was a long wooden workbench cluttered with offcuts of cardboard, corrugated paper and balls of string.

'I don't like this,' one of the men said.

'No, neivver do I,' Dolan replied. 'I fink we better be careful what we say.'

'I reckon we should make a run fer it,' the quieter of the two men suggested.

His friend gave him a hard look. ''Ow far d'yer fink we'd get?' he growled. 'They've all got shooters.'

Suddenly a door swung open and two powerful men walked swaggeringly into the room. One was carrying a sawn-off shotgun under his arm and he smiled disarmingly. 'I'm Tony an' this is Mick. First of all, gentlemen, a little demonstration. If yer'd be so kind, Mick.'

The captives watched in puzzlement as Mick the Hammer pulled a large filled sack into the middle of the room and then stood to one side. Tony turned suddenly and let fly with both barrels. The men jumped visibly at the loud bang and they saw the sack explode into shreds. Tony uncocked the shotgun and inserted two more cartridges.

'What's this all about?' Vic Dolan asked.

'Shut it,' Mick told him sharply.

Tony Mancini clicked the gun shut and turned slowly, the twin barrels coming to rest on one of Dolan's thugs. 'Now let's see what effect this 'as on the 'uman body,' he said coldly.

The man stepped back a pace, his face ashen. 'No! Please don't point that at me,' he whimpered.

Tony laughed aloud. 'Come 'ere,' he told him.

The man moved forward slowly, wondering what to expect. As he got within range the Maltese suddenly swung the butt of the shotgun and caught him a vicious blow on the side of his head. The man dropped like a stone.

'Pick 'im up,' he ordered.

Dolan and the remaining thug grabbed the unconscious man by his arms and raised him up into a chair that Mick brought up.

'Take 'is shoes an' socks off,' Tony ordered as he walked over to the workbench and came back carrying a large bucket. 'Right, now stick 'is feet in it,' he said, grinning at the shocked faces.

'Fer Gawd's sake!' Dolan shouted.

'Do it!' their captor said sharply, then he pointed to the thug with his gun. 'You. Bring that cement over.'

Vic Dolan's eyes were wide with terror as he stared at Tony

Mancini incredulously. 'No yer can't! It's cold-blooded murder!' he screamed out.

'Did you lot fink o' that on Saturday night?' Mancini said calmly.

'We wasn't gonna kill the bloke. It was just a pastin',' the thug whined. 'Honest, guv. Honest ter Gawd.'

'Mick, would you do the mixin'?'

'Sure fing, Tony.'

''Ow long d'yer fink it'll take ter set?'

'A few hours, I should fink.'

Mancini looked at the two terrified men. 'Move! Over there,' he shouted.

'Give us a break, guv, fer Gawd's sake,' Dolan pleaded.

'Like you did on Saturday night?' the gunman sneered. 'Now get in there.'

Dolan and the other man did as they were told and the door was slammed shut behind them. It was dark, the only light coming through a grille in the door. Dolan tried looking through it. 'I can't see what's goin' on,' he said.

Mick the Hammer banged his fist on the door. 'Sit down an' no talkin',' he barked. 'Yer gonna need yer strength later on when yer carry yer pal down ter the river. That concrete's pretty 'eavy.'

The thug slumped in the chair slowly regained consciousness to find himself securely bound, and when he looked down at his feet in the bucket and saw the bag of cement lying near him he gazed up wide-eyed at Mancini. 'No! Please don't do it!' he gasped.

'D'you know why you're in this little predicament?' Mick asked him. 'Because yer stepped on our toes, that's why. We don't like small-time villains takin' the law inter their own 'ands. Not on our manor.'

Tony Mancini walked over and bent down until his face was only a few inches from the bound man. 'You're a very lucky boy, my ole son,' he whispered. 'Shall I tell yer why? It's 'cos I'm feelin' very charitable terday. So what I'm gonna do is give yer a chance. Untie 'im, Mick.'

As the ropes fell to the floor, the captive rubbed his wrists to restore the circulation, hardly able to believe that he wasn't going to the bottom of the river in a pair of concrete boots. 'Fanks, guv. Yer'll never 'ave cause ter worry over me again,' he said sincerely.

'Get yer shoes an' socks on an' piss off before I change me mind,' Mancini told him.

283

Mick smiled with amusement as the man rushed to put his socks on. 'What about those two?' he said, pointing to the locked storeroom.

'We'll let 'em roast fer a few hours,' Tony replied. 'In the meantime we'll sort somefing out.'

Mick saw the crafty look on his colleague's face as he followed him out of the room.

Vic Dolan sat hunched in the corner of the dark storeroom, his head in his hands. 'I wonder what the time is,' he said.

'I dunno. It seems like we've bin 'ere fer hours,' the thug replied.

'Who is this mob? That's what I keep askin' meself,' Dolan said. 'Why should they be so concerned about our little caper?'

'That geezer you wanted sorted out must 'ave some powerful friends, that's all I can fink,' the thug replied. 'I tell yer one fing fer nuffink. If I ever get out o' this alive I'm clearin' well out o' the neighbour'ood fer good.'

Footsteps outside made the two captives jump to their feet.

'Right you two. Out,' Mick said. 'It's time ter do the dumpin'. Don't worry, your pal won't know anyfing.'

The two men were prodded forward and suddenly they stopped dead in their tracks. There in front of them they saw the hunched figure of the other captive bound in the chair with his back towards them. He was slouched forward and a red pool of blood had spread out around him.

'Yer've killed 'im!' Dolan gasped.

Mick nodded solemnly and stroked his chin. 'On second thoughts I fink we'll save yer the trouble o' disposin' of 'im,' he told them. 'Me an' Tony'll dump 'im in the drink later ternight. Now you two piss off, an' just fank yer lucky stars it ain't eivver o' you in that chair. One ovver fing. If we 'ear any more o' you two, or any o' yer pals, we won't be so generous next time. Right then. Out!'

Dolan and the thug hurried into the yard and out on to the busy Cable Street, hardly able to believe they were still alive.

'I wish I knew who they were,' Dolan said as he strode along the evening street.

'I ain't bloody interested,' the other man replied.

'They must 'ave cut 'is froat,' Dolan went on.

'Will yer shut up about it!' the thug screamed at him. 'You got us inter this, an' now Lennie's dead.'

'Piss orf an' make yer own way 'ome if that's the way yer feel,' Dolan told him.

'I will at that, an' don't come round the club any more. Yer won't be welcome,' the angry man told him.

Back in the large room behind the yard, Tony Mancini and Mick the Hammer felt that it had been an entertaining morning, and Mick whistled tunelessly as he removed the stuffed sack from the chair and mopped up the tomato sauce.

Chapter Thirty-seven

Colin Brennen clambered down from the personnel carrier along with his friends and hurried into Richmond Railway Station late on Friday afternoon. The small Yorkshire terminus was surrounded by sombre moors, looking even more bleak in their winter covering of hard-packed snow, and Colin shivered despite his heavy army-issue greatcoat. All the trained soldiers carried a small pack, and as they passed through the barrier and boarded the services leave train they appeared to be strangely subdued. It was as though all the fire and individuality had been squeezed out of them, and to a certain degree it had. For a solid month they had been subjected to a strict and vigorous twenty-four-hour routine, in inhospitable surroundings and with no respite from the bullying, foul-mouthed sergeants.

Now that they were trained soldiers, the men understood the rationale behind the methods employed. They now thought pragmatically, acted as a unit and relied on each other implicitly. They felt fit, confident, and competent with the various weaponry. In the four hectic weeks they had acquired the basic knowledge to become fighting soldiers, but there was more to come. The Royal Signals was a technical regiment and the recruits had now to learn the various specialised skills required. They had all left the basic training camp, and after their weekend leave they were to report to training regiments.

The friends settled down in the carriage for a long and tiring journey to London's King's Cross Station, and as the train drew out on to the cutting between the bleak moors and picked up speed, they slipped off their overcoats, removed their berets and breathed a little easier.

'Well, we made it, lads,' Mick Jackson remarked with a grin.

'I'm glad ter see the back o' that Sergeant Kellerman,' Pete Willis added. 'If we 'adn't 'ave won that drill-stick I'm sure 'e would 'ave shot 'imself – after 'e'd shot us.'

The men chuckled and Colin cast a glance around the carriage at his comrades. There was one man missing from the same group who had shared the journey north just four weeks ago, and he felt a mixture of sadness and anger. Signalman Stanley Upjohn had failed miserably to become a trained soldier, and at this moment he was confined in the guardhouse awaiting a medical report. After three weeks of unbearable bullying and harassment, Upjohn had deserted. He had run off in the middle of the night, dodging the camp guards and the patrolling military police, and reached the main arterial road south. He had hoped to hitch a lift on a lorry bound for London but he was picked up by an army patrol and escorted back to camp. They put him in a cell, first removing his belt, lanyard and shoelaces, but Upjohn still managed to attempt suicide, cutting his wrists on the sharp edge of his metal camp bed. Fortunately the duty corporal had decided to check his prisoner at the crucial moment and the misfit was rushed to the military hospital to have his wounds stitched.

'I knew 'e wouldn't make it,' Ken Moseley said suddenly, as if reading Colin's mind.

'Yeah, so did I,' Mick remarked. 'Yer could see what 'e was like right from the start.'

Colin nodded his head slowly. 'Poor ole Stanley,' he said. 'I wonder 'ow long it'll be before they give 'im a medical discharge.'

'They'll most likely put 'im in the loony-bin fer a few months,' Ken replied callously. 'They won't part wiv 'im too easily.'

Colin glanced at the young man from Poplar. Ken Moseley had been the most vociferous of them all at the beginning, but he had seemed to take to life in the army very quickly. His equipment was always immaculate, his uniform smartly pressed and he carried himself upright, thus dodging much of the bullying the rest had been forced to suffer. Ken had been a bit of a mystery at first, Colin recalled, but close confinement had encouraged him to open up a little and the real man emerged. Ken Moseley's parents had been killed during the blitz and he had been looked after by his ageing grandmother. From a young lad he had had to fend for himself for most of the time and he had become very self-reliant. On the surface he seemed unfeeling and callous, but underneath he had a heart of gold, and Colin smiled to himself to have guessed right in his initial

287

assessment of the young man. Although he had appeared to take an immediate dislike to Stanley Upjohn on the journey to the camp, Moseley was the only one of them who had stopped to gather up the unfortunate man's possessions on the station platform, incurring the inevitable screams and verbal abuse from the military police.

'Well, I'm gonna see about 'avin' it off this weekend,' Mick told them all with a cheeky grin. 'I'm sex-starved.'

'I dunno about that,' Pete cut in. 'I'm still sufferin' from that bromide they put in the tea-urns. I still can't raise a gallop.'

'I reckon that's just a wind-up,' Mick replied.

'Well they must put somefing in the tea. I've never tasted anyfing like it. It's bloody putrid.'

Colin rested his head back against the hard cushion and thought about what was ahead of him, now that the initial training was completed. He had been accepted as a trainee driver and was to be posted to a camp in Durham very soon. Ken Moseley was going there too, and Mick Jackson. Pete Willis, however was going to stay on at Catterick to train as a wireless operator, and he was very pleased. Pete had come from a naval family and he had designs on going into the Merchant Marine as a ship's wireless officer.

The train rumbled along through the snow-covered landscape and the soldiers started to nod off to sleep. It slowly grew dark outside and Colin tried to make himself comfortable. His legs twitched, his back itched and his mouth was becoming increasingly dry. Ken Moseley was sitting directly opposite and he seemed to be in a peaceful sleep, hardly moving and breathing very shallowly.

'I fink 'e could sleep on a clothes-line,' Pete remarked, nodding at Ken. 'I can't get comfortable.'

'No, nor can I,' Colin told him.

''Ave you got a bird?' Pete asked.

'Not a steady one,' Colin replied.

'I got a steady bird, but I didn't say anyfing while we was in camp,' Pete went on. 'They'd all be askin' if I'd got a picture of 'er. I got one, but it ain't a very good likeness. Wanna see it?'

Colin nodded and watched while Pete flipped through his wallet.

'That's 'er. I bin goin' wiv 'er fer over a year now,' Pete told him. 'We was gonna get engaged before I got called up but 'er farvver put the block on it. 'E reckons we're too young.'

Colin studied the dog-eared photograph. The young woman wore glasses and she looked very serious. ''Ow old is she?' he asked.

'She was only sixteen when that was taken,' Pete replied. 'She's eighteen now. 'Er name's Peggy. I was sick when 'er ole man stuck 'is oar in. Silly ole bastard don't know what 'e's talkin' about. It makes yer laugh really. We're old enough ter vote an' fight fer our country, but in 'is eyes we ain't old enough ter get engaged. It'd be different if we needed ter get married right away 'cos she was up the duff. As it is we gotta wait till I get demobbed. Anyway, I'm gonna 'ave it out wiv 'im this weekend.'

Ken Moseley started to mumble in his sleep and Mick was snoring loudly. Pete twisted and turned in an effort to get comfortable and he finally gave up. 'It's no use. I can't sleep a wink,' he groaned.

Colin closed his eyes and thought about his family. They would be looking forward to the weekend and his father would no doubt have something derogatory to say about the uniform. It was ill fitting and the battledress blouse was slightly too big. Maybe his mother could take it in a bit, he thought. One thing was for certain: he would change into civvies as soon as he got home and not put that uniform on again until it was time to leave.

The young soldier felt the train lurch and he opened his eyes. Pete was snoring now but Ken Moseley was rousing. He rubbed his eyes and glanced through the steamy window.

'I wonder where we are?' Colin said.

'Doncaster,' Ken told him.

'It'll be hours yet before we get ter London.'

'We should get in about six in the mornin'.'

'I 'ope the buses are runnin'.'

Moseley yawned widely. 'They'll be runnin'.'

Colin shut his eyes again and finally sleep claimed him.

Jim Carney had enjoyed watching Errol Baines suffer and he smiled to himself as he walked to the freight yard on Saturday morning. Not so long ago it had seemed very unlikely that he would ever get the references he needed to be considered for membership of the exclusive order of the Jolly Boys, but now it was looking quite promising.

'Mornin', Charlie. Just the bloke I wanted ter see,' Jim said cheerfully.

'I got no time ter chat,' Charlie replied irritably. 'I got a full day's work an' we clock off at midday.'

'This won't take long,' Jim continued. 'I was told ter see yer about those references.'

'What references?' Charlie queried.

'You know what references. The ones I need ter join the Jolly Boys.'

''Ow many yer got?'

'One.'

'Only one? That ain't no good.'

'Yeah, but I'm gettin' anuvver one off Errol an' 'e suggested I see you.'

'What for?'

Jim puffed loudly. ''E reckons yer might be disposed ter take three instead o' four.'

'I dunno about that,' Charlie replied, rubbing his stubble with his knuckles. 'Yer say Errol's gonna give yer one? An' yer've got one already. Yeah, anuvver one might do, but it's got ter be from someone important. Errol ain't anybody, really. Yer need a very good one from someone who's respected. If it is a very good one the committee might be disposed to acceptin' three instead o' four. Now if yer could get one from the mayor it might do.'

'I've already tried,' Jim told him. 'I tried me doctor, an' the Salvation Army too.'

Charlie thought for a few moments. ''Ave yer considered goin' ter the police?'

'I didn't give 'em a thought, ter tell yer the trufe, but it's a possibility,' Jim said, scratching his head vigorously.

'Right then, I'll see yer later,' Charlie told him.

Jim went to work feeling rather encouraged. He nodded a greeting to Errol and was rewarded by a scowl. The man looks miserable this morning, Jim thought. He had seemed a little strange all week. If he was being offhand over what happened on Saturday night it was too bad. Like Sara had said, it was a taste of his own medicine.

A little while later, as he was pushing his two-wheeled barrow along the loading bank, Jim saw Errol sidling up to him. 'I 'ope yer not gonna put it all around the yard about Saturday night,' the ganger growled.

'Course I ain't,' Jim reassured him. 'Yer've 'ad a bad shock, I don't wanna rub yer nose in it.'

'Did yer speak ter Charlie?' Errol asked him.

'Yeah. 'E said three would do, providin' the third one is a good 'un,' Jim replied. 'Charlie reckons your one won't be important. 'E said you ain't anybody really. 'E reckons I might get a result if I go ter the police fer one.'

'Don't talk rubbish. Why should they give yer a reference? They don't know yer from Adam,' Errol said scathingly.

'I know the copper who's on the local beat. Me an' 'im often pass the time o' day,' Jim countered. 'Besides, I used ter do a bit o' firewatchin' at the Dock'ead nick.'

'Well, it's up ter you,' Errol said as he walked off, wishing he had never started the thing off in the first place.

When Joe Brennen got home from work that Saturday lunch-time Ada met him at the front door. 'Our Colin's in there,' she said excitedly. ''E got in early this mornin'. Just after yer left fer work. The poor little sod looks fair whacked. Mind you, it's bin a long journey an' 'e's gotta go back Sunday evenin'.'

Joe hurried into the parlour and saw the bleary-eyed young man sitting in the armchair being fussed over by his sisters.

'Give the lad a bit of air,' Joe said as he held out his hand. ''Ow yer doin', son? Yer look very well.'

Colin shook his father's hand. 'So we're gonna 'ave a party ternight,' he said, grinning.

Barbara pulled a face. 'Yeah, it'll be a real ding-dong,' she said sarcastically. 'Mum's 'ad the pianer tuned up an' she's bin ter see Emily Toogood.'

Dawn smiled collusively. 'Yeah, all we need is a few song sheets,' she added.

Colin was feeling too tired to join in and he fought his way up out of the armchair. 'I'd better get a couple of hours' shut-eye then,' he said, feeling embarrassed by the attention he was getting.

Ada sat down in the parlour with Joe after the girls had gone to the market. ''E's lost weight, Joe,' she said. 'I can see it in 'is face.'

'Nah, it's just tiredness. After a good sleep 'e'll look different again,' he replied. 'Ter be honest I thought 'e looked well, considerin'. After all, it ain't a picnic that trainin', is it?'

'I'm gonna do a nice meat pie this evenin' fer tea. 'E needs fattenin' up,' Ada told him.

Joe sat back in his armchair and kicked off his boots. 'Where's our Kay?' he asked.

Ada jerked her thumb towards the window. 'She's at the Kellys'.'

'She seems a different gel this last week,' Joe remarked. 'I'm pleased ter see it. She's bin walkin' round like a bear wiv a sore 'ead fer ages.'

'As long as it all works out,' Ada said, a note of caution in her voice. 'Pat Kelly's bin a bit of a cow-son where the gels are concerned.'

'I wouldn't worry too much,' Joe said reassuringly. 'I was talkin' ter Tom Kelly this mornin'. 'E's over the moon about it all. 'E told me Pat's a changed man. 'E took a bad beatin' by all accounts. Mind yer, 'e's a tough lad is Pat. I wouldn't like ter be in those blokes' shoes if 'e caught up wiv 'em one ter one.'

Ada tutted. 'There yer go again. It's all you blokes seem ter fink of, gettin' revenge,' she said sharply. 'I should fink it'd be better fer 'im ter put all this be'ind 'im an' concentrate on gettin' 'imself fit again. Besides, I don't want our Kay gettin' mixed up in it all.'

'Yeah, yer right, luv,' Joe said quietly. 'As a matter o' fact I'm lookin' forward to 'avin' a quiet chat wiv the lad when 'e comes round ternight. 'E is comin', ain't 'e?'

''E'll be 'ere, along wiv 'alf the street,' Ada said, smiling happily.

'I've told the Catchpoles ter come. Yer don't mind, do yer?' Joe asked drily.

'Nah, the more the merrier,' Ada replied. 'It's years since we 'ad a good ole-fashioned party. Just one fing though, Joe. Yer've not bin drinkin' all that much since yer operation. Don't go gettin' too boozy. I remember the last time.'

'That was ages ago,' Joe said, grimacing.

'Yeah but people don't ferget that easy,' she told him. 'Stan Brady copped the needle wiv you last time.'

'There was no 'arm in it. Sara Brady's a good dancer,' Joe replied.

'Yeah, I know it an' you know it, but Stan wasn't too sure, especially when you an' 'er started doin' the samba,' Ada reminded him.

'I fink we done it very well,' he said defensively.

'Oh yeah, yer did,' Ada replied, 'except it was a waltz Emily was playin' at the time.'

Chapter Thirty-eight

They started to arrive early. The Catchpoles brought a crate of stout, the Kellys brought Guinness, and Emily Toogood brought a small bottle of gin in a carrier-bag along with her music sheets. Emily was an accomplished musician who played with gusto when fortified by a few gin and lemons and she was looking forward to the party. Emily's husband Cyril remained at home, which suited the virtuoso. As she was ready to explain when asked, Cyril was not exactly antisocial, more shy and retiring, as well as being a pain in the arse at times. He preferred to sit at home after working at the ticket office at London Bridge Station, listening to radio talks or reading true crime magazines with bloodthirsty covers which he bought at Jack Springer's paper shop.

The Catchpoles were looking forward to the party too. Ivy had had her bright ginger hair permed for the occasion, and Charlie put on his lavender tie, which he detested, but he wore it for Ivy's benefit. She had bought it as a peace offering and Charlie made the sacrifice, telling himself that he would remove the sickly-looking thing as soon as possible during the evening and lose it down the back of Ada's settee.

The Brennens' parties had once been the talk of the street, and the Kellys, like the rest of the guests, were anticipating a lively evening. Tom Kelly had had his instructions.

'I don't want you singin' any o' those rebel songs, d'you 'ear?' Mary told him. 'You was born 'ere, not in Ireland. I don't want people finkin' you're mixed up wiv the Irish republicans.'

Both of Tom's parents came from Ireland, and he had a full repertoire of rebel songs which his father had taught him long ago. Tom delighted in giving a rendering of 'Kevin Barry' after a few drinks, and saw no harm in it. Mary felt differently, however, and he heeded her wishes. Tom was a man who liked to keep peace in the family.

Ada wanted the evening to be as enjoyable as possible. She had laid out sandwiches in the scullery and moved the furniture around in the parlour to accommodate a wooden bench which she had borrowed from the Mason's Arms. The potman from the Mason's had delivered it that morning, along with a carton of beer glasses and crates of beer which were now piled up in the backyard. Ada and the girls had also changed the net curtains and the cushion covers and cleaned the place from top to bottom.

Elsie arrived early with young Billy. She had asked Kay to do her hair for her and help her with her make-up; she had also tried on her best black dress which had been hanging in her wardrobe for a couple of years, and she was pleased with the result. It hugged her closely and showed off her shapely figure, and Kay had loaned her a pair of black high-heeled shoes to complement it.

'You look smashin',' Dawn enthused. 'I love that dress.'

'Kay's really done yer 'air nice,' Barbara added. 'It suits yer face.'

Elsie was gratified by the compliments and she smiled happily as she and Billy sought out her mother, who was busy organising Joe and Colin.

'Put them glasses over there on the sideboard. No, not there, they'll get knocked over. That's right, over the back,' she instructed Joe. 'Right, now, Colin, get a few more crates in so yer don't 'ave ter keep runnin' in an' out the yard, an' make sure everyone's got enough ter drink. 'Ello, Elsie. You look nice. An' look at our Billy. Doesn't 'e look smart? I like yer 'air, Elsie. Give us a minute, I'm just sortin' these two out. Yer gotta be be'ind 'em all the time.'

Emily was making herself comfortable at the piano and she ran her fingers along the keys. 'It sounds nice,' she said, sipping her gin and lemon. 'They need regular tunin'.'

Annie Thomas and Bet Greenedge came in together, as expected, and Joe and Colin were kept busy filling glasses. Sara and Stan Brady were among the last to arrive, closely followed by Dot Adams.

'I left Jim dozin' in front o' the fire,' Sara told Ada. 'I 'ope 'e don't let it go out.'

294

'I wouldn't take a bet on it,' Stan said, giving Joe a quick look.

Dot Adams sat down heavily on the wooden bench and accepted a glass of stout from Joe. 'Danny said 'e might pop over later, Ada,' she said.

Elsie was standing nearby and she turned to her. ''Ow is 'e, Dot?' she asked.

'Touch wood 'e's not bin too bad lately,' Dot replied. ''E 'ad a nasty 'eadache on Thursday but it didn't last too long. I'm just 'opin' that job of 'is will make a difference. 'E seems ter like it.'

Elsie sat down next to her. 'Danny's gonna do some more work fer me next week, Dot,' she said. ''E's gonna put a couple o' shelves up in Billy's room.'

'Yeah 'e was tellin' me,' Dot replied. ''E's bin doin' a bit o' work round at ole Muvver Dines's place this week. She wanted 'er street door chain fixed by all accounts. I told 'im ter make sure 'e got paid fer it. She's a right ole skinflint.'

'Did she give 'im any trouble?' Elsie asked.

'Nah, she paid up, but Danny was tellin' me 'ow she gets on at that boy of 'ers. Treats 'im like a doormat, she does. I don't fink our Danny'll be too keen ter do any more jobs fer 'er. Mind you, 'e enjoyed workin' at your 'ouse. 'E said you an' 'im 'ad a nice chat an' you spoiled 'im wiv cups o' tea.'

Billy was pottering about amongst the guests, enjoying the fuss being made of him, and Elsie found herself dwelling on the quiet chat she had had with Danny. He had seemed so innocent and childlike that day, and yet he had seen and experienced so much during the war. She was hoping he would decide to come to the party and talk with her some more. She wanted him to feel that she was a good friend, someone he could turn to when he felt the need, though Elsie knew she would have to be careful about having Danny in her house. Ernie did not like him and he would be sure to make the young man feel uncomfortable. Any further jobs of work would have to be done when Ernie was on long-distance runs, she told herself.

After Kay had finished helping her sister prepare for the party, she hurried up to her bedroom and got herself ready to meet Pat Kelly. She had been looking forward to this evening all week. There had been no time to be alone with Pat since he came home by taxi on Monday morning. Every evening she had visited him and they chatted with his mother and father, and she had watched his steady progress. The facial bruises were now almost gone and his cracked ribs were mending nicely. He had regained his ruddy complexion too and was almost back to his normal, cheerful self. Tonight there would be an opportunity to be alone with him for a few minutes before they went to the party, and she was eager for him to take her in his arms and kiss her passionately, instead of the usual brief goodnight kiss at his front door. They had joked about their roles being reversed, and as she thought about Pat waiting for her to go to him this evening, Kay felt excitement building up inside her.

Gordon and Jamie arrived together, and Dawn immediately fussed over her young man. Barbara was less attentive, however, and Ada noticed it. 'Don't leave that lad standin' out there on 'is own,' she told her daughter. 'Get 'im a drink.'

Tom Kelly took the opportunity to have a quiet few words with Joe about the Jolly Boys' plans for the spring get-together, and Jamie and Gordon settled down to talk about the merits of football, as opposed to rugby union, causing Dawn and Barbara to sigh in resignation. Emily had warmed up and she had started tinkling on the keyboard, eyeing her dwindling gin and lemon and hoping it was soon going to be replenished. The gathering filled the small house and Ada passed round amongst them, chatting to everybody.

'Where's Kay, I ain't seen 'er?' Annie Thomas asked.

'She's just gone over ter collect Pat Kelly,' Ada told her. 'She'll be back soon.'

Outside in the scullery there was a conspiracy going on. Barbara had a plan. 'She'll play all night as long as she don't 'ave too much ter drink, so I reckon we should make sure she don't go short.'

Colin snorted. ''Ave yer seen that gin bottle?' he said. 'It's 'alf empty already.'

Barbara took her purse down from the dresser shelf and handed him a pound note. 'Be a luv an' run up the off-licence, Colin. Get anuvver 'alf bottle o' Gordon's,' she told him.

Colin grabbed the money and slipped on his coat. 'I won't be long. While I'm gone, fill 'er glass up,' he said, grinning.

Kay stepped into the warmth of Pat's house and immediately felt his arm go around her waist. He enfolded her to him and she threw her arms around his neck and closed her eyes as he hugged her close. Their lips met in a passionate, open kiss and Kay felt her knees going weak, it was so delicious. As he caressed her she ran her fingers through his dark, wavy hair.

'I've thought about this moment all day,' he whispered.

'Me too,' she gasped. 'I love you, Pat.'

'I love you too,' he said softly, his lips brushing her ear.

Kay moved back a little, her hands resting firmly on his arms. 'We should go over there now, Pat,' she told him.

'I'd sooner stay 'ere,' he replied with a smile hovering at the corners of his mouth.

'So would I, but they'll be talkin' about us.'

'Let 'em,' he whispered.

'Please, Pat. Don't make it more difficult than it is,' she sighed.

'OK, darlin', lead on,' he told her.

Emily was feeling slightly heady and she enjoyed the sensation. It seemed years since she had last played this piano, she thought, and as her nimble fingers darted over the keys she glanced occasionally at the dancing couples. Joe was stepping it out with Ada, and Tom was with Mary. Dawn and Gordon were dancing very close as they competed for space in the small room, and other couples sat around watching. Charlie was sitting passively with Ivy enjoying a pint of beer, his foot tapping in time with the music. It was like old times, Emily sighed, reaching up at opportune moments to take a quick sip of her gin and lemon which was perched on the top of the piano.

Outside in the scullery, Colin was talking with Gordon, who had been deferred from call-up, and Jamie, who had served in the Rhine Army of occupation.

'I did my trainin' at Aldershot,' Jamie was saying. 'It was bad there, but I 'eard it ain't a patch on Catterick.'

'Bloody right too,' Colin replied spiritedly. 'They're a load o' sadists up in Catterick. They sent one o' the lads stark ravin' mad. Ended up in a loony-bin, 'e did.'

'Colin, 'adn't you better top Emily's drink up?' Dawn cut in.

'I just filled it up,' he replied quickly.

Just then their mother walked into the scullery. 'Don't go givin' Emily no more just yet,' she told them. 'She's startin' ter miss the notes.'

Barbara gave Dawn a wicked smile before turning to Ada. 'She's all right. Just a bit rusty I expect.'

As soon as Ada had left, Colin rubbed his hands together gleefully. 'Where's that gin?' he growled.

A few minutes later the young soldier walked into the parlour holding Emily's refill down by his side. He heard the faltering notes of 'Moonlight Bay'. The pianist was flushed and grinning happily as she swayed from side to side on the piano stool, a strand of hair hanging down her forehead.

'There we are, Emily,' Colin said with a large wink as he quickly changed the glasses over.

'You're a little dear,' she told him, trying to focus her eyes on him.

'I reckon anuvver 'alf hour should do it,' Colin said grinning as he returned to the scullery. 'Yer better go an' sort those records out, Barb – we're gonna be needin' 'em soon.'

Elsie was sitting by the room door as Danny came in. He self-consciously sat down next to her. 'I wasn't gonna come,' he told her quietly.

'Why? Don't yer feel very well?' Elsie asked him with concern.

'I feel fine, but I don't usually go ter parties,' he replied.

Joe came over. 'Nice ter see yer, son. What'll it be? We got brown ale, lights, or stout an' Guinness, unless yer'd care fer a drop o' tiddly?'

'A light ale'll do fine, Joe,' Danny said, giving him a quick smile.

'Yer muvver told me yer done some work at Mrs Dine's,' Elsie said.

Danny nodded. 'She wanted the door chain fixed. I 'ad ter cut a piece out the jamb an' put a new piece in. It'd take a tank ter break in there now.'

'She keeps a lot o' money in that 'ouse,' Elsie remarked. 'She needs that chain.'

'It's like a fortress,' Danny went on. 'She's got nails 'ammered in the winder-frames too, though they've split the wood. She was sayin' somefing about 'avin' 'em done prop'ly, but I dunno.'

'Does she want you ter do 'em?' Elsie asked him.

Danny nodded. 'I wouldn't mind, although it'd be an awkward job, but the trouble is she don't leave yer alone. She nags away all the time. I wonder 'ow that son of 'ers sticks it.'

''E's a weird bloke, ain't 'e,' Elsie said shaking her shoulders. ''E gives me the creeps.'

Danny took the glass from Joe and said thanks. ''Ave you bin in the 'ouse then?' he asked her.

The young woman gave him a bashful smile. 'I 'ad ter borrer some money once – twice as a matter o' fact.'

Danny looked at her, his soft dark eyes becoming sad. ''Ave you got yerself in 'er clutches?' he asked.

'It was some time ago,' Elsie said quickly. 'Not any more.'

'If you ever need ter borrer any money, yer can always ask me,' Danny told her. 'I got a few bob put away. It's not much, mind, but it might 'elp tide yer over if you ever need it.'

Elsie wanted to hug him as she looked into his warm eyes. 'Well, that's very nice of yer, Danny. I won't ferget,' she said gently.

Danny looked a bit embarrassed as he sipped his drink, spilling some down his trousers. 'I managed ter get two nice pieces o' pine fer Billy's room,' he told her. 'I can do it next week, if yer want me to.'

'Ernie's away next Tuesday an' Thursday. Can yer manage any o' those days?' she inquired.

'Yeah, next Thursday. I got me day off then,' he replied.

Elsie looked over at the struggling pianist and grinned. ''Ere, look at Emily. She's 'ad enough. Me an' you'd better 'ave a dance while we can. C'mon.'

Danny looked nervous as he got to his feet, but Elsie did not hesitate. She wrapped her arms around him and led him into the centre of the small parlour. There was little room to manoeuvre and they were compelled to dance closely. Danny moved clumsily at first until he felt Elsie's hips and shoulders guiding him. He let her take the lead and began to relax.

''Ave you ever bin dancin?' Elsie asked him.

'Never.'

'You could be a good dancer.'

'D'yer fink so?'

'Yeah, yer got good movement.'

He smiled shyly. 'It's easy wiv you.'

Elsie suddenly felt a warm, excited glow flow through her. He was a nervous young man, younger than her, but there was something about him. His large brooding eyes seemed so sad, yet they were vibrant too. His manner was totally self-effacing, but there was something about him that moved her in a strange way. She could not understand why she should feel this way, yet as she danced with him to Emily's erratic playing, Elsie's neck began to redden and her heart beat faster at her secret thoughts.

Kay and Pat had been standing in the scullery talking together with

Joe and Ada for a while when they heard the thump and raised voices. As they hurried into the parlour they saw Emily Toogood being helped into a chair.

'She just toppled over,' Colin said, trying to keep a straight face. 'I fink she's pissed.'

Ada gave him a blinding look. 'I told yer ter watch that gin. She's drunk the 'ole bottle.'

Colin looked appropriately serious. 'I only give 'er the one. Somebody else must 'ave bin feedin' 'er wiv it.'

Emily began to sing a song in a garbled voice, several strands of hair now hanging down over her forehead, her face bright red.

'Don't let 'er sing,' Ada warned, 'she'll go out when she reaches the 'igh note, she always did.'

'What d'yer want me ter do, stuff a cushion in 'er mouth?' Joe said sarcastically.

'Come on now, Emily, let's me an' you get a nice bit o' fresh air,' Ada coaxed. She and Joe each took an arm and helped her stagger out into the backyard.

''Ere, sit 'er on this,' Joe said, sliding up a rickety chair.

They made the drunken woman comfortable and Ada turned to her husband looking concerned. 'Make 'er a strong cup o' coffee, Joe,' she told him, 'I'll stay wiv 'er fer a while.'

Barbara and Dawn were gathering their latest records together while Colin switched on the radiogram and checked the stylus with the tip of his finger. Ten minutes later the strains of Glen Miller's orchestra playing 'Moonlight Serenade', filled the room. Barbara and Jamie were locked in a tight embrace as they swayed to the music, and Dawn and Gordon joined them in the tiny dance area. Pat and Kay stood watching for a while as they sipped their drinks, then the young man took Kay's hand and led her into the little space left and they swayed dreamily, her head resting on his shoulder, her heart full of love and her body aching with desire.

At ten o'clock the records were turned off and the revellers took refreshment in the scullery. Pat and Kay awaited their opportunity and slipped away. They crossed the dark street hand in hand, entered the house and went straight up to the back bedroom. There was little for either of them to say at that moment: love burnt like a fire inside them and they trembled with hot passion. Kay hung at his neck in the darkness while he slowly and deliberately undid the zip of her skirt. His lips were brushing her neck and ears with whispered

kisses and she sighed with ecstacy. She had waited so long for this
moment. She loved him desperately, and losing all inhibition she
quickly unfastened the buttons of her white satin blouse. Pat slowly
slipped it over her shoulders then his lips strayed down along her
body, kissing her bare midriff and her belly as he gently pulled down
her slip. She was trembling with passion now, wanting him so badly,
and his lips brushed her mound of venus prominent under her tight
knickers. He rose slowly, his hands caressing her sensuously. She
undid her bra and let it fall to the floor, and with a quick movement
she guided his face to her breast and felt his hot lips close over her
hard nipple.

Kay felt herself being lifted up and gently lowered down on to the
bedcovers. He stood over her smiling as he unbuckled his belt and
removed his trousers and shirt; then he lay down beside her, his
eager mouth finding hers, and he hungrily slipped her knickers
down over her thighs. His hands were experienced and she shivered
with pleasure, moving gently, responding to his soft touch. She
ached for him to take her, to love her with a fierce passion, and
when she could bear it no longer she let out a moan of ecstatic
desire. 'Do it, Pat. Do it now,' she whispered.

He entered her and it was as though she was being carried away to
a higher world as they made love together. They moved in unison,
he holding himself above her and she thrusting her hips forward and
gyrating against him as the pleasure intensified. Their nude bodies
were hot and wet and Kay licked the beads of sweat from her lip and
moaned, biting his ear as his movements became urgent. Suddenly
he shivered and let out a deep groan, and at that moment she came,
her whole body tensing and then slowly relaxing in a liquid wave of
boundless ecstasy.

For a few moments they said nothing as they lay in each other's
arms, lost in love, their wet bodies still joined as they clung to each
other; then Kay kissed his chest. 'I waited so long fer you, Pat,' she
whispered. 'I love you so much.'

'I'll never let yer go now, darlin',' he said softly, gently stroking
her smooth bare back.

Outside, the moon slipped through a layer of cloud and bathed
the room in a pale, cold light as the two young lovers kissed tenderly
once more.

Chapter Thirty-nine

Elsie dropped Billy off at the school gates on Monday morning and then walked the short distance to her part-time job at the factory. The morning was damp and foggy but the young woman felt buoyant. The Saturday night party had gone off very well, she thought, and there had been lots to talk about on Sunday morning when the family gathered together for lunch. Her mother had been very pleased with the way things went, except for the slight hitch with the pianist. Poor Emily, she had looked all-in when Joe and Tom helped her to her front door just after midnight, but she was a tough character and she looked bright as a button when she popped in on Sunday to apologise for letting herself get 'tiddly', as she put it.

Elsie smiled to herself as she entered the factory and put her card into the time-clock. It had been good talking to Danny and dancing with him. He was a very nice young man, and Billy seemed to think so too. It was lovely to see how the boy came up to him and sat next to him, and how he rested his head on his lap and fell asleep with Danny stroking his head gently. It was good of Danny to help her home with him, carrying him in his arms to the front door. It would have been nice if he could have come in for a cup of tea, but Ernie was dozing in the chair and he would have raised the roof.

Elsie set to work along with the other women, hardly listening to the usual small talk, her mind dwelling on other things. Ernie was being a pig lately, she thought resentfully. He seemed to have stopped griping about being given all the long runs. Instead he only seemed happy when he was going off on a long-distance trip, especially to Manchester. It was quite probable that he had met someone there. The idea of him having an affair should have devastated her, and it would have done a few years ago, but now it

302

didn't matter any more. Their marriage was a sham. They hardly talked, and even Billy was beginning to notice certain things.

When she left work, Elsie decided to call in on her mother before picking Billy up from school, and she arrived at the family home to find a fresh pot of tea on the hob.

'Our Colin looked a bit low when 'e left 'ere last night,' Ada remarked. ''E said 'e was lookin' forward ter learnin' ter drive, but I fink 'e misses the family.'

'Nah, I don't fink 'e's 'omesick, Mum. Colin's a young man now an' it's a big adventure,' Elsie said reassuringly. ''E was tellin' me 'ow much 'e's lookin' forward ter gettin' posted abroad, an' yer gotta admit, 'e did look well.'

'Did yer fink so? I reckoned 'e looked a bit thin in the face,' Ada replied as she poured out the tea.

'Anyway 'e'll be 'ome again soon,' Elsie told her encouragingly. 'They'll be gettin' leave at Easter, so 'e said.'

Ada handed her a cup of tea. 'I noticed you seemed ter be enjoyin' yerself too, chattin' an' dancin' wiv young Danny Adams,' she said, giving her daughter an inquiring look. 'Barbara an' Dawn were talkin' about it after yer left yesterday.'

'Oh they were, were they?' Elsie said quickly.

'It was nuffink detrimental,' Ada was quick to add. 'They just said it was lovely ter see yer enjoyin' yerself so much. As a matter o' fact they was both sayin' 'ow nice yer looked.'

Elsie sipped her tea quietly for a few moments then she glanced up at her mother. 'I fink Ernie's got a bit o' spare,' she said matter-of-factly.

'Nuffink would surprise me wiv that man,' Ada snorted. 'I just can't understand 'im. All right, maybe it's all over between you two, but why ignore that boy? That's what I can't make out. 'E never takes the lad out anywhere like ovver farvvers do. It's as though the boy don't exist as far as 'e's concerned.'

'Trouble is, Ernie's never at 'ome lately, an' when 'e is Billy's in bed an' asleep,' Elsie pointed out.

'That's the way it is wiv a lot o' farvvers, but at least they spend their weekends wiv their kids,' Ada replied. 'All Ernie seems ter do is go on the piss.'

Elsie finished her tea and put the cup down on the table. 'Let's ferget Ernie. When's the next party?' she said cheerfully.

Ada forced a smile. 'We used to 'ave some good 'uns, didn't we,' she said brightly. 'P'raps this one might encourage someone else ter lay one on.'

Elsie glanced up at the mantelshelf clock. 'I'll 'ave ter be goin' ter pick Billy up from school in a minute,' she said.

Ada nodded. 'Dot Adams was tellin' me 'ow pleased she is wiv Danny lately,' she remarked. 'She said it's since 'e's bin doin' those carpentry jobs.'

Elsie got the impression that her mother was probing. 'Yeah, 'e seemed fine when 'e called on me the ovver day,' she answered. 'I s'pose the tongues'll soon be waggin' about Danny bein' there while Ernie's away.'

'Well, there's no need ter worry about what ovver people fink, if there's nuffing goin' on between yer,' Ada told her.

'There's nuffing goin' on between me an' Danny, Mum. I just fink 'e's a nice, friendly young man,' Elsie said frankly. 'Mind yer, though, I might be tempted, if I wasn't already married.'

'One fing worries me though,' Ada went on. 'If the word gets back to Ernie 'e'll cut up rough, that's fer sure. If 'e lays a finger on yer I want you ter come 'ome 'ere, fer Billy's sake as well as yours.'

'Don't worry, Mum. 'E won't dare touch me,' Elsie said firmly. 'I wouldn't put up wiv it.'

'Watch yer time,' Ada said, looking up at the clock.

'Yeah, I'd better get goin',' the young woman replied, stretching as she stood up. 'I'll try an' pop in again this week.'

Elsie walked quickly to the school, just in time to see the children coming out. Billy came bouncing over, his face glowing as he held up a sheet of colouring-paper. 'I did this terday, Mum. It's you, look,' he said proudly.

Elsie studied the drawing. Two figures with large round faces and big smiles appeared to be clasping hands and one of them had long hair.

'Which one's me?' Elsie said jokingly.

'That's you, Mummy,' Billy told her, 'an' that's Danny. See, 'e's dancin' wiv yer.'

'That's very good,' Elsie said as she took his hand to walk home.

'Can I show Daddy?' the lad asked her.

'Yer farvver's gonna be tired when 'e comes 'ome, an' yer'll be in bed by then, Billy,' she said quickly, reminding herself to hide the drawing.

They turned into Dover Lane and suddenly spotted Danny

Adams. He was coming towards them, his head held low and his shoulders hunched.

'Look, Mummy, it's Danny,' Billy said.

The young man came up and passed them without a glimmer of recognition, and Elsie turned to watch him as he swung into Waggoner's Way.

'Why didn't 'e say 'ello, Mummy?' Billy asked her, looking puzzled.

'Danny's not very well terday, luv,' she said sadly, her heart sinking.

Jim Carney accosted PC Fuller in the street with his usual manic enthusiasm, but the railwayman was soon disappointed.

'You're wastin' yer time, Jim. They'll just tell yer ter piss off,' Fuller told him.

'But I'm a law-abidin' citizen. Yer'd fink they'd only be too glad to oblige,' Jim replied. 'After all, it's fer a good cause.'

'Look, mate, they're only interested in villains at the moment, an' they've got their 'ands full wiv them, believe me,' PC Fuller explained.

'So if I was a villain I could walk in there an' get a result,' Jim said sarcastically.

'Nah, yer'd end up in a cell,' Fuller replied drily.

'Can't you give us one?' Jim asked him.

'I'd like to oblige but I'm not allowed to.'

'Can't you 'ave a word wiv the boss? Tell 'im yer know me well?'

'Sorry, but like I said, it'd be a waste o' time.'

Jim looked downcast and the beat bobby felt sorry for him. 'Look, why don't yer try yer boss at work?' he suggested.

'I've got one from 'im.'

'What about yer doctor?'

'I've already tried.'

'Well, I don't know who else I can suggest,' Fuller said, shrugging his shoulders. 'What about the priest?'

'I've tried 'im too,' Jim replied.

'Sorry, Jim, but I can't fink of anyone else,' Fuller said, moving away.

'Fanks anyway, mate. Mind 'ow yer go,' Jim told him as he carried on to work.

The morning fog was still hanging in the air as Jim Carney walked into the freight yard to start his shift, and when he reached the loading bank he saw the men milling around Errol Baines.

'What's up?' he asked.

'The chairman o' the Southern Railway's on 'is way,' Errol told him. 'We gotta look busy.'

'What's 'e want?' Jim inquired.

'I dunno, 'e never told me,' Errol growled.

'Didn't you ask 'im?' Jim said with a big grin.

''E don't take me into 'is confidence these days,' Errol replied. 'Now let's get started on that truck. The supervisor's told me that the chairman's gonna stop off ter see the waggons bein' loaded. The newspaper reporters are gonna be wiv 'im, so backs into it, lads.'

Jim joined the rest of the gang and soon the cargo of tinned soup was being stacked into a waiting waggon.

'The chairman's comin' ter present Joe Brennen wiv a bravery certificate, so I 'eard,' one of the men told his mate.

Jim overheard and he leaned on his two-wheeled barrow. 'I fink 'e deserves a bit o' recognition,' he remarked. 'Joe Brennen could 'ave bin killed that night. Mind you, I fink we should all get a certificate come ter that. We all done our bit.'

'You'll get a certificate ter take down the labour exchange if the chairman cops yer leanin' on that barrer,' Errol called out to him.

Jim went back to work grumbling to himself, and after a while Charlie Catchpole stepped on to the bank. 'I've just 'eard the chairman's on 'is way,' he told Errol. 'Thought I'd warn yer.'

A few minutes later a slick-looking Humber saloon drove into the yard and stopped outside the railway club. The loaders craned their necks and caught sight of a uniformed chauffeur opening the rear door of the limousine. A tall, lean man with sleeked-down grey hair got out and entered the building, followed by a handful of fussing officials. Soon afterwards a man came running over to the loading bank. 'Right, stop everything,' he said brusquely. 'Everyone's to assemble in the clubroom to watch the ceremony.'

The chairman stood on the raised dais along with Gerry Preston the depot manager; he looked a little bored as he waited for the workers to assemble.

'Good morning, gentlemen,' Gerry began. 'I'd like to welcome Sir Thomas Kilcline, chairman of the Southern Railway, to our depot. Sir Thomas has kindly agreed to present an award this morning to one of the employees for outstanding services rendered during the fire here in the yard a few weeks ago. Now I know you are all keen to get back to work, so I'll delay you no longer and introduce the chairman. Gentlemen, Sir Thomas Kilcline.'

Fitful applause ceased suddenly as the chairman raised his hands.

'Gentlemen, it gives me great pleasure to be here this morning,' he began. 'As you are well aware, the fire in this yard that Sunday evening could have been a disaster of no mean proportion. As it was, the serious conflagration was contained by the brave action of the London Fire Brigade, and by the prompt action of the railwaymen on duty at the time. Some of you men present here this morning will be part of that brave band who risked their lives to help put out the fire.'

''Ear, 'ear,' Jim shouted out, and was promptly hushed by a flustered official.

'I have to tell you that one man's actions that night were over and above the call of duty,' the chairman went on. 'Without thought for his own life and limb he shunted a burning line of waggons along the track to a place of comparative safety. Gentlemen, it gives me great pleasure to present this certificate of bravery to Mr Joseph Brennen.'

Joe stepped on to the dais, looking ill at ease as applause filled the hall. He shook hands with the chairman and exchanged a few words. Bulbs flashed and newspaper photographers jockeyed for position as the two men posed for a moment or two with their hands clasped.

Jim Carney ambled out of the hall and stood casually by the limousine. 'Nice car this,' he remarked to the miserable-looking chauffeur. 'I bet it cost a packet.'

The chauffeur's lack of response did not deter the railwayman. 'What's 'e like ter work for?' he asked.

'Very good,' the driver said, staring ahead.

'I bet you 'ave ter go all over the place, don't yer?' Jim went on.

'He'll be out in a minute,' the chauffeur mumbled, still looking ahead.

'I'd like ter chauffeur 'im about,' Jim remarked. 'It must be better than bein' a loader.'

Suddenly the chairman appeared in the doorway, and as he made for his car the chauffeur moved briskly to open the door. Jim was quicker and he pushed him to one side and flung the car door open, saluting smartly as the bemused chairman came towards him. Errol Baines was standing nearby and he put his hand to his forehead and groaned. Gerry Preston raised his eyes to the heavens and all the officials looked shocked. Thomas Kilcline looked perfectly relaxed, however, and as he stepped up to the open door he smiled at Jim. 'Thank you,' he said pleasantly.

'Jim Carney, sir. Freight loader.'

'Thank you, Mr Carney.'

'I was there that night, sir. I dug the buffers out so the waggons could get frew,' Jim told him proudly. 'We all did our little bit.'

'Well done,' the chairman replied. 'You all did a very good job.'

'One request, sir.'

'Oh, and what's that?'

'I need a reference, sir. I wanna be a Jolly Boy.'

'Well, I'm sure Mr Preston can take care of that.'

'Beggin' yer pardon, sir, but I've already got one from 'im. Can you give me one?'

The chairman stepped into his car and then looked up at the railwayman. 'I'll get my secretary to speak with Mr Preston,' he said.

Jim slammed the car door shut and gave another smart salute as the vehicle drove away.

Everyone seemed to be frozen to the spot, but Jim was unabashed as he looked at Errol Baines and then the rest of the gang with a satisfied grin on his wide, flat face.

'C'mon then,' he told them, 'we've got a waggon ter load.'

Chapter Forty

Many of the Bermondsey backstreets had their own corner shop, but Waggoner's Way was very fortunate in that it had one on each corner. The little shops not only provided a service, they acted as relay stations as well. Customers invariably stood chatting in Basil Cashman's oil shop while he filled their cans with paraffin, weighed up their requirements of nails, tin-tacks and screws, and cut up chunks of whitening and hearthstone for their front doorsteps and fireplaces. Basil never seemed to hurry himself with the orders and there was little else to do except pass the time away with local news.

Jack Springer's paper shop was also a hotbed of gossip. His wife Alma did the morning paper orders and she knew everyone. If Mrs So-and-so had fallen out with a neighbour, or if one of the husbands was off work, Alma would be sure to know. If someone did not come in for their morning or evening paper, Alma would make inquiries, and inside twenty-four hours she knew why, as did most of the street.

The same could be said about Joe Mezzo's grocery shop. It took time to go through a shopping list, and while the customers queued up they chatted together. Maria kept them informed, too, and not only about the condition of Mrs Smith's leg or Mrs Jones's back. She advised them of the current food shortages and the expected delivery dates of scarce items of food, and she made them all aware of the difficulties involved in trying to stock everything they wanted. She produced Food Ministry forms in buff, green and pink, and showed them application forms, Ministry bulletins, food factsheets and sundry other items of information and bits of paper, which tended to set heads shaking and raise eyes at the complexity of running a grocery business nowadays.

The fourth corner shop was rather different in one respect from the other three. Sammy Dinsford the bootmender did not encourage gossip. He was a quiet, thoughtful man, but he was always good for a few minutes of his time, no matter how busy he was. Sammy was a good listener and he could always be relied upon to respect a confidence, and for that reason he knew more about the personal lives of the neighbourhood folk than anybody.

When Emily Toogood walked into Joe Mezzo's shop on Tuesday morning, she was greeted with a knowing smile by Maria. ''Ow d'yer feel terday, Emily?' she was asked.

'I'm fine, fanks,' she replied, wondering why she should be expected to feel any differently on this particular morning.

'Annie Thomas told me about the party at Ada Brennen's on Saturday night,' Maria went on. 'She said you really enjoyed yerself.'

Emily smiled back. 'Oh, so yer know about me gettin' a bit merry then?' she asked.

'Annie just told me you was playin' the pianer an' everyone enjoyed themselves,' Maria replied guardedly.

'I got sloshed, ter tell yer the trufe,' Emily said, knowing that Annie Thomas would have said more than Maria was letting on.

'Well, it makes a nice change, as long as yer feel all right the next day,' Maria remarked. 'What can I get yer?'

'A quarter o' cheese an' a tin o' baked beans, please – oh, an' a packet o' cream crackers.'

Maria placed a large block of cheese on a freshly scrubbed board and cut off a portion with the thin steel wire. 'Ada's boy was 'ome on leave then,' she said as she deftly wrapped the cheese up in greaseproof paper.

Emily nodded. 'Nice lad is Colin. Looked after me, 'e did. Every time I turned round there was anuvver drink in front o' me. If I 'adn't known better, I'd 'ave thought 'e was tryin' ter get me sozzled.'

'By the way. Young Danny Adams ain't too good,' Maria said. 'Dot came in 'ere this mornin' an' she looked really worried.'

''As 'e 'ad anuvver bad turn?' Emily asked with concern.

''E came 'ome early yesterday, accordin' ter Dot,' Maria told her.

'Bloody shame,' Emily said. 'She must be worried sick.'

'Anyfing else, luv?'

Emily fished into her purse. 'Nah, that'll do fer now,' she replied. 'See yer later, gel.'

Dot Adams had not felt disposed to tell Maria the full story, but when she crossed the street to Sammy Dinsford's she was more expansive. 'Sammy, can yer fix the 'andle on me shoppin'-bag?' she asked him.

The bootmender took a quick look and nodded. 'It won't take a minute. Wanna wait?' he asked.

'Yeah, I might as well,' she replied.

Sammy sat down at his leather-stitcher and worked the treadle. 'I'll put a couple o' rivets in each side fer extra strength,' he told her.

The job was soon done. ''Ow's the boy?' he asked her as he gave her change from the ten-shilling note.

Dot shook her head slowly. 'Not too good at the moment,' she replied. ''E was gettin' on so well an' I was beginnin' ter fink 'e'd seen the last o' those 'eadaches, but yesterday 'e come 'ome lookin' really ill.'

'What d'yer put it down to?' Sammy asked her.

'Gawd knows,' she said sighing. 'It could be anyfink.'

'What are they like at the baths? Do they know about the 'eadaches?' he asked.

'As a matter o' fact, Danny's guv'nor came ter see me last night,' Dot replied. ''E seems a real nice feller. The man at the labour exchange 'ad told 'im about Danny's condition. They 'ave to, 'cos of 'is disability wotsit. Anyway, 'e told me not ter worry. 'E said 'e'd watch out fer 'im. 'E was tellin' me that 'is boy was a flyer in the RAF an' luckily 'e came out of it all right.'

''E sounds a nice bloke,' Sammy remarked.

Dot smiled slyly. ''E's about me own age an' 'e's a widower. Quite a smart man too.'

Sammy gave her a sideways glance. 'Oh yeah, an' do I take it yer gonna get ter know 'im better?'

Dot shrugged her shoulders but the look in her eyes gave her away. 'I dunno. Yer tend ter get set in yer ways when yer've bin on yer own as long as I 'ave,' she told him.

Sammy was not fooled. 'It's never too late, Dot,' he said smiling. 'You're still a good catch.'

Dot felt pleased at the compliment and she leaned forward over the counter. ''Is name's Len an' 'e said 'e'd like ter call again.'

'Yer put 'im off of course,' Sammy said, grinning.

'I just told 'im ter please 'imself,' Dot answered as she picked up her repaired shopping-bag from the counter.

'Yer know the ole sayin',' Sammy called out as Dot reached the door. 'The older the fiddle the better the tune.'

By the end of the day, most of the Waggoner's Way folk knew about Danny Adams. It had been relayed via Maria Mezzo to Annie Thomas and then to Bet Greenedge, who passed the news on to Mary Kelly. Mary told Ada that afternoon, and when the Brennens sat down for tea the conversation came up.

'I was surprised when Mary told me,' Ada went on. 'Danny looked really well when 'e was 'ere on Saturday.'

'Yeah, but wiv that sort o' fing yer can never tell,' Joe replied. 'Anyfing could trigger it off. It might be the job 'e's doin'. It gets very 'ot in those baths, what wiv all that steam.'

'Danny looked very at ease wiv our Elsie on Saturday,' Barbara remarked.

'Danny always got on well wiv 'er,' Ada replied. 'I remember 'ow 'e used to 'ang around 'er in the street.'

Joe scooped up the last of his shepherd's pie on the edge of his knife and wiped it on to a thick slice of crusty bread. 'It's a pity she didn't marry someone like 'im instead o' that no-good git Ernie,' he growled.

Kay pushed back her plate and looked across at Dawn. 'C'mon, it's our turn fer the dishes,' she reminded her. 'You wash, I'll wipe. I gotta 'urry up, I'm goin' out ternight. Pat's takin' me ter the pictures an' I promised ter pop over to Elsie's first.'

The fog had hung around all day and by early evening it was getting noticeably thicker. The inclement weather had put Grace Dines in a bad mood and she took it out on Simon.

'I dunno why yer 'ave ter go out this weavver,' she moaned.

''Cos I get fed up o' stayin' in 'ere, that's why,' he replied caustically. 'That bloody fire don't give out no 'eat an' I gotta sit 'ere listenin' ter that load o' rubbish on the wireless. They've got a nice banked-up fire at the pub an' I get ter talk ter people. We can't even 'ave a poxy chat in this 'ouse wivout yer start rantin' an' ravin'.'

'Nah, that's all yer fink of, yer own comfort. Never mind about yer poor ole muvver sittin' 'ere freezin',' the old lady went on. 'Anuvver son would at least show some concern.'

312

'Yer wouldn't 'ave ter sit 'ere freezin' if yer'd let me bank the fire up,' Simon shouted at her.

'Yer know I gotta be careful o' that chimney,' she shouted back. 'D'yer want it ter catch light?'

Simon felt that he would like to strangle her there and then. ''Ow many times 'ave I said I'd get the chimney-sweep, but no, yer won't let me,' he retorted angrily.

'I told yer why,' the old lady growled. 'Those sweeps make a bloody mess o' the place. I ain't well enough ter go cleanin' up after 'em. It wouldn't be so bad if you'd 'elp me, but yer won't lift a finger.'

Simon was getting furious. 'That's it, keep on,' he sneered. 'It's little wonder I can't stop in, the way you go on.'

'Sod yer then, go out,' she told him. 'I could get murdered in me chair while you're guzzlin' them pints.'

'I only 'ave a couple,' the young man shouted. 'An' as fer somebody breakin' in, a poxy army couldn't get in 'ere, what wiv that chain on the door an' the nails in the winder-frames.'

'That's anuvver fing yer mucked up,' the grimalkin reminded him. 'Yer split all the frames wiv those bloody great nails yer banged in. Yer should 'ave used screws. Gawd knows what's gonna 'appen if the sashes snap.'

'Don't talk wet,' Simon growled. 'Winder sashes only snap wiv constant use. Those bloody winders ain't bin open fer years.'

Grace Dines reached into the pocket of her apron and pulled out a snuff-stained handkerchief. 'If yer goin' out yer better get goin' now,' she sniffed. 'An' don't be too long. Yer know 'ow scared I get on bad nights.'

Simon stared down at his mother and sighed deeply. 'I said I wouldn't be too long, didn't I? An' if yer worried about the winder-frames, I'll get that bloke in again ter put screws in,' he said in an effort to pacify her.

'Make sure yer do,' she replied.

Simon stepped out into the foggy night, and as always he waited until he heard the chain being drawn across the front door before setting off.

The old lady returned to the parlour and immediately put a shovelful of coke on to the fire, then she reached down inside her bodice and pulled out her key, mumbling to herself as she slipped it over her head. She picked up the small metal money-box from the shelf beside her armchair and locked it away in the sideboard drawer, and before settling down for a nap she glanced through the tattered notebook that contained the names and accounts of her clients. It had been a bad spell since Christmas, she grumbled to herself.

The charade at Wapping the previous week had had the desired effect. Vic Dolan had been lying low, and when he finally surfaced he went to see the seamen's club owner and learned that Benny Carter was running scared.

'If I'd known the implications I would never 'ave got involved,' Benny told him. 'Those geezers don't mess about. They're big-time. I've bin warned off in no uncertain terms, so yer better not show yer face 'ere again. I can't afford ter be put out o' business. I've told the ovvers the same. They're not welcome 'ere any more. Spiv Norris is movin' out the area anyway an' I don't expect Jo-Jo an' Lennie are gonna 'ang around neivver after what's 'appened.'

Dolan looked at the club owner in astonishment. 'Lennie?!'

'Yeah. Lennie told me they scared the livin' daylights out of 'im,' Benny replied. ''E really thought they were gonna put 'im in the river. 'E was still shakin' like a leaf when 'e come in 'ere that Monday afternoon.'

Dolan left the club feeling very angry. It had been a put-up job and he had fallen for it. The message had been crystal clear though. If there was a next time they wouldn't bother with dummies. He and the three heavies he had employed were marked men. All through that bitch Margie opening her mouth, he thought. Margie and that interfering git Chippy. Well, he had to get out of the neighbourhood while he was ahead, but he would make sure the publican got a going-away present, one he would never forget.

Mick Mollison had been invited to Hoxton by Nick Zanti for a few drinks and a chat.

'The business was sorted out perfectly,' the Maltese villain assured him as the two men sat drinking in the saloon bar of Zanti's local pub. 'They were all very frightened men by the time we'd finished with them. There's no need for you or your friends to lose any sleep. You won't be troubled by that load of filth any more.'

'I'm really grateful,' Mick replied. 'If there's anyfink I can do ter return the favour, just let me know.'

Nick Zanti looked intently at the docker for a few moments, then he smiled. 'I'll get us a refill,' he said.

Mick watched as the well-dressed villain sauntered to the counter. It had been a chance encounter in the first instance, and he remembered it well. It had been late last year, at a time when the wharves and docks were very busy and good wages were being earned. He was amongst a group of rivermen who were enjoying a Friday night out; the pub they happened to be using was playing host to the Maltese faction the same evening. One of the dockers had had too much to drink and he began to take umbrage at the Malts, as he put it, using a docker's pub. It was a stupid attitude to take, Mick thought. The man had become loud-mouthed and his comments were being picked up by the Maltese. The situation became volatile and it looked as though it could spill over into a nasty fight. Common sense had to prevail, and a bit of diplomacy was employed. The drunken docker was quickly dispatched out of the pub through another bar and then Mick went over to the Maltese group to apologise. A round of drinks lowered the tension drastically and Nick Zanti thanked him for his token of goodwill. They had chatted for some time, and by the end of the evening a rapport had been established.

Nick returned with large whiskies. When he had made himself comfortable the villain leaned forward over the table. 'If you meant what you just said, I might take you up on it,' he said quietly.

Mick nodded. 'I meant it, an' I'm listenin'.'

Zanti studied his drink for a few moments and then looked up. 'Very soon there's a special cargo coming in from Gdańsk on board the SS *Jaroslav Dabrowski*,' he began.

Mick frowned in puzzlement. 'That's a Batavia Line freighter,' he replied. 'It comes in regularly, but it's a food ship. It docks at Mark Brown's Wharf in Tooley Street. It only carries eggs an' sides o' bacon, stuff like that. Mind you, there's often a stowaway on board. Yer not talkin' about one o' them, are yer?'

Nick smiled indulgently. 'I'm going to tell you something and I want you to listen very carefully,' he said in a low voice. 'During the war the Nazis looted valuable art treasures as they ploughed through Europe. Field Marshal Goering himself hoarded some priceless paintings and had them stored at a secret location inside Poland. It was common knowledge: you may have read about it.

Anyway, when the war turned against them and the Russians began to advance, the hoard had to be moved before the Russian army overran the country. The people involved decided to transfer the paintings to Gdańsk and through the Baltic via submarine to South America. Are you still with me?'

Mick nodded enthusiastically and Zanti went on. 'Those paintings never reached the Baltic port, and to all intents and purposes they disappeared off the face of the earth, until the summer of last year. In July a German industrialist who had served on Goering's staff was murdered during a robbery. His safe was blown open and amongst the haul was a document listing the "Goering Treasures", as they were called. The list was recognised as being the real McCoy because of two things. Firstly, it included famous paintings alleged to have been looted by Goering personally and subsequently confirmed at the Nuremberg war trials. Secondly, because the document also mentioned Cracow, which is a large town on the River Vistula.'

Mick Mollison looked confused. 'Just a minute,' he cut in. 'Fergive me fer bein' fick, but why should that make the list genuine? What's Cracow got ter do wiv it?'

Nick sipped his drink before replying. 'It makes sense,' he continued. 'Cracow is on the Vistula, and that river flows out to the Baltic, at Gdańsk. Also, in October last year, one of the paintings on the list surfaced in Cracow. In fact it was sold to a private collector. It was assumed that the hoard was still in the secret hideaway and that the one painting sold was to finance the shipment of the rest out of the country. Now do you see?'

Mick looked a little shocked. 'You mean ter say that the paintin's are comin' over on the *Jaroslav Dabrowski*? It sounds unbelievable.'

Nick Zanti smiled at the docker for a moment, enjoying his surprise. 'Only four. The rest have already been moved and it's more than likely they're adorning the walls of private collectors throughout the world by now. The four paintings I'm talking about are priceless and they've been bought by a collector in this country. How he's going to take delivery is not known yet, but the plan is to make sure those paintings never reach him.'

'Why are yer tellin' me all this?' Mick asked.

Nick Zanti's face became serious. 'I'll tell you in a moment, but first a word of warning,' he said in a hushed voice. 'I don't need to remind you that what you've just heard is strictly confidential. No one, and I mean no one, must ever get as much as a whisper of this. I'm deadly serious, Mick.'

The docker understood the implication of the warning and he nodded firmly. 'No fear. I'm struck dumb,' he replied.

Zanti looked satisfied. 'Right then. Now to the basics. The regular sailing dates and docking times we know. What we don't know yet is which trip the paintings are coming over on. In the meantime we need as much info as possible on dock security, and future cargoes coming into the Dockhead wharves. That's where you come in. You see, Mick, we need a diversion. We're riding our luck at the moment. We've had two hoists from the Dockhead wharves recently and security is tightening up all the time now. There's a lot of planning going into this one. You get us the info we need and there'll be a nice little earner for you at the end of it. You know your methods best, but be very careful not to make anyone suspicious. Heed the warning, or you and I could end up standing in concrete at the bottom of the Thames.'

Chapter Forty-one

Elsie brought Billy home from school on Thursday afternoon, wondering as she did so whether Danny was going to turn up. He had promised to fix the shelves in the young lad's bedroom that afternoon, but after what Kay had told her on Tuesday evening Elsie wondered whether he was going to be well enough. She had seen nothing of him, though she had heard that he was back at work. It was sad to think that after getting on so well Danny had suffered a set-back.

The young woman took Billy to play with his young friends next door and then she hurried round the place, dusting and tidying up in general. She wanted the house to look nice for when Danny came. It was being silly, she knew, but it was important to her. For him to walk into a scruffy home was like her openly saying that she had failed in her marriage. She couldn't allow him to think that. She had to make sure that the house was always clean and tidy, meals were always ready on the table when Ernie came home, and that it was clear she loved Billy and cared for him as well as any other mother could. There must be no fingers pointing in her direction nor tongues wagging about her failings as a homemaker and a mother.

The kettle was coming to the boil as Danny arrived carrying his tool-bag. He looked pale and drawn but his face broke into a wide grin as she let him in.

'I was wonderin' if you could make it terday,' she said, offering him a chair.

Danny put his bag down and sat down puffing. 'I wasn't feelin' too good when I got up on Tuesday mornin',' he told her, 'but I decided ter go in anyway. I thought the 'eadache might wear off but it got worse. I don't remember much about Tuesday. Me supervisor said I just left wivout a word to anybody.'

318

'I passed yer in the street when I was comin' 'ome wiv Billy but yer didn't see me,' Elsie told him. 'I guessed what 'ad 'appened.'

Danny gave her a sheepish grin. 'So I ignored yer, did I?'

'It doesn't matter,' Elsie said, touching his arm momentarily. 'Just as long as yer feelin' better.'

Danny watched her pour the boiling water into the teapot. 'I shouldn't take long puttin' the shelves up,' he told her.

Elsie stirred the tea and slipped a patchwork cosy over the china pot. 'Just get yer breath first an' 'ave a cup o' tea. By the way, did yer bring the planks?'

Danny looked down at his bag and winced. 'I fergot 'em,' he replied, looking worried.

'It doesn't matter,' she said.

Danny watched her pour the tea. 'It was stupid ter ferget the planks. After all, I've come ter put 'em up. I must be losin' me marbles.'

If it had been anyone else Elsie would have made a joke of his remark, but in Danny's case it was different. Deep down he probably meant it. 'I do some silly fings at times,' she said reassuringly. 'I'm very fergetful too. I used ter worry about it, but I don't any more. OK, so yer fergot the planks. At least yer never fergot ter call in.'

'I wouldn't 'ave fergot, Elsie,' he replied. 'I got a sheet o' paper pinned up in the scullery. I didn't need ter be reminded in your case though.'

The young woman's heart went out to him. 'I fink that's very nice o' yer ter say so,' she said smiling. 'I enjoy yer callin' too. It's nice to 'ave a chat wiv yer.'

Danny's eyes fixed on hers. 'I should 'ave asked yer ter marry me before 'e did, even though I was only fifteen,' he told her.

'Pity yer didn't,' Elsie said smiling affectionately. 'I could 'ave waited till yer got ter be sixteen.'

Danny chuckled, his eyes still fixed on her as she poured out the tea. 'Wouldn't that 'ave bin somefing,' he replied.

Elsie handed him his tea and the young man sipped it with a serious look on his handsome face.

'Is there anyfing troublin' yer, Danny?' she asked after a while.

He shook his head. 'Not really. Do I look worried?'

'P'raps it's more a thoughtful look,' she said.

'Yeah, there is somefing.'

'D'yer wanna tell me?'

'It's nuffink really.'

'OK then.'

Danny stared at his tea for a moment or two then he looked up at her. 'That Dines woman wants anuvver job done,' he said.

'Don't yer fancy doin' it?' Elsie asked him.

'I wouldn't mind, but I told yer 'ow she is, especially towards 'er lad,' he explained.

'Tell 'er straight yer not interested, then.'

'It's not as simple as that.'

'All yer gotta do is say no.'

Danny put his empty cup down on the table. 'Simon Dines called round yesterday while I was at work. 'E said 'is muvver's bin drivin' 'im mad about the winders. Apparently the ole lady's terrified o' someone breakin' in while Simon's up the pub in the evenin'. Anyway, me mum told 'im I wouldn't be off till Thursday, terday, but I'd be busy doin' a job fer somebody else. She said Simon looked really agitated so she told 'im I might be able ter pop round after I finished 'ere.'

Elsie leaned forward in her chair facing him. 'Look, Danny, yer don't 'ave ter go round there if yer don't want to,' she told him. 'Simon'll just 'ave ter stand up to 'er, or fix it 'imself.'

'That's the problem,' Danny replied. ''E mucked the job up in the first place. I saw the nails 'e banged in that frame. It's all split.'

'What can you do about it?' she asked him.

'It just means pullin' those nails out an' puttin' screws in the sides. It's easy enough, but I just get the creeps finkin' about goin' in there. It smells to 'igh heaven, an' that ole lady walks around all the time cursin' an' moanin' at the boy. She did when I was there, anyway.'

'Well, it's up ter you, Danny, but if yer really fink yer shouldn't go, just ferget it,' Elsie advised him.

Danny stood up and reached for his tool-bag. 'Well, I'd better make a start,' he said, smiling at her. 'I'll put the end pieces on first then I'll slip back 'ome an' get the planks. Can yer come an' show me just 'ow 'igh yer want 'em?'

Elsie followed him up the flight of stairs to Billy's room, and when Danny stepped inside he nodded in approval. 'Yer've done this lovely. I like the wallpaper. Did yer do this all by yerself?'

She smiled proudly. 'Yeah. All my own work.'

They were standing close and Danny's face suddenly became serious. He could smell the eau-de-Cologne she had on and saw how the light from the window played on her fair hair. Her eyes seemed to be laughing and her partly open mouth appeared to be inviting him, challenging him to be bold, and he stood looking into her wide eyes for what seemed an age. It was only a few brief seconds, but it was long enough for Elsie to notice and she turned quickly, suddenly afraid of her own feelings.

'That's the place I'd like 'em, Danny,' she said in a voice she hardly recognised. 'Can yer put 'em about a foot apart so I can put Billy's books on there?'

Danny swallowed. 'No trouble,' he told her.

Elsie could hear him working in the room above as she leaned over the stone sink in the scullery. He was once again getting to her, just like he always had. It had been Danny the boy, a charming lad who hung on to her every word and trailed her like a pet dog. Then it was poor Danny, a grown man but a sad figure, a victim of war who many regarded as an imbecile. She had taken to him then in pity, trying to protect him and encourage him in her own way, but now she glimpsed the whole man behind it all, desirable and exciting to be with. He exuded an innocence and at the same time held an animal attraction for her, and she did not know what to do.

Danny came down into the parlour. 'I better go an' get them planks now,' he said.

As he made to leave, Elsie called out, 'I'm gonna cook tea fer me an' Billy an' there'll be plenty if yer wanna eat wiv us.'

'If you're sure,' he replied with a smile.

Outside the weather had deteriorated. The fog had returned during the early afternoon and as darkness fell it became dense, compounded by smoke and coke fumes pouring out from the chimneys as fires were stoked. Inside the cosy parlour Elsie set the table. There was one extra place this evening and Billy was curious.

'Don't Danny like 'is mum's food?' he asked.

Elsie ruffled his blond hair. 'Course 'e does, but 'e's doin' your shelves, so me an' you are gonna let 'im 'ave 'is tea wiv us.'

Billy sat down at the table and twirled a knife. 'Why doesn't Daddy 'ave 'is tea wiv us?' he asked.

''Cos yer daddy works on the lorries an' 'e 'as ter go a long way away,' Elsie explained.

'I like Danny,' the lad said.

'I like 'im too,' Elsie replied, reaching out and taking the knife away from him.

'Does 'e like us, Mum?'

'Yes, I fink so.'

Danny walked into the room and winked at Billy. 'Well, that's all fixed. Two shelves fer yer books an' fings,' he told him.

'I wanna see,' Billy said, running from the room.

Elsie felt a little embarrassed. 'Sit down, Danny. I'm gonna serve up now,' she said.

Billy was soon back. 'It's really good, Mum,' he told her, climbing on to his chair. 'I can put all me books an' fings on there. Can I do it after tea?'

'If you eat all yer tea up,' she said, filling his plate with beef stew from a large tureen in the middle of the table.

Danny tucked into his meal with relish, occasionally glancing across the table at Elsie. 'That was really good,' he said finally, taking another hunk of bread and wiping it round his plate.

'Are yer gonna go over there?' Elsie asked him as he leaned back in his chair.

He nodded. 'I'd better go. It shouldn't take long.'

'Why don't yer call in on the way 'ome?' she suggested.

'If it's all right,' he replied.

'Of course. I'll 'ave a cuppa waitin' an' you can tell me 'ow yer got on,' she said, smiling.

Joe Mezzo looked out at the thickening fog and then closed the heavy curtains. 'It's gonna be a pea-souper by the look of it,' he said.

Nick Zanti eased his position in the armchair. 'So it's definite then? Next Wednesday?'

Joe lifted his hand in warning as footsteps sounded outside the room. Maria came in carrying a large tray laden with a tall coffee-pot, a jug of cream, a sugar bowl and several cups and saucers.

'Splendid. Maria you're an angel,' Nick said winsomely as she placed the tray down on the low table in the centre of the room.

The big woman gave him a flashing smile as she left and then Joe looked around at the assembly.

'The ship comes into the Pool on the mornin' tide,' he began. 'By the time it's berthed an' the customs 'ave finished it'll be early afternoon before they start unloadin'. It's carryin' a full cargo of

322

eggs this time. Now I've got a detailed map of the wharf lay-out. It's gonna be tricky. Let me show yer.'

Nick, Tony Mancini and Mick the Hammer moved over to the dining-room table as Joe spread out the rolled-up sheet of paper and secured it with two ashtrays. 'This is Potters Fields and it leads ter Mark Brown's Wharf,' he told them. 'Now this is the dock office on the right. The gate next to it leads inter the transport yard. It's where they service the electric trucks the dockers use. That's our point of entry. There's a back entrance in that yard which leads directly on to the quayside and smack bang facin' the SS *Jaroslav Dabrowski*. We go in on Wednesday night.'

'We?' Mick queried.

'Yes we,' Joe said smiling. 'We're all in on this one.'

Mick turned to Zanti who nodded affirmatively. 'Me too.'

Joe poured out the coffee and passed the filled cups round. 'On Sunday night we'll go over the plan. There's no margin fer error on this one, so it's important we meet early ter make sure we get everyfing straight. By the way. This weekend I'm goin' ter church,' he announced.

Nick frowned. 'You, church?'

'That's right. I'm gonna get meself religion,' Joe told them. 'Maria goes ter church every Sunday. She's devout an' she's bin on at me ter take up the faith once more. I told 'er I'd never abandoned it but she said as I didn't go ter church I couldn't repent me sins an' I didn't know 'ow many 'Ail Marys I 'ad ter say. So there we are, gentlemen, I'm goin' ter church. Now remember we meet 'ere at seven sharp on Sunday evenin', not at the pub. Comprendi?'

Chapter Forty-two

Danny humped his heavy tool-bag through the thick fog in Dover Lane and knocked on the weather-beaten front door. He heard footsteps in the passage and the scratchy voice of Grace Dines. 'Simon. Who is it? Who's there?'

''Ow the bloody 'ell do I know?'

'Well, find out, sod yer.'

The door opened and Danny saw the flushed face of Simon Dines.

'I was 'avin' a doze,' Simon said apologetically. 'Come in.'

'Who is it, I say?' the old lady called out.

Simon led Danny into the parlour. 'I said 'e'd come ternight, didn't I?

Grace Dines snorted. 'Fine time this is. Couldn't yer come earlier?'

Danny shook his head. 'I 'ad anuvver job ter do terday,' he replied. 'Me muvver explained it ter Simon.'

The old lady eased herself down in her armchair and glared up at him. 'My son can't get anyfing right. 'E didn't tell me you 'ad anuvver job ter do first,' she croaked.

'Oh yes I did,' Simon said quickly.

'Oh no yer didn't,' she countered. 'Never gets anyfing right.'

Simon glanced at Danny and raised his eyes to the ceiling in exasperation. 'It's no good arguin' wiv 'er,' he said quietly.

'What yer say? Don't whisper. I can't 'ear yer if yer whisper.'

Danny took his tool-bag over to the window and set it down. 'I'd better make a start,' he said, sighing.

'What yer say?' the old lady shouted.

''E's gonna make a start,' Simon told her.

'Yer better make a start or you'll be 'ere all night,' she moaned.

Danny took out a pair of pincers from the bag and then pulled the filthy net curtains to one side before levering the first of the protruding nails out of the frame. He saw that some of the nails had been sunk below the surface of the wood and he puffed. It was going to be a tricky job, he realised. If he applied too much pressure to raise them he could well splinter the whole frame.

''Ow long d'yer reckon yer gonna be?' Grace Dines asked him in her crackly voice. 'I don't want yer messin' about there too late. I don't like people in my 'ouse when it's gettin' late.'

'It's only quarter past six,' Simon told her.

'I don't care. It's gettin' late,' she insisted.

'I'll be as quick as I can,' Danny told her, beginning to sweat as he struggled with the sunken nails.

Simon made to leave the room but the old lady stopped him.

'Where you goin'? You ain't leavin' me 'ere on me own, are yer?' she said indignantly.

The young man flopped down in the armchair, puffing loudly. 'Shut up, you silly ole cow,' he mumbled.

'Don't mumble. I can't 'ear yer when yer mumble,' she shouted.

'I'll mumble as much as I like, you scatty ole witch,' he muttered.

'What yer say?'

'Wash yer ears out, yer scatty ole rat-bag.'

The old lady got up out of her chair and picked up the evening paper. 'I said don't mumble,' she cried, beating him about the head with it.

Simon raised his hands to fend her off and she stepped back a pace and glared at him. 'Get out there an' put the kettle on, yer great big lummox,' she shouted.

Danny stood watching what was happening until the old lady turned to sit down again and she spotted him. 'Don't just stand there. Get on wiv it,' she ordered him.

Danny felt his face getting hot and he gritted his teeth as he set to work once more. It seemed to him as if he was slaving away with some hideous monster at his back, and as he struggled with an obstinate nail he heard the window crack. He looked in horror at the line running down the length of the glass and he turned quickly to see if the old lady was aware of what he had done, but she was sitting slumped in her chair. He went back to work with a vengeance, wanting to get out of this madhouse as quickly as possible. Finally he gained a purchase on the last of the stubborn nails and levered it free of the wood. Now for the screws, he told himself thankfully.

'Where yer puttin' them?' the old lady crackled.

Danny jumped with fright, realising she had come up behind him. He stood in front of the cracked pane of glass, hoping she would not notice it, and pointed to the side frame. 'I'll put a few screws in eivver side just 'ere,' he explained. 'That should do the job.'

'It better, or yer don't get paid,' she growled as she went back to her chair once more.

Danny worked as quickly as he could, feeling the sweat running down his back and trying to ignore the tension building up at the base of his skull. He shouldn't have come, he knew he shouldn't have.

'Ain't that kettle boiled yet?' the old lady called out.

'No, it ain't,' came the sharp reply.

Danny finished tightening the last of the screws and he sighed with relief. He was beginning to feel a bit nauseous and he quickly gathered up his tools.

Grace Dines got out of her chair and came over to him. 'Move aside, I wanna see,' she shouted at him.

Danny stepped away from the window, waiting for the outburst, and he did not wait long.

'Look what yer've done! Yer've smashed the winder!' the old lady screamed out at him. 'Yer clumsy oaf. I knew yer'd mess it up. I just knew it. Simon! Get in 'ere. Look what 'e's done.'

The young man came hurrying in and when he saw the window he gave Danny a look of commiseration before turning to face his irate mother. 'It was only an accident. 'E didn't do it on purpose,' he said quietly.

'Accident! Accident!' she screamed. 'It was just downright bloody carelessness, that's what it was. Well, 'e ain't gettin' paid, not till 'e replaces that broken winder. Yer gotta replace it. D'yer 'ear me?'

'All right, I'll fix it termorrer,' Danny said meekly as he picked up his bag.

Simon led him to the front door. 'Sorry about this,' he said, his weak eyes blinking nervously.

Danny nodded and started off along the turning, only to hear the old lady's cackling voice behind him. 'I want that done termorrer or yer won't get yer money. Did you 'ear me?'

Danny saw the curtains move back next door as he hurried off and crossed the street. When he reached Elsie Gates's house he was trembling.

'Whatever's wrong?' Elsie asked as she let him in.

Danny dropped his tool-bag in the passage and walked unsteadily into the warm parlour. 'It's me 'ead. It's bad. I can't see prop'ly,' he gasped.

Elsie guided him into the armchair and loosened his shirt. 'Can I get yer anyfing?' she asked anxiously.

'Just some water.'

She was soon back from the scullery. 'Did that ole cow upset yer? Was she the cause o' this?' she asked angrily as Danny sipped the glass of water.

He nodded slowly. 'She was goin' on an' on,' he told her. 'She wouldn't stop. I wanted ter leave it but I finished the job.'

Elsie took the glass from him and began to gently massage the back of his neck and his shoulder muscles in an attempt to ease the pain, but he groaned in agony and his whole body seemed to knot up.

'There, there,' she said, as if talking to a child. 'It'll pass off soon. Just stay still, you're all right now.'

Danny looked up at her, his eyes narrow slits. 'I can't stay 'ere. I must get 'ome,' he told her.

'You can't go yet. Wait till the pain eases,' she said with concern in her voice. 'It's a bad night out there.'

'All right. Just fer a while,' he said, wincing and raising both hands to his head.

Elsie stood up straight and gazed helplessly at him for a few moments then she reached for the teapot. ''Ow about a nice cup o' strong tea?' she suggested.

Danny nodded faintly. 'It'll be over in a while and then I'll go,' he replied.

When he had finished his tea, Elsie made him comfortable with another cushion and then she went upstairs to Billy's room. The little boy was sleeping soundly and she bent over his bed and kissed him gently on his forehead before creeping out again. She came back into the parlour and looked anxiously at the figure sitting slumped before the bright fire. He looked ashen and his eyes were closed. Elsie picked up the paper and tried to read but she could not concentrate. Her eyes strayed constantly to the young man and, after staring fixedly at him for a while, she realised that he was sleeping. Her heart went out to him. She wanted to take him in her arms and comfort him, press his head against her breast and stroke him, and she sighed deeply as she leaned her head back against the cushion and finally closed her eyes.

Strange thoughts and half-conscious feelings swirled through her mind, and the energy was draining from her tired body, ebbing away in waves of deep fatigue. The old lady was screaming, her toothless smile mocking, her dark evil eyes staring wildly. She came forward, her long dirty fingernails like talons. Elsie tried to cry out but her voice had gone. She was struck dumb, frozen with terror as the long sharp claws reached out towards her unprotected eyes.

Elsie woke up with a start and found herself panting. Her heart was pounding and she could feel the cold beads of sweat on her forehead. She sat up straight and took a few deep breaths, glancing up at the clock. It was ten minutes after nine o'clock. Danny was stirring and he ran his fingers through his hair as he opened his eyes.

'D'yer feel better, Danny?' she asked him.

He nodded and looked up at the clock. 'It's gettin' late. I'd better get goin',' he said.

Elsie watched as he climbed unsteadily to his feet. She took down his coat and helped him into it. 'Why don't yer stay a bit longer? You're still shaky,' she said.

Danny held the door-jamb as he stepped into the dark passage. 'I'll be all right,' he told her.

Elsie took him by the shoulders. 'Please stay.'

He kissed her gently on her cheek and then reached for the front door catch. 'I better go. Fanks fer everyfink, Elsie,' he said quickly, suddenly feeling panicky as the pounding in his head started up again.

As the night settled in over the Bermondsey backstreet, so the fog grew more opaque, thick with sulphur fumes and coke grains which burnt the eyes and clung to the face. Folk hurried home and built up their parlour fires, adding to the noxious vapours. They coughed and wheezed, and they cursed the fog and said that it was the worst one for many a year.

At nine o'clock, as usual, Simon Dines stepped out of his house into the dense yellow pall, cursing the old lady. 'Put the chain on,' he called out, then he set off for the sanctity of the pub. He walked carefully, his hands held out in front of him, feeling his way along.

He reached the Mason's Arms, a pub he hardly ever used, but it would do tonight, he thought.

Simon drank two pints of beer that evening, savouring the respite in the quiet public bar. Very few people had ventured out in the suffocating fog, and the young man was able to sit by the fire and ponder things. At ten minutes to ten he said goodnight and left. He carefully walked the fifty or so yards to his front door and knocked. There was no answer and he knocked again, louder this time. Still there was no answer. Simon shouted through the letter-box. 'Muvver, wake up! Let me in!'

He kicked at the door loudly and then stepped back as the woman in the next house came out holding a handkerchief up to her mouth.

'I wondered what was goin' on,' she mumbled from under her handkerchief.

'Somefing's wrong, she's not answerin',' Simon told her.

'P'raps she's fell asleep,' the woman said as she went in and closed her door.

Simon banged on the front door with his foot, then he went to the window and rapped on the upper pane. Still there was no answer. The young man went back to the door and then stepped back a few paces. With a sudden rush he threw himself at it and it crashed open.

Frances Harper had put up with shouting, insults and every other form of neighbourly cussedness ever since she had had the misfortune to move next to Grace Dines and her son. From experience she had found it was best to ignore them as much as possible, and on that cold and foggy night she did not wish to leave her banked-up fireside to go and find out what the noise was all about. Earlier that evening she had been moved to peep through the curtains when she heard the old lady shouting at someone outside, and she had caught a brief glimpse of a young man hurrying past her window.

'The old bag next door is at it again,' she told her husband.

Herbert Harper was dozing in the armchair and he puffed irritably. 'Take no notice, it's nuffink ter do wiv us,' he told her.

Frances saw the figure disappear into the fog and she adjusted the curtains. 'I dunno what it is wiv that woman,' she growled. 'Bloody ole cow ain't got a good word fer anybody. They'll end up buryin' 'er upside down if she's not careful.'

Herbert settled down again and Frances got on with her knitting.

The fire burned brightly and soft music on the wireless made her feel contented. She worked away on the difficult cable stitch, pleased with her efforts, and when her eyes began to prickle with fatigue she put down her knitting and dropped off to sleep. The banging outside woke her with a start. She looked up at the clock to see it was five minutes to ten and she sat up straight as the banging continued.

''Erbert. Wake up,' she said loudly. 'It sounds like next door.'

'What does?' he mumbled.

Frances gave her sleepy husband a hard look, then she slipped into her coat and went to the front door to listen. She could hear Simon Dines shouting to be let in and she took out her handkerchief and put it over her mouth as she opened the door. After a few words with the young man she came back inside. 'If the silly ole cow didn't stick that chain across the door 'e'd be able ter let 'imself in, instead of 'avin' ter wait fer 'er to open it,' she grumbled.

The crash sounded loudly in the room and Frances and Herbert looked at each other. It went quiet for a few moments, then there was a hammering on their front door, and this time Herbert went to answer it. Simon stood wide-eyed, his mouth hanging open. 'Me muvver! She's dead!' he cried out.

Herbert hurried next door, followed by Frances. They went into the parlour and saw her. Grace Dines was lying on her back in front of the low fire. Her head was turned to one side slightly, and a copious mess of clotted blood clung blackly in the hair above her left temple. The blood had poured down her face and neck, too. Her lifeless eyes stared up at the ceiling and her hands were clenched in fists at her side. On the floor beside her was a blood-stained flat-iron.

Chapter Forty-three

Detective Sergeant Moody leaned his heavy bulk back in his office chair early on Friday morning as he studied the initial report on the killing of Grace Dines. Simon Dines had left a lot of questions unanswered, Moody thought, and he threw down the folder and rubbed his bleary eyes with his thumb and forefinger. He would need to check out the statement himself and visit the scene of the crime in the hope of gleaning some clues to the old lady's killer. There were neighbours to talk to as well, and a visit to the mortuary. There seemed to be no doubt as to the way she had died, but there were always other factors to consider.

At ten o'clock that morning, Moody knocked at the house in Dover Lane and was shown in by a dishevelled-looking young man.

'I'm sorry, but I fell asleep in the chair,' Simon told him.

The detective sat himself down facing him. 'I'm sorry to 'ave ter trouble yer, but I've gotta tidy up this report,' he began. 'You said 'ere that yer went out at nine o'clock an' yer muvver put the chain on the door as yer left.'

'That's correct,' Simon replied.

'Yer went ter the Mason's Arms an' stayed there until ten minutes ter ten, an' when yer got 'ome yer couldn't get in. Is that right?'

'I ain't got a key. Me muvver always lets me in, yer see,' the young man explained.

'Why 'aven't yer got a key, Simon?'

'There's no point. Me muvver chains the door.'

'Why would she do that?'

'She was a moneylender an' there was money lyin' about,' Simon replied.

331

Bill Moody studied the folder on his lap for a few moments. 'Whoever killed your muvver did it between nine o'clock an' ten minutes ter ten if your statement is correct.'

'It's correct,' Simon said quickly. 'I always look at the clock before I go out, an' me muvver never liked me ter stay out too long. That's why I always keep a check o' the time.'

'Now you say 'ere that when yer broke in the door yer saw that the chain wasn't on,' Moody continued. 'That means that the killer was known ter yer muvver an' she let 'im in, unless it was a stranger an' 'e tricked 'is way in.'

'Nah, she wouldn't let anybody in while I wasn't there, unless she knew 'em well.'

'Like a customer?'

'Yeah, a customer.'

'Did she 'ave any enemies ter your knowledge?'

Simon smiled cynically. 'She was a moneylender. They don't 'ave many friends,' he replied.

Moody's face hardened. 'I'm not talkin' about friends. I said enemies.'

'Not that I know of.'

Moody studied the folder once more. 'Right now, you said 'ere that yer muvver's notebook is missin' as well as all the money from the cashbox. Could she 'ave just mislaid the notebook an' it's still in the 'ouse somewhere?' he asked.

Simon shook his head unequivocally. 'She always 'ad that book by 'er side on that shelf,' he said, pointing to the corner of the room.

'What else was taken?' Moody asked.

'Just the money an' the notebook. I told the policeman that,' Simon answered.

'An' that book was always by 'er side.'

'Yeah, it was, till she locked it away at night.'

'Where did she put it?'

The young man pointed to the sideboard. 'In that drawer wiv the cashbox.'

'Is the drawer locked?'

'Yeah.'

'Could it be in there?'

'I shouldn't fink so. In fact, I'm sure. Why should she put the notebook away an' leave the cashbox out?'

'Yer've not actually looked in the drawer then?' Moody queried.

'I couldn't. Me muvver always carried the key round 'er neck. It never leaves 'er.'

'So the key is still on 'er body?'

Simon nodded. 'It must be.'

'Tell me somefink, Simon,' Moody said slowly. 'You knew where the key was. Why didn't yer check that the notebook wasn't locked in the drawer before yer reported it stolen?'

'I didn't wanna disturb the body. I didn't even close 'er eyes in case I was doin' wrong,' the young man replied.

'So the notebook could be in that drawer.'

Simon shook his head vigorously. 'Me muvver never put the fings away until she was goin' ter bed.'

'Never?'

'No, never.'

Sergeant Moody studied the young man for a few moments. 'If you're right, the notebook was taken fer a special reason, wouldn't you say?'

Simon nodded. 'Whoever killed 'er was let in. It must 'ave bin one of 'er customers. The man's name would be in the book, that's why 'e took it.'

'It might 'ave bin a woman,' the detective reminded him.

'I s'pose it could've bin.'

'Can yer fink of anyone else, ovver than a customer, who yer muvver might 'ave let in?' Moody asked.

Simon thought for a while. 'No, I can't fink of anybody.'

Moody got up and went into the passage to inspect the heavy steel chain. Then he came back into the parlour and pulled the curtains to one side. ''Ow long 'as this bin cracked?' he asked.

'Last night,' Simon told him. 'The man who put the screws in done it, but 'e's comin' back ter put a new winder in.'

'Last night?' Moody queried. 'When last night?'

'About six o'clock or just after. 'E's the same bloke who mended the chain,' Simon replied.

'Was you 'ere all the time, until the man left?'

'Yeah.'

'What's 'is name?'

'Danny Adams. 'E lives at number Seven Waggoner's Way.'

Moody wrote in his notepad then looked up again. 'Would Danny Adams 'ave 'ad any reason ter call back after yer'd left fer the pub?' he asked.

Simon shook his head once more. 'Nah. Me muvver wouldn't 'ave let 'im in anyway.'

'Not even if 'e'd told 'er 'e left one of 'is tools be'ind?'

'I don't fink so.'

'Yer don't sound very sure.'

'Nah, I don't fink she'd 'ave let 'im in. She was upset anyway about 'im breakin' the winder.'

Sergeant Moody put the notepad back into his coat pocket and buttoned up his overcoat. 'That'll be all fer now,' he said. 'Oh, just one fing more. Do yer 'ave any idea 'ow much was in the cashbox?'

'I dunno. It could 'ave bin about forty or fifty pounds, maybe a bit less,' Simon told him.

Moody nodded and walked to the front door. 'I'll be in touch,' he said as he let himself out.

News of the Dines murder swept through the backstreets like a forest fire. Everyone was talking about it, and when Dot Adams met Annie Thomas and Bet Greenedge in the street, she was quick to tell them that Danny had only that evening fixed the old lady's window.

'Good Gawd, Dot, they wouldn't fink 'e 'ad anyfing ter do wiv it, would they?' Annie asked with her hand up to her face.

'Course not. The ole lady's son was there all the time,' Dot told them.

Mary Kelly and Ada Brennen were talking about the murder as they stood together at Ada's front door. 'Somebody 'ad it in fer 'er, that's fer sure,' Mary remarked. 'People like 'er make a lot of enemies.'

'Yer right, Mary. Look at the mess our Elsie got into when she got in 'er clutches,' Ada replied. 'The interest charges was pullin' 'er down.'

''Ere, yer don't fink the ole lady's son 'ad anyfink ter do wiv it, do yer?' Mary asked. 'She used ter make 'is life a misery by all accounts.'

Ada shook her head. 'Nah, the boy come back from the pub an' found 'er dead on the floor. 'E 'ad ter break in, accordin' ter Mrs 'Arper. She lives next door ter the Dineses an' she told Sara Brady about it. Sara said that Mrs 'Arper went in wiv the boy an' saw the ole lady sprawled out on the floor wiv 'er 'ead bashed in.'

'Good Gawd. What a shock.'

'I s'pose it was the money they was after,' Ada said.

'I 'eard she kept it all under 'er bed,' Mary remarked. 'I bet she 'ad a nice few quid stuffed away somewhere. I wonder 'ow much they got away wiv.'

'Gawd knows. I expect it'll all come out when they catch 'im,' Ada replied. 'Well, I s'pose I'd better get goin'. I'll be glad when the shift changes over. It's one mad dash when they're on earlies.'

Mary nodded. 'I know what yer mean. 'Ere, is your Joe gonna get that certificate framed?'

Ada smiled. ''E's stuck it in the dressin'-table drawer. I bet 'e'll ferget all about it in a few days' time.'

Mary picked up her shopping-bag. 'Be seein' yer, luv.'

'See yer, Mary.'

Kay was ready and waiting when Pat Kelly called to take her out on Friday evening, and as she stepped out into the street, the young man slipped his arm around her waist and gave her a squeeze. 'I've missed yer,' he said smiling.

Kay grinned and snuggled against him as they set off along the street. The fog had cleared during the day and now it was cold and crisp. The night sky was full of stars and a crescent moon was rising as the two young lovers walked over the railway bridge in the direction of the river.

'Wasn't it terrible about that ole lady?' Kay remarked. 'Mum said she was a moneylender. She said Danny Adams was doin' some work for 'er that same evenin'. Apparently 'er son found 'er lyin' dead on the floor when 'e came back from the pub.'

Pat's arm tightened about her waist. 'What a night it was too,' he replied. 'It's the sort o' fing yer'd expect in a Charlie Chan film. The murders always seem ter take place on foggy nights.'

They reached the foot of the bridge and carried on under the long arch which led to Jamaica Road.

'I don't fancy sittin' in Chippy's place too long, Kay, but I should go an' see 'im after what 'e did,' Pat told her. 'If it wasn't fer 'im gettin' a couple of 'is pals to 'elp me out, I might not be 'ere now.'

'Don't talk like that, Pat,' she said quickly, 'it frightens me.'

He gave her another reassuring squeeze. 'Anyway, we'll just say 'ello an' then we'll go along ter the Gregorian. They've got a good singer in there at weekends.'

They crossed the quiet thoroughfare and walked into the narrow maze of backstreets. As they neared Chippy's pub, Pat glanced into the dark archway where he was attacked and gritted his teeth tightly at the memory of that night.

'Well, if it ain't young Patrick me lad,' Chippy said loudly as the two youngsters walked into the grimy bar. 'An' look who's wiv 'im, no less.'

Pat shook hands with the landlord, who leaned over the counter to plant a kiss on Kay's cheek. 'I never turn down the opportunity ter kiss a pretty gel,' he laughed.

'Chippy, I wanna fank yer fer what yer did that night,' Pat told him.

'There's the two blokes yer need ter fank sittin' over there,' he replied. 'Ole Solly too, but 'e ain't bin in fer a few nights. Solly was the one who saw it 'appenin'. 'E come runnin' in 'ere like a bat out of 'ell.'

Pat looked over at the two hefty men who were playing cards in the far corner of the bar. He took Kay's arm and led her over. He knew them both by sight and he had exchanged a few words with Mick Mollison on occasions.

'I'd like ter fank you two lads fer comin' ter the rescue that night,' he said.

They looked up, cards in hand. 'Fink nuffink of it,' Mick said pleasantly.

'This is my lady friend, Kay,' he told them.

Kay smiled. 'I wanna add my fanks as well,' she said.

The two dockers looked embarrassed at the fuss, and Tubby grinned as he spread his hand of cards out on the table in front of him. 'It was nuffink really,' he said, 'they was just a load o' rubbish. They won't be showin' their faces round 'ere again, yer can take that fer gospel.'

'Let me buy yer a drink. It's the least I can do,' Pat said grinning.

'That's neighbourly of yer. We're drinkin' bitter,' Tubby replied.

Pat stood talking to Chippy for a while after he had taken the drinks over and Kay stood at his side, her arm through his. 'I bin worried about any comebacks, Chippy,' the young man said. 'Whoever they are they'll guess that Tubby an' Mick came from this pub.'

The publican leaned forward over the counter with a knowing look on his unshaven face. 'There'll be no comebacks, take my word fer it,' he told him.

'D'you know somefing I don't?' Pat asked.

'Mick Mollison mixes wiv some dodgy characters an' 'e was owed a favour,' Chippy explained. 'As it 'appened, Tubby recognised one o' the geezers who jumped yer. 'E drinks at the seamen's club in Rovverhithe an' Mick passed the word on. The result was there's bin a visit paid there. People were named an' they've bin spoken to. It was all very civilised, but the fright'ners were put in. Take it from me they're all runnin' scared.'

Pat nodded. 'That's comfortin' news, Chippy, but where does that leave Margie? What if Vic Dolan takes it out on 'er?'

''E was spoken to as well,' the publican replied. 'Dolan won't dare lay a finger on 'er now.'

'These people Mick knows. Why should they concern themselves?' Pat asked. 'All right, Mick was owed a favour, but would they bovver ter sort Dolan out if 'e took it out on Margie, say in six months' time?'

Chippy looked at Kay and shook his head slowly. 'This feller o' yours is a disbelievin' son of a bishop, ain't 'e?' He turned to the young man. 'Listen, Pat, I'll explain. These people are organised. They're family, like the Mafia. They know the score an' they've got backin'. They don't do fings by 'alves. If you cross 'em you'll pay, 'ave no fear. But if yer call in a favour like Mick did, then it's honoured. If Vic Dolan tried anyfing wiv Margie it'd be seen as a direct insult ter the family. Dolan knows this. 'E's bin around long enough ter take 'eed. I tell yer now, if 'e don't, 'e's dead.'

Pat looked closely at Chippy and saw the candour in his eyes. 'I don't doubt yer,' he replied.

They finished their drinks and bade the friendly publican a goodnight, then walked out into the cold night air.

'It's scary when yer fink of it,' Kay remarked as she snuggled against him.

Pat nodded. 'It'd be more scary if I still 'ad ter keep lookin' over me shoulder. Anyway, let's ferget it. C'mon, it'll be music time in the Gregorian.'

Chapter Forty-four

Detective Sergeant William Moody had been officially placed in charge of the murder investigation and he was in no doubt that his credibility was on the line. Already there had been two wharf robberies and a lorry theft which were almost certainly planned by local villains, and as yet no progress had been made. If this investigation were to go on too long, questions would be asked in many quarters, not least by the press.

As he sat at his desk on Saturday morning, Moody pondered over the murder. The woman who lived next door to the victim had stated that she came out and saw the victim's son calling out to his mother and that she went into the house along with her husband after the young man had broken the door down. The woman had also stated that earlier that night she had heard shouting, and she had looked out through her curtains to see a young man passing by. He was being verbally abused by the victim. The neighbour had gone on to state that she had only caught a brief glimpse of him but assumed that he had just left the house next door.

The detective stood up and went over to the window, gazing out at the overcast sky for a few moments, then he hurried out of the office to speak to the desk sergeant. 'Can someone go round ter see the Dines boy?' he asked. 'I need 'im 'ere ter clear up a few points.'

While he waited for the young man to arrive, Moody sat smoking a cigarette, turning the details over in his mind. Whoever murdered the old lady had to have known of her and her son's habits. The person would also have been known and trusted: such as a customer, perhaps, or a visitor on business.

Twenty minutes later, Simon Dines arrived at the police station and was shown into an interview room. Sergeant Moody studied the young man through a glass panel for a few moments before going in. He noticed that Simon was wearing dark glasses and held his head low.

The detective entered the room and sat down facing him. 'I'm sorry ter trouble yer again but we need a few more details,' he told him.

Simon leaned forward and put his elbow on the table, shielding his eyes with his hand. 'It's OK,' he replied.

Moody stared at him. ' Is there somefing wrong?' he asked.

'It's the bright light,' Simon told him. 'I got weak eyes, yer see.'

Moody got up and flicked the light switch. 'Is that better?'

The young man nodded. 'I 'ave ter wear these glasses when I go out,' he explained.

The sergeant sat back in his chair. 'You were tellin' me about the notebook your muvver kept. Do yer know any o' the names in that book?'

Simon shook his head. 'Nah, me muvver never let me near it.'

'But yer must 'ave seen people comin' in ter borrer money from time ter time. They would be known to yer, wouldn't they?' Moody queried.

'I wasn't encouraged ter be there,' the young man replied. 'Muvver used ter tell me ter keep out o' the room unless she called me in. She liked ter do 'er business in private.'

'In private? But you're 'er son. Surely she didn't mind you bein' there?' the detective pressed him.

'Yer didn't know my ole lady,' Simon countered. 'She was very funny in 'er ways.'

'Did yer get on wiv 'er? I mean, did she nag yer a lot?'

Simon smiled bitterly. 'She was an old cow, an' I'm not afraid ter say so 'cos it's the trufe. I couldn't do anyfing right. It was always Norman this, an' Norman that.'

'Norman? Is 'e yer bruvver?'

'Yeah.'

''E doesn't live wiv yer, does 'e?'

''E's in the Merchant Navy.'

'What about when 'e comes 'ome? Does 'e stay wiv yer then?'

Simon shook his head. 'Norman wouldn't spend a minute longer in the 'ouse than 'e 'ad to. 'E can't stand our muvver.'

Moody leaned forward and rested his clasped hands on the table. 'Are you certain yer never saw any o' the names in that notebook?'

'I never looked at it. That's the trufe,' the young man said, his face flushing up with discomfort.

'It's OK, I'm not doubtin' yer,' Moody reassured him. 'I 'ave ter make sure. Just take it easy.'

Simon pushed his glasses up on to the bridge of his nose and sighed deeply. 'I know I should be feelin' bad about me muvver, but I can't feel anyfink,' he confessed. 'I'm sorry she got killed, of course I am, but I'm not grievin' over 'er. I know it sounds terrible but I'm bein' honest. She led me a dog's life.'

Moody studied the pitiable figure for a moment or two, then he stood up. 'Would yer like a cup o' tea?' he asked.

'Yes please.'

The policeman left the room and returned with two mugs of weak tea. 'It's not much good but it's wet an' warm,' he remarked.

Simon sipped the tea and then took his glasses off to wipe his watering eyes. 'I expect yer a bit shocked by what I said,' he went on.

Moody shrugged his broad shoulders. 'Not really. You were tellin' the trufe,' he replied. 'I just wonder why yer never left 'er an' got a place o' yer own.'

'Me eyes are too bad fer me ter go out ter work. I 'ave ter live on me sick money,' Simon told him. 'I couldn't afford the rent.'

The detective nodded. 'We're gonna 'ave ter check that sideboard drawer. I'm seein' the coroner this afternoon an' I'll collect the key.'

Simon stared down at his tea. 'I s'pose there 'as ter be a post-mortem?'

'Yeah, it's standard procedure,' Moody answered. 'It's ter determine the cause o' death.'

'I should 'ave thought that was obvious,' Simon replied.

'On the surface, yeah, but the blow itself might not 'ave killed 'er. It could 'ave brought on an 'eart attack or a stroke.'

'Would that make any difference ter the charge?'

'Nah, it would still be murder.'

Simon nodded slowly. 'Well, I 'ope you 'urry up an' find whoever done it,' he said quietly. 'Like I say, I never got on wiv me muvver, but that was no way fer 'er ter go.'

Moody leaned back in his chair. 'Before yer go, there's somefing else I wanna ask yer,' he said. 'This bloke who came ter mend the door an' the winder. What's 'e like?'

The young man shrugged his shoulders. 'I don't know 'im. I'd only 'eard that 'e done carpentry jobs.'

'Yeah, but yer saw 'im work. Was 'e shifty? Did 'e seem ter be interested in the cashbox? After all, 'e must 'ave noticed it lyin' there,' Moody prompted.

'All I can say is 'e seemed a decent sort o' bloke,' Simon replied. ''E got a bit nervous though, especially when me muvver started shoutin' at 'im.'

'Fer crackin' the winder?'

'Yeah. She screamed at 'im an' 'e started 'oldin' the back of 'is neck, like 'e 'ad an 'eadache or somefing.'

'She shouted out at 'im in the street too, didn't she?'

Simon nodded. 'Yeah, she did. I expect all the neighbours 'eard it.'

'Next door did. Well, it's bin very interestin' talkin' to yer,' the detective said. 'That'll be all fer now. Fanks fer comin' in. I'll talk ter yer again. By the way, I'd like ter see inside that sideboard drawer after I collect the key.'

'I'll be in all day,' the young man replied.

Len Taylor glanced up at the wall clock and then made his way along the tiled corridor to check on all the cubicles. The baths were closing in five minutes and he wanted to get away sharp. There was much he had to do before going out that evening, and he did not want to be late. He had faced considerable resistance, and after a lot of beating about the bushes he had finally come out with it and told Dot in plain English that she would be quite safe in his company. She had laughed at him then, explaining that it wasn't him she was frightened of but herself. She told him that since her husband had died she had never been out with a man, especially an attractive man, and she was nervous of making a mess of it.

Len smiled at the thought of her finding him attractive and he began to whistle as he did his final daily check. All looked well. The cubicles were all clean, the baths spotless, and the dirty linen gathered up. The last job was to shut down the main valve which controlled the water supply, and as he turned left at the end of the corridor and went into the storeroom where the valve was situated, he saw Danny Adams sitting on a wickerwork linen basket with his head in his hands.

'What yer doin' 'ere, Danny?' he asked anxiously. ' I thought you left ages ago.'

Danny looked up and his sunken eyes were almost closed. 'It's bin bad, I couldn't see properly,' he groaned.

'D'yer wanna go ter the 'ospital?' Len asked him.

'Nah, it's wearin' off now.'

'Look, I fink the tea bar might still be open. I'll go an' see. You stay right where you are,' Len told him.

Five minutes later, the supervisor came hurrying back carrying two large mugs of steaming tea. 'There we are, get that down yer, it'll make yer feel better,' he said quietly.

Danny took a sip from the mug and then put it down beside him. 'I'm sorry ter be a nuisance, but I couldn't leave the way I felt. I was almost blind,' he said in a husky voice.

'It's all right. Don't worry. Just take it easy,' Len said, sipping his tea. ''Ere, I'm gonna be callin' round ternight. I'm takin' yer mum out fer a drink.'

'That's good. I'm pleased,' Danny mumbled.

'What brought this one on? Was it the chlorine? They've bin changin' the water in the swimmin' bath this afternoon an' the fumes always seem ter carry up 'ere when they add that fresh chlorine.'

Danny shook his head. 'This 'as bin 'anging' on since Thursday night. I can't even remember what I did Friday. It's a complete blank.'

Len looked at him in surprise. 'You came in same as normal yesterday. I was kept busy fer most o' the day an' I didn't get much time fer a chat, but I saw yer cleanin' out the cubicles as good as gold.'

'I must 'ave bin workin' instinctively,' the young man said, rubbing his forehead. 'I just can't remember anyfing. Y'know, Len, I fink I'm goin' mad.'

The supervisor rested his hand on Danny's shoulder as he saw him starting to tremble. 'It'll come back. Don't torture yerself,' he said kindly. 'Now c'mon, finish yer tea an' I'll walk 'ome wiv yer.'

Late on Saturday afternoon, Sergeant Moody had the coroner's report in front of him. Grace Dines had died from a single blow to the left side of her head which had fractured her skull and caused a massive brain haemorrhage. The death had occurred between nine and ten p.m. Moody closed the folder and slipped it into his desk drawer, then he picked up a thin wedding ring and a small key which was secured to a length of white string and put them into his coat pocket. He could have used a car to take him to Dover Lane but he preferred to walk. Things were beginning to sort themselves out in his mind and the fresh air would help stimulate him.

The long paired lines of wet steel railtrack gleamed beneath the thunderous sky as the policeman crossed the railway bridge, and as he turned into Dover Lane, spots of rain started to fall. Simon Dines answered the knock and Moody noticed that his eyes looked red and swollen, though he seemed composed.

'I've got yer muvver's weddin' ring 'ere,' he said, taking it from his pocket and laying it down on the bare tabletop. 'I brought the key too. Now let's take a look, shall we?'

Simon stood back while the officer inserted the key, pulled the wide drawer out and brought it over to the table. It contained a well-worn photograph album, a long, buff-coloured envelope which was stuffed with papers, and a small tin box which contained various small trinkets.

'I knew the notebook wouldn't be in there,' Simon said quietly.

Moody nodded. 'Yeah, yer did say. I'll need ter go frew these papers, wiv your permission,' he replied, taking the key out of the drawer and slipping it into his coat pocket. 'I can do it now if yer like. There might just be somefing amongst this lot that'll give us some sort o' lead.'

Chapter Forty-five

Early on Sunday morning, Joe Mezzo took a number 63 bus to Clerkenwell. The area in north-east London near King's Cross Station had become the new home for thousands of Italian immigrants since the rise of Fascism had driven them from their native country. Many Maltese people too had made the area their home, and the settlers strove to keep their national identity. Shops and businesses bore Italian names, and marriage within the community helped to preserve the culture and traditions. The area was popularly known as Little Italy, and it was there that Joe was going to worship.

The large Catholic church was packed and the service was about to begin when the shopkeeper from Bermondsey stepped inside, crossed himself reverently, and then took his place in a back pew. He had gone to church before, to be christened, and to be married, and once after his ship had gone down, when he had joined the survivors in a service of remembrance to those who had perished.

The service was conducted in Italian. Joe bowed his head when everyone else did and stood when they stood. His grasp of the language was very limited, but he mouthed the words of the hymns and responded in a mumble to the chants. The shopkeeper said his own prayer that morning during the service. He prayed for the success of the coming robbery, and he did not feel that he was blaspheming in any way. Robberies were not the kind of activity that the Lord smiled upon, he knew full well, but in this case Joe Mezzo was confident that the Almighty would at least afford Himself a wry smile and a shake of His holy head at the vagaries and irony of human affairs, before promptly bestowing His blessing.

When the congregation left their seats and took the sacrament,

Joe remained where he was, his head lowered as if in prayer. In reality he was gathering his thoughts for his coming meeting with the eminent Monsignor Franco Vincenti, officer of the papal court and special messenger from the Vatican. It was more a courtesy visit Joe was paying him, a formality in effect, but it was still awe-inspiring, and he considered it a matter of personal honour to conduct himself with decorum.

The congregation moved slowly from the church, and it was not until the last of them had left that Joe Mezzo got up from his pew and walked towards the altar. The priest who had conducted the morning mass was talking quietly with a younger member of the church and he turned as Joe came over.

'Would you be . . . ?'

'Mr Mezzo, Father, yes,' Joe replied.

'His Eminence will see you now, if you'll just follow me,' the priest told him.

Joe was shown into a large room and found himself facing a huge figure dressed in papal robes and wearing a large crucifix. The monsignor was completely bald, except for a few wisps over each ear. His pate was shining and his heavy face was flushed. He came forward and held out his hand, palm down, as though showing off his ring, and Joe hesitated momentarily, wondering whether he was supposed to shake it or kiss it. He decided to clasp it and recoiled inside as he felt its clammy limpness.

'It is very nice to meet with you, Mr Mezzo,' the monsignor said in perfect English. 'I want you to know that we are very gratified by your response and your commitment, and our prayers go with you.'

'Fank you, your Grace,' Joe replied, talking to the back of his head as the man went over to a long carved yew cabinet.

'Will you partake?' the priest asked. 'The weather is not very sympathetic in these latitudes this time of year, especially to a constitution accustomed to Rome.'

Joe nodded as he held up a bottle of Napoleon brandy invitingly, and watched as he poured two large measures into lead-crystal goblets. Hoping that the papal priest had a sense of humour, he chanced to quip, 'That looks a mite stronger than communion wine.'

A huge belly laugh came out of the monsignor as he handed Joe his drink and offered him a seat facing the huge desk. 'I regret to say that time is rudely short, Mr Mezzo, so I suggest we begin while we enjoy our brandy,' he said. 'Is everything prepared?'

Joe took a sip of the excellent spirit and put the glass down carefully. 'Well, your Grace, the situation is this . . .'

Barbara halved the last of the peeled potatoes with her sharp knife and laid the pieces in a large tray. 'That's it, Mum. Want the greens done?'

Ada shook her head. 'There's plenty o' time. I'll stick them taters in, though. The joint's doin' nicely an' I've mixed the batter.'

Dawn was still wearing her quilted pink dressing gown and she sniffed loudly as she dabbed at her red nose. 'Anyfing else ter do?' she asked without enthusiasm.

'Go an' sit in the parlour, or go back ter bed,' Ada told her.

Dawn looked sorry for herself as she shuffled into the passage and Ada turned to Barbara and said, 'She's like a bear wiv a sore 'ead when she gets a cold. Yer'd fink she was dyin'.'

Barbara smiled. 'She reckons she's got a touch o' the flu. 'Ow can yer 'ave a touch? Yer've eivver got it or you ain't.'

Ada sprinkled some salt over the potatoes and then soaked them with hot water from the kettle. She added a small knob of cooking fat and sizzling gravy from the beef joint before popping them into the top of the oven. 'Is there anyfing in the papers about the ole lady's murder?' she asked.

Barbara shook her head. 'The papers'll be full of it next week,' she replied.

Ada sat down and opened the *News of the World*. 'Kay was tellin' me this mornin' that Mary Kelly told 'er she saw the Dines boy gettin' in a police car yesterday.'

'I wonder if 'e 'ad anyfing ter do wiv it?' Barbara remarked. 'It's common knowledge 'e didn't get on wiv the ole gel. She treated 'im like a chattel apparently.'

'There's gonna be all sorts o' stories comin' out now,' Ada told her. 'They won't let the poor ole woman rest. It don't do ter listen ter such talk. All right, maybe she was a bit of an ole cow, but no one knows what sort o' life she 'ad wiv that boy.'

Joe came into the scullery. 'Anyone seen the *News o' the World*?' he asked.

Ada passed it over to him with a quick, meaningful glance at her daughter as she waited for the response.

'I mighta known,' Joe grumbled. 'If I 'adn't come out fer it, yer'd be doin' the spuds on it.'

'No I wouldn't. I was only tryin' ter find some juicy bits o' scandal,' Ada told him with a grin.

Joe shook his head slowly as he walked out with the paper under his arm, and Barbara turned to her mother. 'Did our Else say she was comin' over fer dinner?' she asked.

'She didn't say she wasn't so I presume she is,' Ada replied. 'Why d'yer ask?'

'Well, she's normally 'ere by now.'

'P'raps young Billy ain't well.'

'Could be.'

'If she's not 'ere soon I'll pop over an' find out what's wrong,' Ada said.

Five minutes later, Elsie walked in with Billy, who ran straight into the parlour to see his doting grandfather. Elsie joined her mother and Barbara in the scullery and sat down with a deep sigh. 'I dunno why I bovver,' she said dejectedly.

Barbara and her mother exchanged quick glances.

'I can see what side o' the bed you got out of,' Ada said.

'I'm sorry, Mum, but I just 'ad a big row wiv Ernie an' 'e stormed off out,' Elsie told her.

'What was it all about?' Barbara asked her.

'Yer know I got Danny Adams in ter put a couple o' shelves up in Billy's bedroom,' Elsie began. 'Well, Ernie went in there this mornin' an' 'e came out lookin' all mean an' 'orrible. 'E asked me who put 'em up an' when I told 'im 'e went crazy. I thought 'e was gonna whack me. I should 'ave asked 'im first, an' I shouldn't 'ave 'ad Danny in there while 'e was away. Gawd almighty, I dunno what 'e would 'ave said if 'e'd known Danny stayed fer tea.'

''E stayed fer tea?' Ada queried. 'It's takin' a chance, ain't it, Elsie? S'posin' young Billy let the cat out o' the bag?'

The young woman looked up quickly. 'What was I s'posed ter do?' she replied. 'Yer know what a terrible night it was on Thursday. Danny 'ad ter go an' do anuvver job after 'e put the shelves up, so I said 'e was welcome ter stay fer tea. There was no 'arm in it, an' as far as Billy goes 'e never 'ardly sees 'is farvver these days. Anyway, I warned 'im not ter say anyfing. I put it in a way 'e understood. 'E's a sensible boy.'

'Yeah, but 'e's only a child,' Ada told her. 'Ernie can wheedle fings out of 'im. Yer gotta be careful 'ow you 'andle it or it'll seem like there is somefing goin' on between you an' Danny.'

''E can fink what 'e likes from now on,' Elsie said angrily. 'I've just about 'ad enough o' bein' treated like a dish-mop.'

Barbara felt it was time to change the subject. ''Ere, what d'yer fink o' the ole moneylender gettin' murdered?' she said.

'Terrible, wasn't it?' Elsie replied. 'Danny repaired the ole gel's winder the same night. Just a couple of hours before she got done in.'

'They won't fink 'e 'ad anyfing ter do wiv it, will they?' Ada asked with concern.

'Nah, the ole lady's son was there all the time,' Elsie said.

'I wonder who it was killed 'er?' Barbara cut in.

'Whoever it was got away wiv a nice few bob, I bet,' Ada said. 'It was common knowledge she kept a lot o' money in the 'ouse. She must 'ave made a packet over the years.'

Billy came bounding out into the scullery. 'Gran'ma. Danny put some shelves up in my bedroom,' he said excitedly.

Ada pulled him to her and gave him a big kiss on his cheek. 'So my little man's got shelves up in 'is room. Ain't you lucky?'

'Daddy didn't like 'em,' the lad replied.

''E prob'ly does, Billy.'

'No 'e don't, Gran'ma. I 'eard 'im shoutin' at Mummy after I showed 'im the shelves. Why don't 'e like 'em? I do.'

Ada could not think of a good answer and she hugged the lad to her. ''Ere, why don't yer go in the parlour an' ask yer grandad if 'e knows where yer sweets are,' she prompted.

Billy hurried out of the room and Ada puffed. 'It's a bloody shame that child 'as ter be a party ter what's goin' on wiv you two,' she said sharply.

Elsie bit back an angry reply and shook her head slowly. 'I try ter shield 'im from it all but it's difficult, Mum. 'E's growin' up fast. 'E can sense fings are not right.'

Ada nodded acquiescently. 'It's always the kids who suffer in these sort o' situations,' she remarked, 'as much as yer try ter keep it from 'em. Yer'll just 'ave ter keep a special eye on the boy, Elsie. 'E's doin' all right at school, ain't 'e?'

'Yeah, 'is teacher's very pleased wiv 'im,' Elsie told her.

'That's a blessin'. Schoolwork's the first fing ter suffer,' Ada replied. 'Does 'e 'ave nightmares or wet the bed occasionally?'

'Mum!' Elsie cut in quickly. 'Billy's fine. Really 'e is. I'll tell yer now, if I thought it was affectin' the boy I'd up an' leave Ernie termorrer, honest ter God I would, even if it meant gettin' a room fer us somewhere.'

'Yer won't do that,' Ada told her sharply. 'Yer'll both come 'ere ter live. We can manage some'ow.'

Barbara put her arm round her sister's shoulders affectionately. 'We could all pile in tergevver. Remember 'ow we used to?' she said, beaming.

Elsie forced a smile. 'Anyway it ain't come ter that yet,' she replied.

Ada stood up and stretched. 'Why don't you two get out from under my feet an' go an' pester yer farvver. I gotta do the greens,' she told them.

Jim Carney sat in the Bradys' parlour, sipping his tea with a satisfied grin on his flat face, while Sara read his application. 'There's gonna be a few surprised people when they get this,' he told her. 'They didn't fink I'd get the references, I know.'

Sara looked up at him over her tin-rimmed spectacles. 'There will be a few surprised people if yer send 'em this letter,' she said coolly.

'What's the matter wiv it?' Jim asked her.

'Well fer a start,' she told him, 'yer can't address an application like this: "Dear to who it may concern". You should start it, "Dear sir". Then there's the bit about gettin' the reference from the railway chairman. Yer can't say that Sir Thomas Kilcline's a pal o' yours. There's also this bit about you goin' ter the town 'all an' bein' let down by the deputy mayor. Yer've called 'er a silly ole bag.'

Jim looked put out. 'Well, she was. It wouldn't 'ave 'urt 'er ter gimme a reference,' he said.

'Best fing I can do is write a proper letter out an' then you can copy it,' Sara told him.

'Would you do that fer me, Sara?'

'I might as well,' she sighed. 'I ain't got nuffink else ter do, apart from washin' an' ironin', an' clearin' up, an' makin' the beds.'

'You're a diamond an' I'm gonna tell that ole man o' yours 'ow lucky 'e is, strike me if I don't,' Jim said with passion.

''E'll strike yer if yer do,' Sara replied quickly.

'I really appreciate it, gel. Yer bin like a muvver ter me.'

'Don't get carried away. Sister'll do,' she growled.

Chapter Forty-six

Maria Mezzo considered herself to be a devoted wife and a devout Catholic. It was all she had ever aspired to be, and she was contented with her lot. Joe was a good husband who saw to it that she wanted for nothing, and they enjoyed a happy life together. The only thing which sometimes saddened Maria, however, was that Joe did not share her strong religious feelings. Although he had been brought up in the faith, he was not a devout Catholic. He never went to church, and she had long since given up trying to persuade him to accompany her when she attended St Mary's for Sunday Mass.

As Maria prepared coffee and sandwiches for Joe's guests on Sunday evening, she worried. Something was going on, she felt sure. Normally Joe would meet with his friends at the pub on Sunday evenings, but tonight they were all gathered in the lounge, and she had felt the tense atmosphere in the room when she went to find out what they would like to eat and drink. The talking had suddenly ceased when she walked in, and Joe himself had appeared to be a bit edgy. She would speak to him about it later, although she knew full well that he would not be forthcoming. Neither would he be disposed to enlighten her about the mysterious trip he had made that morning to Clerkenwell. That was the way he was, and Maria sighed as she picked up the laden tray.

Danny Adams went to bed early on Sunday night, but he could not get to sleep. The latest attack had been a severe one and he felt drained. The pain had left him but his stomach was churning and he was tormented by a sense of impending doom. The police would soon find out about him doing that job of work at the Dineses' house and they would want to talk to him. He would have to be very careful how he answered their questions, and he hoped that they would not try to browbeat him.

The night sounds of waggons being shunted carried into his darkened room and Danny twisted on to his back. It had been very nice doing those jobs for Elsie, he thought. She was a pretty, desirable woman, and it was sad the way she was trapped in a miserable marriage with little to look forward to. She was kind and caring and she had made him feel like a normal human being again, instead of an object of pity and derision.

The young man turned over on to his side and closed his eyes. The spectre of the old lady snarling at him kept flashing into his mind out of the darkness. He could hear her grating voice calling out after him. Her haggard face and cruel rheumy eyes stole towards him, minatory, accusing, and he fought to shut them out. He could smell her stale breath as she came near, her long, talon-like fingers pointing, clutching at him, and he shouted out in terror, suddenly finding himself bolt upright in his bed, his body bathed in sweat as he stared across the room at the first light of dawn.

Heavy rain fell from a leaden sky as Waggoner's Way came to life. The coalman drove his lorry into the turning and carried hundred-weight sacks of best bright, nutty slack and coke into the homes. The daily milk was collected from doorsteps and people went off to work and to the market. The bedraggled paper boy delivered the morning newspapers, and PC Fuller ambled through the street looking forward to a chat and a cup of tea at the grocery shop. Basil Cashman opened up his oil shop, bemoaning the fact that the rain would stop him displaying his bundles of wood outside on the pavement. Jack Springer had been up since the crack of dawn sorting out the deliveries, and he was enjoying a mug of tea after the initial early morning rush, unlike Sammy Dinsford, who never bothered to open before nine o'clock. Sammy had come to realise that, for some unknown reason, most of his customers discovered their boots and shoes required mending after the streets had been aired, which allowed him time to get a good fire going, make a mug of tea and read the morning paper.

The day had started as usual for the Waggoner's Way folk, and Dot Adams had no reason to suspect that today would be different from any other Monday. She had made sure Danny was up for work and then gone off to the office cleaning job she did in Tooley Street.

351

She was home by eleven o'clock and had time to put her feet up with a cup of tea and a read of the paper. She settled down in front of the fire, and after reading her horoscope, and an article on the build-up of Russian forces in Eastern Europe which she found very depressing, Dot leaned her head back in the armchair and thought about Saturday night.

Len had taken her to the pictures, the first time she had gone in years. The film was a thriller and Len had actually held her hand during the frightening bits. She recalled feeling like a young woman again, a little silly in fact, but it was nice, and nobody had seen them holding hands in the darkness of the theatre. He seemed a very nice man who was lonely and needed a woman's company. He was also good to Danny and had been instrumental in his settling down at the job. He wanted to see her again and she was looking forward to a night out, though she did not want to rush things. Better she took it slowly, for both their sakes.

A double knock on the door brought Dot out of her reverie with a start, and she was shocked to see a policeman standing on the doorstep.

'Mr Adams?'

'No, I'm Mrs Adams,' she said with a note of sarcasm.

'I mean does Mr Adams, a Danny Adams live 'ere?' the constable asked.

'Yeah why? What's wrong?' Dot said quickly.

'Is 'e in?'

'No 'e's at work. What d'yer want wiv 'im?'

'Could yer ask 'im if 'e'd mind callin' in Dockhead Police Station when 'e gets in from work?' the policeman replied.

'What's 'e done?' Dot asked anxiously.

'It's just routine. 'E might be able to help with some inquiries,' he told her.

The day had suddenly soured for Dot, and try as she might she could not get rid of the anxiety that was working away at her stomach. Her horoscope had warned her of her ruling planet coming into conjunction with Mars, which could pose problems before Wednesday. She was being silly again, she told herself firmly. The stars were not to be taken literally. Danny was most probably going to be asked if he had noticed anything unusual when he was working in the old lady's house. It was nothing to worry about. Nothing at all.

'Ada, I'm fair worried about my Danny,' Dot said to her neighbour that afternoon when they met in the street.

Ada Brennen put down her shopping-bag on the wet pavement and rubbed her numb hands together. 'What's wrong, luv?' she asked.

'I 'ad a copper call on me this mornin',' Dot told her. ''E wants Danny ter go down the station when 'e gets in.'

'Is it about the Dines murder?'

'I dunno. I expect so.'

'I shouldn't worry,' Ada said encouragingly. 'They just wanna ask 'im a few questions about the ole gel an' 'er son, I should imagine.'

'That's what I keep tellin' meself,' Dot replied. 'I wish I'd told the Dines boy that Danny wasn't interested in doin' any more jobs.'

'You wasn't ter know anyfing like this would 'appen, was yer?' Ada said. 'Danny's got nuffink ter worry about anyway.'

Dot nodded her head in agreement and told herself Ada was right, but as she made her way home she was feeling more and more anxious.

Sergeant Moody had had a trying day and he was feeling jaded as he walked into his office and slumped down at his desk. The lead into the salmon robbery at Dockhead had gone nowhere. A shopkeeper in the Old Kent Road had been found with a case of red salmon for which he could not provide a receipt or a Food Ministry permit, and the hopeful sergeant had decided to follow it up. It turned out that the brand of salmon did not correspond to that which had been stolen and, as for the receipt, it was miraculously found by the shopkeeper's wife, who had managed to lose it down the back of her sofa whilst doing the books. Moody was not going to wait around while the woman searched for the missing permit, and he left with a scowling face, much to the delight of the relieved shopkeeper, who knew that if the detective had given himself time to study the receipt properly he would have seen by the date that it was an old one.

At six o'clock that evening, Sergeant Moody was informed by a constable that Danny Adams was waiting in the interview room and his immediate response was to ask the PC for a mug of tea. It wouldn't do any harm to let him wait, he thought. The interview room was not very comfortable and it tended to put the fear of God into many suspects and interviewees. It was strange how that room tended to frighten people, even those who had done nothing wrong.

353

He would finish his tea and smoke a cigarette before going along to do the interrogation, by which time the atmosphere of the place would have had the desired effect.

'Mr Danny Adams?'

The young man stood up and said yes and was motioned back into his seat.

'Yer don't mind if I call yer Danny, do yer?' Moody said quietly.

'Course not.'

'That's fine. It gets us off to a better start,' the detective said in an agreeable voice.

''Ow can I 'elp yer?' Danny asked.

'I need some information on the Dines boy an' yer might be able ter provide it,' Moody told him. ''Ow well d'yer know 'im?'

''Ardly at all.'

'That doesn't tell me much.'

'Well, I'm sorry.'

'Fer what?'

Danny began to get warning bells and he took a deep breath. 'I only met Simon Dines a couple o' weeks ago when I repaired 'is front door chain,' he said.

'What did yer do to it?'

'I put a new piece o' wood in the door-jamb ter secure the fastener better,' he replied. 'The old piece o' wood was split.'

'Yer went back last Thursday and secured the winders wiv screws, so the Dines boy said,' the detective continued.

'That's right.'

'Was Simon Dines in the room all the time you was workin' there?'

'Yes.'

'Did you 'appen ter notice a cashbox on the shelf by the ole lady's side?'

'No.'

'Are you sure about that?'

'Yes, I'm sure.'

'What about the notebook? Yer must 'ave seen the notebook.'

'I didn't see any notebook.'

Moody took a packet of Woodbines from his top pocket. 'Want a fag?' he asked.

Danny shook his head. 'I don't smoke.'

'Tell me, Danny. 'Ow come yer didn't see that cashbox?' Moody

354

pressed him. 'It was right next ter the winder. There was a lot o' money in it apparently.'

'I wasn't interested in anyfing else except gettin' the winder done an' gettin' out,' Danny replied in an irritated voice.

'Why was that?'

'The ole gel was gettin' on ter me.'

''Ow?'

'She was standin' over me. Tryin to 'urry me up.'

'An' yer got annoyed.'

'Sort of.'

'What about Simon Dines, did 'e get on ter yer as well?'

'Nah, 'e just stood there watchin'.'

Moody toyed with the packet of Woodbines before taking a cigarette out and lighting it. 'I understand yer made a balls-up o' the job,' he said offhandedly.

'No, I never,' Danny replied sharply. 'As I was gettin' one o' the nails out, the winder cracked. I said I'd replace it.'

'I bet the old lady was mad at yer, wasn't she?'

'Yeah, she started shoutin'.'

'What did yer do then?'

'She started screamin' at me an' it started me 'ead poundin', so I left as quick as I could,' Danny explained.

'She came out an' stood at the front door screamin' after yer, didn't she?' Moody prompted. 'She didn't pay yer neivver.'

'No, she never.'

'So yer went back later an' asked fer the money.'

'No.'

'Yes yer did,' Moody said quickly. 'Yer went back after 'er son went out an' she let yer in. But she decided she wouldn't pay yer, so yer lost yer temper an' clouted 'er wiv the flat-iron. Then yer took the money from the cashbox an' scarpered. That's right, son, ain't it?'

'That's not true,' Danny said in a loud voice, his eyes flaring. 'Why should she let me in again if she wasn't gonna pay me?'

'That's easy. Yer tricked yer way in by sayin' you 'ad the glass ter replace the cracked one. Then yer killed the ole lady fer 'er money. The money in the cashbox.'

'No I never.'

''Ow much was in the cashbox, Danny? Fifty pounds? Sixty pounds? Maybe it was nearer seventy.'

'No, it wasn't.'

'Was it less? Say forty-five? Forty maybe? That was it, wasn't it? Forty pounds. Yer killed that ole lady fer forty pounds. You 'ammered 'er ter death wiv a flat-iron. Just one blow. That's all it'd take from someone who was used to 'andlin' tools. Just like knockin' a nail in, wasn't it?'

'Yer mad!' Danny shouted. 'I never killed the ole lady. I never touched the flat-iron. Check fer fingerprints if yer like.'

'We already 'ave,' Moody said in a low voice. 'The flat-iron was 'eld wiv a cloth. Women always 'old flat-irons wiv a cloth, or they'd burn their fingers. The cloth was beside the iron an' yer picked it up by the cloth 'cos o' leavin' fingerprints. You knew we'd check fer fingerprints, didn't yer? That's why you was cocky about it.'

Danny lowered his head, trying to keep his composure. He felt the tension building up in the base of his skull and he prayed that it would pass. 'I never went back ter the 'ouse,' he said flatly.

'Yes, you did, an' yer picked a good night fer it. No one would see yer in the fog, yer thought, but somebody did,' Moody told him with a malicious smile playing on his thick lips. 'The woman next door did.'

'She's a liar. I never went back, I told yer.'

'She saw yer leavin' an' gave a good description. She'll remember seein' yer pass by 'er winder again when we ask 'er, that's fer sure. Why did yer take the notebook?'

'I never took the notebook.'

'Yes, yer did. Yer took it ter transfer suspicion. Yer wanted us ter fink one o' the ole lady's clients killed 'er. That's why yer took it, wasn't it?'

Danny stared into the cold, menacing eyes of his tormentor. 'I never took anyfing.'

'Oh, I see. Yer jus' killed 'er in a temper an' then ran out. Then that no-good son of 'ers took the money an' the notebook ter cover yer. You were both in it tergevver.'

'God Almighty!' Danny groaned as the searing pains cracked through his head. 'I never killed anyone.'

'Where did yer go when yer first left the ole lady's 'ouse?' Moody asked quickly.

'I dunno. Me 'ead was poundin' an' I just . . . I dunno . . .'

'Yer just waited. Yer knew the son was goin' up the pub. Simon told me the ole lady was gettin' on to 'im about goin' out every night while you was there. Yer waited yer opportunity an' then went back. C'mon, Danny, admit it. You killed that ole lady fer forty pounds. Didn't yer?'

The young man could see lights flashing sickeningly in front of his eyes now and he clenched his hands into tight fists. 'No. God, I dunno.'

The detective suddenly changed tack. 'It's understandable,' he said in a soft voice. 'You were tryin' ter do the ole bitch a good turn an' shit was yer fanks. She was known fer 'er vile tongue. She slagged yer off all the time you were workin', an' ter top it all she refused ter pay yer. It's understandable, son. Many people would 'ave bin tempted ter do what you did. I understand perfectly. Don't feel too bad about it. Yer went back ter get yer rights, an' when she refused ter pay yer, you saw red. The iron was 'andy an' yer picked it up. Just one little moment of anger an' it was all over. I understand. You can see it now, can't yer? That's why yer didn't remember goin' back at first. You was still so shocked an' overcome wiv it all that yer wasn't finkin' straight. You are now though. Yer went back an' killed 'er, didn't yer?'

Danny felt the policeman's voice becoming louder and louder as the pounding in his head grew overwhelming. It was like a giant drum, an endless thump that threatened to tear the top of his head off. 'Please. Please 'elp me,' he groaned in agony.

'I'm on your side. 'Ere, 'ave a fag,' the detective said quietly.

Danny waved it away. 'I gotta sleep. I gotta close me eyes. They're burnin'.'

'I'll let yer get some sleep soon. We'll just need ter get a confession made out an' you can sign it. OK?'

Danny gulped hard, trying to make sense of what his tormentor was saying. He tried to nod, praying that the torture would end soon, and he let out a deep sob as he covered his throbbing eyes with the palms of his hands. He could get no relief from the searing, lacerating pain, and in the blackness he could see her outline glowing, just like in his dream. She was coming towards him with her hands reaching out to him, her long dirty fingernails inches from his eyes, and he lashed out. He had killed her. It wasn't a dream after all. He had smashed her head in with the flat-iron as she clawed at him. Yes, that was it. That was how it happened.

The voice seemed to resonate around the room as the words were slowly pronounced. 'Danny Adams, I'm chargin' you wiv the murder of Grace Dines an' I 'ave ter caution yer that you do not 'ave ter say anyfing at this time, but if yer do it'll be taken down an' may be used in evidence against yer.'

Footsteps came and went and then Danny heard his own voice responding to the prompting as he faced the policemen across the table. He saw them in a haze, their faces like fragmenting patterns, and he forced down nausea as he sought to get it all over as quickly as possible. He lowered his head as it mercifully went quiet, then he heard the rambling voice start up again. It seemed to go on and on as the statement was read out to him, and then he felt the pen being placed in his hand and the voice, louder still, urging him to sign. It was over. It was at an end, and now, as the heavy door closed behind him, he slumped down with exhaustion on the hard camp bed. He could close his eyes in glorious peace and rest alone and undisturbed, until sleep bore the excruciating pain away.

Chapter Forty-seven

The Brennen household was quiet that evening. Barbara and Dawn had gone to the pictures together and Kay was spending the evening with Pat at his home. Ada Brennen had been dozing in her favourite armchair for a while and when she slowly roused herself she moved her stockinged feet away from the heat of the fire. 'Dear oh Lor', it's nearly nine o'clock,' she remarked, yawning. 'Draw them curtains, luv, we don't want everybody lookin' in.'

Joe put the evening paper down and got up out of his armchair to close the heavy drapes over the freshly laundered net curtains. He heard the sound of a car pulling up outside and he pushed the nets back a little.

'Don't muck them nets up, Joe, I've got 'em 'anging' right,' Ada told him irritably.

'There's a taxi just pulled up opposite,' he told her.

Ada got up and hurried over to the window. 'That's Dot Adams, an' it's that feller wiv 'er. The one I saw go in there the ovver night,' she said. 'There's somefing wrong wiv 'er. It looks like she's cryin'. She's got an 'anky up to 'er face.'

'P'raps somefink's wrong wiv young Danny,' Joe suggested.

'Gawd, I 'ope not,' Ada replied. 'D'yer fink I should go over there?'

'Trouble is, yer don't know if yer doin' right, do yer?' Joe said.

Ada nodded and adjusted the curtains as soon as the taxi drew away. 'I fink that's Dot's chap who's gone in there wiv 'er,' she remarked.

'Oh yeah?' Joe said, grinning.

''E seems a nice bloke,' Ada told him as she sat down again.

'Why, 'ave yer spoke to 'im?'

359

'Nah, but I've seen 'im an' Dot walkin' up the street an' they was laughin' tergevver. Smart man too.'

'Oh yeah?'

'Mind yer it'd be nice fer Dot Adams. She's bin on 'er own fer years now,' Ada went on.

Joe tried to get interested in the paper again but he found himself watching his wife. He could see that she was uncomfortable: she was twiddling with her thumbs, a sure sign that something was troubling her.

'If yer sittin' there wonderin' whevver yer should go over an' see what's wrong, why don't yer go?' he said. 'Yer won't rest ovverwise.'

'Yer right, luv. I fink I will,' she replied.

Ada took down her coat from behind the room door and slipped it on quickly. 'I might be some time, so don't ferget ter keep that fire in, Joe. It's bleedin' cold ternight,' she remarked.

The street was deserted as Ada hurried over to the house opposite and knocked on the front door. She could hear Dot's voice and she sounded distressed. The door was opened by a tall, well-built man who Ada took to be in his fifties. He looked worried and she gave him a quick smile. 'I'm Ada Brennen an' I live opposite,' she told him. 'I 'ope yer don't fink I'm pryin', but I saw you an' Dot gettin' out the cab a little while ago an' I could see that Dot was upset. Is there anyfing wrong?'

Len stepped back a pace. 'P'raps yer better come in,' he replied.

Ada walked into the tidy parlour and saw Dot Adams hunched in her chair with a handkerchief held up to her face.

'It's my Danny, Ada,' she said in a choking voice. 'They've charged 'im wiv murder!

'The Dines woman?'

'Yeah. They said it was 'im.'

'That's ridiculous!' Ada said as she went over and put her arm round Dot's shoulders. 'Danny wouldn't 'urt a fly.'

''E's admitted it, Ada. 'E's made a statement,' Dot sobbed.

'Where is 'e? At Dock'ead?'

She nodded. 'They wouldn't let me see 'im. 'E's up at Tower Bridge Court termorrer mornin'.'

''As 'e got a solicitor?'

'Yeah, 'e's gonna be there termorrer.'

'I jus' can't believe it,' Ada said, moving over to the vacant armchair opposite her.

Len Taylor looked uncomfortable as he stood by the door. 'Should I make a cuppa?' he asked.

Ada nodded. 'Make it a strong one.'

Dot took the handkerchief away from her face. 'Ada, this is Len Taylor. 'E's a good friend o' mine.'

Ada exchanged a quick nod as Len went out to make the tea and she turned back to Dot. 'Yer mustn't worry, Dot,' she told her. 'Danny was 'ome 'ere at the time the Dines woman was murdered, wasn't 'e?'

Dot shook her head. 'No, 'e wasn't. That's the trouble.'

'Where was 'e? Don't yer know?'

''E went out ter put some shelves up at your Elsie's.'

'Then Elsie can vouch fer 'im, surely?'

'It was in the afternoon that Danny done the shelves,' Dot told her. ''E came back about tea-time 'cos 'e'd fergotten ter take the pieces o' wood, an' yer remember 'ow bad the weavver was last Thursday night. Anyway, 'e said that your Elsie was gonna get 'im a bit o' tea, ter save 'im walkin' backwards an' forwards frew the fog. Danny 'ad promised ter do a job over at the Dineses' 'ouse, yer see.'

'So after Elsie gave 'im 'is tea Danny went over ter do the job an' 'e came 'ome late, did 'e?' Ada queried.

Dot shook her head. 'No, Ada. Danny never came 'ome that night.'

Ada looked puzzled. 'Yer mean 'e stayed at our Elsie's all night?'

'I presume so,' Dot replied. 'Yer see, when 'e came back ter collect the wood an' told me Elsie was gonna get 'im 'is tea, 'e also said if the fog got any worse 'e'd kip down on Elsie's sofa. Well, yer know it did get worse. Yer couldn't see more than a couple o' feet in front o' yer, so when 'e didn't come back that night I wasn't worried. I knew that's where 'e'd be.'

Ada drew a deep breath and blew through her lips. She thought it unlikely that her daughter would have allowed Danny to stay the night, bearing in mind the current state of her marriage. Ernie might well have got to know of it and caused a great deal of trouble for everyone concerned. 'Didn't you ask Danny later if 'e stayed at Elsie's that night?' she queried.

Dot looked at her friend with barely suppressed panic showing in her red eyes. ''E musta gone straight off ter work from Elsie's. I never saw 'im till Friday evenin' an' I couldn't get any sense out of 'im when 'e got in,' she explained. ''E was in a bad way. 'E just picked at 'is tea an' then 'e went up ter lie down. I went up later an' 'e was fast asleep so I just left 'im. There was nuffink else I could do. There's nuffink anybody can do when 'e gets those attacks of 'is.'

'Did Danny go ter work on Saturday?' Ada asked her.

'Yeah, but 'e wasn't over it,' Dot replied. 'Len 'ad ter bring 'im 'ome when 'e finished. 'E was almost blind. 'E was better yesterday, fank Gawd, but I could see 'e was different, some'ow.'

'Different?'

'Yeah. Like there was somefink on 'is mind.'

'Did yer ask 'im about it?'

Dot shook her head. 'I know it's difficult fer people to understand about Danny, but I know 'im better than anybody. If I try ter pry or ask 'im questions when 'e's not prop'ly 'imself it tends ter get 'im agitated, an' that's what I 'ave to avoid. 'E's not mad, Ada. That boy's as sane as you or me.'

'Yer don't 'ave ter tell me that, Dot. I know you're right,' Ada assured her. 'Everyfing's gonna be all right. Once the solicitor's 'ad time ter talk to 'im it'll all be sorted out.'

Dot Adams bent her head and started to sob loudly, and Ada got up out of her chair and put a comforting arm round her distraught friend. 'C'mon, Dot, don't cry,' she whispered. 'It'll be fine. You'll see.'

Len came in carrying three large mugs of steaming tea. 'I'll stay wiv 'er fer a while,' he said quietly.

The three sat sipping their tea in silence for a few moments, then Len looked across at Ada. 'We're just 'opin' your daughter can clear it all up,' he said.

'I'm sure she can,' Ada replied. 'I'll go over an' see 'er first fing termorrer mornin', soon as 'er 'usband's gone off ter work. I'd go ternight but I daren't, not while 'e's there.'

'I understand,' Len told her. 'I'm takin' the day off, so I'll be in court wiv Dot.'

Ada nodded and put down her empty mug. 'Is there anyfing I can do, Dot?' she asked.

The distressed woman remained staring down at the mug she was clasping in both hands. 'Why did 'e sign that statement, Ada? 'E confessed 'e'd done it,' she said in a low voice.

'The boy was mixed up. 'E didn't know what 'e was doin',' Ada told her quietly.

Len took the empty mug from Dot and patted her back gently. 'Why don't yer try an' get some rest, luv,' he said kindly. 'I'll let meself out.'

'It's a good idea,' Ada said as she got up and put on her coat. 'I'll go an' see Elsie soon as I can an' then I'll come over. What time 'ave yer gotta be in court?'

'Ten o'clock,' Len replied.

Ada left the house and crossed the dark street to her own home with a feeling of dread. What was Elsie thinking about, allowing the young man to stay there? she thought. Did he stay there, or had he walked the streets all night? Surely not in that fog. Was it at all possible for a nice young man like Danny Adams to kill someone? It wasn't in his nature, whether or not he was in control of his faculties. It wasn't possible.

Joe sat listening in shocked silence until Ada had finished telling him everything, then he stood up and leaned his hand on the mantelshelf, staring thoughtfully into the bright fire. 'I can't bring meself ter believe that Danny would 'ave stayed at our Elsie's all night, Ada,' he said. 'Nor can I believe that 'e could 'ave killed the ole woman.'

'I feel the same way, but could 'is mind 'ave snapped?' Ada asked him.

Joe shook his head slowly. 'I know that the Dines woman was an ole witch, an' she was inclined ter shout an' scream at people, but even if she'd gone off at Danny fer some reason, I can't see 'im reactin' violently. ''E'd just walk away, I'm sure.'

Ada reached for the teapot. 'We'll know more in the mornin',' she said as she poured out two cups of tea. 'Let's 'ave this an' get ter bed, not that I'm gonna get any sleep ternight.'

Simon Dines sprawled his legs out in front of the fire as he sipped his cup of tea thoughtfully. The money had to be here somewhere, he told himself. Mother had been thrifty all her life. Nothing was wasted and not a penny spent on luxuries. She had skimped on coal for the fire, and sixpences for the gas meter. She had moved around the house in semi-darkness rather than burn lights, and she had even bought the cheaper cuts of meat and made do with half-rotted vegetables sooner than spend a few coppers more. She had distrusted banks and the post office and it figured that there must be quite a large amount of money stashed away somewhere in the house. The locked drawer had not revealed any money, nor had any other of the drawers. A thorough search of the parlour had revealed nothing either, and it was unlikely that the scullery could be a hiding-place. It had to be the old lady's bedroom, Simon decided.

As soon as he finished his tea, the young man got on with the search. He lit the light in his mother's back bedroom and drew the curtains. His first job was to check the bed. The flock mattress was lumpy, but it was obvious to him that the hoard wasn't there. Next he tried the dressing table. The drawers contained various bits and pieces as well as clothing, but there was money there and Simon cursed loudly as he looked around the room. The tallboy was next, but once again the result was the same. The single wardrobe creaked open to reveal nothing more than a couple of dark dresses, a tweed coat, three or four hats and some shoes.

The young man sat on the bed for a few moments, rubbing his chin thoughtfully, then he went back to his search. He took down a dusty suitcase from on top of the wardrobe and opened it. Inside there were old newspapers, some song sheets and a bundle of *Hobbies* magazines. These must have belonged to Father, he thought as he put the suitcase back. The iron storage trunk at the foot of the bed produced nothing apart from bedding, and Simon began to feel agitated. It just had to be here somewhere, he growled to himself. This would be the obvious room to keep the money in. There was just the corner cupboard to be searched and he opened it slowly, half expecting to see the hoard lying there waiting for him. A cut-glass chandelier was resting on the floor of the cupboard and Simon lifted it out carefully. It might have brought a few bob, he told himself, except that some of the glass pendants were missing. He put it back and saw that the other shelves were packed with blankets, sheets and a couple of grubby candlewick bedspreads. The top shelf was empty, apart from a large biscuit tin, and the young man's heart leapt as he gingerly took it down and laid it on top of the bed. He pulled off the lid with bated breath and swore loudly at what he saw. The tin was full of toy building-bricks in assorted colours.

Simon hurried down the stairs and went into the parlour. She could have buried it in the yard, he thought, smirking as he pictured his ageing mother wielding a pick and shovel. No, it was here in the house. It was somewhere he had missed, but where? He twisted his mouth angrily as he leaned on the mantelshelf and stared at himself in the smudgy mirror, and his weak eyes blinked like an owl as he looked at the bits and pieces on the shelf. There was a small wooden-framed picture of him and Norman at Southend and a matching framed picture of the old lady as a young woman, and a few hairclips, a pencil, a thimble and a packet of needles were lying around on each side of the seven-day clock which was set in the centre, mounted on half-inch-thick metal discs.

The young man stood for a while, trying to think of any place he had not looked. Then he spotted something shining under the base of the clock. It looked like a piece of jewellery. He picked up the pencil and fished it out. It was an elongated glass pendant with a gold-coloured ring attached to one end. He recognised it as belonging to the damaged chandelier and wondered what it was doing under the clock. The old lady might have found it on the floor of her bedroom and stuffed it into her apron pocket, he thought. She might have remembered it later and put it under the clock out of the way. Suddenly he looked at the picture of Norman and his face broke into a broad smile. He hurried up the stairs to his mother's room once more, opened the cupboard and removed the chandelier. The centre of the three small floorboards was loose and Simon prised it up easily. He reached down into the hole and withdrew an oblong wooden box. He held his breath as he raised the lid and then gasped as he saw the money. There was a bundle of rolled white five-pound notes and a thick wad of one-pound notes secured by an elastic band. He lifted them out and found a bundle of ten-shilling notes and beneath them a dozen gold guinea pieces. He had been right. His mother had dislodged one of the glass pendants from the chandelier when she last used the secret cache. Norman had been shown the secret location when they were both children. Simon recalled how his brother had often taunted him about his secret place under the floorboards where he kept his treasures. He had never divulged the location, not even when they had joked about it as young men.

'Your secret's out, Norman,' Simon said aloud as he rested back on his haunches. 'The money's mine, all mine.'

Chapter Forty-eight

Ada was up early on Tuesday morning. After seeing Joe off to work with a peck on his cheek, she made herself a cup of strong tea. It was no use going round to see Elsie until Ernie had left for work, she thought.

'You all right, Mum?' Kay said as she came into the scullery.

'Danny Adams 'as bin charged wiv the ole lady's murder,' Ada told her.

Barbara walked in yawning widely just at that moment and heard it too. 'I don't believe it,' she gasped.

Dawn came in then and the three girls gathered round their mother while she told them the full story.

'Elsie wouldn't take the chance wiv Danny,' Barbara said firmly, glancing at her sisters.

Dawn shook her head, concurring with her, but Kay made no sign as she stared at her mother's worried face.

'What d'you fink, Mum? Do you fink Danny killed that ole lady?' Dawn asked her.

'Certainly not,' Ada replied with conviction. 'Danny's a lovely boy.'

'I bet 'is muvver's goin' out of 'er mind,' Barbara remarked.

Ada got up to remove her curlers. 'C'mon, you lot, get yerselves ready fer work,' she told them. 'I'm goin' over ter see Elsie in a minute.'

After Barbara and Dawn had left for the factory, Ada sat drinking tea with Kay who did not have to get into work until nine o'clock.

'I'm all on pins, but it's no use goin' over there just yet,' Ada said. 'I'll wait till you go out an' we can walk along tergevver.'

'I could skip work an' come wiv yer, Mum,' Kay offered.

'No, there's no sense in that,' Ada replied. 'I'll tell yer all about it ternight.'

The clock showed half-past eight as Kay and her mother put their coats on and left the house. They walked along towards Dover Lane and as they turned the corner past the bootmender's they saw Ernie Gates running towards them. His face was ashen and he fought for breath as he reached them. 'I was just comin' round ter tell yer,' he gasped. 'It's Elsie! She's 'ad an accident!'

'Oh my Gawd!' Ada cried. 'What's 'appened?'

'I found 'er lyin' unconscious at the foot o' the stairs,' he puffed. 'They've took 'er ter Guy's. I found 'er lyin' there when I come in ter get me overnight bag.'

'Is she 'urt bad?' Kay asked him quickly.

'We dunno yet. I took Billy next door after I phoned fer the ambulance,' Ernie said, still gasping for breath.

'Did 'e see Elsie fall?' Ada asked.

'No, I woke 'im up.'

'I'll make sure Billy's OK, then I'll go straight up the 'ospital,' Ada told him, biting back tears.

'I'm comin' wiv yer, Mum,' Kay said, taking her by the arm.

Ernie nodded. 'I'll take the lorry back then I'll see yer up there.'

Len Taylor sat beside Dot Adams on the long polished wooden bench at Tower Bridge Magistrates' Court and tried to console her. 'Look, luv, it's gonna be all right. That solicitor seems a sensible sort o' bloke. 'E knows what 'e's talkin' about. It'll be all right, I tell yer.'

'Why didn't Ada Brennen come ter see us this mornin? She promised,' Dot sobbed.

'I dunno, luv. We'll find out when we get back 'ome,' Len replied.

'Did you see Danny's face? 'E looked like 'e didn't know what was goin' on,' Dot fretted, her voice wavering. 'I wanted 'im ter look at me but 'e just stared in front of 'im. 'E's ill, Len. What's 'appenin? When can I see 'im?'

'Look, the solicitor's comin' ter talk to us in a minute, as soon as 'e sorts it out in there,' Len told her.

''E's gonna be tried at the Central Criminal Court, the magistrate said. That's the Ole Bailey,' she murmured, dabbing at her eyes. 'I jus' can't believe this is all 'appenin'. It's like a nightmare an' I'm waitin' ter wake up.'

A side door opened and a tall thin individual came towards them carrying a briefcase, his footsteps echoing on the tiled floor. The man wore thick-rimmed spectacles and his carroty red hair stood up on top of his head like a wire brush.

'I'm sorry for the delay, Mrs Adams. I've been making representations about your visiting rights,' he said in a reedy voice. 'There's often some confusion in these cases, but don't you worry. This is just a committal hearing. Your son's being sent on remand to Brixton prison while the date of the trial is set.'

'When can I see 'im?' Dot asked tearfully.

'I'm going to fix that now, if you'll bear with me for a little longer,' the solicitor said quietly.

'What about Danny's medical condition? Yer said yer was gonna see into it,' Len reminded him.

'I'm applying for your son's medical file from his panel doctor and I'm getting on to the War Office for their medical file too,' he replied, looking at Dot over his glasses. 'Mrs Adams, you may rest assured that everything possible will be done to help your son.'

Joe Brennen climbed down from the tender and pulled his silver watch from his waistcoat pocket to check the time while he waited for Tom Kelly.

'It'll be an hour at least before those food waggons are loaded,' the shunter told him as he came up.

The two old friends walked across the tracks to the railway canteen and got their mugs of tea from a large urn.

'What was Errol Baines on about this mornin'?' Tom asked as they sat down at a vacant table.

'It's that Carney business,' Joe replied with a grin. 'The silly git gave Errol a letter ter pass on ter Charlie Catchpole an' Errol told 'im ter do it 'imself.'

'I wondered what the ruck was about.'

'The trouble is, Carney's already tried ter give it ter Charlie an' 'e told 'im ter go frew 'is foreman,' Joe explained. 'Yer know what Charlie's like.'

'This bloody episode's got out of 'and,' Tom remarked as he slurped his tea.

'Episode?' Joe snorted. 'It's more like a saga. 'Ow long's it bin goin' on?'

'We'll be expected ter respond now, though,' Tom replied. 'What we gonna do about it? We can't accept 'im. It was agreed right from the start that we're a closed shop.'

'The way I see it we've got two choices,' Joe told him. 'Eivver we turn 'im down flat, or we make 'im some sort of honorary member. Poor ole Jim's gonna be upset if we give 'im the elbow ter say the least, 'specially after the trouble 'e's gone frew ter get those references.'

'It's all down ter Errol Baines. 'E started geein' Carney up,' Tom growled.

'Anyway, we've got a meetin' next week. It's up ter the full committee ter make a decision,' Joe replied.

Charlie Catchpole came into the canteen and, spotting Joe, he hurried over. 'I guessed I'd catch yer 'ere, Joe,' he said breathlessly. 'Yer gotta go over ter the office straight away. There's a message for yer.'

Joe got up quickly, a worried frown appearing on his weather-beaten face. 'I wonder what that's all about?' he said anxiously.

Ada and Kay sat beside a bed in the surgical ward and stared down at the still figure of Elsie Gates. The young woman lay on her back with her eyes closed and her face was almost the colour of the crisp white pillowcase. Her lower arm was encased in plaster and stretched out at her side, the purple bruising on her knuckles showing up against the whiteness.

'She's beginnin' ter come round,' Kay said in a whisper.

'I don't like the look o' that bruise on the side of 'er face,' Ada remarked. 'It looks like it's got bigger since we've bin 'ere.'

'She'll be all right, won't she, Mum?' Kay asked, her voice choking with emotion.

Ada gulped hard and gripped her daughter's hand. 'Course she will,' she said in a quiet voice. 'Elsie's a tough 'un.'

The ward sister came into the room. 'Doctor Ramsey's coming up now, if you'd like to follow me,' she said softly.

The two women followed the sister into her office and she invited them to sit down. The doctor came in almost immediately and smiled at them.

'I'm Mrs Brennen, Elsie's muvver, an' this is my ovver daughter, Kay,' Ada said. ''Ow is she, Doctor?'

The doctor sat down and crossed his legs, then he cleared his throat. 'Well, apart from the broken wrist, your daughter's concussed and there's extensive bruising,' he replied. 'I've given her something for the pain and it'll make her very drowsy for a time. It's important that she gets plenty of rest, so I would have to ask you not to stay too long. She should be more awake when you visit this evening.'

'Fanks fer yer time, Doctor,' Ada said, forcing a faint smile as he got up to leave.

'Would you both like some tea?' the sister asked.

Ada nodded and then suddenly she let go of her feelings and bowed her head, sobbing quietly. Kay too shed a few silent tears, reaching her hand out to her mother.

'Don't cry, Mum. Dad'll be 'ere soon,' she said softly.

'I'm worried about yer farvver meetin' up wiv Ernie. I can see there'll be fireworks,' Ada said fearfully.

The sister came back into the office with two teas on a tray. 'Your daughter's husband's arrived. He's just gone in,' she told Ada.

Mother and daughter exchanged worried glances. 'We'd better drink this tea an' see if we can catch Joe before 'e goes in ter see Elsie,' Ada said quickly. 'I don't want 'im an' Ernie gettin' at it.'

They walked out on to the landing and stood looking down the wide stone staircase. 'Yer know what yer farvver finks of Ernie,' Ada said nervously. 'It'll only take one word out o' place an' 'e'll plant 'im one.'

'Not in an 'ospital, surely?' Kay replied.

'Nah, but 'e'd ask 'im outside. I know yer dad,' Ada told her.

'There 'e is now,' Kay said quickly. 'I'd better warn Ernie.'

Joe came hurrying up the stairs and when he reached the landing he looked anxiously at Ada. ''Ow is she?' he asked breathlessly.

'She's got a broken wrist an' concussion,' Ada told him. 'She's just comin' out o' the anaesthetic. We've just bin talkin' ter the doctor.'

'What'd 'e say?' Joe asked quickly.

Kay walked along the ward and saw Ernie Gates sitting slumped in a chair beside the bed. 'Me dad's just arrived,' she said softly.

He nodded and stood up. 'I s'pose it'll be better if I make meself scarce fer a while,' he replied.

He walked the length of the main ward to the far exit door, and Kay breathed a sigh of relief. It was terrible the way things were between him and her father, she thought, but Ernie was to blame.

370

He had made himself unpopular right from the start and things had got steadily worse.

Joe came into the ward and bent over the bed, kissing Elsie on the forehead, then he sat down and took her hand, stroking it gently. She opened her eyes and mumbled something unintelligible, and Kay could see her father's eyes filling with tears. Ada came back to the bedside and stood next to Joe, her arm going around his shoulders.

Kay walked out on to the landing feeling sick with shock, and she wished Pat was there with her at that moment just to hold her in his arms and comfort her.

Mick Mollison worked as a casual docker, which meant that he did not have a regular gang. He preferred it that way. He took his chance every morning at the call-on, and being a popular character who was not afraid of hard work he usually got picked to make up a casual gang. The casuals went wherever extra men were wanted, and on that particular Tuesday morning, Mick found himself working on the quayside at Wilson's Wharf, just a few berths away from Mark Brown's Wharf, where the Polish ship normally docked.

The docker and the rest of his gang were busy rolling casks of Madeira wine up on to electric trucks for transportation to the bonded warehouse when the ganger called a halt. 'We're gonna make ourselves scarce fer a while,' he told them. 'The bowler-'at mob are on the way down.'

'What's that in aid of?' one of the men asked.

'They're security geezers an' there's a couple of insurance people wiv 'em, so I've bin told,' the ganger replied.

'They're worried about the booze, I should fink,' the docker remarked. 'There's a poxy fortune bein' stored in that ware'ouse.'

The ganger nodded. 'I 'eard they're gonna double up on the night patrols. It's the insurance people who's insistin' on it,' he said, waving his gang to follow him.

'Yer can't blame 'em,' the docker went on. 'I could pick that gate lock meself an' drive a lorry up on the quay wiv no trouble. It only wants a couple o' blokes ter roll the casks on the lorry.'

'An' 'ow would yer get in the ware'ouse?' the ganger said, smiling.

'Easy. I'd back the lorry inter the door.'

'They're steel-plate doors, yer silly git.'

371

'I know that,' the docker said contemptuously, 'but the frames are bolted inter the brickwork an' it's all crumbly. You take a look at it next time yer go in there.'

Mick tried to look nonchalant as he listened to the conversation. With the raid due to take place tomorrow night, it was bad news that the patrols were being doubled up.

The gang sat down on some empty casks near the front gate and the ganger took out his tobacco pouch. 'Those dock coppers 'ave got their 'ands full if you ask me,' he remarked as he began to roll a cigarette. 'I 'eard they've got a rocket up their arse over that turn-out a couple o' weeks ago at Mark Brown's.'

'Yeah, I should fink so,' the talkative docker agreed. 'The crane driver landed two stowaways on the quay an' they only caught one. The ovver bleeder scarpered. 'E could 'ave bin a Russian spy fer all we know. That's 'ow 'alf of 'em get in the country, off them commie ships.'

'Well, they'll find it 'ard from now on, even if they wait till it's dark, what wiv the added security,' the ganger told him.

'I don't fink them blokes are from the insurance at all,' another docker remarked.

'No?'

'Nah. They're from the Government. What they call 'em?'

'MI5.'

'Yeah, that's right.'

'Yer could well be right, Lofty,' the ganger said grinning. 'So yer better be careful what yer say. If they 'ear you talkin' about strikes an' stoppages they'll fink you're a Commie agitator.'

Mick joined in the laughter, but inside he was feeling anxious. Nick Zanti and his men would be walking into a lot of trouble, and it looked very unlikely now that they would even be able to reach the Polish freighter, let alone board her.

Chapter Forty-nine

When Joe Brennen arrived back at work later that morning, he was called into the depot manager's office. 'It must have come as a shock,' Gerry Preston said sympathetically after Joe had finished explaining what had happened. 'Are you going to let your boy know?'

'I'll 'ave to,' the railwayman replied. 'Wiv my lot, if one gets cut they all bleed. If I don't let Colin know, 'e'll go off alarmin' when 'e does find out.'

'What'll you do, phone the camp?' Preston asked.

'Yeah, but I'll 'ave ter find out the phone number first though,' Joe told him. 'I popped indoors an' picked up Colin's latest letter on me way back from the 'ospital. 'E's just bin moved to a new camp. I was gonna ask if I could slip out an' make the call.'

'No need. Do it from here,' the manager said.

'Yeah, all right,' Joe replied, 'as long as yer don't mind?'

Gerry Preston got up from his desk. 'Come on, I'll get my secretary to connect you.'

Five minutes later, Joe looked into the office. 'I've just spoken ter the adjutant at Colin's camp in Durham, Gerry,' he told him. ''E seemed a nice bloke. They're arrangin' fer 'im ter get a forty-eight-hour pass on compassionate grounds. 'E'll be leavin' the camp this evenin' an' 'e's ter report back by first parade on Friday.'

On Tuesday evening the Maltese fraternity met at the Falcon, a small pub off the Old Kent Road. The pub was never very busy, and on this particular evening the group were able to find a quiet corner out of earshot.

'I've asked yer all ter meet me 'ere ternight 'cos there's bin some developments an' it don't look good, gentlemen,' Joe Mezzo began.

'Our contact came ter see me this mornin' an' 'e wasn't very optimistic about our chances. The *Jaroslav* left Gdańsk on time wiv the paintin's on board, an' it's due in termorrer mornin' as scheduled, but the courier's bin changed. They may 'ave sussed that 'e intended jumpin' ship an' they're takin' no chances. I 'ave ter tell yer that the items are now in the care of a Communist Party official.'

'That's bad news,' Mick the Hammer growled.

Joe sipped his whisky then he took out a dog-eared photograph from his coat pocket. 'This is Boris Mikloski, the party official,' he said, placing the snap in the centre of the table. ''E's a Pole an' 'e's got a bad reputation amongst 'is own countrymen. The man's ruthless an' dedicated ter the party, which makes our job much 'arder. 'E's not gonna pass the items over wivout a struggle, an' we'll 'ave no time ter bandy words wiv 'im.'

'I fink we can persuade 'im ter be a good boy,' Mick said, thumping his clenched fist into the palm of his hand.

Joe Mezzo looked around at each of the men in turn. 'There's somefink else,' he said sternly. 'Mick Mollison rang me this evenin'. They've doubled up the security on all the quays, an' Mark Brown's Wharf is gonna be tighter than a drum when that ship docks. They're worried about the amount o' stowaways who've bin gettin' frew the net.'

'So what 'appens now?' Tony Mancini asked.

Joe leaned forward over the table. 'Let's look at the original plan first,' he went on. 'After we picked up our Polish interpreter we were goin' on ter the quay via the transport yard in Potter's Fields. That's out now. Wiv the added security it'll be too risky. We could get ourselves cornered in that yard. Once aboard ship we planned ter grab the captain, locate the courier who would 'ave bin ready an' waitin' wiv the items, an' then escort 'im off, takin' the captain wiv us as 'ostage ter prevent anyone comin' after us. We would 'ave left the same way as we went in, an' finally dumped the skipper at the gates as we drove off.'

'Have you had time to formulate another plan?' Nick Zanti asked.

Joe took a large gulp from his glass. 'As I see it, the money we'll get fer this caper is very substantial, but it's not the prime consideration 'ere,' he told them. 'Every one of us agreed in the beginnin' that this was somefing special, a conscience fing first an' foremost. So I'm gonna suggest anuvver way forward.'

'We're listening,' Zanti said quietly.

'Right then. We've already scrapped the diversion plan, as yer know, which is just as well. There'll be enough police an' security present as it is, wivout us tippin' 'em off that somefing's goin' on. Now this is the plan. We pick up our Polish friend an' then go in via the front gate. I'll explain 'ow we do that later. We grab the captain as planned, then collar the party official. Once we've got the items we'll lock up the official an' the captain, then we'll go over the side o' the ship an' make our getaway via the river. I've 'ad a word wiv Mick Mollison an' 'e's assured me 'e'll be able ter lay 'is 'ands on a small boat. We go under Tower Bridge an' moor up at Dock'ead. That's where we part company. Mollison'll stow the goods in a safe place local till our man can take delivery; meanwhile we walk away from the area clean. If we do get a pull by the law we're just out fer a night's drinkin'.'

'Why don't we use the van fer the getaway?' Mick asked.

'If Mollison don't show wiv the boat we'll 'ave to, but I don't fink we'll 'ave any worries on that score,' Joe replied. 'If we use the van an' one o' the crew raises the alarm we might get stopped before we get out the gate. It'll be safer by river, apart from the police launch. It's the best bet, as I see it.'

'What about this Mollison geezer? Is 'e reliable?' Tony queried.

'He got us the info on the salmon and he's to be trusted. I'll vouch for him,' Zanti said confidently.

'It sounds good so far, but what about the crew?' Tony asked. 'Will they be likely ter give us trouble?'

'That's where our Polish friend comes in,' Joe replied. ''E'll be talkin' to 'em. Everyone on board knows who the party man is. They make it their business to. Yer gotta remember that party officials are the same as secret police. They report any anti-government talk an' unrest amongst the crew an' the poor bastards concerned get sorted out when the ship gets back ter Poland. They're not gonna risk their necks 'elpin' 'im. As fer makin' Comrade Boris tell us where the goods are stored, I 'ave no doubt 'e can be persuaded.'

'It's a pity we don't know exactly what time Thursday the 'and-over's gonna take place,' Mick remarked. 'We could've waited till the goods are off the ship an' out o' the wharf an' then pounced.'

'We couldn't do it that way, it's out o' the question,' Joe told him. 'The Russian embassy are sendin' an official car ter the ship. The

375

party official is gonna be a guest at some sort o' diplomatic banquet. 'E's supposed ter be deliverin' the paintin's ter the embassy in person so the buyer can collect 'em there. Our contact seems ter fink it's one o' the Western ambassadors. Anyway, the Russian car'll be well shepherded by the police an' we wouldn't get near it.'

'You were saying we'll go in via the front gate, Joe. How do you propose we manage it?' Nick Zanti inquired.

'First I'm gonna get us all a drink, then I'll tell yer,' Joe replied with a sly smile.

The few old men sitting around the bar sipped their drinks and dreamed of yesteryear, blithely unaware of the drama unfolding at the far table.

Joe explained the rest of the plan, then he took out a piece of paper and a pencil stub from his coat pocket. 'I'd like us ter take a vote on whevver we go or not,' he said quietly. 'It's gotta be unanimous or we scrub it. We'll each put eivver a tick or a cross on the paper an' if there's one cross then we forget it.'

The men watched while Joe tore the paper up into five pieces and passed them out. He put his mark first, then folded his slip into four and dropped it into an empty whisky glass. The rest followed suit and then Joe picked up the glass and turned it over on his palm, shaking it before releasing the folded slips. The men all watched intently as their leader unfolded each slip and laid it out in the centre of the table. As the last mark on the last of the slips was revealed, Joe slapped the table with his open hand. 'We go, lads,' he said, grinning.

Joe and Ada Brennen walked anxiously into the ward that evening and saw that Elsie was propped up in bed. She gave them a strange smile as they leaned over to kiss her on the cheek.

''Ow yer feelin', luv?' Ada asked her softly.

Elsie nodded slowly as she looked from one to the other.

''Ow did yer manage that?' Joe asked, nodding to her plastered arm.

'I don't know. I can't remember,' she said in a hollow voice.

'Billy's fine. We've got 'im wiv us,' Ada told her.

The young woman turned to her with a frown. 'Billy?' she muttered.

Joe gripped his wife's hand tightly as the realisation dawned on him. 'Elsie, yer know who we are, don't yer?' he said gently.

'Everyfing's blank. I've bin tryin' ter fink, but I can't concentrate,' she replied languidly. 'I just can't . . .'

Ada brought her hand up to her mouth in horror as her daughter closed her eyes. 'She's lost 'er memory, Joe!' she whispered.

'It's the drugs. She's dropped off ter sleep,' Joe said comfortingly. 'She'll be all right termorrer. Maybe we'd better go an' let 'er get some rest.'

Ada shook her head. 'No, I wanna stay,' she told him.

They sat beside the sleeping figure, occasionally glancing along the ward at the other patients and their visitors.

'I'll try an' see the doctor before we leave,' Joe said.

Ada nodded. 'I've 'eard lots o' people get amnesia after concussion,' she remarked.

'They do get their memory back, don't they?' Joe asked her quickly.

'Course they do,' she told him. 'Like yer say, it's the drugs. Elsie's not 'erself yet.'

Joe patted her hand. 'Colin'll be 'ome termorrer. It'll buck 'er up when 'e walks in,' he said.

Ada smiled briefly and stared at Elsie for a while. 'It's strange 'ow fings work out,' she said finally. 'I dread 'avin' ter tell Dot Adams the news. I'm sure she'll fink we're lyin' to 'er. She was really upset when I went over this mornin' ter see 'er.'

'I know we've got ter find out the trufe fer Danny's sake, but we can't go quizzin' the gel as soon as she does come round,' Joe told her.

Ada nodded. 'Yeah, yer right, Joe. I just feel so 'elpless sittin' 'ere like this,' she sighed.

'I don't s'pose she knows about Danny anyway, unless someone knocked an' told 'er,' Joe said.

'I doubt it,' Ada replied. 'We only found out last night an' the gel was in 'ere first fing this mornin'. She 'adn't bin out the 'ouse, 'ad she?'

'It'll be a shock when she does find out. We'll 'ave ter break it to 'er gently. She's really fond o' that boy.'

Elsie was still sleeping, unaware of the anxious discussion going on at her bedside, and when she moved slightly and groaned, Ada reached out and stroked her forehead. 'There, there,' she whispered.

Joe looked at his wife with fondness. It was almost as if the years had fallen away and she was tending their baby once more.

The ward sister rang the bell and the visitors started to leave. Ada caught the sister's eye and the imperious-looking figure strode up to the bed.

'She's bin sleepin' all the time, Sister, an' she doesn't know us,' Ada told her.

The sister's stern face relaxed as she bent over the bed and lifted Elsie's eyelids. 'She's getting the rest she needs. It's very common for concussion cases to suffer a brief loss of memory,' she explained calmly. 'I'm sure she'll remember everything within a few days. I know it's difficult but you must be patient. Don't try to prompt her, it could make matters worse. Just let her come round in her own time. At the moment she's feeling the effects of the pain-killers the doctor prescribed. They're morphine-based, you see. They act like a tranquilliser, though tranquillisers themselves are not normally prescribed to patients with head injuries.'

''As she bin in a lot o' pain?' Ada asked.

'Your daughter was uncomfortable this afternoon when the doctor saw her,' the sister replied. 'She got slightly agitated too. I think that could have been a sudden recollection of what happened to her, which is a good sign in itself, you understand.'

Ada buttoned up her coat and took Joe's arm as they bade the sister goodnight.

'C'mon, I'm takin' you fer a quiet drink,' Joe told her.

'We'd better get back 'ome, Joe,' she replied. 'The gels are gonna be worried an' we gotta fink o' young Billy too.'

'We'll only be a few minutes longer,' he insisted. 'A stiff drink'll do yer good after the shock yer've 'ad.'

They turned the corner and walked into a small pub, where Joe found them a seat near the fire.

'I'm really disgusted wiv Ernie,' Ada said as they sipped their drinks.

Joe nodded. 'I expect 'e's gone on that two-day journey, after all.'

''E told me an' Kay 'e was gonna take the lorry back this mornin',' Ada went on. 'I'm sure 'is firm would 'ave put somebody else on the run if 'e'd asked 'em.'

'I dunno,' Joe replied. 'Elsie was tellin' me they've bin puttin' on 'im ever since 'e 'ad that lorry stolen.'

'That's as it may be, but any man wiv feelin' would 'ave told 'em

378

where ter stick their job if they refused 'im time off ter see 'is wife,' Ada said with passion.

They finished their drinks and Ada held on to her husband's arm as they stepped out into the cold March winds. 'Please God we'll see a difference in Elsie termorrer night,' she said, sighing anxiously.

Pat Kelly sat at the table in the Brennens' parlour, cutting pieces of folded coloured paper for Billy. The young lad's eyes sparkled as he watched the sheet open to reveal a pattern of small holes.

'There we are, Billy boy. Now see if you can make me one,' Pat told him.

Kay sat with her sisters, occasionally sneaking a glance over at Pat and exchanging secret smiles.

'They should be 'ome by now,' Barbara remarked.

'I 'ope nuffink's wrong,' Dawn said anxiously.

'I bet Dad's took Mum fer a drink,' Kay told them.

Pat leaned back in his chair. 'If Elsie's feelin' better termorrer, p'raps we could go in an' see 'er, an' then go down Chippy's fer a farewell drink wiv Margie afterwards,' he suggested.

'Yeah, we said we was gonna 'ave a drink wiv 'er, didn't we,' Kay replied.

The key turned in the front door and Joe and Ada walked in. 'Sorry we're late. Dad took me fer a drink an' then we popped over ter see Dot Adams,' Ada explained.

''Ow's Elsie?' they all said at once.

'She's sleepin'. They've given 'er some strong pain-killers,' she told them. 'She'll be all right, please Gawd.'

Joe was glad that Ada had not mentioned Elsie's amnesia. There was no sense in adding to their worries for the time being.

Ada picked Billy up and gave him a big hug. 'An' 'ow's my little soldier?' she asked.

Billy grinned and grabbed up the coloured paper. 'Look what Pat done fer me, Gran'ma.'

''Ow's Dot Adams copin'?' Barbara asked.

'She's in a terrible state,' Ada replied. ''Er feller was there wiv 'er. 'E seems a nice chap.'

'Did Ernie go in the 'ospital ternight?' Kay asked them.

Joe shook his head. ''E's prob'ly gone on a run, the no-good git,' he growled.

Pat's face set hard as he heard Ernie's name mentioned, and it did

379

not go unnoticed by Kay. She felt sure that before very long the two men would come together to settle their differences. It would be in a bloody battle, and she felt suddenly cold.

Chapter Fifty

Colin looked pale and drawn as he hurried into Guy's Hospital on Wednesday morning. He had arrived home in time to catch his father before he left for work and had been brought up to date with all that had happened. He had managed to snatch a couple of hours in the armchair, but he was still feeling the effects of the long journey home from Durham. His uniform was creased from the travelling and he was conscious of the dark shadow round his chin as he looked into the ward office. 'I'm Elsie Gates's bruvver an' I've jus' got 'ome. Can I see 'er please?' he asked.

The sister gave him a smile and nodded. 'It's outside visiting hours, but it'll be all right, as long as you don't stop too long,' she told him. 'The doctor will be doing his rounds soon, and he'll be wanting to take a look at your sister. You'll find her in the third bed on the right as you go in.'

Colin walked into the ward trying not to make too much noise, but his Army boots sounded loudly on the tiled floor. Elsie was propped up with pillows and she looked at him blankly as he came up to her bed. The young man's heart sank. She did not recognise him.

''Ello, sis. What you bin doin' ter yerself then?' he asked, giving her a kiss on her cheek.

'I'm sorry I . . .' she faltered.

'It's OK. I'm Colin, yer bruvver. Your only bruv,' he said, trying to make her feel at ease. 'Are yer feelin' better?'

She nodded, her eyes searching his face for some clue to help her remember him. 'I'm feelin' stiff an' achy, but me 'eadache's gone,' she replied.

Colin reached out and gently touched the swollen fingers of her damaged arm. 'It'll all come back ter yer very soon,

381

so don't worry,' he said reassuringly. 'Dad an' Mum said yer doin' fine.'

Elsie shook her head slowly. 'I've bin lyin' 'ere tryin' ter remember who I am an' what I'm doin' 'ere, an' every so often I get little flashes in me mind,' she told him.

'I can tell yer who you are an' what yer doin' 'ere,' Colin volunteered with a broad grin.

'Yeah, but it doesn't mean anyfing,' she said with a deep sigh. 'I know I was found at the foot of some stairs, but 'ow did I get there? What 'appened?'

'I can make a guess 'ow yer got there,' Colin replied. 'It was early mornin' when it 'appened. You were prob'ly still 'alf asleep an' yer tripped. Yer could 'ave overslept an' bin rushin' about.'

'I s'pose so,' she said flatly.

'I was gonna bring yer in some flowers, but I thought yer might like these instead,' he told her, taking a small box of chocolates out from inside his battledress blouse.

'That was nice of yer,' she replied, giving him a brief smile. 'Are you on leave or did yer get time off ter come an' see me?'

'I got forty-eight-hours' compassionate leave,' he said. 'I'm stationed in Durham. I'm doin' a drivin' course.'

Elsie made to say something but drew back, and she closed her eyes for a few moments. Colin looked at her closely and noticed how pale she was. He could see the pulse beating in her neck and the purple patch of bruising on her temple.

She opened her eyes and saw him studying her. 'I just got anuvver flash,' she said, her eyes going up to the ceiling as she concentrated. 'I was standin' somewhere. I was wrappin' somefing up, an' then it went. It's frightenin' ter fink I might never remember the rest of it.'

'Course yer will,' Colin told her firmly. 'Don't push it. It'll 'appen soon. I bet yer'll wake up after a nap an' it'll all be back.'

Tears filled the young woman's eyes and she looked away with embarrassment. 'I'm sorry,' she said, swallowing hard in an effort to control herself.

Colin leaned forward over the bed. 'I'd better not stay too long, the sister keeps lookin' at me,' he told her. 'She said the doctor's comin' round soon. I'll pop in ternight, all right?'

Elsie nodded and gave him a wan smile. 'Fanks fer comin' in,' she replied.

Colin stood up and straightened his jacket before leaning over and planting a soft kiss on her forehead. 'Bye, Elsie,' he said. 'See yer ternight.'

Charlie Catchpole sat with Joe and Tom in the railway canteen, his thin, lined face creased with a grin as he waited for a response.

'I dunno,' Joe said, shaking his head slowly as he threw the letter down on to the table. 'It's a bleedin' potted life 'istory.'

Tom Kelly had already read the letter and he nodded. 'I bet Sara Brady told 'im what ter put,' he replied. 'I can't imagine Jim Carney writin' that off 'is own bat.'

'What we gonna do, that's what I wanna know?' Charlie said quickly. 'Accordin' ter that, 'e's bin to everyone except the Pope fer a reference. 'E's gonna be really upset if we say no.'

'Yeah, especially after 'im gettin' that reference from the railway chairman,' Joe growled. 'I reckon 'e'd be bold enough ter complain to 'im if we black-balled 'im.'

'Errol Baines didn't know what 'e was doin' when 'e primed Jim Carney up, that's fer sure,' Charlie muttered. 'I told 'im so too, bloody idiot.'

'The only way I see it is ter make 'im an honorary member,' Joe suggested.

'Yeah, that's an idea,' Charlie replied, grinning. 'We could give 'im some sort o' cardboard badge. Jack Springer could make one up, 'e's a bit artistic.'

Charlie took out his tobacco pouch and proceeded to roll a cigarette. 'I wonder 'ow that poor bleeder Danny feels right now,' he remarked almost to himself.

'I still can't believe a lad like Danny Adams could 'ave killed that ole lady,' Tom replied. 'All right, I know 'e gets dizzy spells an' loses 'is memory at times, but 'e ain't mad, an' 'e ain't a violent boy. It's just not in 'im to 'urt anyone.'

Joe was silent, his mind dwelling on his eldest daughter and what she would say when she regained her memory. Would she be able to help the lad clear his name? Supposing she never fully recovered until after the trial: Danny could well be sentenced to death, unless the defence made a good case for him. At the best they could only ask for the charge to be changed to manslaughter, or plead temporary insanity.

'Gawd knows what poor ole Dot Adams must be goin' frew,' Charlie remarked.

Joe remembered the look on Dot's face when he and Ada called in after their visit to the hospital. She had been hollow-eyed and haggard and she had collapsed into her chair when Ada told her about Elsie. The poor woman was beside herself with grief and convinced that Danny would hang. It seemed as though she had decided that nothing could save him from the rope. Did she know something that no one else did?

The Grace Dines murder was on everyone's lips that Wednesday. Bet Greenedge and Annie Thomas discussed it at Joe Mezzo's shop and Maria sighed in resignation as Emily Toogood walked in ready to add her thoughts. It was bad enough her having to cope on her own this afternoon, she thought, without being dragged into a major conference.

'Where's Joe?' Emily asked as she fished into her purse for her soap coupons.

''E's 'ad ter go out on business,' Maria told her.

'Nice fer some,' Emily replied, looking at her friends.

'We was just talkin' about poor Danny,' Bet said to her.

'I just bin chattin' to Ivy Catchpole about it,' Emily told her. 'She was sayin' it's the second time someone's bin done fer murder in the street. It was Charlie's muvver who told 'er about it.'

'Is that a fact?' Annie butted in.

'Yeah, it was way back in ninety-seven or ninety-eight, accordin' to Ivy,' Emily went on. 'The family lived at number Fourteen. Appleby, their name was. Mae an' Jim Appleby. Apparently Jim come 'ome from night shift at the railway yard an' caught Mae in bed wiv anuvver feller. 'E took 'er up a cup o' tea an' found 'im there.'

'Dear o' Lor',' Annie said.

'Anyway, Jim put the cup o' tea down beside the bed wivout a word then went downstairs an' sat in the armchair. A few minutes later 'is wife came down bold as brass an' asked 'im point-blank what 'e was gonna do about the ovver man.

''E just looked at 'er an' said, "Sod 'im, let the lazy bleeder get 'is own tea."'

Bet, Annie and Maria looked at Emily in astonishment. 'You're 'avin' us on,' Bet said.

'It's the trufe, as sure as I'm standin' 'ere,' Emily assured her. 'Anyway, a few minutes later the bloke comes down the stairs an'

384

Mae Appleby tells 'im ter pour 'imself out a cuppa. 'E goes ter the scullery an' Mae follers 'im out. A few seconds later Jim Appleby walks up be'ind 'im an' clouts 'im on the back o' the 'ead wiv a chopper. Terrible turn-out it was. Blood everywhere. As a matter o' fact, they carted the dead bloke off wiv the chopper still stickin' out of 'is 'ead.'

'Good Gawd!' Annie gasped.

'Jim Appleby swung fer it,' Emily told them. 'Accordin' ter Charlie Catchpole's muvver, all the neighbours got up a petition ter save the poor bleeder, but it came ter nuffink.'

'What must Dot Adams be goin' frew right now?' Bet said, shaking her head slowly. 'The lad comes 'ome from the war an' then ends up bein' 'ung fer murder. Gawd Almighty, she must be goin' out of 'er mind.'

'We'll 'ave ter get a petition up if they do say 'e's gotta swing,' Emily said forcefully.

'The barrister might plead insanity,' Maria cut in. 'After all, Danny does 'ave those funny turns at times.'

'They'll lock 'im away fer life anyway,' Bet replied. 'Fancy 'avin' ter spend the rest o' yer life locked up in Colney 'Atch or Broadmoor.'

'Terrible. Bloody terrible,' Emily said with a shudder. 'I fink I'd sooner swing than end up in a place like that.'

The women finally left the grocery shop and immediately bumped into Sara Brady. The discussion went on out in the street beneath the dull March sky, while along the small turning, other women stood talking together on doorsteps. One front door remained closed, however, and the curtains were drawn tight.

In a run-down factory in Wapping, the last-minute preparations were taking place.

'I've stuck that ovver number-plate on the van,' Mick the Hammer told Nick Zanti.

'Right, now let's get the sign pasted on the side,' Nick told him.

Tony Mancini came in the yard carrying a large bundle. 'It's all 'ere,' he said triumphantly.

Joe Mezzo stroked his chin thoughtfully. 'We must sort out a long rope,' he reminded them. 'A lorry rope'll be ideal.'

'What's the name o' this Polish geezer we're takin' wiv us?' Tony asked.

'Jan Krazinski,' Joe replied. ''E was in the Polish army durin' the war an' 'e's inclined ter be a bit crazy at times, but 'e's a man ter be trusted, an' 'e speaks good English too, accordin' to our contact.'

Tony Mancini had unwrapped the bundle and was sorting out the overalls. 'We're gonna look the part in this get-up,' he grinned.

'We'd better,' Joe told him. 'It's the only way we can get on that quay.'

Nick Zanti called Joe to one side. 'I've just checked the hardware,' he said matter-of-factly.

Joe walked into the littered office with him and closed the door. 'I'll take the shotgun an' you can 'ave the revolver. OK?'

Nick nodded. 'What about the others?' he queried.

Joe shook his head. 'I don't want Tony an' Mick tooled-up, nor that crazy Pole,' he replied. 'They might get carried away. We don't want any shots fired if we can avoid it. Apart from someone gettin' 'urt, the noise'll bring the law runnin'. Let's just 'ope the mere sight of a shotgun'll do the job.'

Nick smiled. 'Yeah, let's hope. Our sponsors are not going to be very pleased if it turns into a shooting-match.'

Joe slipped his arm round Zanti's shoulders. 'Are yer sure yer wanna be up the sharp end on this one, Nick?' he asked quietly.

'Positive. I feel the way you do about this job,' he replied. 'Anyway, I feel I'm getting desk-bound.'

Joe nodded acquiescently. 'This one could get a bit rough, an' I'd sooner yer didn't get involved, you bein' family, but I understand yer feelin's,' he told him.

Nick gathered up the firearms and slipped them into a cupboard. 'Shall I call them in now?' he asked.

Joe nodded. 'We'll go over it from start ter finish, then we'll get a few hours' rest. I fink we're gonna need it.'

PC Fuller strolled along Waggoner's Way and entered the grocery shop. 'Joe not in?' he queried.

''E's bin called away on family business,' Maria told him.

The policeman took off his helmet and scratched his head. 'I was 'opin' to 'ave a chat wiv 'im,' he said.

Maria did not know exactly what was planned for this evening, but from all the activity recently she guessed it was something big. 'Is it anyfing important?' she probed.

'Nah, it'll keep,' he said, smiling.

'Joe did say there was a parcel 'ere for yer,' Maria told him.

PC Fuller was about to reply when Sara Brady walked into the shop. 'There's no rush. I'll slip in an' see Joe termorrer,' he said, putting on his helmet and adjusting the chinstrap.

The beat bobby walked slowly along the street, thinking about the bit of news he had intended telling Joe about. The Russians were coming. They were sending a car from their embassy that evening to pick up someone of importance from the Polish ship which had docked at Mark Brown's Wharf on the early tide. The visit had been planned for Thursday originally, but it had been put forward a day, and along with some of his colleagues, PC Fuller had been recruited to patrol the Tooley Street area as part of a big security operation. As the chief superintendent had stressed, there was a cold war going on, and it could prove catastrophic if some lunatic decided to mess with the Russians.

Chapter Fifty-one

Night had settled over the Bermondsey dockland and the rising moon was obscured behind heavy cloud as the 'Industrial Fumigation and Pest Control Services' van drew up outside the public convenience in Tooley Street. A heavily built man climbed into the back. The van drove off and then turned right into Potters Fields. The pick-up was wearing a black reefer jacket and a woollen hat pulled down over his thick dark hair. His eyes were deep-set in a broad, flat face, and he looked impassive as he crouched on the metal floor.

'Now remember what I said,' Joe told Mick the Hammer as he pulled the van up at the wharf gates. 'Just look pissed-off. Fumigation vans go in these wharves all the time ter fumigate the ships, an' it's always after workin' hours. They're not likely ter suspect anyfing, but don't stand there arguin'. If they say yer can't go in, just walk away, got it?'

Mick nodded as he got out of the van. He walked casually up to the gate and rang the bell.

A uniformed man from the dock police came out of an office and walked over to the gate. 'Yeah? What can I do fer yer?' he asked.

'We gotta fumigate the *Jaroslav*,' Mick said, yawning.

'Did they get yer out o' bed?' the policeman joked as he slipped the gate bolt.

Mick smiled and walked back to the parked van.

'Stop just inside the gate,' Joe reminded him.

Mick did as he was told and waited while the gate policeman jotted down the van registration number. Joe leaned out of the passenger seat. 'They normally give us a bit more warnin' fer these sort o' jobs,' he told the policeman. 'The geezer who phoned us said their embassy people were comin' termorrer.'

The dock policeman tucked his clipboard under his arm. 'There's bin a change o' plan. The embassy car's comin' ternight now,' he said.

Joe hid his anxiety with a smile. 'What time's it due?' he asked.

'About eight o'clock,' the policeman replied.

'It's quarter-past seven now, so we'd better get started,' Joe told him.

Mick drove the van along the cobbled path between the high wharf buildings and out on to the illuminated quay. The SS *Jaroslav Dabrowski* loomed up in front of them, and Joe saw that a few of the ship's crew were already looking over the side.

'Take it easy, don't rush,' he said quietly as the men began to unload the equipment. 'Jan, you go on in front o' me.'

The Pole climbed the gangway to the deck, followed by Joe, who carried a roll of flexible piping, and behind him Nick Zanti, who held a large canister in his arms. They were followed by Mick and then Tony, who was holding a large bottle containing a green liquid. As Jan reached the deck he was stopped by a crewman who seemed rather excited. Words were exchanged, and then the man hurried off. Jan turned to Joe. 'He said he don't know anything about fumigation.'

The crewman came walking back along the deck accompanied by a short, thick-set man with closely cropped hair. He was wearing a light brown suit and he had on a pair of metal-rimmed glasses. Jan turned to one of the curious deck-hands who were standing nearby and mumbled something. The sailor looked serious as he muttered a reply.

'This is the party official,' Jan whispered to Joe.

'Yeah, I recognise 'im from the photo,' Joe growled under his breath.

The official stopped in front of them and addressed Joe in perfect English. 'We have no need for fumigation. There must have been some mistake,' he said curtly, dismissing the crewman who had summoned him with a wave of his hand.

'I'll need ter get confirmation from the captain. 'E'll 'ave ter sign me works docket in any case,' Joe told him.

'I can sign that,' the official said sharply, reaching for the slip of paper in Joe's hand.

Nick Zanti put down the canister he was carrying and moved in front of the official, one hand inside his overalls. 'Take us ter see the captain or I'll blow your stomach out,' he hissed.

The official's face went suddenly white. 'The captain's not on board,' he replied in a hoarse voice.

'We'll go ter your cabin then. We need ter talk,' Joe told him firmly.

The official led the way along the slippery iron deck to the cabin area at the stern of the ship. The few crew members who were standing some way back were unaware that anything was happening, and they ambled away as the fumigation team stepped into a companionway behind the blank-faced party man.

'Don't try anyfing stupid or yer won't be goin' ter the banquet ternight,' Joe told him sharply.

They reached a cabin door and Joe turned to Tony Mancini. 'You an' Mick wait outside,' he said quickly. 'Make sure nobody comes in.'

Nick pushed the Pole inside roughly. They were followed by Joe and Jan, who closed the door behind him. The small cabin was on the starboard side of the ship and a porthole looked out on to the illuminated Tower Bridge. There was a tiny table hinged to the superstructure with a seat beside it; to the right was a made-up bunk. Above that there was a shelf containing a variety of books and in the far corner a full-length cupboard.

Joe motioned the official to sit. 'Right, now listen carefully,' he growled, undoing the top buttons of his overalls to expose the muzzle of the sawn-off shotgun. 'We want the paintin's you've got, an' quick.'

'Paintings? I don't know what you are talking about,' the official replied.

'Don't try bluffin' us, an' don't stall fer time,' Joe growled, his face moving closer. 'We know you're s'posed ter be deliverin' 'em ter the Russian Embassy ternight. Now where are they? C'mon, I ain't got time to argue the toss. I wouldn't like ter use this on yer if we can possibly avoid it.'

The man pushed his glasses up on to the bridge of his nose. 'If you kill me, the noise will bring the dock police, and you'll never find what you are looking for,' he said calmly.

'I don't intend ter kill yer,' Joe replied, equally calmly. 'I'll just use the butt on yer face. Now shall we get down ter business? The parcel, please.'

'I don't know what you're talking about,' the official said, his shifty eyes going from one to the other.

Nick Zanti slipped his revolver into his shoulder-holster and suddenly pulled the party man up by his coat lapels. 'Now listen to me,' he hissed. 'One of the men standing outside the door is a disturbed, sadistic bastard. He'd take extreme pleasure in neutering you. Do you understand what I'm saying? Do you understand?'

The official nodded his head as Nick pulled him closer and stared at him.

'You'll save yerself a lot o' pain an' sufferin' if yer tell us where the paintin's are,' Joe warned him.

'The captain has them,' the man replied quickly as Nick threw him back in the chair.

Joe stared at him for a few moments. 'OK. You've 'ad yer chance,' he told him.

At that moment there was a tap on the cabin door. Nick Zanti opened it quickly and saw a crewman dressed in a white tunic standing between Mick and Tony.

'I fink 'e wants ter talk,' Tony said.

Nick pulled the crewman in and closed the door again, and Jan addressed the frightened-looking man in Polish. There was a quick exchange of words, the diminutive newcomer becoming more and more excited, then Jan held up his hand to stop him and turned to Joe. 'This man is the ship's cook and he wants us to help him jump ship,' he explained. 'He wants asylum.'

The official shouted angrily at the cook in his native tongue, but Jan shouted back at him to shut up. The cook stepped in front of him and screamed out a torrent of abuse, and suddenly the official sprang at him, his large hands locked round the man's throat. Joe and Nick finally succeeded in freeing the choking crewman and he fell sideways on to the bunk coughing and spluttering. Nick pushed the official down into the chair and drew his gun from the holster. 'I've a good mind to kill you here and now,' he snarled, forcing the revolver under the official's chin.

'All right, Nick. Take it easy. We need that package, an' quick,' Joe said urgently.

Nick Zanti stepped back a pace, still pointing the revolver. 'Where is it?' he growled.

All eyes were on the party man, and no one was quick enough to stop the irate cook as he climbed from the bunk, grabbed an ashtray

391

from the table and brought it down on the official's head with a resounding crack. The man toppled sideways from his chair and sprawled in a heap on the floor.

'Gawd Almighty!' Joe gasped.

Nick bent over the crumpled figure. 'He's out cold,' he told them.

Joe looked at his wristwatch. 'It's twenty minutes to eight. The embassy car'll be 'ere any time now,' he groaned.

Nick pulled the cupboard open and tossed out the contents. 'It's got to be somewhere,' he growled.

Joe rubbed his hand over his face in frustration. 'We've got no time ter search the 'ole ship,' he puffed.

The cook was sitting quietly on the bunk looking very pleased with himself. Jan spoke to him again and there was another, longer exchange of words, then Jan grinned widely and patted the cook on his back.

'Would yer mind tellin' me what the 'ell's goin' on?' Joe shouted.

'I told him we're looking for a package and he stopped us finding out where it was hidden. He said not to worry. He can take us to it, if we help him jump ship,' Jan told them, still grinning.

'We could 'ardly leave 'im 'ere now,' Joe replied quickly. 'Tell 'im we'll take 'im wiv us, but if 'e tries ter pull a fast one I'll personally blow 'is 'ead off.'

'Who's going to watch him?' Jan said, pointing to the unconscious party man.

Joe opened the cabin door. 'Our friend Boris 'as 'ad a mis'ap, Mick. You wait 'ere an' keep an eye on 'im,' he said, taking the sawn-off shotgun from under his overalls. 'Be careful wiv this. We don't want blood on our 'ands.'

They hurried from the cabin, with the cook leading the way along a companionway to a Jacob's ladder and down into the bowels of the ship. They followed him along another gangway and into the galley. The man smiled and held out his hands as he spoke.

'He said welcome to the galley,' Jan told them.

'Never mind about that. Where's the package?' Joe said impatiently.

There was another exchange and Jan nodded as the cook went over to a box of eggs in one corner. Some of the trays were missing from one side of the box, but the other side was packed full. The

392

cook carefully lifted out the first tray and placed it on the floor, then after removing two more he bent down and gingerly lifted out a parcel wrapped in oilskin and bound with tape. It was ten inches by eight and stood roughly six inches high, an ideal size to fit down into an egg crate. Jan took the package from the cook and put it down carefully on the long wooden table. Everyone gathered round and stared at the bundle and Joe touched it reverently with the tips of his fingers.

The diminutive ship's cook began speaking excitedly to Jan, who nodded frequently.

'It was hidden here away from the customs men when they came aboard,' Jan told them when the cook paused for breath. 'The galley is the only place they never seem to bother with. The party official told the cook that if he mentioned a word to anyone about where the package was hidden, he was going to be put in irons and thrown overboard on the voyage home.'

'It's hard to believe there are four priceless paintings there,' Nick said in a quiet voice.

'C'mon, let's go, we're runnin' out o' time,' Joe told them urgently as he picked up the parcel.

They hurried back up the ladder and along the companionway to the party official's cabin. ''E's still out cold,' Mick said as they all rushed up on to the main deck.

They stepped out into the cold night and suddenly stopped dead in their tracks. A glare of headlights lit up the ship and the throaty roar of motorcycle engines carried up on to the deck as the Russian embassy car drew on to the quay. Mick tore open his overalls and pulled out a coiled length of rope.

'Quick as yer can, an' make sure it's secure,' Joe told him anxiously as they all hurried to the starboard side, out of sight of the police escort. Mick reached the rail first then ducked down quickly. 'River police,' he grated.

The raiders huddled down in the scuppers, and it seemed their luck had finally run out. Police were on the quay in numbers, and a river police launch was patrolling in the Pool. Joe scowled restively. When the party official failed to make an appearance, the messenger and the police would come aboard, he thought. It was either capture, or taking a chance in the Thames. On a dark night in the cold, murky water, with a fast-flowing tide and swirling eddies, it was suicidal.

Boris Mikloski, the party official, opened his eyes and winced as he felt the large bump on the top of his head. That traitorous little rat Ludeck was going to pay for this, he vowed, pulling himself up painfully into the chair. He looked up at the small clock on the shelf and blinked to focus his eyes properly. It was ten minutes to eight. The car would be arriving at any minute, he realised. He had to attract attention in some way, but how? If the gangsters were still on board they would surely shoot him to avoid capture, and they would have left someone on guard outside the door. He stood up and steadied himself against the bulkhead as he glanced out of the porthole at the imposing Tower Bridge. That was it, he told himself, reaching into the table drawer.

PC Holden hunched his shoulders against the rising gusts and paced the centre-span for the umpteenth time that evening. His colleague was beginning his walk back on the other side, and they would meet in the middle and inevitably moan about the cutting wind on that exposed bridge.

PC Bradley cursed the wind as he paced back towards the middle of the bridge, his thoughts centring on a mug of steaming cocoa and then a warm bed. Night duty on the bridge was the most unrewarding duty possible, he moaned to himself. Nothing exciting ever happened at night, not up here, anyway. Even the lost souls who wanted to use the river to end it all tended to do it in the daytime. He glanced over at his chum and past him to the quay cranes and the hull of the Polish freighter moored near the bridge. Suddenly he saw a light flash on and off from a porthole of the ship. It appeared to be signalling, and PC Bradley crossed over to take a closer look.

PC Holden had already spotted it. 'That looks like a signal,' he remarked as his colleague walked up to him.

The two stood watching the light for a few moments, and then Bradley nudged his chum. 'It's Morse. Look, three short, three long, an' three short again. It's an SOS!'

'I'll use the bridge phone an' contact the river police. Flash a reply,' PC Holden shouted above the wind.

Mick Mollison walked down the slippery stone steps at Dockhead and jumped aboard as Tubby Wallis manoeuvred the small boat alongside.

'We'll 'ave ter be careful,' Tubby told him. 'The bloody police boat's bin up an' down this stretch a dozen times. It's like they know somefink's on.'

Mick sat beside Tubby in the forward section, shielded from the weather by a cuddy. Spots of rain and spindrift made it difficult to see, but the lighterman handled the small boat expertly.

'I'll moor up just under the bridge. Bill Risley keeps it 'ere most nights,' Tubby said, easing back the hand throttle.

The small craft was used for ferrying lightermen and tug crews back and forth on the river, and Tubby knew it would attract no attention at its regular mooring. He cut the motor and let the boat drift in against the wooden stanchions, enabling Mick to reach out for the iron mooring-ring.

The big docker looked at his watch. 'I make it seven-thirty. They should be ready fer pick-up soon,' he told Tubby. 'Listen out fer the whistle.'

'Keep yer 'ead down, there's that police launch back again,' Tubby warned him. 'We can't afford ter be seen on board while there's no activity on the river.'

The police boat turned near London Bridge and came back slowly. The two men watched it slip under Tower Bridge and disappear into the darkness.

'It's bin comin' back every fifteen minutes by my reckonin',' Tubby remarked. 'It could be tricky.'

Mick looked at his watch every couple of minutes, his teeth gnawing on his lip. Tubby seemed quite relaxed as he sat slumped in the control seat with his arms folded over his large belly.

'What's keepin' 'em?' Mick growled.

Joe Mezzo and his team crouched low on the freighter's deck and they heard the embassy car's horn blast out twice.

'They're gettin' impatient. They'll be comin' on board any second now,' he groaned.

Jan suddenly stood up and walked quickly over to the port side, watched by curious crew members who were at a loss to know just what was going on. He leaned over the bulwark and shouted something down to the chauffeur who was standing by the car. The answering wave reassured the Pole and he came back over. 'I've just told the driver his passenger sends his apologies and he'll be there shortly,' he said, grinning.

Joe nodded. 'Soon as that police launch passes under Tower Bridge, we go,' he told them.

The raiders watched the slow progress of the launch as it reached London Bridge, and then suddenly everything started to happen. They heard police whistles and running footsteps on the quayside.

'They're on to us!' Joe screamed. 'We go now.'

Mick threw the coil of rope over the side and checked the knotted end for strength while Joe leaned over the rail and gave two loud blasts on his own whistle. They heard the throaty roar of the tiny ferry boat as it revved up and sped across out of the darkness to draw alongside. Joe looked at the frightened cook and pointed to the rope. The man wanted no prodding and he swung his legs over the guardrail and slid down into the boat. Mick, Tony and Nick Zanti followed and then Joe motioned Jan to go. The Pole shook his head and pointed over at the port side. 'You go. I'll delay them,' he shouted.

Joe clambered over the side and gripped the rope between his legs, holding on with one hand while he clasped the package tightly with the other. He could hear shouting and a crashing noise and he guessed that the police were already on the deck, unaware that Jan had recruited some crewmen to help him couple up the ship's hosepipe. The sailors responded quickly, thinking that maybe war had broken out and they were being asked to repel a boarding party who were trying to take over the ship. The fierce jet of water hit the first policemen who were clambering up the gangway, and sent them sliding back down on to the quay. Jan left the hose in the hands of a determined-looking sailor and ran over to the starboard side, slithering quickly down the rope. The police launch was sweeping round on full throttle at the London Bridge end of the Pool.

'They're on to us too,' Mick shouted as Tubby swung the wheel over and pressed the hand lever right down.

The ferry boat surged forward and slipped round the bows of the freighter, causing a wide wash. The following launch was closing but the spreading wake slowed it enough for Tubby Willis to gain a few vital yards. The fumigation team stripped off their overalls to reveal suits underneath, and stared back at the pursuing boat as their own craft powered under Tower Bridge. Tubby steered it against the Dockhead steps and Mick jumped ashore, pulling the stern of the ferry boat on to the stonework. Everyone hurried off, then Tubby cut the engine and quickly tied the painter rope to a mooring-cleat before following them. Joe was carrying the work overalls and, as he reached the top of the steps, he stuffed them into a nearby sand-bin.

The plan had worked so far, but they were not out of the woods yet, Joe realised as he passed the oilskin-bound package to Mick Mollison. 'Guard this wiv yer life, an' take the cook wiv yer, Mick. 'E'll be a dead giveaway wiv us,' he shouted as they turned into a dark cobbled lane. 'We'll meet termorrer.'

Tubby and Mick each grabbed an arm and propelled the scared cook along the deserted riverside walk. Mick the Hammer and Tony Mancini followed on some way behind the rivermen, while Joe, Nick Zanti and Jan set off in the opposite direction and turned away from the river, making their way towards Tooley Street. They walked slowly, as though they were out for an evening stroll, and Joe breathed more easily.

Suddenly he frowned. 'Careful, there's a copper in front,' he said quietly.

The constable stepped out of the shadows. 'D'yer mind tellin' me where you're goin?' he asked, looking suspicious.

'Yeah, we're on our way ter the Gregorian. There's some music on by all accounts,' Joe told him.

'Where 'ave yer come from?' the constable pressed him.

'We've bin 'avin' a drink in the Tower Bridge 'Otel,' Joe replied amiably.

The constable's colleague stepped out of the darkened doorway and came up. 'I thought I recognised that voice,' he said smiling.

''Ello, mate, you're keepin' late hours,' Joe quipped.

PC Fuller nodded and turned to his fellow officer. 'It's OK, Mac, I'll vouch fer this man,' he told him.

'Albert, I'd like yer ter meet Nick an' Alberto. They're my nephews from Wappin',' Joe said, smiling. 'I'm takin' 'em out fer a drink.'

'Pleased ter meet yer,' PC Fuller said, nodding to the men. 'We've gotta do a check on everybody round 'ere ternight,' he told Joe. 'There's bin some activity on the river.'

'Yer don't say,' Joe replied.

'Yeah, apparently someone stole a boat an' took off a group o' stowaways from the Polish ship,' PC Fuller told him.

'I dunno what it's comin' to,' Joe remarked. 'They could be Commie spies fer all we know. Anyway, we'd better be on our way.

All the best, mate, an' pop round fer a chat when yer get five minutes.'

'Ole Joe Mezzo's a diamond,' PC Fuller said to his colleague as the men walked off. ''E owns a grocer's shop on my beat. That man's as straight as a die.'

Chapter Fifty-two

Ada Brennen called a family conference at tea-time on Wednesday evening. She was insistent that they all heard her out, and Joe knew from experience that when Ada was in one of her insistent moods, it was good policy to remain quiet until she finished what she had to say.

'Now, I know you're all keen ter go in the 'ospital ternight, but I don't fink it's a good idea,' she began. 'When I spoke ter the doctor last night 'e felt that what our Elsie needs more than anyfing is rest, an' too many visitors in an' out will only tire 'er. After all, it's only 'alf an hour visitin' time an' two round the bed, an' she won't get a chance ter say much. Besides, Ernie's likely ter be there, an' as much as we don't get on wiv the man, 'e is 'er 'usband.'

Barbara looked at her mother questioningly. 'Yer not 'oldin' anyfing back are yer, Mum? Elsie is gonna be all right, ain't she?'

'Course she's gonna be all right, but when me an' yer farvver went in last night she was a bit confused, that's all,' Ada told them. 'Yer gotta remember she's 'ad a nasty fall, an' in some cases people tend ter ferget what 'appened to 'em.'

'Are yer tellin' us that our Elsie's lost 'er memory?' Dawn asked quickly.

Ada nodded. 'I didn't tell yer last night 'cos I didn't want you all worryin' unnecessarily,' she explained. 'The doctor assured us that it'll only be fer a few days. That's why I fink it'll be best if only me an' yer farvver go in ternight. Once she's feelin' better, everyone can go in.'

The girls looked disappointed, and Kay was first to break the silence. 'What about Colin?' she asked. ''E's gotta go back termorrer night.'

'I could slip in termorrer afternoon fer five minutes,' the young man replied. 'If I tell the ward sister I'm due back off leave, I fink she'll let me spend a few minutes wiv 'er.'

'You knew Elsie 'ad lost 'er memory,' Dawn said to him in a peeved voice.

'Yeah, but Mum said not ter say anyfing,' Colin replied.

'That's right, I did,' Ada told her.

'Yer mum's right,' Joe said, taking out his watch and consulting it. 'She knows best.'

The girls recognised the final tone in their father's voice, and they knew it was useless to argue. Barbara got up from the table and proceeded to collect up the plates with a sigh of resignation, while Dawn picked up the empty teapot with a pained look on her face. 'I s'pose I'd better make anuvver cuppa,' she said grudgingly.

Colin and Kay exchanged furtive glances. Their sisters would no doubt have something to say to each other while they were busy in the scullery, and both knew it was better leaving them to their own devices.

'Why don't yer come out fer a drink wiv me an' Pat ternight?' Kay suggested. 'We're goin' ter Chippy's.'

Colin pulled a face. 'That's a right ole dump ter go fer a drink,' he replied. 'Surely yer can find a better pub than that.'

Kay smiled indulgently. 'We gotta meet someone there. Besides, Pat an' Chippy are ole pals. Why don't yer come along? Pat won't mind, I'm sure 'e wouldn't.'

Colin dived into his father's armchair while it was empty and sprawled his legs out in front of the fire. 'Nah, I fink I'll give it a miss. Why don't yer ask those two?' he said, nodding towards the scullery and pulling a comical face.

Kay threw the tea-cosy at him. 'I love 'em both, but there's a limit ter what a gel can stand,' she replied, grinning widely.

The night had turned cold and damp, with the Thames mist drifting into the cobbled riverside byways. The wet mist swirled along Dockhead, cloaking the faded picture of a ship's bell on the old pub sign as the two rivermen hurried along with their frightened charge. They found a welcoming warm fire inside and a friendly landlord who turned away from his conversation to stare at them curiously.

'Give us the usual, Chippy, an' one fer our pal,' Mick Mollison said as he put the package he was carrying down on the counter.

'Where did yer find 'im?' Chippy asked as he pulled down on the beer-pump .

'This is our pal, Franz Lubeck. We got that much out of 'im anyway,' Tubby told him.

Chippy looked at the stranger, who stood grinning at his helpers. 'What'll it be, Franz?' he asked.

'It's no good askin' 'im,' Mick said. ''E's a Pole. 'E can't speak a word of English.'

'Is 'e off that ship in the Pool?' Chippy inquired.

'Yeah, but 'e can't go back,' Tubby cut in. ''Cos if 'e does the bastards are gonna chuck 'im overboard on the way back ter Poland, so 'e said.'

Chippy pointed to the line of optics behind the bar and shook his head. 'Polish vodka, no,' he said slowly. 'Whisky, yes.'

Franz grinned even more widely as he pointed to the upturned bottle of Haig's whisky. 'Is good,' he said.

Mick paid for the drinks and then pointed to the package. 'Chippy, can yer put this away somewhere safe fer the time bein'?' he asked.

The landlord nodded. 'I won't ask what yer got there, but tell me, is it valuable?'

'Priceless,' Tubby said with a smile.

'I'll put it upstairs in my bedroom,' Chippy told them as he picked it up.

'Be careful, it's delicate,' Mick warned him.

Margie Dolan happened to stroll over. ''Ello, boys, who's yer friend?' she asked, looking Franz up and down saucily.

'This is Franz Lubeck, but 'e can't speak a word of English, Margie,' Mick told her. 'What's more, 'e's done a runner from 'is ship, so I don't s'pose 'e's got any dosh on 'im.'

Franz was enjoying the attention Margie was paying him, and he pointed to his drink with raised eyebrows.

Margie winked at him and the Pole felt into his trouser pocket and drew out a thick wad of notes.

'Where there's a will there's a way,' she said, smiling. 'C'mon, Franz, come an' talk ter me.'

Chippy shook his head slowly. 'She's incorrigible,' he remarked. 'She's come in 'ere ternight all upset about leavin' the area, an' now look at 'er.'

'What's she leavin' for?' Tubby asked.

'I fink she wants a change o' scenery if you ask me,' Chippy told him. 'After all, she ain't 'ad it too good this last few weeks, what wiv that ex-'usband of 'ers.'

''E ain't cuttin' up rough again, is 'e?' Mick asked quickly. 'I thought 'e'd bin warned off.'

'Vic Dolan's a frightened man, accordin' ter what Margie told me,' the landlord replied. 'She said 'e went round ter see 'er yesterday. Told 'er 'e was gonna move away. 'E wanted a stake, by all accounts, but she told 'im ter piss off in no uncertain terms.'

'Good fer 'er,' Tubby said. 'I'm gonna miss 'er round the place.'

'Yeah, so am I,' Chippy replied. 'She's a good 'un, is Margie. 'Elp anyone out, she would.'

Mick leaned forward over the counter. 'Chippy, I was wonderin' if you could put our Polish pal up ternight,' he asked. ''E's got nowhere ter go until this bloke we know takes 'im off our 'ands.'

'When's that likely ter be?' Chippy inquired.

'The geezer's comin' fer 'im termorrer. Apparently Franz 'as got relations up north. They're gonna sort it all out fer 'im, but 'e needs ter be kept out of 'arm's way till then.'

'Not ter worry, I'll put 'im up on the sofa,' Chippy told him.

'You're a good sort. You'll get yer reward one day,' Tubby said, smiling.

'I'd prefer it sooner than later, an' in 'ard cash,' the landlord replied. 'Just look at the state o' this pub. I bin on ter the brewery fer ages now ter fix it up, but they keep puttin' me off. I fink they're waitin' fer me ter get the needle an' turn it in. They'll 'ave ter wait a long time though. Where could I go if I left 'ere?'

Loud laughter came from the far table and Chippy shook his head. 'Some'ow I don't fink I'm gonna 'ave ter worry about puttin' your pal up,' he remarked. 'It looks like Margie's gonna sort that one out.'

There was a gush of cold air as the door opened, and Chippy's face lit up as Pat Kelly and Kay Brennen walked in. 'Well, well, if it ain't the lovebirds themselves,' he joked.

Pat slipped his arm around Kay as they reached the counter. 'Nice ter see yer, Chippy,' he said smiling. He nodded over to the far table. 'I see Margie's enjoyin' 'erself.'

The landlord cast his eyes over to where Tubby and Mick were sitting. 'They brought that geezer in,' he told him. ''E's off the Polish freighter that's berthed at Mark Brown's Wharf. 'E's jumped ship by all accounts.'

'I dunno if it's got anyfing ter do wiv it, but we saw a couple o' police cars flyin' about on our way 'ere,' Pat replied. 'There were some coppers flashin' their torches along the lane as well. They may decide ter call in, so I'd warn Margie if I were you.'

Chippy stroked his chin thoughtfully. The police could be looking for the Pole, but it was just as likely they were looking for something else, he realised. Tubby and Mick had looked a bit agitated when they came in, and they'd been keen for him to hide the package they had with them. What was going on?

'Chippy?'

'Sorry, Pat, I was just finkin',' the landlord said quickly.

''Adn't yer better tell Margie ter put that seaman on 'is guard?' Pat urged him.

'Yeah, I'll do it right away. What yer 'avin' ter drink, by the way?'

'Later, Chippy. Tell 'er first,' Pat pressed him.

''E looks very nervy,' Kay remarked as Chippy walked over to Margie.

'Somefing's goin' on 'ere, I can sense it,' Pat told her.

'Like what?' she asked.

'I dunno. It's just a feelin' I got.'

'D'yer wanna stay or would yer sooner us go?' Kay asked him.

Pat glanced around at the few old men sitting over their drinks and then he kissed her quickly on the cheek. 'Did I ever tell yer you look beautiful?' he said, smiling.

'Not this week, but that's not answered me question,' she told him. 'Shall we stay or what?' Kay asked.

'Yeah, I'm intrigued. It's unlike Chippy ter be on edge, an' those two don't look very relaxed,' he pointed out.

Kay looked over to where the two rivermen were sitting, and she saw that they were huddled over their drinks in earnest conversation. 'Yeah, you're right,' she remarked.

Tubby and Mick were in fact feeling a little uneasy after their brush with authority.

'I was given to understand that they were after some sort o' paintin's which are s'posed ter be priceless,' Mick was saying. 'Yer not gonna tell me that package contains paintin's.'

'If it's paintin's in that parcel then my dick's a bloater,' Tubby

403

replied adamantly. 'I reckon it's more like precious stones, like diamonds, or rubies.'

'Yer don't fink it's anyfing else, do yer?' Mick asked him. 'I wouldn't like ter be mixed up in anyfing really dodgy.'

'Yer mean like opium or somefink?' Tubby queried.

Mick nodded. 'There's bin a few ships turned over by customs in the West India Docks an' they found opium, on its way ter Lime'ouse. It makes yer fink.'

Tubby sipped his drink and rubbed his chin thoughtfully. 'I 'ope Bill Risley won't be too upset about where I left that boat of 'is,' he remarked. 'There weren't much else I could do under the circumstances.'

'I 'ope the river police don't impound it,' Mick said.

'Nah, I don't fink so. They'll just moor it back in its usual spot,' Tubby replied. 'They're not a bad crowd really. We get on OK wiv 'em.'

'Anyway, it's over an' done wiv now, so let's get anuvver drink in an' ferget it,' Mick said, draining his glass.

The shadowy figure lurking in the wharf doorway had been hard pressed to avoid the patrolling policemen, but they had moved off now and it was very quiet. Several yards along the cobbled lane, the lights from the pub glimmered out into the fog and he mumbled a curse as he reached into his overcoat pocket. He tore the wrapping from the milk bottle and then took out a short length of oil-lamp wick, which he partially stuffed inside. The petrol immediately soaked up into it right to the end left dangling, and Vic Dolan stepped out of the shadows. He was being forced out of the neighbourhood, made to feel like a pariah, he scowled, and it was that interfering bastard of a publican who was to blame. This was a going-away present, something to remember him by. He lifted the storm-guard of his cigarette lighter and flicked the wheel. It lit on the second attempt and he put the flame to the petrol-soaked wick and threw. The flaring bottle went through the window, and Vic Dolan ran off into the darkness.

Margie Dolan had found herself a willing customer, and she smiled to Pat and Kay as she walked over. 'I'm glad you two could come ternight,' she said happily. 'Let me get yer a drink.'

''Ello, Margie. We're OK fer the time bein',' Pat told her.

'Me an' Franz over there are good friends already. Just look at 'im,' she said sighing. 'Ain't 'e sweet?'

The Pole was looking over, grinning broadly as he sat at the far table with his arms folded.

'When yer leavin', Marge?' Pat asked her.

'Termorrer, darlin',' she replied. 'I'm gonna be sorry in one respect. I made a lot o' lovely friends round this area, an' I'm gonna miss Chippy somefing painful, but there comes a time when a gel 'as to ask 'erself a few important questions. I didn't like the answers I was gettin', so I come to a decision, luvvy.'

Pat grinned and pulled Kay to him. 'We're both gonna miss yer, Margie,' he told her.

'I'm gonna miss you too, but I'll send Chippy me address soon as I get fixed up, then you can send me an invite ter yer weddin',' she said to Kay. ''E's a nice feller, luv. Just you keep a tight rein on 'im.'

Kay was just about to make a witty reply when it happened. There was a crash of glass and in a split second the corner of the pub had become a roaring inferno. There were no customers sitting under the window, and the curtains had cushioned much of the impact but they were burning fiercely and the flames were rapidly spreading throughout the bar. The landlord's face had gone white as he jumped over the counter. Pat quickly grabbed the two women and pulled them away from the flames, while Tubby and Mick went to the aid of the two old men who were standing in the far corner as if mesmerised. The Polish cook jumped up and went to help the rivermen get the old men away from the advancing flames.

'Everybody out the back way,' Chippy shouted.

The fire had spread to the counter and the heat was intense. The large mirror behind the bar suddenly cracked and bottles of spirits began to burst, adding fuel to the flames. Black, acrid smoke from the burning carpet and draperies filled the bar and the ceiling began to peel.

Chippy led the way out into the backyard and fought to slip the rusted bolts of the small gate. Tubby pushed him to one side and threw his heavy bulk at the planking. The door crashed outwards on to the cobbles and everyone tumbled through as the flames rose up behind them.

'Is everyone accounted for?' Pat shouted.

Chippy looked around and nodded, then he saw Mick Mollison

suddenly run back into the yard. 'The package! 'E's gone back fer the package!' he cried out.

'Bloody 'ell!' Pat shouted, making after him.

Kay clung on to him. 'No, Pat! No!' she screamed.

'Grab 'er, Tubby, quick!' Pat called out, and as the big lighterman pulled Kay away, he rushed back into the yard.

The flames were already eating away at the stairs, and Pat held his handkerchief to his mouth as he raced up to the room above. He could hear Mick coughing and spluttering and as he reached the landing he saw him standing in a doorway clutching the oilskin package. Suddenly the whole staircase was enveloped in flames and a shower of sparks flew up as the woodwork collapsed. Pat saw Mick fall to his knees as smoke filled his tortured lungs and he realised that they were cut off. He looked around in desperation as he too felt the billowing fumes beginning to take their toll. With a supreme effort he managed to drag Mick and the package he was still clutching back into the bedroom and close the door. He could feel the heat beneath his feet and knew that very soon the whole of the floor would fall into the inferno. He picked up a handful of bedding and, wrapping it round his fist, he punched out the window-frame.

Mick was dragging himself towards the parcel which had fallen out of his arms just inside the room. 'Get the parcel! Don't leave it be'ind!' he gasped as Pat pulled him over to the window.

Kay held her hand up to her face when the window-frame fell on to the cobbled lane, and she stared transfixed as Pat eased the docker out through the opening. He was holding on to the man's wrists and his face was contorted with sheer effort as he lowered him down.

'Let 'im go,' Tubby shouted up.

The unconscious docker fell into the arms of the bulky lighter-man, and then Pat threw out the package. He swung his legs over the windowsill as the floor collapsed behind him and he hung for a moment by his fingertips and then let go. Once again Tubby was waiting below, and he broke the young man's fall. Kay ran over as Pat staggered to his feet, her arms going round his neck. 'Oh, Pat. I was so scared,' she sobbed.

'I'm all right. What about Mick?' he asked her.

''E's unconscious but 'e's breavvin',' she told him.

They heard bells and then they saw the glare of headlights along the lane as the fire-engine roared towards them.

'Yer'd better take the Pole off 'ome wiv yer, Marge, before the police get 'ere,' Chippy told her. 'Take this, too. I'll be glad ter see the back of it, ter tell yer the trufe.'

'What's in it?' Margie asked him as he handed it over. 'Cor, it's 'eavy, ain't it?'

'I dunno what it is, but guard it wiv yer life,' he told her. 'Mick nearly lost 'is life goin' back fer that bundle.'

Chapter Fifty-three

Colin turned over in bed and stretched, his eyes going up to the alarm clock on the chair beside his bed. It was ten-thirty. He could do with another half-hour, he thought drowsily. There would be little chance of sleep on the journey back to Durham tonight.

The young soldier finally dragged himself out of bed at ten minutes past eleven and dressed quickly. He went downstairs, half expecting to see his mother there, but the house was empty. The fire was burning brightly, however, and there was some tea in the pot. The morning paper was lying on the table and he cut two thick slices of bread and slipped them on to the toasting-fork. It was no use going to the hospital until early that afternoon, he decided. The sister had already warned him that the doctor did his rounds about midday.

Colin toasted the bread until it was black and then thickly coated the slices with margarine. The tea was over-brewed but it was hot, and he scooped two large spoonfuls of sugar into the mug to disguise the taste. He spent the rest of the morning reading the paper beside the fire, occasionally glancing up at the clock. His mother would have gone to the market and then stopped off for a chat with one of the neighbours, he guessed.

It was nearly one o'clock when Ada walked in and flopped down wearily in the armchair. 'I've bin sittin' wiv Danny's mum fer the past two hours,' she told him. 'That woman's gonna 'ave a total breakdown, mark my words.'

''As she managed ter see Danny yet?' Colin asked her.

'Yeah, that's what's got to 'er,' Ada replied. 'The boy looks like a zombie, so she said. She couldn't get any sense out of 'im.'

Colin shook his head slowly. 'I can understand 'ow she feels,' he told her. 'If they don't certify 'im, 'e'll 'ang. What a terrible fing.'

Ada shuddered. 'I saw a few o' the neighbours down the market. They're talkin' about gettin' up a petition, though I dunno what good that'll do. I've never known anyone gettin' reprieved frew a petition.'

'It just don't seem real,' Colin replied, picking up the empty teapot. 'That ole gel must 'ave really got to 'im. I've 'eard she was a wicked ole cow.'

'She was, by all accounts, but that don't warrant 'er gettin' 'er 'ead caved in,' Ada retorted.

'I reckon Danny Adams must 'ave 'ad a brainstorm,' he remarked. 'I'm certain they'll find 'im insane. They'll put 'im away fer life.'

'Go an' make that tea, fer Gawd's sake,' Ada said quickly. 'Yer gettin' me all depressed.'

Eddie Chipperfield had spent the night on Margie Dolan's sofa and had then had a busy morning. He'd gone along to the local St Olave's Hospital to visit Mick Mollison, only to be told that the docker had discharged himself earlier. He then had to go to the police station at Dockhead to make a statement, and he had next contacted the brewery who were sending someone down that afternoon. He spent some time sifting through the burned-out ruins of his pub, and finally he met Tubby for a lunch-time drink.

'That dopey git Mick's discharged 'imself from 'ospital this mornin', would yer believe,' Tubby said grinning.

'Yeah, I know,' Chippy replied. 'I went up there first fing terday.'

''E come round ter see me,' Tubby went on. 'It's lucky I'm on nights this week. 'E looked a bit rough, but that's understandable, considerin' what 'appened. I told 'im I was meetin' you 'ere an' 'e said 'e'd pop in.'

''E was lucky last night,' Chippy remarked. 'If it 'adn't bin fer Pat Kelly, 'e'd 'ave snuffed it.'

'Gawd knows what's in that parcel ter make 'im risk 'is life fer it,' Tubby muttered.

'Don't you know?' Chippy asked him.

'Nah, nor does Mick. We was only talkin' about it just before that petrol bomb come flyin' frew the winder,' Tubby said. 'By the way, did yer tell the police who yer fink did it?'

Chippy shook his head. 'Nah, I told 'em I didn't 'ave a clue.'

'But why? It's obvious it was that no-good git Dolan.'

'I know that, an' so do you, but I didn't want the law makin' a big issue of it. It'd only delay fings,' Chippy explained. 'If the brewery knew that the police were lookin' fer Dolan in connection, they'd 'ang fire 'cos o' the insurance. As it is, they've promised me anuvver pub till they've rebuilt the Bell. Dolan's 'ad 'is bit o' fun an' I'm pretty certain we won't 'ear any more from 'im now. It's best fer everyone concerned, not least Margie, that fings stay the way they are.'

'I s'pose you're right,' Tubby conceded.

Just then Mick walked into the pub and sat down wearily at the table, refusing the offer of a drink.

'You look like yer done fifteen rounds wiv Joe Louis,' Tubby said, grinning.

Mick ignored the remark. 'Margie's still got that package in 'er place, ain't she?' he asked anxiously.

'Yeah, course she 'as,' Chippy told him.

'Fank Gawd fer that,' he replied. 'I've bin in touch wiv the Malts. They're sendin' a car round this afternoon fer it. I told 'em where ter go. Someone'll 'ave ter be in.'

'I'll be there, I got nowhere else ter go,' Chippy remarked. 'Margie's put off movin' fer a couple o' days till I get meself sorted out. She's a diamond.'

'I saw Bill Risley this mornin',' Tubby said, pulling a face.

'Was 'e all right about the boat?' Mick asked.

''E gave me a bit o' verbal,' Tubby replied. 'The police knocked 'im up last night ter go an' claim it.'

'Ole Bill's as good as gold,' Mick said as he stood up. 'I still feel a bit groggy, so I'm off 'ome ter get a bit o' shut-eye. See yer later, an' don't ferget they're comin' fer the parcel this afternoon.'

Colin Brennen walked into Guy's Hospital that afternoon and hurried up to the ward. He met the sister coming out of her office. 'I'm goin' back ternight, so can I—'

'Yes, you may,' she interrupted with a friendly smile, 'but don't stay too long.'

Colin walked into the ward and saw Elsie sitting on the edge of her bed, clad in a white dressing gown. She looked up and gave him a welcoming smile. ''Ello, Colin,' she said.

The young soldier's face lit up and he bent over and planted a kiss on her cheek. 'Yer know me. Yer got yer memory back.'

Elsie nodded. 'There's a day-room along the corridor. Let's go there.'

He took her by the arm and he could feel her trembling as they left the ward.

Once they were seated in the comfortable armchairs in the quiet day-room, Colin looked at her expectantly, but his sister seemed hesitant, as though not wanting to talk.

'Ernie came in this mornin',' she said flatly.

'I bet that cheered you up,' Colin answered with a cynical smile.

'It was while 'e was 'ere that it all came back ter me,' she said, her voice breaking suddenly.

Colin leaned forward in his chair as he saw tears in Elsie's eyes. 'What's wrong?' he asked her.

She dropped her head and began to sob. 'Nuffink. I just feel awful,' she spluttered.

''E didn't—'

'No,' Elsie interrupted him. 'I was asleep when 'e called. I woke up an' saw 'im sittin' there. 'E was just sittin' there starin' at me an' then when I opened me eyes 'e reached out an' touched me face. It was then that everyfing came back like a flash. It was 'im touchin' me face.'

Colin raised his sister's chin gently with the tips of his fingers. 'Look at me, sis,' he said quietly. 'What is it? Why are yer so upset?'

She held her head up self-consciously and the young soldier saw the pain and anguish reflected in her eyes. Tears fell down her cheeks and she reached out her hands to him. Colin felt the lump in his throat as he knelt by her chair with his arms around her. 'Tell me,' he whispered. 'Yer must tell me everyfing.'

Elsie fought to compose herself, and after a while she leaned back in the chair and gave a deep sigh of resignation. He had to be told, she realised. They all did.

Colin rested his hands on the arms of her chair, still kneeling in front of her. 'Go on, Else,' he said encouragingly.

The young woman reached into the pocket of her dressing gown and drew out a handkerchief. Colin watched while she dabbed at her eyes and then blew her nose hard. He got up and went back to his chair, almost dreading what he was about to hear.

'I remember oversleepin' on Tuesday mornin',' Elsie began. 'When I got up I looked in on Billy an' saw that 'e was still fast asleep, so I went downstairs an' made a pot o' tea. I poured Billy's first, an' as I was takin' it up the stairs, Ernie walked in. They'd put 'im on a journey an' 'e was comin' in fer 'is overnight bag. 'E shouted up ter me that it was Danny Adams who killed ole Mrs Dines an' the police 'ad charged 'im. 'E'd 'eard it at the yard. Ernie was leerin' up at me an' sayin' that Danny was a maniac an' it was a good job they'd caught 'im before 'e killed anyone else. I shouted back that there must 'ave bin a mistake. I told 'im that Danny couldn't kill anybody, then 'e got really mad. 'E ran up the stairs an' put 'is face right up ter mine. 'E said I fancied the nutter an' I was too stupid ter see what Danny was really like. Yer gotta remember, Colin, I'd only just got up, an' I couldn't take 'is screamin' an' shoutin' that early, so I told 'im ter piss off.'

'Good fer you, Else. Yer should 'ave done that ages ago,' Colin said angrily.

'Listen ter me, Colin, that wasn't all,' the young woman went on. 'Ernie took no notice. 'E just went on an' on about what an idiot Danny was an' 'ow 'e'd battered a defenceless ole lady ter death. I couldn't stand it no more so I told 'im point-blank that Danny couldn't possibly 'ave killed that ole gel, fer the simple reason that 'e was wiv me all night.'

'Gawd Almighty!' Colin gasped.

'I've never seen Ernie in such a rage,' Elsie continued, screwing up her handkerchief. ''E called me a liar an' everyfing from a pig to a dog. 'E said I was just sayin' that ter get Danny off, but then I really drove it 'ome to 'im. I swore on Billy's life that every word I said was true. Danny did spend the night wiv me. Ernie let out one yell an' then 'e swung the back of 'is 'and an' caught me on the side of me 'ead. I remember topplin' sideways an' then it was blackness. The next fing I'm wakin' up in 'ere wiv Ernie sittin' by the bed. 'E reached out ter me an' I screamed. The nurse came runnin' an' told 'im 'e'd better go. I was cryin' an' shakin'. It was like it was 'appenin' all over again.'

Colin's face had gone white and his hands were clenched in hard fists. 'I'll kill the bastard,' he hissed through gritted teeth. 'I'll maim 'im fer life.'

Elsie reached out and gripped his fists in her hands. 'No, Colin. No,' she pleaded. 'Me an' Ernie are finished fer good now. There can't be any goin' back after what 'e did. There's ovver, more important fings ter sort out. We gotta get Danny Adams freed. 'E didn't kill that ole lady, I can swear on a stack o' Bibles that 'e's innocent.'

Colin took a deep breath and tried to control his raging temper. 'What 'appened wiv you an' Danny?' he asked her in a strained voice.

'Danny came round ter put a couple o' shelves up in Billy's bedroom,' Elsie explained. 'It was a really foggy night. Yer couldn't see more than a yard in front of yer. Anyway, when 'e finished the shelves 'e stayed fer tea. 'E 'ad this ovver job ter do at the Dineses' 'ouse afterwards, yer see. I thought it'd save 'im goin' back 'ome an' then comin' back. The Dineses' place is only across the street from me. Well, as it 'appened, Danny got a lot of abuse while 'e was doin' the repair ter the winder, an' 'e accidentally cracked a pane o' glass. The ole cow went mad an' she refused ter pay 'im until 'e put it right. Danny told 'er 'e would but she still wasn't satisfied. She screamed at 'im all along the street, an' by the time the poor sod got ter my 'ouse 'e was shakin'. Yer know 'ow fings like that can set 'is 'ead off an' that's what 'appened. Danny was in agony an' 'e finally fell asleep in the armchair.'

'Was Simon Dines there all the time Danny was?' Colin asked her.

Elsie nodded. 'From then on 'e was wiv me all night.'

''E slept in the armchair all night?' Colin queried.

'No. 'E woke up later an' told me that 'e felt a bit better,' Elsie replied. 'I could see 'e was still groggy an' I urged 'im ter stay. I wasn't finkin' of me, I was more concerned about 'im. Anyway, 'e put 'is coat on an' went ter the front door. By that time the fog was like a blanket. 'E said goodnight an' then suddenly 'e staggered. I caught 'im in me arms an' I could see that 'is eyes were all funny, like they couldn't focus. So I dragged 'im back in the parlour an' told 'im I wasn't gonna be responsible fer anyfing 'appenin' to 'im an' 'e'd 'ave ter stay the night. I let 'im sleep in my room an' I settled down on the settee.'

Colin could see that his sister was becoming distressed again, and he gripped her hands in his. 'Take it easy, luv,' he told her softly.

'I'm all right,' she replied, sighing. 'I'm tellin' yer all this 'cos I want yer ter know the full story. Before I went ter sleep I crept up the stairs an' looked in on Danny ter see if 'e was all right. I could 'ear 'im cryin' quietly, like a frightened young child. I felt a terrible urge ter take 'im in me arms, just as I would if it'd bin Billy cryin' like that. I got inter bed next to 'im an' 'eld 'im tightly all night long. There was nuffink sexual. I just felt a pure love fer that feller. I do love 'im, Colin. Can you understand what I'm sayin'?'

'Yeah, I do,' Colin replied quietly, stroking the backs of her hands. 'If yer really love 'im, nuffink else matters, except gettin' 'im freed as quick as possible.'

'What should I do though?' Elsie asked him anxiously.

'Nuffink. You leave it ter me. Just you rest,' he told her. 'I'm gonna get goin' now. I'll start the ball rollin' right away. There's time yet before I catch that train back ter camp. The police'll come an' take a statement off yer, but there's no need fer yer ter worry. Just tell 'em what yer told me. Don't 'old nuffink back.'

They hugged before he left and then, as Colin reached the door, Elsie called out to him. 'Promise me yer'll stay clear of Ernie,' she urged him.

'I've got no time ter worry about that mongrel,' he told her. 'It's Danny we gotta fink of.'

Colin hurried from the hospital into the cold late afternoon, his fists clenched tightly and his face set hard with the burning anger inside him. Ernie Gates was going to pay for what he had done, he vowed. Things would have to be handled very carefully, though. He would tell the family the good news that Elsie had regained her memory, but keep the full details to himself. If his father got to find out about Ernie he would take off after him. This was something Colin had to do himself. He would wait until later that evening. Ernie Gates had been into the hospital that day so he wasn't on a two-day journey. He would find him somewhere, most likely propping up a bar in one of the neighbourhood pubs. One thing was for sure: Bermondsey was not big enough for that evil bastard to hide in. He would find him.

Chapter Fifty-four

Margie Dolan peeped out through her crisp lace curtains as she heard the car draw up. 'They're 'ere,' she called out. 'Blimey, one's a priest by the look of it.'

Joe Mezzo walked into the house and exchanged introductions with Chippy and Margie. 'This is Farvver Ryan from St Mary's Church,' he told them. ''E's gonna take charge o' the package.'

Margie was decidedly uncomfortable as she shook hands with the priest, but his disarming smile made her feel a little more at ease.

'Joseph and I have been given the full story of what happened last night,' he said. 'It seems that we of the Church owe you a great debt of gratitude. May I please see the package you have?'

Chippy left the room and came back carrying the small bundle which he put gingerly on the table. 'There we are, Farvver. All in one piece. There's not even scorch-marks on it,' he said, grinning.

The priest went over to the table and passed his fingers over the package, closing his eyes for a few moments as though in prayer. 'I won't try to explain what's inside this parcel, nor just what it means to the Catholic Church, but you shall know, all of you who have been instrumental in the recovery,' he told them. 'I am going to take this with me to St Mary's and I want to extend to you both an invitation to meet someone very important from Rome. He will tell you everything and I feel sure you'll find it fascinating. Can you come to St Mary's Church tomorrow evening at seven?'

Chippy and Margie nodded, both feeling a little overawed by it all.

'I'm gonna let Pat Kelly know,' Joe said. 'Can you tell Mick an' Tubby that they're invited too? By the way, did our little Polish friend get away OK?'

'Yeah, a man came in a taxi early this mornin',' Margie told him, suppressing a smile.

'That would be Jan Krazinski,' Joe replied. ''E's takin' 'im up ter Sheffield ter stay wiv some of 'is family. It was arranged by the Church.'

'Ah yes,' Father Ryan cut in. 'After all, we could hardly leave the poor fellow to his own devices, considering his contribution. We are also going to support his application for the right to stay in the country, and when the full story emerges, I don't see too much of a problem; but of course it's in the Lord's hands.'

'Would yer care fer some tea?' Margie asked them.

'No, thank you kindly. We have much to do,' the priest replied, smiling warmly. 'Until tomorrow evening, then.'

Margie and Chippy watched intrigued as Father Ryan picked up the package from the table as though it were made of fragile glass, and after the front door closed behind him and Joe Mezzo, they looked at each other in bewilderment.

'This is like somefing out o' one o' those Peter Lorre, Sidney Greenstreet films,' Chippy said, scratching his head.

'Yer can say that again,' Margie replied, shaking her head slowly.

Chief Superintendent Roger Cranley leaned back in his office chair and sighed irritably into the internal phone. 'As soon as he gets back I want him in here,' he ordered the desk sergeant.

It had been a bad day and it was not over yet. The top echelons had shown their displeasure at the crime clear-up rate for the district, and the file was growing. They were also concerned about the Mark Brown's Wharf fiasco. A top-level complaint had been made by the Russian ambassador on general policing and lack of protection for a Communist ship in the Port of London. He had also openly accused the Metropolitan Police and security services of aiding and abetting defection by a crew member. That in itself was bad enough, but the police commissioner had gone on to demand a full report on how the ship's boarders were allowed to make a clean getaway despite extensive police presence in the immediate area.

It was enough to be getting on with, Cranley thought, but then to cap it all a young soldier had walked into the station during the afternoon and pulled the ground away from a murder prosecution. The subsequent bedside statement he had taken himself just an hour

416

or so ago at the hospital had backed up the soldier's information and yet another unsolved crime was added to the ever-growing list.

Detective Moody had already been warned by the desk sergeant what to expect, and he walked into the chief superintendent's office prepared for the worst. Nevertheless, the severity of it took him aback.

'Sergeant Moody, how long have you been in the force?' Cranley asked him quickly.

'Fifteen years, sir.'

'Long enough to understand correct police procedures?'

'Yes, sir.'

'Good. Then why did you not follow correct procedures during the Grace Dines murder investigation?'

'I don't understand, sir.'

'Oh, you don't? Then let me enlighten you, Sergeant,' Cranley said scathingly. 'You bring in a suspect. You cross-examine him and then come to the conclusion that the man is guilty. Fine. Then despite the fact that the man you subsequently charged with murder had a medical history dating back to a war injury, you did not deem it necessary to follow up with your inquiries to substantiate that he was telling you the truth, whether or not he had confessed to the murder.'

Moody bit back an angry reply. ' I originally contacted PC Fuller, the local beat constable, for any leads 'e might 'ave, sir. When I drew a blank there I acted on the only information I 'ad at the time. After I questioned Danny Adams I went back ter PC Fuller fer 'is opinion of the young man, an' Fuller said that as far as 'e was concerned, Adams was quite normal in 'is be'aviour, apart from occasional bouts of 'eadaches an' confusion due to a war injury. I took that inter consideration when interviewin' Adams. 'Is answers didn't lead me ter believe that the man was confused at that time. In fact, 'e finally admitted ter the killin' wivout any pressure on my part. If I 'ad felt 'e was coverin' fer somebody or 'e wasn't *compos mentis*, I would 'ave gone furvver. That wasn't the case though. There was no alibi ter check out eivver. I still feel that the man is guilty as charged.'

'Then let me tell you that Danny Adams was elsewhere at the time of the murder,' Cranley said quietly as he reached into his desk drawer. 'There's the statement I took a short while ago. Coupled with that statement are medical reports from both the man's panel

417

doctor and the War Office. In other words, Sergeant, you charged the wrong man.'

At ten minutes past seven on Thursday evening, Joe Brennen helped Ada on to a number 21 bus and they took their seats on the lower deck.

'I was so pleased when Colin told me the good news about our Elsie,' Ada said as she made herself comfortable. 'I knew it would only be a matter o' time before she got 'er memory back. The poor little cow must 'ave bin scared out of 'er wits.'

'Gawd knows what she was goin' frew,' Joe replied as he fished into his pocket for the fare.

Ada stared out of the bus window at the shuttered shops. 'I thought our Colin seemed a bit edgy this evenin',' she remarked after a while. ''E nearly bit Barbara's 'ead off when she asked 'im if there was anyfing wrong.'

'I s'pose it's the thought o' goin' back off leave,' Joe answered. 'I don't fink that camp's much good, right up there in the wilds. It's next door ter Scotland, is Durham, an' the journey can't be very nice.'

'P'raps yer right, but I dunno. Our Colin's never bin one ter let yer know what's troublin' 'im,' Ada went on. 'Remember when 'e 'ad that pain in 'is stomach an' it turned out ter be appendicitis? The little cowson never let on fer ages 'e was in pain. If we'd 'ave left it much later before we took 'im up the 'ospital, it would 'ave turned ter peritonitis.'

Joe nodded thoughtfully. 'I 'ope 'e ain't 'oldin' somefing back about Elsie. 'E would, yer know, if 'e thought it was gonna worry us.'

'Anyway we're nearly there, we'll soon find out,' Ada replied. 'There's a flower stall on the station forecourt. I'll get 'er some nice flowers ter cheer 'er up. She loves flowers.'

Ada and Joe stepped off the bus and Ada bought a small spray of carnations from the stall at the top of the steep flight of steps leading down opposite the hospital entrance. They hurried in through the gates and Ada held on to Joe's arm, feeling a little apprehensive.

'If Ernie 'appens ter come in ternight, I don't want no trouble, d'you 'ear what I say?' she warned.

Joe looked the picture of innocence as he glanced quickly at her. 'I'd just ignore the cowson,' he replied.

They climbed the wide staircase to the ward just on the half-hour, and when they hurried through from the corridor, Ada immediately knew that something was wrong. Her daughter's face looked pale and there were dark shadows around her eyes.

''Ello, luv, 'ow are yer?' she asked, kissing her on the cheek.

'Is Colin all right?' Elsie asked straight away.

'Yeah, course 'e is,' Joe replied as he greeted her with a quick kiss. 'Why d'yer ask?'

Elsie turned to her mother with a worried look on her face. ''Ow much did Colin tell yer, Mum?' she asked.

'Only that yer got yer memory back an' yer looked well,' Ada replied.

Elsie eased her plastered arm and winced as she raised herself up in the bed. 'I bin worried out o' me life ever since 'e come in ter see me this afternoon,' she told them.

'Why?' Ada asked her, frowning.

''E's gonna go lookin' fer Ernie, I'm sure of it,' she answered.

'What for? Did Ernie do this to yer?' Joe asked her quickly.

Elsie nodded slowly, dropping her head. 'I wasn't gonna tell Colin, but I 'ad to. Fer Danny's sake.'

'That little bleeder never said anyfing to us,' Ada told her, a note of anger in her voice.

''E knew I'd go after 'im, that's why,' Joe cut in. ''E'll be lookin' for 'im now. You was right, Ada. Yer said 'e looked a bit edgy before we came out. 'E was just waitin' fer us ter leave.'

'What can we do now?' Ada asked him anxiously.

'Ernie'll kill 'im,' Elsie groaned. ''E's an animal. Colin won't stand no chance wiv 'im.'

Joe got up quickly. 'I know what ter do. I'll ring Jack Springer. I'll ask 'im ter pop along an' warn Kay. She can get Pat ter stop 'im.'

''Urry up then, luv. There's no time ter lose,' Ada said urgently, She turned to Elsie. 'I fink you'd better tell me exactly what did 'appen.'

Colin waited until his parents had left the house, then he went to his bedroom. There was time yet, he thought. Ernie Gates would no doubt be out drinking this evening as usual, and it would most likely be in one of the local pubs. He would try the Mason's Arms first. Elsie had told him he often used that pub. He would have to be careful how he approached him. Ernie would not be above using a weapon to defend himself with, and a broken beer glass could be lethal.

The young man sat on the edge of his bed and tried to steady his rapid breathing. Ernie Gates had a reputation. He was a hard man, but like all hard men he had his Achilles' heel. He was easily angered, and that could be made to work against him, Colin told himself. Ernie Gates was the stronger, but he had youth on his side. He felt extremely fit from his Army training and he had learned a few things about dirty fighting during the unarmed combat lessons.

Colin got up and reached under his bed. If Gates did try to use a broken glass on him, then he would get a taste of this, he thought, smiling to himself as he drew out a two-foot length of heavy chain.

'What time 'ave yer gotta leave fer the station, Colin?' Dawn asked when he came down into the parlour.

'About ten o'clock,' he replied. 'I'll be goin' out in a minute, though. I gotta see one o' me mates.'

'Don't leave it too late or you'll miss yer train,' Dawn warned him, catching a warning glance from Barbara.

'I won't,' the young soldier said sharply as he sat down in the armchair.

'Sorry I spoke,' Dawn muttered.

Barbara shook her head quickly as she met her sister's eye. Dawn was taking a chance, she thought, with the mood Colin was in.

After an uneasy silence, Barbara got up and stretched languidly. 'Anyone fancy a cuppa?' she asked pleasantly.

'Not fer me, I'm off out now,' Colin told her as he stood up and left the room.

Five minutes later, the young soldier was striding purposefully along Waggoner's Way, his battledress blouse buttoned up to the neck, concealing the length of chain which was draped over his shoulder.

Back in the Brennen household, Barbara was lounging in the scullery waiting for the kettle to boil when there was a knock on the front door. She was surprised to see Jack Springer standing there. He looked anxious.

'I got a phone call from yer Dad, luv,' he told her. ''E said ter tell Kay that Colin's goin' after Ernie Gates. 'E said she'd know what ter do.'

'I knew it. I knew somefing was wrong,' Barbara replied. 'Fanks,

Jack. Our Kay's over at the Kellys'. I'll go an' tell 'er straight away. Colin's only just gone out.'

Arthur Selby the landlord of the Mason's Arms, was busy discussing football with a few of his cronies in the saloon bar while Vera his wife stood leaning against the public bar counter buffing up her long red fingernails. It was one of those tedious nights, she thought. There were hardly any customers to speak of, and there was little to do except be on hand. Arthur could manage quite well on his own, but the selfish pig was too wrapped up in his own little world to spare a thought for her. She had to look after the two bars while he prattled on about things he knew very little about, if the look on his friends' faces was anything to go by.

The heavily built man sitting at the counter suddenly pushed his empty glass forward. 'Same again,' he growled, burping loudly.

Vera sighed in resignation as she complied. Ernie Gates was a pig, too, she thought, a pig of a different order. He was one customer she could well do without. He frightened her with his general manner. He was abrupt and off-putting, and when he did get into conversation with anyone, it usually ended up in a row.

'There we are, luv,' she said sweetly as she placed the full glass in front of him.

Ernie pulled it towards him and slid a half-crown across the counter. 'This place is like a morgue,' he remarked sarcastically.

'It's early yet,' Vera replied, trying to hold her temper. 'It's a cold night too. That don't 'elp our trade.'

Ernie took a deep draught from his glass and then wiped the back of his hand across his lips, to Vera's disgust. She turned away to continue with her manicure when the door opened. After many years in the licensing trade the blonde landlady had developed a certain kind of intuition, but even without it she would have known at that moment as she stared at the young soldier standing there with clenched fists and his feet spread apart that this was trouble.

'I'm lookin' fer a dirty, no-good son of an 'ore who gets 'is kicks beatin' up defenceless women,' he snarled.

Chapter Fifty-five

Mary Kelly slipped her coat on and turned to Tom. 'C'mon, luv, look sharp,' she told him. 'I wanna pop in an' see poor ole Dot Adams before we go ter the pictures. She's really down.'

Tom gave Pat and Kay a quick glance and a secretive smile as he got up out of his armchair. 'We'd better not stop too long, gel, or we'll miss the start,' he reminded her.

As soon as the Kellys had left, Kay got out of her chair and went over to where Pat was sitting. He put his newspaper down and slipped his arm around her shoulders as she curled herself up on the hearthrug and leaned against his legs.

'D'yer still love me?' she asked him, looking up into his dark eyes.

'Yeah, I fink so,' he replied teasingly.

Kay pulled a face. 'We never seem ter get much chance ter be on our own,' she said, lowering her head on to his knees.

Pat ran his fingers through her long fair hair and planted a kiss on her neck. 'We're alone now, darlin',' he said softly.

Kay looked up again and saw his suggestive look. 'Do yer remember that night, the night o' Colin's party when we slipped away? Well, I've not stopped finkin' about it since,' she said, sighing.

He smiled and leaned down, his lips brushing against hers. 'Finkin' about it keeps me awake at night,' he whispered. 'I see yer standin' in the darkness an' you come towards me, very slowly, an' then yer slip inter bed beside me. We make love all night, an' I can smell the perfume an' yer 'air, an' . . .'

'Stop it, Pat, yer gettin' me goin',' she said in a husky voice, her arms going up around his neck and her lips closing on his.

Pat savoured her warm, moist kiss and the feel of her fingers through his thick hair. He stood up, pulling her up with him, and

422

then put his arms around her waist. They kissed sensuously, their tongues touching, teasing as the embrace intensified. Her body was stirring, pressing against his and feeling his growing passion. His hands were exciting her, caressing up and down until she moaned with pleasure.

The loud double knock on the front door made them part suddenly, and Pat gulped as he ran his fingers quickly through his dishevelled hair. 'Who the bloody 'ell could that be?' he growled.

He pulled open the door to find Barbara looking agitated. 'Pat, it's Colin!' she said quickly. ''E's gone after Ernie Gates!'

Kay rushed into the passage on hearing her sister's voice. 'What for?' she asked her.

'Elsie's accident. It was down to Ernie,' Barbara blurted out. 'Elsie told Colin terday an' now 'e's gone after 'im. Dad phoned Jack Springer from Guy's an' 'e come round. We've gotta stop 'im, Kay. Colin's no match fer Ernie.'

Pat went into the parlour to collect his lumber jacket. ''Ow long's 'e bin gone?' he asked urgently as he came back, zipping it up.

'About five minutes or so,' Barbara told him.

Pat went to rush out into the street and Kay grabbed his arm. 'Wait fer me. I'm comin' wiv yer,' she told him.

Ernie Gates sat staring down at his drink, his eyes unblinking as he thought about the past few days. They would come looking for him now, he knew, but it was too late for regret. What had happened was her doing. She had provoked him, taunting him about her carryings-on with that Adams boy. The marriage was finished, and she was welcome to the halfwit. It was time to move on, away from the area he had come to detest. It was a shame that he had not managed to form any lasting bond with the boy, though, but how could he? He could never really be sure that Billy was his. After all, Elsie was not exactly altar-pure when he married her, by her own admission. Perhaps it would have been better if she had not been so honest with him at the outset. It didn't matter now, though. He had money salted away, enough to get him a new start in another place.

Ernie heard the taunts levelled at him and he turned round slowly on his stool, narrowing his eyes menacingly as he looked the young soldier up and down. 'Are you addressin' me?' he growled.

'Yeah, I'm talkin' ter you, Gates.'

'Yer better get off 'ome, sonny, before I ferget you're family,' Ernie replied.

'Outside! Me an' you!' Colin spat out, fighting to keep his voice under control. 'Let's see if yer got any bottle when yer up against a man instead of a woman.'

Vera Selby stood open-mouthed as the two men stared at each other and Arthur came from behind the bar. 'Look, I don't want no trouble 'ere,' he said quickly.

'Yer won't get any trouble, if that cocky young git pisses off 'ome right now,' Ernie told him.

'I've asked yer once, an' if yer don't get outside I'll drag yer out,' Colin snarled as he took a few paces forward.

Gates got up from his stool and moved forward. 'Right, sonny. You asked fer it, an' by the time I'm finished wiv you yer'll wish yer stayed 'ome instead o' tryin' ter play the big man.'

Pat Kelly slipped into the pub and stood behind the young soldier. 'Move aside, Colin,' he said quietly.

'I don't need no one ter fight my battles,' the young man said as he turned to face Pat.

'It's not your battle. Not any more,' Pat told him. 'Take 'im 'ome, Kay.'

'I'm goin' nowhere, an' you can keep out of it,' Colin replied angrily.

'So the big man's takin' it on 'imself, I see,' Ernie said, a smile playing on his lips.

'It's unfinished business, Ernie. Me an' you. It's time we settled it once an' fer all,' Pat replied, his face set hard.

'I don't want no trouble in 'ere,' Arthur Selby protested.

Ernie turned on him. 'Shut yer trap,' he growled.

Pat Kelly walked up to Ernie and stood, feet apart, his hands tucked into his belt provocatively. 'Where's it gonna be, 'ere or outside?' he asked calmly.

Ernie lowered his gaze, and then without warning his fist came round in a wide swinging loop and caught Pat on the side of the head. Pat staggered back and dropped to one knee, stunned for a moment.

Kay had slipped into the bar behind Pat, and she gasped at the suddenness of the attack. Colin moved sideways as he unbuttoned his jacket, his eyes fixed on the two combatants. Pat was rising slowly to his feet, shaking his head and grinning ruefully.

'Now why don't you all piss off 'ome before I get really mad,' Ernie snarled.

Pat lunged forward, his straight left catching Ernie full in the mouth. The man staggered back but stayed on his feet. Suddenly he reached over to his empty beer mug, took it by the handle and brought it down sharply on the counter. The glass shattered in pieces and he was left holding a jagged weapon. Pat stopped dead in his tracks, his eyes fixed on the spiky chunk in Ernie's large fist. 'That figures wiv you,' he growled. 'Yer never like ter be at a disadvantage, do yer, Gates?'

'This 'as bin goin' on too long wiv me an' you,' Ernie replied, his eyes narrowing to slits. 'It's time we finished it fer good. I'm gonna cut yer, Kelly. I'm gonna put me mark on yer.'

Pat backed away as Ernie stabbed towards him with the glass, brandishing it with a leer. Suddenly Colin lunged forward and brought his chain down hard on Ernie's wrist. The glass flew from Ernie's grasp and he screamed in pain. Pat sprang forward and hit Ernie with a hard left and a right in his face, but he was gripped in a bear-hug. Though he was the more lithe and quick of the two, Ernie Gates was the stronger, and as he struggled and wriggled trying to break the bear-hug, Pat felt his feet leave the floor. Ernie was straining to crush the breath out of him, and he snarled like an animal as he tightened his hold. Pat began to feel panic, and in a last desperate effort he brought his head down sharply, smashing Ernie on the bridge of his nose. Blood spurted as he lost his grip and Pat struggled free. The bull-like man came at him again, his head held low as he rushed forward. Pat was ready and he stepped smartly aside and delivered a crashing blow to the side of Ernie's head. He went down on all fours and blinked through blood as he struggled to rise, and Pat stood with his feet apart as he waited for him.

Vera and the few customers in the bar stood horror-struck as they watched the encounter, and Arthur's hand shook as he picked up the phone.

'I'm gettin' the police,' he shouted out.

Ernie Gates suddenly lunged forward, and this time he managed to grab the lighter man. They careered out through the door and into the street, and Pat fell backwards into the road with Ernie on top of him. Colin rushed out after them with Kay at his heels, and they stood helpless as the battle went on. Ernie was trying to pin Pat beneath him, his fists pummelling his face, but the lighter man twisted and managed to roll over until he was on top. Pat Kelly pounded into him but Ernie's superior strength told again as he shoved Pat off. They rolled apart and staggered to their feet, both bloody but unbowed, and the fight became a trade of heavy punches, each man staggering backwards from the impact. Ernie was gasping, each breath coming in a loud wheeze, and Pat forced a grin through bruised and cut lips. 'Yer tirin', Ernie,' he taunted.

The big man knew that it was now or never, and with a last lunging movement he ducked forward and caught Pat Kelly in the midriff with the top of his head. They went over again in a heap, all the breath knocked from the lighter man. They were fighting to rise to their feet and, as they struggled upright, Pat's fist caught Ernie full on the jaw. The big man staggered backwards, and before he could recover, another looping right-hand punch cracked him on the temple. Pat felt a numbness travel up from his broken knuckles to the pit of his arm, and he watched as Ernie dropped forward on to his face. This time he did not struggle to get up, and Pat slouched wearily over to the prone body of his defeated opponent. 'It's finished,' he gasped. 'It's bin settled once an' fer all.'

Ernie rolled over slowly and painfully crawled to the kerbside where he sat holding his battered face in his hands. Colin walked up slowly and stood looking down at the bloodied man. The sight of Ernie's battered face had a strangely calming effect on him, and he suddenly found that there was no more hatred left inside him. 'Just stay away from Elsie,' he said in a quiet voice.

Kay had gone to Pat and she stood holding him around the waist as he dabbed at his bleeding lips with a handkerchief. 'C'mon, darlin'. It's all over,' she said in a strained voice. 'Let's go 'ome.'

They started off, the three of them, with Pat walking rather unsteadily between brother and sister. They heard the sound of a police bell and a roaring motor as they walked back into Waggoner's Way.

The police car screeched to a halt and the crew hurried into the pub, the driver stopping to look down at the beaten figure in the kerb. 'What's bin goin' on 'ere then?' he asked.

'It was a private fight,' Ernie growled.

'Are you all right?' the driver asked him.

'Yeah, I'm just winded,' Ernie replied, spitting out blood from his cut mouth.

'You'd better get off 'ome then,' the policeman told him.

Inside the pub, Arthur was making his point. 'I told 'em I wasn't standin' no ole nonsense in my pub,' he said, puffing out his chest. 'Didn't I tell 'em, Vera?'

'Yeah, you told 'em right enough,' she said sarcastically. 'Anyway, it's all right, officer. They decided ter settle it outside.'

'What was it all about?' one of the policemen asked her.

'It was an old feud,' she told him. 'It started over a woman, right 'ere in this pub, a long time ago, an' it ended up over a woman, but it's finally bin settled, fank Gawd.'

Chapter Fifty-six

Chief Superintendent Cranley stormed into the police station early on Friday morning and glared at the desk sergeant. 'Is Moody in yet?' he asked abruptly.

'Yes, sir.'

'Locate him and tell him to report to my office right away,' Cranley ordered.

When the detective presented himself two minutes later, Cranley dispensed with the niceties. 'Bring me the Dines file. I shall be taking over the murder investigation myself,' he said sharply. 'Oh, and by the way. Keep yourself available. I'll need to discuss the case with you later.'

Sergeant Moody made a quick exit and was soon back with a buff-coloured folder which he put down on the desk. Cranley picked it up and immediately felt a solid object amongst the papers.

'What's this?' he asked as he withdrew a small envelope from between the sheets of reports.

'It's the key ter the Dineses' sideboard,' Moody told him. 'It was around the dead woman's neck. I fergot ter return it.'

'All right, Sergeant. We'll speak later,' Cranley told him.

Once his subordinate had left, Superintendent Cranley set to work reading through the statement from Simon Dines, and then he pored over the confession of Danny Adams. Finally he took out the police crime photographs and studied them for a while. His cup of coffee grew cold as he became more and more involved with the case documents, and it was some considerable time before he stood up and went to the window. Down below he could see the busy Jamaica Road with its passing trams and buses, horsedrawn carts and pedestrians going to and fro. It seemed like a typical March morning, when the river mists and winter fogs were beginning to

428

give way to the early spring sunshine and budding trees. It was a time of year he enjoyed, with the promise of a colourful garden and roses in abundance in his Kentish garden, but on this particular morning Cranley had no time to dwell on anything except the contents of the murder file lying there on his desk.

The day grew dull as heavy clouds rolled in from the west, and rainspots began to dapple his office window, but by now Superintendent Roger Cranley was oblivious to everything, totally immersed in the case. On the surface it looked cut and dried. The statements of both young men were concise and without any ambiguity, and to Sergeant Moody's credit they had been professionally prepared, but a persistent gut feeling that he had overlooked something kept niggling away in the superintendent's mind. He sent for more coffee and once again let it get cold as he pored over the papers.

It was beginning to get dark when the truth hit Cranley like a blow on the head. He quickly took out the photograph which showed the murdered woman lying on her back, and he fished into his desk drawer for his magnifying-glass. For a while he studied the photo through the powerful lens, then he took up the key which was lying on one side of his desk and let the grubby white string pass slowly through his fingers.

'Sergeant. Send Moody in right away,' he barked into the phone.

As soon as his subordinate showed his face, Superintendent Cranley said, 'I want you to bring in Simon Dines.'

'This evenin'?' Moody queried.

'Now. Right away.'

Sergeant Moody left in a hurry and Cranley went back to work. He used a jotting-pad to record his conclusions, and then he picked up the key by the string and gripped it tightly in his clenched fist. There was always something, he told himself with a satisfied smile.

Forty-five minutes later, Sergeant Moody looked in. 'I've got 'im sittin' in the interview room, sir,' he announced.

Cranley leaned back in his comfortable desk chair. 'I'll interview him in here, Sergeant,' he replied.

Simon Dines was wearing his dark glasses and he looked hesitant as he was shown into the small office. He stood in front of the desk in his grey overcoat, his light brown hair plastered down with brilliantine.

'Take a seat, Mr Dines,' Cranley bade him pleasantly.

Simon sat down and folded his hands in his lap. 'I was told yer wanted ter discuss a few points,' he said, his mouth twitching nervously.

'That's right, Mr Dines,' Cranley replied. 'Do you mind if I call you Simon? It sounds less formal.'

'That's all right,' the young man answered.

'Tell me, is the light bothering your eyes?' Cranley asked him.

'Yeah, it's a bit strong,' Simon said.

'If I turn off the main light and just leave this desk light on, can you remove your glasses?' Cranley asked.

Simon nodded and the superintendent got up and flicked the wall switch. A pale light flooded the desk-top, and Cranley adjusted the stand as he made himself comfortable at his desk once more. 'There we are, is that better?' he asked.

Simon took off his glasses and wiped his eyes with a grubby handkerchief. 'I 'ave ter wear these all the time when I'm out,' he remarked.

Cranley opened the case file and took out a sheet of paper. 'There's a few points I'd like to clear up,' he began. 'Tell me, Simon. When you came back from visiting the pub, why did you break into the house?'

'I already told the policeman that,' the young man replied.

'Yes, I know, but I must go over the main facts once more, so please bear with me,' Cranley explained. 'Why did you break into your home?'

'I never 'ad a key an' there was no answer when I knocked,' Simon told him.

'Yes, but you've stated here that every time you went out you waited until your mother put the chain on. You also said that on the night of her murder you did the same as usual. You called out for her to put the chain on. Is that correct?'

'Yes, I told the policeman that,' Simon replied.

'So why did you immediately seek entry by charging at the front door when you knew that the chain was on?' Cranley pressed him. 'After all, you knew that it was a heavy-duty chain and it was installed to prevent that very thing happening.'

'Yeah, but it wasn't on, an' I got in easy,' Simon replied.

'But how did you know the chain was off? You had no way of knowing. When you left the house your mother immediately put the chain on. That's what you said in your statement.'

Simon looked down at his clasped hands in silence for a few

moments. 'When me muvver never answered I got panicky. I expected the worst so I charged the door down,' he said hesitantly.

'Common sense tells me that you would have gone in through the window.'

'But the winder was nailed down. I wouldn't 'ave bin able to open it.'

'But you knew the window-pane was already cracked. And it would have been the obvious way to get in, by smashing the glass.'

'I didn't fink.'

Cranley studied the sheet of paper in front of him once more, then he looked up suddenly. 'Now, Simon, I want you to clarify a very important point. It says here that you did not touch the body at all after you charged in. Is that correct? You would swear to that?'

Simon nodded his head vigorously. 'When I went inter the parlour an' saw me muvver lyin' there, I looked down at 'er fer a few seconds then I run next door ter the lady.'

'So you never at any time touched your mother's body?'

'No, I never.'

'Do you recognise this key, Simon?' the policeman asked quietly.

'Yeah. It's the key me muvver wore round 'er neck. She wore it all the time.'

'This is the key which opens your sideboard drawer. Correct?'

Simon nodded again. 'Yeah, but it's left opened now, so I didn't fink of askin' 'im fer it back.'

Cranley leaned forward in his chair. 'This key was always around your mother's neck?'

'Yeah.'

'It was on your mother's body when she was taken to the mortuary, but it wasn't around her neck when she was battered to death with that flat-iron, Simon,' Cranley said sharply.

'It must 'ave bin. She never took it off,' the young man replied.

'This key was put back around your mother's neck after she was killed.'

'I don't understand.'

'You will, in good time,' Cranley said quietly. 'You see, down through the years, people have always sought to commit the perfect murder, but they invariably forget one thing. One little slip-up which gives them away. In this case it was the key. Before your mother's body was taken to the mortuary, a police photographer took photos. It's the usual procedure. It shows quite clearly on the photographs that the wound had bled profusely. The blood had run down the side of your mother's head on to her neck and chest. Yet there's no sign of blood on the key string. You can see for yourself.'

Simon stared at the string held up in front of his eyes, and he blinked nervously. 'Whoever killed me muvver must 'ave took it off 'er then put it back afterwards,' he faltered.

'No, Simon. If someone had come in to rob your mother they wouldn't have hung around until the blood congealed before replacing the key around her neck,' the policeman continued. 'They would either have snatched the key from her forcibly, in which case the cord would have snapped, or they would have taken it from her after killing her, and in that case there would have been blood on the string. In any case they would have opened the drawer and searched for valuables and money, then they would have left as soon as they could. Yet you would have me believe that they relocked the drawer and then put the key back where they found it, around your mother's neck. No, Simon. I put it to you that you took the key from around your mother's neck, when she was asleep maybe, and then you searched through that drawer for money. Your mother then woke up and discovered what you were doing. During the row that followed you took up the flat-iron in a temper and battered her to death. You then had to think hard. You hid the notebook to make it look like one of her customers had done the killing, and then you went out and closed the door after you, calling out to your mother to put the chain on, just for the benefit of the neighbours. That was at nine o'clock, and while you were drinking in the pub you suddenly remembered that you'd left the key in the drawer lock. You went back home around ten o'clock and made a big thing about not getting any answer. You broke in through the door, aware that the chain wasn't on, and immediately put the key back around your mother's neck before running out to sound the alarm. That was it, wasn't it, Simon? Your mother was dead when you left for the pub. Because you killed her.'

The young man's face had gone ashen, and suddenly he dropped his head into his hands and sobbed.

'She never 'ad any time fer me,' he gulped. 'It was always Norman. What did 'e do fer 'er? 'E run off ter sea ter get away from 'er as soon as 'e could, an' she was gonna leave 'im all 'er money.'

'Did she tell you this, that she intended to leave her money to Norman?' Cranley asked quietly.

'No, but I found out.'

'You opened the drawer and found a will?'

'Nah, there wasn't any will. It was the letter Norman sent to 'er fankin' 'er fer leavin' 'er money to 'im. It was in the drawer,' Simon said, wiping his hand over his eyes.

'How did you manage to get the key?' Cranley asked him.

'Muvver wasn't feelin' too good so she went ter lay down after tea. I went in 'er bedroom a bit later ter see 'ow she was, an' she was sittin' propped up in bed fast asleep, so I took the key from round 'er neck an' opened the drawer. She came out while I was readin' the letter, an' when I confronted 'er about it she went mad at me. She told me I was useless an' too lazy ter go out ter work. She said that ter me, even though she knows 'ow me eyes are. I can't stand daylight. She knew that right enough, but it didn't stop 'er.'

'So you lost your temper and grabbed the first thing that came handy, the flat-iron?'

Simon nodded. 'I didn't mean ter kill 'er, even though I didn't get on wiv 'er.'

'After you killed her you took the money from her cashbox, hid the notebook, then you went out, forgetting that you had left the key in the lock. You put it back round your mother's neck as soon as you got back from the pub, am I right?'

'Yeah. I didn't want Danny Adams ter be suspected. 'E's a nice bloke, so I tried ter make it look as though someone else did it.'

'One of her clients?'

'That's right.'

'Where's the notebook, Simon?'

'I put it up the chimney at first, then I burnt it in the fire later,' he replied.

'Along with the letter?'

'Yeah.'

'I see from the report that there were no bank books or post office savings books amongst your mother's possessions?' Cranley queried.

Simon shook his head. 'She never believed in banks. She kept the money in the 'ouse. I found it. It was in 'er bedroom cupboard under a floorboard.'

'What did you do with the money?'

'I put it in the bank.'

Cranley picked up the phone and ordered coffee, then as he

returned to his desk he laid a hand briefly on the distressed man's shoulder. 'Take it easy,' he said quietly.

'I should 'ave waited fer a few more weeks,' Simon mumbled, looking down at his clenched hands.'

'I don't understand,' Cranley replied.

'I went ter the Moorfield's Eye 'Ospital yesterday. They told me I'm goin' blind,' Simon said flatly. 'If she'd 'ave known that it might 'ave made a difference ter the way she treated me.'

Cranley stood up as the coffee arrived and he passed one of the cups to Simon Dines. For a few moments he studied the young man. 'Danny Adams was charged with your mother's murder,' he said finally. 'He was remanded in custody at Brixton prison, facing a possible death sentence. Would you have come forward to save him?'

Simon was staring down at his hands, and after a long time he looked up. 'I don't know,' he replied helplessly. 'I don't know.'

Cranley picked up his cup and walked with it to the window. Down below, the lights of the city shone out in the darkness as workers hurried homewards. It had ended on a satisfactory note, casewise, the detective thought. But there was no sense of achievement, no feeling of a job well done. Only a sadness that seemed to rise up within him until it soured the coffee. He turned and looked at the pathetic figure, and suddenly thought about his roses. They would be bursting forth soon.

Chapter Fifty-seven

On Friday evening, a meeting of the Jolly Boys was convened in the railway club to finalise plans for the June charity social. There was much to discuss, but before they could set to work there was one outstanding item on the agenda that had to be resolved.

'Get 'im in 'ere fer Gawd's sake,' Walter Smith the chairman growled.

Charlie Catchpole grinned evilly as he hurried out of the clubroom.

'Don't let's make too much of it or we'll never get rid of 'im,' Joe Brennen advised.

Tom Kelly eased back in his chair and folded his arms in anticipation, and Maurice Woodley the secretary fiddled with his papers in an effort to look important.

'I got the badge 'ere,' Jack Springer announced, tapping his coat pocket.

Alec Broomfield and Bill Cosgrove exchanged amused smiles and tried to look serious as Charlie walked back into the room accompanied by Jim Carney.

'Take a seat, Mr Carney,' the chairman said without looking up.

Jim made himself comfortable. 'I appreciate yer seein' me. It's bin a bloody nightmare gettin' those references,' he said pointedly.

Walter Smith looked up and lowered his thick-rimmed spectacles on to the end of his nose. 'Now I 'ave ter tell yer that we've all given your application a great deal of thought,' he began. 'As you are aware, the Jolly Boys is a closed shop, but in your case, due ter your persistence in drivin' us all round the bloody twist, we've decided ter make you an honorary independent member, which means that you can give us a bit of 'elp wiv the charity social an' come along to informal meetin's. What yer can't do is vote on any decisions we might 'ave ter take, is that clear?'

Jim nodded his head forcefully. 'I got yer, mate,' he replied.

'You'll address me as Mr Chairman at meetin's,' Walter said sharply.

'Sorry, Mr Chairman.'

'Right then, give 'im 'is badge,' Walter ordered.

Jim Springer took out a large circular cardboard disc from his pocket and handed it to Jim Carney. 'Yer gotta wear this at all functions,' he said solemnly.

The new, honorary independent member's face lit up as he saw the bold letters 'H-I-M' on the disc. 'Cor, fanks,' he said, grinning broadly.

'You're one of us now – well, nearly,' Charlie Catchpole remarked.

'I 'ope you'll wear that badge wiv pride,' Maurice told him.

The members hid their amusement as Jim removed a safety pin from under his coat collar. 'All right if I stick it on now?' he asked. 'I'd like ter walk 'ome wiv it on.'

'We'll adjourn fer refreshment now,' the chairman announced. 'C'mon, Jim, I fink we can buy yer a pint out o' the club funds.'

One hour later, the rather merry honorary independent member of the Jolly Boys ('HIM' for short), arrived back at his lodgings, proudly wearing his cardboard badge. 'Well, I finally done it, Sara,' he told her with a big smile.

'Yeah, yer sure did, Jim,' Sara Brady replied, not knowing whether to laugh or cry.

Pat Kelly sat holding hands with Kay in a side room of St Mary's Church on Friday evening. The Maltese confederates were all there too, along with Mick Mollison, Tubby Willis, Edward Chipperfield and Margie Dolan. Facing them on a table covered with a purple cloth was the small package, still in its oilskin covering. Father Ryan stood near it, along with a bareheaded priest dressed in a purple robe which was tied with a thick cord. A large bronze crucifix hung down from the priest's neck and he smiled at the gathering as he stood with his hands concealed inside his wide sleeves.

Father Ryan coughed to clear his throat. 'I would like you all to meet Monsignor Vincenti from the Vatican,' he said.

The priest raised a hand in a papal blessing, then he went round the table and laid his fingers on the package, his eyes studying the small assembly. 'I have come from Rome to take possession of this package,' he told them solemnly. 'It would be unthinkable, however, to leave without meeting you all and thanking you for your involvement in the recovery of these treasures. Father Ryan, will you assist me?'

Everyone present watched with fascination as Father Ryan picked up a paper-knife from the table and slit open the outer wrapping. The monsignor then opened the flaps of the cardboard box inside and slowly lifted out the first of the small pictures. He stared at it reverently for a while, then held it up for everyone to see. It was a painting of Christ on a gold background inside an embossed edging. The second picture was of the Virgin Mary, and it had been created in the same style. The remaining two paintings were of the disciples, and as the monsignor put the last one down on the table, he crossed himself and closed his eyes for a moment or two in silent prayer. The huge ring on the priest's finger flashed in the light as he waved his hand over the table. 'What you see here are the *Ignatius Icons*,' he announced. 'To understand what the recovery of these icons means to the Catholic Church you have to know the full story.'

The monsignor folded his arms as he began. 'When Christianity was flourishing in Tsarist Russia, many churches were built, and in 1605 an artist called Ignatius was commissioned to design stained-glass windows and paint frescos in the newly erected churches. His fame grew, and then in 1630 he decided to travel outside the country to improve his knowledge and talents. He made his way through neighbouring Poland but unfortunately he was caught up in severe weather. Some Franciscan monks discovered him lying in a snowdrift, starving and near to death. They took him to the monastery of St Francis in the hills above Cracow and nursed him back to health. Before he left to continue his travels, Ignatius painted these four icons and presented them as a gift to the monastery. They were hung in the chapel and admired by everyone who prayed there. In 1683 King John of Poland was requested by Austria to come to the aid of their capital Vienna, which was being besieged by a Turkish army of three hundred thousand. King John raised an army of forty thousand, and before he left he prayed in the chapel of St Francis. The Turks were finally routed and the king became convinced that the icons, the same ones that you see here now, were truly blessed.'

437

Everyone in the small side room of St Mary's Church remained silent as the priest continued. 'The icons hung in the chapel of St Francis for over three hundred years, but in September 1939, with the German Army already nearing Cracow, the monks of St Francis decided to transfer them to the safety of the cathedral in Cracow. They believed that their monastery would be ransacked and probably destroyed in the shelling, but that even the Germans would not dare ravage the Cathedral of Cracow. They were wrong. The icons and many other treasures were taken away on orders from the Gestapo, but with the Allied and Russian Armies approaching from the west and East, it was decided to hide the spoils within the city. Goering had claimed the icons for himself, but he was captured before he could collect them, and they remained hidden.

'A lot of hard, dangerous work went into locating the cache, and when our investigators discovered that the icons had been secured by a British buyer and were coming over on a Polish ship, we had to lay our plans for their recovery. You know the rest. These blessed paintings survived the war, were recovered by the brave men who are present here tonight, and then nearly perished in a fire. I can only say to you all that the Lord was with you in your hour of trial and tribulation. The icons are safe and sound, and they will be returned to their rightful place. Unfortunately they cannot go back to the monastery of St Francis, for it was destroyed during the war, but one day soon they will be hanging once more in a bastion of Christianity, the Cathedral of Cracow.'

Pat slipped his arm around Kay as they left St Mary's after the short benediction. They walked home deep in thought, Kay's head resting against his shoulder. The young man had spent some time thinking about the fire at Chippy's, wondering what had possessed him to chase into the flames after Mick Mollison. He now felt that he knew the answer.

Danny Adams walked into the ward at Guy's Hospital and saw Elsie smiling at him. Colour had returned to her cheeks and she looked radiant as she held out her arms to him. He bent over the bed and kissed her softly on her eager lips. 'They let me go,' he said simply.

'I missed yer, Danny,' she whispered.

He sat down beside the bed and touched her plastered arm tenderly. 'I brought Billy wiv me,' he told her. ''E's waitin' outside the ward.'

438

Elsie slipped her feet on to the floor and reached for her dressing-robe. 'Let's go an' see 'im,' she said excitedly.

Danny took her arm and gave her an encouraging wink as they walked slowly to the door. 'You can make it,' he joked.

She looked up into his deep-set eyes, her heart full of happiness. 'I can now,' she said.

Epilogue

It had rained for most of the week but on Saturday morning the June sky was clear. Everyone was out early. The shopping over, the women of Waggoner's Way congregated together to organise the children's street party. It was the first stage of a community programme, and by the time the men had set up trestle-tables and forms in the small turning, the women were ready. Emily Toogood and Sara Brady laid the tables with coloured paper, while Annie Thomas and Bet Greenedge brought out the jellies they had made the night before. Dot Adams and Mary Kelly helped Ada Brennen make the sandwiches, and Jim Carney strolled up and down, wearing his badge and getting in everybody's way.

Joe Mezzo and Maria brought round a huge bowl of Sockeye Salmon that had been mashed with pepper and vinegar, and a dozen tins of fruit, and Jack Springer delivered a jar of boiled sweets and bars of chocolate as well as a batch of paper hats. A churn of ice-cream had been donated, and Jim Carney was delegated to stand guard over it.

The children arrived and the party began. Ada's piano had been manhandled into the street, and Emily went into her repertoire. It was the beginning of a long day, and the pianist had brought suitable fortification in a carrier bag at her side. Later there was to be a social evening at the railway club, and all money taken from the sale of entry tickets would go to swell the fund. Raffles had been organised, and there were to be sandwiches, jellied eels and cockles and whelks on sale.

During the afternoon festivities, PC Fuller called into the street to see how things were progressing, and he was given a salmon sandwich and a cup of tea by Bet Greenedge. He left soon after, having first called into Joe Mezzo's shop to collect his weekly parcel of bacon. Later on that afternoon, Superintendent Cranley made a brief appearance. Joe Mezzo stood talking to him outside his shop for a while, and then Bet Greenedge came over, having been informed who the stranger was by Jim Carney.

'Would you two gentlemen like a cuppa and a salmon sandwich?' she asked. 'We've got loads o' salmon over.'

'No, thank you,' Cranley replied with a friendly smile.

'If yer sure. It's best red salmon,' Bet said blithely as she strolled off.

'Not Sockeye I hope,' Cranley said quietly, staring into the middle distance.

'I shouldn't fink so,' Joe replied with a dignified air.

Across the turning, the men were standing talking together. 'I see the Adams boy looks fit and well,' Cranley remarked.

Joe nodded. 'Yeah, 'e's courtin' Elsie Gates, the Brennens' gel. She 'elped 'im no end after the Dines business.'

'The outcome of that trial was a surprise, don't you think?' Cranley said. 'Having the charge reduced to manslaughter was a good result for Dines's brief. I wasn't very optimistic about his chances, to tell you the truth, but I expect they took everything into consideration: the constant pressure from the old lady and his medical condition. Seven years is not for ever, not for a man of his age. He could be out in five.'

Joe lit up a cigar. 'Well, I'd better see 'ow Maria's gettin' on,' he said. 'We're shuttin' up early terday so we can get ter the social.'

Cranley nodded. 'I'd better be off too,' he replied. 'I'll be seeing you, Joe. Don't do anything I wouldn't.'

'I wouldn't dream of it,' the grocer told him with a grin, drawing deeply on his cigar and puffing a cloud of smoke to the heavens.

The night sky was filled with stars, and a sliver of moon hung above the railway yard as the local community arrived to support the Jolly Boys. Jim Carney strutted about with his hands clasped behind his back, the badge prominent on his coat lapel. 'Take yer time, there's plenty o' room,' he called out officiously.

'Who's that soppy git?' one of the women from Hastings Street asked.

'That's HIM.'

'Who?'

'HIM. The one an' only Jim Carney. Can't yer see the badge?'

441

''E looks like a pox doctor's clerk, if yer ask me,' the Hastings Street woman remarked.

Music struck up and the dancing got under way. Dawn and Barbara Brennen were whisked around the floor by their proud partners, while Elsie sat talking quietly with Danny, patiently waiting for a waltz. Tom and Mary Kelly were enjoying a lively chat with Joe and Ada Brennen, and Colin, on embarkation leave for Germany, stood at the food counter looking smart in his freshly pressed uniform and being ogled by a young lady from Dover Lane.

Pat took the opportunity to whisper into Kay's ear as they danced together. She smiled impishly and the two of them slowly sidled towards the door, then they slipped out into the cool night air and held hands as they made their way back to Waggoner's Way. Pat turned the key and pulled Kay into the dark passage. She melted into his arms, her lips seeking his. 'I love you, Pat,' she sighed.

He picked her up in his arms and nuzzled her white neck. 'I love you too, darlin',' he said softly.

Back at the railway club, it was time for the raffle.

'I'd like ter call on our honorary independent member ter draw the tickets,' Charlie Catchpole said in a loud voice.

Jim Carney stepped up, looking very pleased with himself.

'Who the bleedin' 'ell's 'e?' someone asked.

'Don't yer know?' the woman from Hastings Street replied. 'That's HIM.'